"I had a silly schoolgirl crush on you."

"What you and my sister had was real, and I messed it up for both of you. Now I have a chance to fix it," Chloe said.

"What if I told you I don't want you to?" Easton asked.

"Why not? Two days ago you were all for the plan."

"I wouldn't go that far." He looked down at her and lifted her chin. "But it's not your sister I want to kiss right now, it's you."

"You want to kiss me?"

Instead of answering her whispered question with words, Easton lowered his head and slanted his mouth over hers. She'd been waiting fifteen years for Easton McBride to kiss her again. But this was not the kiss of the boy she remembered. It was the kiss of an experienced and confident man. There was no more gentleness now. Only heat and passion and hunger. This would not end with just a kiss. This was already more than a kiss. It was . . .

Acclaim for
The Christmas, Colorado Series

Wedding Bells in Christmas

"Romance readers will absolutely love this story of matchmaking and passion rekindled. *Wedding Bells in Christmas* is the very definition of a well-fought-for HEA."
—RT Book Reviews

"I loved this book. For me, it was the perfect example of small-town contemporary done right. It's definitely going on my Top Ten Books of 2015 list."
—SimplyAngelaRenee.blogspot.com

"I completely enjoyed visiting Christmas again. This novel is full of rich, full-flavored characters with a story line that never lets up and keeps you turning page after page to discover what happens next. I would definitely recommend this story to anyone who wants an intense, involved story that brings in the entire town for the celebration of two people falling in love."
—KeeperBookshelf.com

It Happened at Christmas

"Debbie Mason gives the reader an excellent love story that can be read all year long...You must pick up *It Happened at Christmas*." **—NightOwlRomance.com**

"A passionate, liberal environmental activist and a straight-arrow conservative lawyer looking to the senate set the sparks flying in this nonstop, beautifully crafted adventure that skillfully unwraps a multilayered plot, adds an abundance of colorful characters and a familiar setting, and proves in no uncertain terms that opposites do attract." **—*Library Journal***

Christmas in July

"A heartwarming, feel-good story. I have not read anything written by Debbie Mason before, but now I have to read more of her books because I enjoyed *Christmas in July* so much." **—HarlequinJunkie.com**

"Debbie Mason's books are the type of books that leave you with a warm and fuzzy feeling...*Christmas in July* is a great read." **—FreshFiction.com**

"4 Stars! A quintessential romance with everything readers love: familiar and likable characters, clever dialogue, and a juicy plot." **—*RT Book Reviews***

The Trouble with Christmas

"A fun and festive tale, flush with small-town warmth and tongue-in-cheek charm. The main characters are well worth rooting for, their conflicts solid and riveting."
—USA Today's Happy Ever After blog

"4 Stars! This is a wonderful story to read this holiday season, and the romance is timeless...This is one of those novels readers will enjoy each and every page of and tell friends about."
—RT Book Reviews

"The lovers are sympathetic and well drawn...Mason will please fans of zippy small-town stories."
—Publishers Weekly

"I'm very impressed by [Mason's] character develop-ment, sense of humor, and plotting...Ms. Mason wraps this book up as if it were a very prettily wrapped package. Why not open the pages and have a Christmas present early?" **—LongandShortReviews.com**

"Debbie Mason has created a humorous, heartwarming tale that tugged at my heartstrings while tickling my funny bone...a community that I enjoyed visiting and hope to visit again." **—TheRomanceDish.com**

Kiss Me
in Christmas

ALSO BY DEBBIE MASON

Kiss Me
in Christmas

Debbie Mason

FOREVER

NEW YORK BOSTON

Forever
Hachette Book Group
1290 Avenue of the Americas
New York, NY 10104
www.HachetteBookGroup.com

Printed in the United States of America

First Edition: February 2016
10 9 8 7 6 5 4 3 2 1

OPM

Forever is an imprint of Grand Central Publishing.
The Forever name and logo are trademarks of Hachette Book Group, Inc.

The Hachette Speakers Bureau provides a wide range of authors for speaking events. To find out more, go to www.hachettespeakersbureau.com or call (866) 376-6591.

The publisher is not responsible for websites (or their content) that are not owned by the publisher.

This book is dedicated to my children, April, Jess, and Nick. I'm so proud of the adults you've become. You're everything a mother could ever hope for in daughters and a son, and I love you more than I can say. You truly are my world.

Acknowledgments

Thanks once again to the incredible team at Grand Central Forever for all their efforts on behalf of my books, especially my fabulously talented editor, Alex Logan. I couldn't ask for a more dedicated, hard-working, supportive bunch. Thanks also to my wonderful agent, Pamela Harty, for always being there for me.

Many thanks to the members of the Mazzuca and LeClair families, especially my mom, in-laws Bob and Rose, brother, sister, and sister-in-law Connie. I am truly blessed to have you in my world. And to my wonderful husband, amazing children, and adorable granddaughters, thank you for all your love and encouragement and for supporting me in doing what I love to do. Love you all so very much.

Thanks to my writing pals Vanessa Kelly and Allison Van Diepen for the laughs and friendship. Love you both. A special thanks to my daughter Jess, who reads my first drafts, answers my endless questions, and isn't afraid to tell me when something doesn't work.

And to the readers, bloggers, and reviewers who take time out of their busy lives to spend a few hours with me in Christmas, Colorado, you have my heartfelt gratitude. Thank you for the lovely e-mails, tweets, and Facebook posts. You guys are the best.

Kiss Me
in Christmas

Chapter One

The room was dark, the floorboards creaking ominously under the weight of the intruder's footsteps as he approached the bed with murderous intent. His shadow loomed over Chloe O'Connor, and she squeezed her eyes shut. She heard the rasp of his breath behind his mask, and felt a whisper of cool air against her cheek as the pillow beside her disappeared. He was going to kill her, and there was nothing she could do to stop him.

It was the most ridiculous, uninspired ending for a character of her stature that she had ever heard of. The writers hadn't put enough effort or thought into the scene. Chloe had been the star of the daytime drama *As the Sun Sets* for five years. She'd won two daytime Emmys for her portrayal of Tessa Hart, and she refused, absolutely refused, to go out with a whimper.

If they were going to kill her off, and obviously they were, she should be begging and pleading for her life, the camera capturing the sheer terror in her green eyes. Janet

Leigh's famous shower scene in *Psycho* popped into her head. The idea was so perfect Chloe could barely contain her excitement. There was no doubt in her mind that she'd win another daytime Emmy for the scene she envisioned. Now she just had to convince the director, Phil. Rising up on her elbows, she opened her mouth to call *cut* at the same time the killer slammed the pillow over her face.

The vindictive force of the attack lay Chloe flat-out on the mattress and had her second-guessing the assailant's identity. It wasn't a man; it was Molly. The redheaded actress had auditioned for the part of Tessa Hart, but had been given the lesser role of Tessa's sister. Her back-stabbing sister who was going to get everything once poor Tessa was dead. Chloe struggled to breathe. Her heart gave a terrifying flutter, then another, leaving her weak and light-headed.

"Stop! Please, stop," she cried, the pillow shoving the words back down her throat.

The killer had responded to her muffled pleas by leaning their weight onto their hands. They were actually going to kill her! They didn't know she had a weak heart. She hadn't told anyone on the show. Her identical twin, Cat, had acted as Chloe's unauthorized stunt double for the past two years, but she was gone now, abandoning Chloe in her hour of need.

There was no help for it; she had to save herself. Her arms felt like they had twenty-pound weights strapped to them as she pushed ineffectually against her attacker. She concentrated on her lower body. Twisting and turning, kicking her leaden feet, she attempted to wriggle from beneath the pillow. It didn't work. It was hopeless. Tears pooled in her eyes as she lost the feeling in her arms and legs. She was dying. And as though to confirm it, her life began to flash before her eyes.

The hospital stays for her heart condition, the times she was teased and bullied in grade school and high school, her sister standing up for her, Easton McBride protecting her, the day he told her he loved her, the day he broke her heart and she broke her sister's. The images from her past were filled with love, lies, and loss. The images from the last five years were filled with much the same as she clawed her way to the top, stepping on whoever got in her way.

A sob warbled in her throat. She wouldn't get the chance to tell her family she loved them, to have a family of her own, to have someone who loved her, to win an Oscar, to... *Please God, please, I don't want to die. I want to live*.

"That's a wrap. Good job, everyone," Phil called out.

The pressure lifted from the pillow. Chloe barely had enough strength to push it from her face. Once she did, she dragged in great, gulping gasps of life-saving oxygen.

Dame Estelle Alexander, her agent and manager, rushed to her side and offered her a hand. "As soon as I realized Molly was your killer, I went to the dressing room and got your pills, my dear," the older woman whispered, her British accent more pronounced.

Chloe struggled to sit upright. "Thank you," she said, taking the pills while casting a covert glance around the set. The sound stage was empty. Chloe accepted the bottle of water Estelle offered with a small smile, doing her best to hide her disappointment that not one person stayed behind to thank her for her years of dedication. She popped the nitrogen tablets into her mouth at the same time Molly came into view.

The redhead pulled off black gloves as she walked toward them. Chloe's fingers tightened around the water bottle. Molly was the last person she wanted to see, but at least she'd come to pay her respects. Maybe Chloe would forgive her for practically smothering her to death. "Well, Molly—" Before she got out another word, the actress lifted her iPhone. The flash nearly blinded Chloe.

Molly laughed, then turned the screen toward them. "I think I'll caption it 'Chloe O'Connor ends her days on a bender.'"

Chloe squinted at the photo and gasped. She was a hot mess. Her long, dark hair was all over the place, and not in a sexy bedhead kind of way. Her false eyelashes were half-off, half-on, her red lipstick smeared from her mouth to her cheek. If Chloe wasn't afraid she'd have a heart attack, she'd leap off the bed and strangle Molly. "Do it, and I'll sue," Chloe threatened, her voice a weak rasp.

Holding up her phone, Molly smirked and pressed a button. "Consider it payback for all the years I've had to put up with you, Chloe. Good luck, by the way. Word on the street is no one will hire you. Everyone blames you for poor George going off the deep end."

George had been with *As the Sun Sets* from its inception. He'd played Byron Hart, Tessa's husband. He was currently serving time in a psychiatric hospital. "Me? The man tried to kill my sister! He's delusional."

Molly gave a negligent shrug. "That's not how the fans see it. At least they'll stop picketing the studio now that you're dead." She smiled and wiggled her fingers. "Toodle-oo, I have to change for your wake."

"You're having a wake for me?" Chloe blurted, horrified at the thought.

Estelle pointed her cane at Molly. "You won't be so smug a month from now. You're not half the actress Chloe is. You can't carry *As the Sun Sets*. The fans will abandon the show in droves."

A flicker of worry crossed Molly's face. She might despise Chloe, but she respected Estelle. A Broadway actress of some renown, Estelle's opinion held weight with the cast and crew. It's too bad her star status didn't appear to be influencing the casting directors. To date, Chloe hadn't received a single offer for a new role.

She carefully swung her legs to the side of the bed. Still weak from her ordeal, she took a moment before standing. She swayed slightly as she got to her feet and looped her arm through Estelle's. "Don't waste your breath. We have an appointment with Steven at WP24, remember?" She tightened her fingers around the older woman's arm, silently warning Estelle not to call her on the lie. Then Chloe lifted her nose in the air, focusing on her posture to walk away with her patented elegant grace.

Suck on that, Molly.

Getting the best of the other actress felt good for about five seconds before the realization hit that Chloe was washed up at thirty-two. And none of her colleagues cared. They despised her. She wasn't exactly easy to work with, but only because she wanted the daytime drama to be the best it could be. She pushed her co-stars as hard as she pushed herself. But she'd never forgotten one of their birthdays and sent all of them cards at Christmas and Hanukkah.

"I don't suppose Mr. Spielberg called you back, did he?"

"Sorry to say he hasn't, my dear." Estelle patted her hand. "I'm sure he would have if he'd viewed your audition tapes. You're a brilliant actress. Don't let Molly or the others make you doubt yourself. You have a bright future ahead of you."

Chloe managed a weak smile. "You're good for my confidence, Estelle. I don't know what I would have done without you these past few months."

The older woman had moved in with Chloe when Cat decided to remain in Colorado—with Estelle's grandson Grayson. They were a couple now. A bitter pill both she and Estelle had to swallow. Grayson was perfect for Chloe. Even Estelle thought so. But he'd fallen in love with Cat while she'd been pretending to be Chloe. How telling was that? Estelle swore that one day he'd come to his senses and return to LA and Chloe.

"Likewise, my dear. Fluffy and I are very happy at the beach house," Estelle said, referring to her white Angora cat and Chloe's gorgeous home on Redondo Beach. The older woman gave her an apologetic smile when they reached Chloe's dressing room. "I'm afraid I have more bad news."

Chloe placed a hand over her racing heart. She needed another pill, but she'd already taken her limit for the day. "You're not leaving me too, are you?"

"No, it's—"

Her frantic gaze searched Estelle's face. "Are you sick? Because if you are, you don't have to worry. I can afford to get you the best care money—"

"No, no, it's not me. It's your sister and Grayson.

They're engaged. Your mother is hosting an engagement party for them this weekend and expects us both to attend."

* * *

Chloe sat in the back of the stretch limo with Estelle and Fluffy. Her mother had met every one of Chloe's excuses not to come to the party with stony silence. She supposed she shouldn't have been surprised by her mother's hard-headedness, but she was. She'd always been her mother's favorite. Liz O'Connor, now McBride after her remarriage last fall, had been Chloe's staunchest ally, her biggest fan. At least up until Christmas she had been. Everything changed the day Chloe accused her sister of trying to kill her.

But when she'd risked her own life to save Cat from the real killer, Chloe'd thought she redeemed herself. She'd discovered over these past few months that she was wrong. Her mother hadn't completely forgiven her. Which was why Chloe was on her way to the engagement party. She didn't want to risk further damaging their relationship.

Estelle, who was on the phone with Grayson, elbowed Chloe in the ribs with a gleam in her eyes. "Really, she invited your father? Whatever gave her the idea you'd be happy about that, my boy?"

Chloe couldn't work up the energy to get caught up in Estelle's excitement. Returning to Christmas always depressed her. It was a pretty town: quaint, charming, postcard perfect really with its pastel-painted shops and cobblestone lanes. She glanced out the tinted windows to where the majestic Rocky Mountains stood sentry over the valley. When she was a little girl, she believed fairy princesses and knights in shining armor inhabited those rocky outcroppings. Their castles hidden in the dark depths of the forest. Her hometown had seemed a beautiful and magical place to live back then. But everything had changed when she hit high school.

Then her dreams and fantasies had been about leaving Christmas and becoming a star. She'd win an Oscar and prove to them that the girl they thought wouldn't amount to anything had. Only she hadn't, not really.

She rubbed her chest, willing the tightness away. It was so much harder coming home today. Chloe's life was circling the drain, and Cat was getting her happy-ever-after. And there'd been a time last December when Chloe had believed Grayson was *her* happy-ever-after.

That was the problem with being identical twins. Not only did they look alike, Chloe and Cat had the same taste in men. But the men fell in love with her sister. She didn't understand why Cat's happiness always had to come at the expense of hers. Cat got the perfect heart, and Chloe got the defective one. Cat got the man of Chloe's dreams, and Chloe got...no one.

"Hang in there, my boy. We'll see you shortly." Estelle gave Chloe's thigh an enthusiastic pat. "There's trouble in paradise, my dear. Grayson is finally seeing the light. I knew sooner or later that he would. My son is in town."

"Lord Waverly is here...in Christmas?" Whatever was Cat thinking? Even Chloe knew that Grayson and his father were estranged. And for good reason.

"Yes. Your sister invited him without telling Grayson." Estelle rolled her eyes. "She wanted to surprise him."

Chloe twisted the Sisters Forever necklace Cat had given her the day she'd been bullied so bad she'd wanted to quit school. She didn't appreciate Estelle making fun of her sister. Chloe could say what she wanted about Cat, but no one else could. "My sister's thoughtful like that. Family's important to her. She'd want Grayson to have his with him today."

"She'll find out the hard way that Peter isn't much of a father. Never was. I raised Grayson." Estelle frowned at her phone. "But I'm surprised my son hasn't called me. He must be as disappointed in Grayson's choice of bride-to-be as I am. He's all about the title. And, as you know, your sister is hardly ladyship material. But you are, my dear. And if we play our cards right, Grayson will see that, too. Maybe it's a good thing Peter's come to town after all."

"I can't think about that now, Estelle. I'm more concerned someone will discover my career is in the toilet. We should go over that list of movies we talked about. The ones we're going to say I have a part in." She chewed on her thumbnail. "Maybe instead of saying I have a part in all of them, we'll say I've got one, looking good for the others." Oh goodness, the plan was fraught with problems already. Estelle's memory couldn't always be trusted. There's no way she'd stay on point the entire day.

As the limo turned onto her stepfather's street, Chloe caught sight of the long lines of vehicles parked on either side of the road. Her chest tightened again. Breathing slowly in and out, she reminded herself that at least she had the money to play the part of a celebutante. The thought helped ease the anxious knot.

The driver parked in front of the gray stone bungalow and then went to open his door. "We'll need a moment," Chloe said, taking a compact out of her coral Hermès bag. She fluffed her hair and did a quick retouch of her makeup. Estelle did the same.

Ten minutes later Chloe looked out the window, wondering why no one had come to greet them. She noticed the driver tapping impatiently on the steering wheel and nibbled on her bottom lip. She grimaced and rubbed her finger across her teeth, then reapplied her coral lipstick. Obviously Grayson hadn't alerted the family that they were close by. She sighed and informed the chauffeur that they were ready.

Chloe checked to make sure her dress hadn't ridden up before gracefully alighting from the limo. As she placed her hand in the chauffeur's, she looked from under her fake eyelashes, checking to see if they had an audience. They didn't. Her shoulders slumped. So far, the day wasn't going how she envisioned. Smoothing a manicured hand down her Jean Paul Gaultier garden-printed sheath dress, she waited for Estelle to join her on the walkway. At least Chloe's dress was divine, perfect for a garden party in early May. Her Louboutins with the four-inch coral heels were fab, too. And thankfully her hair had cooperated, falling into long, loose waves to her midback.

"You'll be the belle of the ball, my dear. You look absolutely stunning."

"Oh no, I don't want to overshadow my sister. It's her day after all." She pasted a gracious smile on her face. She *so* wanted to overshadow Cat today. Yes, it was petty and mean-spirited, but it was the truth. She didn't like the feeling and wished she could make it go away. The trick was not to let anyone else know how she felt. Thank goodness she was a brilliant actress.

Chloe companionably looped her arm through Estelle's. "You're looking very posh yourself." The older woman had on a gold silk sheath dress with matching jacket, her champagne blond hair smoothed back in a classic chignon. At seventy-seven, she was still a beautiful woman. "Anyone special you were hoping to see today?" she teased, knowing full well there was.

"I thought perhaps I'd look up Fred and Ted." Estelle patted her hair, then made a face. "That nasty old woman isn't going to be here today, is she?"

Chloe knew exactly who she was referring to. Nell McBride was the town's self-appointed matriarch and matchmaker. Ted and Fred were her best friends, and she hadn't been pleased when they'd taken a shine to Estelle. "I'm afraid so. She's my stepfather's aunt."

And that reminded Chloe who else would be here… Easton McBride. She stopped halfway up the stone walk and dug in her purse for her pills. Estelle did the same, then held up a silver flask. "I thought we might need this."

"I'm not sure we should be taking our medication with Scotch, Estelle."

"I watered it down," the older woman said and popped her pills in her mouth. She took a swig before handing Chloe the flask.

She supposed it couldn't hurt. She'd need a little liquid courage to face Easton. He despised her and didn't care who knew it, including her. And yes, he may have had good reason to feel that way fifteen years ago. But my goodness, it was such a long time to hold a grudge.

She wrinkled her nose as she lifted the flask to her mouth.

The front door opened. It was Easton. And like every single time she saw his outrageously handsome face, her heart pitter-pattered in her chest and the theme song from *The Princess Bride* started playing in her head. It was silly. And she wished she could turn off the soundtrack in her mind. But it had been playing there since she was fifteen and Easton saved her from the schoolyard bullies. He'd been her hero from that moment on. Her white knight. She'd thought he was her *one* until he became her sister's. He'd loved Cat. They'd probably be…Chloe's eyes widened…married now if it weren't for her.

"Little early to be drinking, isn't it, Scarlett?"

Chapter Two

Chloe barely registered what Easton said because a lightbulb went off in her head. Her sister's old flame was the answer to her prayers. She opened her mouth to lay out a win-Cat-back plan to Easton and inhaled an excited breath. She choked on the Scotch.

"Jesus," Easton muttered with an irritated look in his sapphire blue eyes as she coughed and sputtered. He came down the front steps and patted her back.

She teetered on her heels, raising her hand to get him to stop with the forceful slaps. "I'm okay," she wheezed.

The man didn't know his own strength. He was built like the star quarterback he'd once been in high school—thick neck, wide shoulders and broad chest, narrow hips and the tightest behind this side of the great divide. Actually, since he stood in front of her, she hadn't gotten a look at his behind. But she didn't imagine it had changed since she'd last seen him naked. His seven-year stint in the military had only served to further strengthen and harden the man.

Her four-inch heels put her eye level with his chin, the cleft she used to delight in kissing barely visible beneath the dark scruff. She lifted her gaze to his beautifully shaped mouth; the hint of a bow in his upper lip, the bottom sensually full. His perfect lips flattened. She briefly closed her eyes and released a disheartened sigh.

Easton McBride would never be the answer to her prayers.

He made an aggravated sound in his throat and dropped his hand, taking a step back.

"Are you all right, my dear?" Estelle asked, touching Chloe's shoulder in concern while slanting a wary glance at Easton.

"I'll be fine, thank you. I just need a moment to catch my breath." And to prepare to see her family and the happily engaged couple. It would have been so much easier if she could convince Easton that Cat was his *one*. He could save them both a whole lot of heartache by simply going along with the plan that had popped into Chloe's head the moment she saw him.

He crossed his arms over the U.S. Army logo stitched onto his sleeveless black T-shirt. "What's with the accent?"

She drew her gaze from his biceps. "What are you talking about? I don't have an accent."

"Don't know why I bothered to ask," he said as if talking to himself, then gave them a mocking bow. "Your highnesses."

She didn't understand why he had to be so rude. The man held a grudge longer than anyone she knew. Still, she couldn't help but watch as he headed across the grass toward the line of cars. His black sweat shorts showed off his tight behind. She'd been right, he did have the best butt, and his legs were...

A shocked cry escaped before she could contain it. His right calf was strong and muscular while his left was ravaged with ugly, vivid red scars from repeated surgeries. She'd heard that an IED had blown up the convoy he'd been traveling in in Afghanistan, but other than a noticeable limp, she hadn't known the extent of his injuries. He was lucky to have kept his leg.

Easton glanced over his shoulder, and those mocking blue eyes held hers. He'd heard her horrified gasp. He wouldn't want sympathy from anyone, least of all her. She turned away, forcing a smile for Estelle. "I suppose it's now or never."

Chloe flinched at the sound of a door slamming. He was angry at her. She didn't blame him; she should have done a better job concealing her reaction. She wondered if she should go to him and try to explain. She glanced over her shoulder. He'd retrieved a football from his truck. He wasn't leaving after all. Still shaken by that brief glimpse of how badly he'd been injured, how close he'd come to losing his life, she thought it best to hold off on the apology and returned her attention to Estelle. She helped the older woman up the steps. "An hour should be long enough to pay our respects to the happy couple, don't you think, Estelle?"

Her manager rubbed her cheek against Fluffy's head. "If it's any longer than that, let's hope the punch is spiked."

Chloe seconded the sentiment and rang her stepfather's doorbell. Technically, she supposed the stone bungalow was her mother's home, too, since she lived here, but Chloe felt uncomfortable walking in without an invitation.

A drawn-out sigh warned her that Easton was close by. Sure enough, he reached around her and opened the door. She hesitated, once again wondering if she should apologize. But given how he felt about her, he'd probably throw her apology in her face. So instead she murmured, "Thank you," and went to step inside. But strong, warm fingers wrapped around her arm, and he drew her out of the way. "Go on in, Dame Alexander. I need a word with Chloe. Everyone's out back." He gave Estelle directions, then closed the door.

Chloe pivoted. "Easton, that's so rude. Estelle doesn't know—"

He stared down at her. "Why are you here?"

She frowned. "Where else would I be? It's my sister's engagement party. I was invited."

"Don't bullshit me, Chloe. I know you too well. If you've come to make a scene, I suggest you head back to LA right now."

"Why are you being so mean to me?" She searched his face, his cold, closed-off expression. This wasn't about her reaction to his injury. This was about their past. "You'll never forgive me, will you? I've apologized over and over again, but you just tune me out. Fifteen years is a long time to hold a grudge, even for you." She hoped he'd forgotten about the little incident at their parents' rehearsal party last fall.

His brow furrowed, then he released a short bark of laughter. "You're unbelievable. This is about Cat. It's her day, Chloe. And if you do one thing to upset her, I'm toss-ing you out on your ass."

She blinked up at him, ignoring the dull ache expand-ing in her chest. "You really do love her."

"Of course I do. We all do. And no one wants to see her hurt again. So if you think you can come here—"

At the reminder of how much everyone adored her sis-ter and despised her, Chloe's bottom lip quivered. She bit down on it. She shouldn't have come. The logo on his T-shirt blurred, and she turned to face the door. "Despite what you think of me"—the emotion she struggled to contain came out in her voice, and she cleared her throat before continuing—"What you all seem to think of me. I love my sister. I won't stay long. I don't want to ruin everyone's fun."

She heard him swear under his breath, then he placed a hand on her shoulder. "Look, maybe I over—"

Her mother opened the front door. She glanced from Easton to Chloe with a tentative smile on her pretty face. "Is everything okay out here?"

"Everything's wonderful. It's so good to see you, Mommsy. I've missed you so much," Chloe said past the lump in her throat. Her smile wobbled. Combined with Easton's hurtful remarks, seeing her mother and knowing how close she'd come to losing her love last Christmas broke what little control she had left over her emotions. A tear rolled down her cheek, and Chloe gave a small, helpless cry, throwing herself in her mother's arms.

* * *

Dammit to hell, he'd done it now. He made Chloe cry. It hadn't been his intention. Granted, since he knew the woman was an emotional drama queen, he should have thought before he spoke. All he wanted to do was ensure that they didn't have a repeat of last December's drama. He didn't want Chloe to ruin her sister's big day. Cat had lived in her sister's shadow long enough. She deserved to be the center of attention today. But he'd wanted to take the words back as soon as he saw Chloe's bottom lip quiver and the shimmer of tears in her green eyes.

Maybe if she hadn't shown up in a stretch limo looking like a cover model in a dress that hugged her curves and probably cost more than half the folks in town made in a year, he wouldn't have laid into her. Only problem with that argument was, he hadn't said anything then. Chloe flaunting her money, along with her newly acquired British accent, wasn't why he'd gone off on her. He was pretty much immune to Chloe O'Connor the beauty queen.

What he wasn't immune to was the sickened expression that came over her face when she got a look at his leg. Did it bother him that the sight of his scars made her look like she wanted to hurl? Nah, he couldn't care less. Chloe lived in a world where people went under the knife for the slightest flaw, imagined or otherwise. Injecting poison into their lips and foreheads to the point they resembled pod people. Chloe hadn't succumbed to the pressure yet, but it was only a matter of time. No one worshipped at the altar of perfection more than Chloe O'Connor.

But thanks to her shocked cry, he'd lost his concentration while walking across the uneven grass to retrieve the football from his pickup. After turning away from her, he'd tripped. The last thing he wanted to do was fall on his face in front of her, and he'd strained the weak muscles in his injured leg to remain standing. The excruciating pain nearly brought him to his knees, and that pissed him off. He was tired of the pain, tired of seeing the worry on his family's and friends' faces.

Chloe had been on the receiving end of his temper and frustration. Typically, he alleviated the anger with the reminder he was damn lucky to be alive. He should have thought about that before taking it out on her. Even though his warning was warranted, he could have toned it down some.

He grimaced when Chloe threw herself into her mother's arms, his fingers tightening around the football. Liz looked at him as she stroked her daughter's long, midnight-black hair. He wasn't sure if it was a here-we-go or a what-did-you-do expression on his stepmother's face. Whatever it was, he probably should apologize.

Just as he opened his mouth to do so, Liz said, "Darling, what's wrong? Why are you crying?"

Easing from her mother's arms, Chloe sniffed loudly and repeatedly. "I-I'm not crying, Mommsy. I must be allergic to Fluffy."

Huh. He was kind of surprised she didn't throw him under the bus. And that made him feel guiltier for the way he'd treated her. Because while she might be a spoiled pain in the ass, he knew she could also be sweet, compassionate, and kind. There was a time, years earlier, that he'd been on the receiving end of her sweetness. Right before she'd played him and ruined his relationship with her sister.

"You've never had allergies before…" Liz trailed off as she searched her daughter's face. "Do you have any other symptoms? Tightness in your chest, swelling of your lips and tongue?"

Oh, Jesus, no, she did not just put out the specter of anaphylactic shock to Chloe. Then again, he supposed he shouldn't be surprised that she did. Liz had been angsting over Chloe's health since they brought her home from the hospital with a hole in her heart. If she could have put her little girl in a protective bubble, she probably would have. Something he could relate to. His father was as much a worrier as Liz. But there was one big difference; Easton and his brothers weren't hypochondriacs. Chloe was. And now her mother had most likely ensured there would be a scene like the one he'd hoped to avoid. Unless…

He moved away from the door, shutting it behind him. "She's fine, Liz." He put his arm around Chloe and gave her a squeeze. "Aren't you?"

"I don't know. I am having a hard time swallowing." She rubbed her throat as though pushing a football down her long, graceful neck, then smacked her coral lips together a couple of times. "My lips feel tingly. Is my tongue swollen?" At least that's what he thought she said. It was kind of hard to make out since she stuck her tongue out at the same time she asked.

"Chloe, you're not allergic to the cat. You—" Easton was working his way to an apology, but she cut him off.

"Are you sure? It feels really thick."

"Put your tongue back in your mouth. You were crying because I hurt your feelings, not because you've developed a sudden allergy to Fluffy."

She stiffened, then removed his arm from her shoulders. "You didn't hurt my feelings, and you certainly did not make me cry."

His father, wearing chinos, a powder-blue golf shirt, and a frown, approached. "What's going on?"

The last thing Easton wanted was to give Chloe an audience. And if they stood here long enough, they'd draw a crowd. He had to move this along. "Look, I'm sorry, Chloe. I didn't mean to make you cry."

His father drew her to his side, narrowing his eyes at Easton. "You made her cry?" Paul had become as protective of Liz's daughters as he was of his own sons.

Before Easton could defend himself, Chloe gave his father a fond smile and patted his chest. "It's all right, Paul. I'm used to Easton. I don't pay attention to what he says to me anymore. It goes in one ear and out the other." She demonstrated this with a manicured, peach-polished finger, then her narrow shoulders raised on a sigh. "If I'm upset about anything"—she touched her damp cheek—"and obviously I am, it's because of the traumatic experience I suffered a couple of days ago. I thought I'd shaken it off, but really, that would be expecting too much of myself. Of anyone, really. It's not every day you're murdered. Smothered to death by a pillow-wielding sociopath."

The three of them stared at her, and she waved her hand. "I'm perfectly fine. Mommsy and Paul, no fussing over me. I absolutely forbid it. This is Cat's big day. All the attention must be on her, do you understand me?"

Oh, she's good, Easton thought, even though he didn't have a clue what she was talking about. Apparently he wasn't the only one.

"Well, yes…" Liz wrinkled her nose. "Actually, no

I don't. What are you talking about, darling? Who was murdered?"

"Me, of course. I...Is it warm in here?" She fanned herself, looking a little panicked when the three of them assured her it wasn't. "I probably shouldn't be talking about dying. That's enough to make anyone's heart race, isn't it?" She pressed the back of her hand to her forehead and pointed to her purse with the other one. "Can...can you get my pills, Mommsy? Please."

Great, she was going into full drama-queen mode. Or as Cat referred to it, "her Scarlett O'Hara act." And Liz and Paul were buying into her performance.

"Of course. Just relax and take deep breaths," her mother said as she dug around in Chloe's purse.

Enough was enough. They'd just make it worse by encouraging her. "Chloe, look at me," Easton said. "There's nothing wrong with you. Those pills aren't—"

His father's eyes widened, and he gave his head a slight warning shake. "Son, I don't think this is the time—"

Easton cut his father off. It was past time she knew what everyone else did. "Chloe, they're sugar pills."

She frowned. "Why would you say something like that? They're nitrogen tablets for my heart condition." She looked up at his father. "Tell him, Paul."

His father rubbed the back of neck. Something he did when he was nervous.

And when his father opened his mouth, no doubt to play into her delusions, Easton gestured to the bottle clutched in her hand. "If you don't believe me, take them to a pharmacist. Cat thought they'd help with your...attacks. There's nothing wrong with you." Nothing a little therapy wouldn't cure.

"Hey, why are you all hanging out in the house?" Cat asked, as she walked through the living room with a smile.

Chloe whirled on her sister, shaking the plastic bottle at Cat. "You changed my prescription to sugar pills! What were you trying to do, kill me?"

Chapter Three

As soon as the words were out of her mouth, Chloe regretted them. And not because she didn't have a right to be furious at her sister's deception, but because of the look of disappointment that came over her mother's face. It was depressingly similar to the expression Liz wore back in December. Chloe may have overreacted then, but she wasn't now.

"Sorry, Cat. I probably shouldn't have said anything." Easton apologized to her sister as if Chloe wasn't standing three feet away from him.

Really? Cat was playing Russian roulette with Chloe's life, and he felt the need to apologize to her sister? It was so easy for all of them to chalk up her attacks to being an overly emotional drama queen. They didn't have to live with the constant fear that their damaged heart would stop beating.

"Don't worry about it, Easton. She was going to find out sooner or later," her sister said, then turned to Chloe.

"I'm sorry. I should have told you. But Easton's right, Chloe, there isn't anything wrong with you."

Right, she just had an unreliable heart. And now they were all watching her as though they expected her to lose it and make a scene. No one wanted to upset Cat. They couldn't care less that she'd jeopardized Chloe's well-being, as long as nothing interfered with her sister's happy day.

His stubbled jaw tight, arms crossed over his chest, Easton appeared ready to make good on his earlier threat. She didn't plan on giving him the satisfaction. The re-alization they'd all been discussing her attacks, laughing behind her back, was humiliating enough.

Chloe lifted her chin and channeled her inner diva, the one who was never humiliated or hurt. "I suppose I should be thanking you, Kit Kat. Lately I've been con-cerned about the amount of medication I have to take. At least now I know those studies about the placebo effect are true. Lucky for me I have such a strong and creative mind at my disposal or I'd be stuck taking medication for the rest of my life." She forced a smile and returned the fake prescription to her purse, hoping her abrupt one-eighty didn't give her away.

Since her mother, sister, and Paul visibly relaxed, it appeared they believed her. She shouldn't be surprised. After all, she was an award-winning actress. She just wished her mother's pleased smile didn't carry a touch of pity as well. Chloe didn't know how she was going to get through the next hour. Especially if Easton kept look-ing at her with a hint of amusement in those startling blue eyes of his.

A distant memory ignited a warm flutter in the pit of

her stomach. He used to look at her that way in high school, and every time he did, she'd have the same reaction. Not something she should be thinking about now. The day was proving painful enough. She needed a distraction. She had to look no further than her mother and sister and their casual attire. What on earth had they been thinking? Liz's white capri pants and sleeveless knit top and Cat's navy shorts and nautical T-shirt weren't suitable for a garden party. For that matter, neither were Easton's and Paul's.

"I thought the party started at two. Did I get the wrong day?" She kept her smile firmly in place even though she inwardly cringed at the thought. More than an hour of faked happiness would be exhausting. Without proper medication, she'd have to be careful to keep her emotions in check until she returned to LA. She'd make an appointment with a cardiologist as soon as she landed.

* * *

Chloe didn't have the wrong time or day after all. Too bad someone didn't think to inform her the garden party was actually a pool party. But they were currently experiencing a heat wave so perhaps it was a last-minute decision.

She sat in a lawn chair beside Estelle, pretending that they were having a wonderful time. Just the two of them. There were at least seventy-five guests milling about Paul's backyard. At the moment, her mother was leading four women on a tour along a gravel path through the extensive gardens bordered by lilac trees and crab apples in full bloom.

Their fragrant aroma mingled with the smell of chlorine from the pool a few feet from where Estelle and Chloe sat. She'd prefer to be sitting in the shade of the soaring pine and aspen trees clustered at the far side of the yard but a large group of older women already sat there, including Nell McBride.

Estelle said something, and Chloe drew her attention back to her manager. As she did, she noticed Paul, who stood on the other side of the pool with a group of his friends, watching her with a concerned frown. She moistened her lips and forced a girlish laugh, then patted Estelle's hand. "You tell the most amusing stories."

The older woman frowned. "I wasn't trying to be amusing. I think Fluffy has heatstroke," she said, tipping the cat's face up.

"Oh, I'm so sorry, Estelle. I couldn't hear above the music." At least her excuse was believable. A boom box sat not ten feet from them, the latest hits blaring from the speakers. If they'd been there for more than twenty minutes, Chloe would suggest they leave. Instead she said, "I'll get her a bowl of water and a cold cloth," and half rose from the chair.

"No, no, I'll take her inside," Estelle said, getting up. She patted Chloe's shoulder. "Don't worry, I won't be long."

Obviously Chloe's panic at being left alone showed on her face. She sighed, wishing Ty was there. At least she'd have someone to talk to. But her mother had mentioned he'd be late. Ty used to be the hairstylist for *As the Sun Sets*. Three months earlier he'd also been Chloe's roommate, and, she'd thought, close friend. Until he decided he liked her sister better and picked up stakes and moved to Christmas to open a salon.

As she watched to make sure Estelle got the patio door

open, Easton's niece yelled, "Get ready, Lily! I'm going to do a cannonball."

Chloe whipped her head around, judging the distance from her to the pool. She raised her hand. "Just a moment, Angie. Let me move my chair, please."

The pretty, dark-haired teenager turned to look at her. "It's Annie. And if you don't want to get wet, why don't you sit over there?" She pointed to where Cat sat laughing with a group of her friends—her casually dressed friends.

"I can't sit in the sun," she told the teenager, and shuffled the lawn chair further beneath the green-and-white-striped awning.

Annie frowned. "How come?"

"It causes skin cancer." She didn't think the young girl would care that it also caused premature aging. "Do you have sunscreen on? I have some 40 SPF if you want to use it." She reached into her purse to pull out a tube.

"No, thanks," Annie yelled mid-run, and then she did a cannonball.

A cascade of water rose up from the pool, splattering Chloe's dress. She released a small cry of dismay and hurriedly wiped at the droplets in an effort to protect the expensive fabric from staining.

"Why the Sam Hill did you get all gussied up? It's not the wedding, you know."

Chloe inhaled a deep breath through her nose. She should have known she wouldn't escape Nell McBride's attention for long. The older woman walked toward her wearing a pair of red capri pants and a T-shirt covered in poppies the exact match to her hair. "Hello, Nell. I see you've been going to Ty. He did a lovely job with your hair."

Nell finger-combed her spiky hair. "He did, didn't he? Fred and Ted tell me I look ten years younger." She pulled a lawn chair beside Chloe and sat down. Estelle had picked a fine time to abandon her. Although it was probably best her manager wasn't there. Chloe didn't have the energy to play referee.

She decided it was safer to keep Nell focused on her hair than on her. "They're right, you do. The cut is very youthful, and the color complements your skin tone. What shade did he use?"

Nell ignored her attempt to distract her. "Didn't expect you to show up today. For your mother's and sister's sake, I'm glad that you did. But you should probably mingle a bit. Doesn't look good you sitting off in a corner feeling sorry for yourself. People will start to talk, you know."

"Whatever gave you the idea I'm feeling sorry for myself?" She forced a laugh, it was sharp enough to cut glass. "Now that I'm finally free of my role as Tessa Hart, I have directors inundating me with scripts. I've hardly gotten any sleep trying to read—"

"So they killed you off, did they? Thought they might. I saw the fans picketing the studio on *Access Hollywood*."

Chloe lifted her chin. "The news hasn't been released yet. Once it is, I'm sure my fans will do the same for me when they learn I've been murdered." Now that wasn't something she'd given much thought to. Probably because she'd expected the offers to be pouring in by now. But if her fans reacted like George's, maybe they'd resurrect Tessa Hart. It wasn't as if it hadn't been done before. Anything was possible on a daytime drama. But could she really see herself going back? She sighed. It was an option if no other offers came her way.

Nell, her attention on Easton, absently nodded in response. He was playing football with his brothers, and Cat's fiancé, Grayson, on the lawn to the left of the pool. Chloe had been doing her best to ignore them. It was difficult to see Easton crippled by his injury. He couldn't run like he used to, and those disfiguring scars... But it was the tall and leanly muscled Grayson, with his pale blue eyes and dark hair, that she'd been avoiding looking at. He was so beautiful he hurt her eyes as much as he hurt her heart.

"You get that thought right out of your head, girlie."

Chloe stiffened. "I don't know what you're talking about. He's my sister's fiancé. I would never—"

Nell's darkened eyebrows drew together. "I was talking about Easton."

"Oh, I... Why can't I look at Easton? Does he have a girlfriend?" She didn't know what made her ask or why the thought caused a small pinch in her chest. Maybe she was still holding out hope for her win-Cat-back plan.

"Not yet, he doesn't. But I intend to fix that. He's the hero in my next book. I just need to find him his perfect match."

Obviously, from Nell's reaction, it wasn't Chloe.

Two years earlier, the older woman had started writing a romance series set in Christmas. Each book featured a couple Nell had a hand in bringing together. All of whom were here today, looking happy and very much in love. Watching them made Chloe realize how much she longed for a family of her own. But where her love life was concerned, she seemed destined to make one disastrous choice after another. Maybe what she needed was a matchmaker with a proven track record. She smiled at Nell. "So when do I get my book?"

Nell grimaced. "Would you look at that, it's already three. I better get in there and help with the food," she said and got up from the chair.

"Wait, you didn't answer..." Chloe trailed off as the older woman made a dash for the patio doors leading off the kitchen. Several people turned from their conversations to look at Chloe. Her cheeks warmed, and she bowed her head, fishing in her purse for her phone. She put it to her ear, pretending she had an important call.

"Oh, Steven"—she released a tinkling laugh—"you'll make me blush. Of course I can. I'm sure my family will understand—" She looked up to see Estelle hurrying toward her and wondered if her manager and Nell had gotten into it in the kitchen. She hoped they did. At least they'd have a legitimate excuse to leave early. Their rooms at the lodge should be ready by now.

Chloe pretended to disconnect. She didn't have to say a fake good-bye. No one was paying any attention to her. "Is something wrong, Estelle?"

Lowering herself onto the chair beside Chloe, the older woman beamed. "I just got off the phone with Peter. The visit went exactly as I expected. My son refused to give his blessing and tried to talk Grayson out of the marriage. They had a terrible row just before they left for the party, and Grayson sent him packing."

She didn't understand what Estelle was so happy about. "That's awful. Poor Grayson."

"He'll get over it. Now all we have to do is play on the doubts Peter planted in my grandson's mind, and the wedding will be off."

Chloe glanced to where her mother stood with her friends. "I don't think that's a good idea. If I do anything

to come between Grayson and Cat, my family will never
forgive me." And she didn't know if she'd forgive herself.
She'd destroyed her sister's happiness once. She couldn't
do it again.

"You'd be doing her a favor, saving her from future
heartache. Look at them, do they look happy to you?"

"It's their engagement party, of course they're..." As
she searched the crowd for her sister, Chloe trailed off.
Grayson and Easton's older brother Chance were no
longer playing football. They were standing under a tree
talking to Cat. Her sister was pinching the bridge of her
nose between her thumb and forefinger, something she
did when she was frustrated. While Grayson raked his
hand through his thick, chocolate-brown hair, looking as
unhappy as his bride-to-be. Chloe leaned forward in an
effort to read the couple's lips.

A familiar voice distracted her, and she twisted at the
waist. Ty leaned half-in and half-out the patio doors, talking to someone in the kitchen. He had on white slacks
and a short-sleeve shirt with a white-and-black geometric
print. Laughing, he slid the glass door closed and
searched the crowd. Happy to see another friendly face
besides Estelle's, Chloe raised her hand, about to call out
to him. Then lowered her arm at the thought he'd want to
see his best friend first.

He turned and caught sight of Chloe, a wide, welcoming smile creasing his handsome face. "Diva!" As soon as
he reached her, he hauled her out of the lawn chair and
rocked her in his arms. "I've missed you."

"I've missed you, too," she said, hugging him tight.

He leaned back, taking her in from head to toe. His
eyes admiring behind his red square-framed glasses, he

said, "Totally rocking the Jean Paul, Diva. And your hair is fabulous as always. Thank God there's someone else around here with a sense of style. Can you believe how they're dressed for an engagement party?"

She laughed, feeling a little less alone than she had earlier. "No. Couldn't you talk my sister into a more elegant affair?"

He snorted, then stepped away from her to greet Estelle. "Duchess, you look marvelous, darling." The older woman preened when he lifted her hand to his lips. "So how are my roomies faring without me?" he asked as he grabbed a lawn chair.

"Wonderful. We no longer have to wait hours to use the loo," Chloe said, moving her chair over to make room for him between her and Estelle.

He grinned and patted her thigh. "You really do miss me, don't you? Okay, now give me the 411. How's everyone at *As the Sun Sets*? Is Molly still being a biatch?"

"Molly killed me. She smothered me to death with a pillow."

"Shut up! She did not."

Sinking her teeth into her bottom lip, Chloe nodded.

"They're a bunch of morons," Ty said, pulling her into his arms. "Without you, the show will be canceled in six months."

"Just so, my boy. That's exactly what I told her," Estelle said.

"Now's your chance to break out. Forget the soaps. Go after a nice, meaty big screen role. You've got the acting chops for it...and the looks. Have you had any bites?"

"Oh, yes, there's a wonderful period piece—" Estelle began.

Chloe cut off her manager before she listed the movies they'd discussed earlier. She didn't have to pretend with Ty. "Not one."

He frowned. "Are you serious?"

"Yes, but I'm sure something will come up soon." She had to change the subject; she was getting depressed. "Enough about me. How are you enjoying Christmas? Did you have the official opening for your salon yet?"

"I wouldn't have it without my favorite celebrity in attendance, now would I? As soon as your mother told me about the engagement party, I scheduled the grand opening for next Saturday afternoon."

"We planned to leave tomorrow morning." She chewed on her thumbnail. She knew what he was going to ask. And no matter how much she wanted to be here for Ty, she didn't think she could handle staying in town.

He pulled her thumb from her mouth. "You have to stay. I need you there."

"You have Cat."

He glanced to where her sister stood deep in conversation with Chance and his very pregnant wife, Vivi. "Between Grayson and her job, she hasn't had much time for me." He shrugged as if it didn't bother him, but Chloe could tell that it did.

Impulsively, she said, "All right, I'll stay."

Ty clapped his hands. "What about you, Duchess?"

"Yes, of course. Anything to support you, my boy." Estelle patted his cheek, then leaned in to him. "Now tell me, how is my grandson? Truly."

"Okay, and this is totally under the dome of silence," he steepled his fingers over his head, "There's trouble in paradise."

"I knew it!" Estelle said, banging her cane on the ground for emphasis.

"What part of 'dome' and 'silence' did you not understand, Duchess?"

"Sorry. Do tell."

The three of them huddled close with their heads touching. "All right, so Pussy just…Oh, get over it," he said when Chloe and Estelle winced at his nickname for Cat, "…took on a case with McBride Security, and Grayson wants her off of it. She's protecting a guy that the FBI's been investigating for the past year. She refused, and then Lord Waverly arrived the next day. Last night I would have laid odds against this little shindig happening."

Chloe sat back in her chair, mulling over the news. Grayson was a special agent with the FBI, so she could see his point. But she could also see her sister's. Several years ago, Cat had been the youngest female detective with the Denver PD. She'd loved working in law enforcement. It had nearly destroyed her sister when she was forced to leave her job under a cloud of suspicion. Chloe imagined working for Easton and Chance at McBride Security had gone a long way in erasing those unhappy memories. Cat took pride in her job, and there was no way she'd cave to Grayson's demands. Now or ever. Estelle was right, the couple were setting themselves up for heartache.

Unless Chloe did something.

She had to save her sister from making another mistake. Even though she'd been positive Cat's ex, Michael Upton, was the scoundrel he turned out to be, she hadn't said anything to her sister. So while it was possible Chloe would alienate her family, she had to take the risk. This was her chance to make up for the hurt she'd caused Cat in the past.

She looked up to see Estelle watching her. The older woman raised her penciled eyebrows as if to say "I told you so." Chloe nodded. She knew what she had to do.

"Ty, darling, come here for a sec." Her mother waved him over to the group of women she stood with.

"Okay, you two, remember." Ty made a zip-it motion with his fingers as he got out of his chair. "Once the party's over, we'll head over to my salon, and I'll give you the grand tour."

"I can't wait," Chloe said.

Estelle agreed. "Looking forward to it, my boy." The moment he was out of earshot, she whispered to Chloe, "What's the plan?"

"Don't you worry about it. I'll take care of everything, Estelle." Chloe stood up and smoothed a palm down her dress. As she walked around the pool, she thought of something her sister-in-law Skye always said, "Everything happens for a reason."

Maybe she was right. If Chloe hadn't been killed off *As the Sun Sets* or if an offer had come in for a movie role, she wouldn't have the opportunity or time to play Cupid and make up for her past mistakes. The thought made her feel better about her lack of job opportunities and reinforced her belief that she was meant to do this.

She stepped off the cement deck to avoid being splashed by the laughing children in the pool. "Careful," she told them, forcing a light-hearted tone to her voice, then she raised a hand and called, "Easton. Yoo-hoo, Easton."

His eyes met hers just as he drew his arm back. Then, as the ball left his hand, he mouthed "oh, shit" and yelled, "Chloe!"

What's the matter with him now? she thought, tipping her head back to watch the football spiral in the cloudless blue sky. And that's when she realized it was headed directly for her.

Chapter Four

Easton ran full-out in hope of intercepting the ball, but his leg slowed him down. He swore under his breath when the football hit Chloe's hands and glanced off her head. His brother Gage, who he'd been throwing the ball to, sprinted past him. Neither of them made it in time to save Chloe from falling backward into the pool. As she hit the water with a blood-curdling scream, Gage shot him a look.

"For chrissakes, I didn't do it on purpose," Easton muttered, closing in on the pool. They all knew how he felt about Chloe, so he supposed it wasn't a stretch that his brother might think the throw had been intentional. But seriously, he should know better. Easton would never hurt a woman, even if she was a pain in the ass. The problem was, Chloe had called out to him as he drew back his arm to throw the ball. She'd distracted him, and possibly made him nervous. There'd been something about the way she looked at him that put him on edge.

Her head popped up when he reached the side of the pool. She sputtered, choking on a mouthful of water as she screamed for help. She kept screaming and flapping her arms.

"No, stay away from her, girls," Gage ordered his daughters Annie and Lily, who began swimming to Chloe's rescue.

It was a good call. The way she was flailing about in the pool, she'd probably drown them. "Chloe, calm down. Grab my hand." Easton knelt on the edge, reaching out to her.

"Help! I'm drowning! Someone help me!"

"You're not drowning. Just give me your damn hand."

She ignored him and kept yelling for help while waving her arms, bobbing up and down in the water. With everyone crowded around the pool calling out to her, it was possible she didn't hear him.

There was no help for it; he had to jump in.

Grayson beat him to it. In three powerful strokes, the other man reached her and wrapped an arm around her waist. "I've got you, Chloe," he said.

She released a shuddering breath, sagging against Grayson as he swam toward the pool's edge. Easton leaned over and grabbed her by the arms. Her eyes were closed, mascara mingling with either tears or water droplets to carve black tracks down her stark white face.

Her eyes opened when he hauled her from the water. "Are you happy now? You nearly drowned me," she whispered, her pale lips quivering.

He sighed and lifted her into his arms, then limped toward the grass. "I didn't mean to. I called out to you. All you had to do is move. Not stand there waiting for the ball to hit you," he grumbled. He wasn't really mad at her. What pissed him off was the sight of his father running toward them with his medical bag followed by a distraught Liz carrying a blanket. Easton had inadvertently given Chloe another opportunity to cause a scene. And this one was too good to pass up. He had no doubt she'd take advantage of the situation.

"Darling, are you all right?" her mother asked as she wrapped the blanket around Chloe's shoulders.

Her teeth chattering, she gave Liz a wan smile. "I'll be fine, Mommsy."

Easton barely managed to contain an eye roll.

"Put her down here, son," his father directed, pointing to a spot on the lawn.

As Easton slowly lowered himself to the grass, his leg buckled, throwing him off balance. In an effort to stay upright, he lost his hold on Chloe. She rolled onto the ground with a shocked cry. Everyone stared at him. "It was an accident, okay? She's fine. Stop treating her like a damn invalid."

Liz and Paul ignored him and knelt beside Chloe, who stared past Easton with a look of adoration on her face. He briefly closed his eyes and stood up. He didn't have to turn around to know who was behind him. There'd been a time when she'd looked at Easton the exact same way. Grayson had done it now.

Chloe clasped her hands to her chest. "Thank you, Grayson. You...you saved me. I owe you my life."

"Oh, come on, don't be so dramatic. You weren't drowning, Chloe. All you had to do was swim four feet—" Easton began before she cut him off.

"I don't know how to swim."

"Of course you do. You—"

"No, I don't." She glared at him.

Okay, so she hadn't been acting after all. Given how overly protective her parents had been, he probably should have realized there was a possibility they hadn't allowed her to learn. And he would have apologized for misjudging the situation if she didn't immediately turn her hero-worshipping gaze back on Grayson. As everyone crowded behind his father and Liz, Easton took a couple careful steps back on the uneven ground. *Here we go,* he thought, when Estelle and Ty crouched beside her. They were almost as dramatic as Chloe.

Cat sprinted toward them. Standing off to the side, Easton was in a position to witness her brief exchange with Grayson. She lightly brushed her hand down his arm, thanking him, Easton assumed, for saving her sister. Obviously, she didn't realize the consequences of her fiancé coming to Chloe's rescue. Grayson looked down at Cat and said something that made her frown. She gave her head a slight, irritated shake, and then went to her sister's side. Sadly, Easton wasn't the only one who witnessed the exchange.

From where she lay on the ground, Chloe's leaf-green eyes flitted from her sister to Cat's unhappy fiancé. The couple were going through a rough patch, and the last thing they needed was Chloe in town stirring up trouble. And he had no doubt she would. She'd caused a crapload of it back in December. They didn't need a repeat. But he didn't know how to broach the subject with Cat. He was a guy; he didn't do relationship shit. But she was his friend, and he owed her a heads-up. Maybe he'd talk to Grayson instead.

Before Easton could take a step in the other man's direction, Chance grabbed his arm and shoved his cane at him. "Don't even think about arguing. You're gray, and you're sweating. You shouldn't have been playing ball, and you sure has hell shouldn't have been carrying Chloe."

"Keep your voice down," he growled, afraid their dad would overhear. That's all he needed. "I bench-press more than Chloe weighs every day." It was true. He'd forgotten how small and delicate she was until he'd held her in his arms. She was almost a foot shorter than him, although her hooker heels added an extra four inches to her height. He glanced in her direction. She was being helped to her feet, the back of her hand pressed to her brow. The woman would never change.

Yet earlier, he'd thought that maybe she had. She hadn't made a scene like he'd expected her to. Oh, she'd been about to. He'd seen the flash of temper in her eyes when she turned on Cat, heard it in her voice. And then, just as quickly, she'd turned it around. The spin she'd put on the situation had amused him. Oddly enough, he seemed to be the only one who realized she was faking it. She'd been humiliated, hurt that she'd been played. He understood how she felt. It's why he'd told her about the sugar pills. And not to embarrass her. In his own way, he was trying to protect her.

Because no matter that she drove him nuts, he couldn't shake the memory of the painfully shy little girl she'd once been. The one who'd light up when he walked into a room, who'd looked at him like *he* was her hero. And while he'd tossed the football with his brothers and Grayson, he'd found himself watching her. An uncomfortable tightness building in his chest at the sight of her sitting alone. He didn't get it. How could a woman as head-turningly beautiful as Chloe be insecure? She was a wealthy, accomplished actress, yet she acted as though she was still that awkward little girl he remembered.

He drew his attention back to his overprotective brother, who muttered, "Knock off the tough-guy act. Take your pain meds and use your goddamn cane."

"Yeah, yeah," he said, taking the cane. He only gave in because he was pretty sure he'd fall on his face if he didn't. Easton wouldn't admit it to Chance, but it felt like someone was stabbing his leg with hot pokers. He leaned heavily on the cane and limped toward the blue Adirondack chair under an aspen tree.

"Where's your meds?" his brother asked.

Easton lowered himself in the chair, briefly closing his eyes as a wave of nausea washed over him. "Just get me an ice pack and a beer, will ya? I'll be fine."

Before Chance could respond, they heard Chloe shriek, "If you take my picture, I'll sue," and then a splash.

"Jesus, did she fall in again?" Easton asked, leaning to the side to see past his brother.

Chance glanced over his shoulder and laughed. "Nope, looks like she pushed Nell into the pool. Or maybe Estelle did."

"Aunt Nell can't swim."

"I know." There was another splash. "Grayson just jumped in to save her."

Easton scrubbed his hand over his face, then looked at his brother. "We have to talk to Grayson and either get him on board with the job or take Cat off the case."

"Already tried talking to him. The man is as stubborn and ornery as Cat. She won't give in either."

"Can we break the contract with Martinez?"

"No, and it wouldn't look very professional if we tried. Besides, I don't agree with Grayson on two counts. One, they've got the wrong guy. Martinez shouldn't be on their watch list, and they know it or they would have brought him in for questioning by now. And two, Cat's a big girl and good at what she does. If they're going to make their relationship work, he has to find a way to support her."

"Yeah, well, that doesn't look like it's going to happen anytime soon. Good thing Chloe's headed back to LA tomorrow."

"In your dreams. She's staying for Ty's grand opening next Saturday."

* * *

A soft breeze rustled the leaves of the trees overhead, the smell of burgers cooking on the grill drifting past Easton's nose. His stomach rumbled, and he thought about getting up. Eyes still closed, he tested his leg. Nope, he'd stay there for a while longer.

"Easton."

He opened his eyes. Chloe stood in front of him with a plate of hamburgers in her hand. She'd changed into a red sundress, the hem fluttering above her knees in the warm breeze. It fit snug at her chest and hips, showing off her curvy figure. Her feet were bare.

He cleared his throat, shifting in the chair. "What's up?" he asked, drawing his gaze to her face. Determined to keep it there. Only looking at her face did nothing to lessen the flare of heat and desire. She was even more beautiful without the dramatic makeup. And her long, dark hair looked…. Jesus, he needed to get laid if Chloe was turning him on.

She gave him a sickly smile and handed him the paper plate. "Chance said your leg's bothering you. I thought you might be hungry."

He was going to kill his brother. Then again, maybe he should be thanking him. The look on Chloe's face as she glanced at his leg did what he hadn't been able to—threw a gallon of ice-cold water on his desire. "Thanks." He raised his eyebrows when she didn't leave, then sighed. She probably expected an apology. "Like I told you, I didn't mean to hit you with the ball, and I didn't know you can't swim."

"Is that an apology?"

"Yeah," he muttered, lifting the burger to his mouth.

"Thank you. But that's not why I wanted to talk to you."

He looked up at the leaves fluttering overhead, then lowered the burger. "What?"

She opened her mouth, closed it, and looked away.

"My burgers are getting cold. You going to tell me what's on your mind, or not?" He was hoping for *or not*. She was nervous, and that made him nervous.

"Do you promise not to yell at me?" She looked at him from under her lashes, nibbling on her full bottom lip.

He gave his head a slight shake, dragging his gaze from her mouth to her eyes. "What did you do?"

"Nothing…yet. And it's more you and me doing something."

He stared at her, stunned. He thought he'd killed her feelings for him their last year of high school. The night he'd discovered he'd been spending time with Chloe and not his girlfriend Cat. For weeks Chloe had pretended to be her sister, and he hadn't had a clue. That wasn't entirely true. There'd been a difference. Cat, who'd actually been Chloe impersonating her sister, had seemed softer, more open with her feelings, more demonstrative. He'd liked the changes, and since they'd recently taken their relationship to the next level, he'd attributed the differences he saw in Cat to that. But he'd been in for another shock; he'd made love to Chloe, not Cat, his girlfriend of two years. The girlfriend he'd planned to propose to the night of their high school prom.

It took a long time for him to forgive Chloe, and Cat. The night he found out he'd been played Cat had admitted to being in on the act. Years later, she confessed she'd lied because she'd been hurt he couldn't tell them apart. She'd had no idea what her sister had been up to.

Just as Easton pushed back the long-ago memories, he remembered he'd kissed the hell out of Chloe when she'd been home last fall for their parents' wedding. So he supposed he shouldn't be entirely surprised she still had feelings for him. But he'd only kissed her because he thought she was Cat. They'd traded places. Again.

The thought reignited his anger, and he released a harsh laugh. "You and I won't be doing anything together, Scarlett. Not now, not ever. So you just get those thoughts out of your head."

"I didn't mean *that*." She cast a nervous glance over her shoulder, then looked back at him and lowered her voice. "You and Cat were meant to be together. It's what your mother would want for you, and I know you do, too. I've been watching you. You're in pain. It comes out as anger, but I know it's because you're sad. I don't blame you. It's my fault you're not together. If not for me, you'd be married by now. But I'm going to fix everything. Cat isn't happy either, and she deserves to be. We just have to come up with a plan to show her you're the one she wants, not…" She frowned. "…Easton, what's wrong? Are you choking on your burger?"

He pushed himself up off the chair and towered over her. "You do one thing, just one thing to mess up what your sister and Grayson have, and I'm going to tell everyone what you're up to. And that includes your mother and your sister. Do us all a favor, yourself included, and head back to LA."

"Why are you pretending this isn't exactly what you want? You told me this afternoon that you love her."

"Chloe, Easton, what's going on?" Cat walked across the lawn with a frown on her face.

"Nothing. Nothing's going on," Chloe said, giving her sister a bright smile. "You promised to show me your wedding dress. Why don't we go do that now?" She tugged on Cat's arm.

Cat looked confused. "Ah, because my dress won't be in for at least a month. I told you that."

"Oh, silly me. Of course you did." She released a phony little-girl laugh that irritated the hell out of him. "But you can show me a picture, can't you?"

"Sure. Just let me talk to Easton for a minute." Cat glanced from him to Chloe. "It's about a case. I need to speak to him in private."

"Oh, right…*a case.*" Chloe winked, then gave Easton a smug smile before heading off. She made a beeline for Grayson.

Easton bowed his head. He didn't want to tell Cat, but she had to know.

"Are you going to tell me what she's up to or should I guess?"

He shouldn't be surprised by her question. No one knew Chloe as well as her identical twin. Once he finished laying out what her sister had said, Cat pinched the bridge of her nose. "I really didn't need to deal with this on top of everything else. Grayson and I are having enough problems without throwing Chloe into the mix."

"So send her packing. Tell Ty to withdraw his invitation to the grand opening."

"I can't do that. She'd be devastated." When Easton crossed his arms and gave her an are-you-shitting-me look, she held up a hand. "I know how you feel about her, but despite what you think, she's not doing this to hurt me. The past few months have been difficult for Chloe. She's putting on a brave face, but her career means everything to her. They killed her off *As the Sun Sets,* and Ty told me she hasn't had any offers. I'm worried about her. I just have to figure…" She trailed off, casting Easton a speculative glance that made him uneasy.

"No. Whatever you're thinking, the answer is no."

"All you have to do is play along with her until next weekend. Please, Easton, you can keep an eye on her. She can stay with you at the cabin—"

"Are you out of your mind?"

"She can't stay at the lodge. We'll never know what she's up to. And I can't have her stay with me and Grayson."

"She can stay here."

"No, Chloe and Mom's relationship is just getting back

on track. My mother will figure out what she's up to, and I won't have this come between them. It's my fault, Easton. George wouldn't have tried to kill me if Michael hadn't stolen his money, and Chloe would still have a job."

Cat had been engaged to Michael Upton, a stockbroker who'd been running a Ponzi scheme from their home. A lot of people believed, as a cop, she'd known what was going on—including the FBI. She'd quit the force. The file on her had still been open when she and Grayson met last year. An agent himself, Grayson had made sure she was fully exonerated. Easton had thought that would be enough to alleviate Cat's guilt. But obviously she was still carrying it around. "Stop blaming yourself. None of this is your fault."

"In my head, I know that. I really do. But it's hard right now when Chloe's the one paying the price. Please, Easton, I'll never ask you for another favor. She won't be able to pull anything if she's with you. You just have to keep her busy."

Easton opened his mouth to say *no*, but at Cat's suggestion that he keep Chloe busy, he changed his mind. It was the perfect opportunity for some well-deserved payback. "Okay, Cat. For you, I'll do it."

Chapter Five

*T*humpthumpthump...*thump*. Chloe's heart pounded an alarming beat at the base of her throat. She rested her head on the backseat of the limo while fumbling in her purse for her nitrogen tablets, and then she remembered they were sugar pills. She closed her eyes. They wouldn't do her any good. She retrieved them anyway. They'd worked before, and she had to do something. She was afraid she was having a heart attack. Shaking two pills into her sweaty palm, she repeated the words *nitrogen tablets* over and over again in her mind. As she chewed them, she visualized her frantic heart returning to a normal beat.

Several moments passed before her pulse began to slow, and while she was relieved that it did, she couldn't help but wonder if everyone was right. Was she a hypochondriac? She didn't understand how that could be. She wasn't faking. The symptoms were real and, at times, terrifying. And she didn't understand why they'd come on so suddenly. Especially now when everything was going according to plan. Maybe that was the problem.

Easton's about-face had been rather sudden and surprising. Though most surprising of all had been his insistence that she stay with him. She supposed it would be easier for them to coordinate their plan with no one the wiser. But it was the last thing she expected him to say. He thought she was a spoiled brat and more often than not gave the impression he couldn't stand to be in the same room with her. And no matter what he said, she was sure he'd hit her with the football on purpose. He'd had the best arm in the league, everybody said so.

But maybe this was the opportunity she needed to repair their friendship. They had been friends once, a long time ago. Before she'd fallen in love with him and ruined everything. And she certainly didn't want Cat to marry another man who hated her.

Michael had hated Chloe. He'd done his best to keep them apart. A true narcissist, he didn't like sharing Cat's love. Her poor sister. After what her ex-fiancé put her through, Cat deserved a happy-ever-after more than most. Chloe had dropped everything to fly to her sister's side when his fraud had been exposed. She'd found Cat curled in a fetal position on her bed. It was an image that haunted Chloe to this day, and one she never wanted to see again.

As for Grayson, she'd offer him her friendship, a shoulder to cry on. She'd help him come to terms with losing Cat. She'd convince him to return to LA with her and Estelle. It would be better if he didn't have Cat's and Easton's relationship rubbed in his face on a daily basis. Chloe would wait at least a year before telling anyone about her and Grayson. She chewed on her thumbnail;

she'd have to look up the proper etiquette for dating a sister's ex-fiancé.

She withdrew her compact from her purse and checked her face. She felt more like herself now that she'd had a chance to redo her hair and makeup. Estelle was staying with Grayson and Cat at the ranch, which worked perfectly for the plan. When Chloe stopped by to drop off Estelle, she'd freshened up before heading to Easton's.

She glanced at her watch and lowered the limo's privacy window. "Are you sure you know where you're going? We've been driving for fifteen minutes."

"Yes, ma'am. It won't be long now."

"All right. Thank you." Ma'am? Did she look old enough to be a ma'am? How depressing to think that she did. She was jobless, loveless, relationshipless, and a ma'am at thirty-two. Ugh. The driver pulled onto a long gravel road, and she glanced out the window.

This can't be right. They were in the middle of nowhere. Granted, it was a beautiful piece of property with the mountains visible in the distance, but she'd expected Easton to live closer to town. The limo came to a stop in front of a shack and the driver got out.

Chloe lowered the window. "Is there a problem?"

"No, ma'am. We're here." He opened her door.

She shook her head and leaned out to pull it shut. "No, you must be mistaken. I'll call—"

"It's the right place." He nodded at something over his shoulder.

Chloe angled her head to see what he was looking at. Easton stood on the dilapidated porch, his broad shoulder resting against a weather-beaten post. A lock of wavy black hair fell over his forehead, a white T-shirt stretched over his muscular chest, his jeans worn and faded in all the right places, his bare feet crossed at the ankles.

She swallowed and worked her way back to his gorgeous face, relieved to see a hint of amusement in his blue eyes. It was a joke. Ha-ha. Thank goodness! But since he'd obviously gone to some trouble to set it up, she'd let him have his fun. It was encouraging to see his sense of humor return. This was more like the Easton she remembered. The one *she'd* fallen in love with.

"Thank you," she said to the driver when he helped her from the car. She smiled at Easton. "Look at you living the life." She flung her arms wide. "Smell that fresh mountain air. Umm, so good. It's really beautiful out here, Easton."

He frowned and started down the rickety porch steps. "Are you drunk?"

"No, why would you think that?" The driver opened the trunk. She leaned back and whispered, "Just leave my luggage there for now." No sense taking it out only to have him put the bags back in.

A slow smile spread across Easton's face. "Aren't you going to pay John? I'm sure he has better things to do than wait around all night."

How did he know her driver's . . . Oh, now she got it. Even her driver was in on the joke. "Silly me, I'm such a scatterbrain today. It must have been the blow I took to my head earlier. You know, from the football you drilled at me." She smiled and retrieved her wallet from her purse.

The driver looked slightly confused when she handed him the money. "Should I take your bags out now?"

She glanced at Easton, who raised his eyebrows at her.

She sighed. He obviously planned on playing this out for a while longer. "Yes. Thank you, John."

The man placed her oversize suitcases beside her, then got in the limo. She watched the black sedan head down the gravel drive, frowning when it turned onto the main road without stopping. It looked like they'd be taking Easton's truck back to town. She glanced at the ominous dark clouds gathering over the mountains and hoped he had a tarp for the open bed.

"Come on. I'll show you around, and you can get settled."

"What about my luggage?"

He stopped on the bottom step, glancing at her over his shoulder. "What about it?"

She sighed and gestured to the bags. "You forgot them."

"Nope. You're going to have to bring them in yourself, Scarlett. I wrenched my leg hauling you out of the water. I can't carry anything right now."

An offended gasp escaped from between her lips. She might have gained a few pounds over the past several months, but she couldn't believe he was making fun of her weight. "I am not fat, Easton McBride." Her cheeks warmed, and she crossed her arms over her chest. "All right, joke's over. It was funny for about two seconds. Take me to your real house before it starts to pour."

He lowered himself onto the top step and started to laugh. A deep, sexy laugh that would have made her smile if she wasn't so annoyed with him.

Raindrops splattered on her head. "I'm glad you find me amusing, but it's starting to rain, so maybe you could—"

Still chuckling, he wiped his eyes and, using the railing, pulled himself to his feet. He gave her a slight bow, gesturing to the door. "Mi casa es su casa."

* * *

The look on Chloe's face when she realized he wasn't joking was priceless. He hadn't laughed like that in a long time. It almost made it worth putting up with her for a couple of days.

Struggling to pull up the handles on her red-and-tan bags, she muttered *bloody hell* when the sky opened up. Easton leaned with his back against the open door, watching her through a sheet of rain while trying not to laugh. By the time she made it to the steps, her hair was plastered to her head, her dress to her body.

The urge to laugh faded. He should have carried the luggage in for her. But the whole point of the next few days was to teach her a lesson. Dragging his gaze from her lush curves and her long, shapely legs in her red "dome" shoes, he was a little worried his plan might backfire.

As she hauled her luggage up the steps, her left heel went through a loose board. She stumbled and shot him a pissed-off look.

He forced a smile and winked. "Don't worry, Scarlett. I'll put a fire on. You'll warm up in no time."

"Stop calling me Scarlett. And I'll take a hot shower over a fire, thanks."

"That might be a problem seeing as how I don't have one. Not in the cabin at least. It's out back."

She stopped in front of him, so close he could smell her sweet, sultry perfume, feel the heat from her body coming through the clingy fabric. He grabbed the suitcases and lifted his chin. "Go on in."

"I thought you couldn't carry anything after hauling my fat butt out of the water."

He really didn't want to go there right now. Not while he was trying to get an image of her in the shower out of his head. "Your butt isn't fat, but if you don't get it in the cabin right now, you can carry your own bags to your room."

She smoothed her hand over her ass and glanced up at him through her long, spiked lashes. "You really don't think it's too big?"

He bowed his head and groaned.

"Okay, okay, I'm going." She walked in, then came to an abrupt stop in front of him.

He bumped into her. "What now?" he muttered, dropping the bags to rub his leg.

Her gaze flitted around the cabin. "Your place is, um, very cozy," she said, then gave him a concerned look. "Is everything okay with you?"

Cozy? He held back a grin. The cabin was about six hundred square feet and barely habitable, but it worked for him. Last week, he'd approved the final plans for the home he was building a couple hundred yards from the cabin. He was breaking ground in ten days and hoped to move in by the end of summer. Not that he'd share the news with Chloe.

"Leg's a little sore, but yeah, I'm good."

"No, that's not what I meant." She gestured to the beat-up brown couch and the battered stove and refrigerator. "Are you having financial problems?"

Considering what he had planned for her, it was best that she thought he was. "Medical expenses tapped me out, but I live off the land, so it's all good." He picked up her bags and walked past her. "You can take the bed." A brown curtain separated the bedroom from the living space.

She followed him. "That's very nice of...That's not a bed; it's a mattress on the floor." She patted the wall. "Where's the light switch?"

"There isn't one." He struggled to keep the amusement from his voice. He should have hidden a camera to film her reaction. Especially when he responded to the next question he had no doubt she'd ask.

She looked around the room, then leaned back to search the outer area. "Where's the loo?"

"Loo? Don't think I have one of those," he said. Her fake accent ticked him off.

She sighed. "A bathroom, Easton. And of course you have one. I just want to know where it is."

"Oh, sorry, I don't speak Brit. But yeah, I do. Out the door to your right and back about ten yards."

"The front door is the..." Her gaze jerked to his.

He grinned. "Yeah, we call it an outhouse here in the good old U. S. of A."

"That's disgust....This isn't going to work. I can't stay here, and neither can you. It's...unhealthy." She chewed on her thumbnail. "I'm sure I can get rooms for us at the lodge. And you don't have to worry about the cost. I'll take care of it."

"Nope, I don't take handouts. I have my pride. And if you don't stay here, our deal is off."

"It's not a deal, it's a plan. You have as much to gain as I do, Easton. And it's not a handout. Consider it...an investment."

Some people might think Chloe was an airhead, but it was an act. She was smart. Something he needed to remember. "Doesn't matter, I can't leave here anyway. Like I said, I live off the land. That means I have to work it. And this plan of yours is going to take time away from my chores, so you'll have to help out."

"What kind of chores?"

He thought about that for a second. He had to make it good. "I have to get the garden in and take care of the livestock."

"You have livestock? I didn't see any animals."

He didn't, but his closest neighbors had a farm. He'd pay them a visit first thing in the morning. "Just a cow and a couple of chickens." There were pens out back. They needed a little work, but he'd take care of that in the morning. He smiled, or Chloe would.

"Why are you smiling?"

Dammit. "I'm real fond of my animals. It's why I stay close to home. I don't like to leave them alone for long."

"Oh, I..." She huffed a breath and ungraciously gave in. "All right, I guess I'll have to make it work."

"Okay, then, I'll let you get changed." He limped to the closet and pulled out a couple of towels from the top shelf. "Here you go. I'll light the fire. Once you're dry, you can make us something to eat."

She stared at him. "I'm your guest. You don't make your guest cook."

"You're not really a guest, you're more like a partner. But don't worry, I'll take my turn tomorrow. The damp weather's making my leg act up." He felt uncomfortable at the admission. It wasn't a lie, but he didn't admit his weakness, his pain, to anyone.

Her eyes narrowed. "I thought your leg was sore because you pulled me out of the pool."

"Yeah, that didn't help. I better rest it tonight or you'll have to take care of *all* the chores tomorrow."

She muttered something under her breath as Easton closed the curtain. Let the fun begin, he thought, pretty sure she'd be on her way back to LA tomorrow. Once he got the fire going, he walked to the Harvest Gold refrigerator and pulled an ice pack from the freezer and returned to the couch. He stretched out and shoved a pillow under his leg, placing the ice pack on top of it. Despite the gnawing ache, he had a smile on his face. A smile that disappeared the moment Chloe pushed the curtain aside. She had on white satin pajamas that left little doubt she was commando and braless. He swore under his breath.

She froze. "What's wrong? Is it your leg?"

"No...yeah." He cleared his throat. "Don't you have something warmer to wear? It gets cold at night."

"I didn't expect to be staying in a sha...cabin in the woods."

Knowing Chloe like he did, he should have realized her wardrobe would consist of soft, sexy, and feminine. That was about to change, he decided, as he set the ice pack on the crate. He got off the couch and gestured to the throw pillow. "Sit in front of the fire."

"All right." She nodded and walked over to retrieve the pillow.

At the sound of clicking, he looked at her feet. She had on a pair of heels with white feathers decorating the strap across her toes. "You have to be shitting me."

"What are you, the fashion police? I'm not walking around in my bare feet. I'll get slivers."

He went into the bedroom and grabbed a sweatshirt and a pair of heavy work socks from the dresser drawers. Chloe screamed. He ran from the room. "What—"

She flung herself in his arms and climbed up his body, wrapping her slender arms around his neck, her long legs around his waist. "There's a-a mouse!"

"Stop moving around," he gritted out, bracing a hand against the wall. He slid his other arm under her ass to hold in her place while trying to ignore how her body felt plastered against his. She was all soft curves and warm woman. And she smelled incredible; like ginger and orange blossoms. He cleared his throat. "Maybe we should stay in town."

She leaned back, the light from the fire casting her beautiful face in an angelic glow. "No, we can't leave your animals alone."

Why the hell had he said he had livestock? Oh right, he was going for a little payback. Teaching Chloe a lesson.

She cast a nervous glance over her shoulder, then slid down his body. "Sorry," she said when he groaned. He hoped she thought he was groaning because of his leg.

She clung to him, the weight of her breast heavy and warm on his arm. "Don't hurt the mouse, just, you know, sweep it out the door."

He drew a frustrated breath through his nose. "Chloe, you're going to have to let go of me—"

She shook her head. "No."

"Yes." He clenched his teeth and picked her up, carrying her to the counter by the sink. He put her down. "This may take a while."

She glanced at his leg—Jesus, he hoped it was his leg and not...She raised her pretty green eyes and touched his jaw. "I hurt you. No, don't deny it, I can see you're in pain. If"—she cleared her throat—"if you'd like, I can massage your leg for you. My brother pulled a muscle in his shoulder once, and he said it helped."

And there she was, the girl he remembered.

Chapter Six

Chloe woke up to a barnyard serenade: a cow mooing and chickens clucking. She thought she was having a bad dream until she remembered where she was. She pulled the pillow over her head. Why on earth had she let Easton convince her to stay? She could be sleeping peacefully in a comfortable bed instead of a lumpy mattress on the floor. It was a rhetorical question. She knew exactly why she stayed.

If she didn't, she had a strong feeling Easton would have withdrawn his support for her plan. And without him, she wouldn't be able to convince her sister she was making a mistake. She needed Easton to remind Cat he was her perfect match—a match made in heaven. Oh, Chloe patted her chest, a little emotional at the thought of her father and Easton's mother cheering her on from up above. She wouldn't let them down.

Which meant she had to get up and help Easton with his chores. Ugh. She pulled the pillow from her head and rolled over to scowl at the ceiling. She'd grown up on a ranch and despised it. The horses frightened her while the smell of manure offended her delicate sensibilities. At least she hadn't been expected to do chores; her heart issues exempted her from strenuous activity. Something she'd have to remind Easton of. Though he'd probably demand a doctor's note.

She couldn't believe he was happy living this far from town. And living off the land...What was that all about? She chewed on her thumbnail, wondering if he was having trouble adjusting to civilian life after his experiences in Afghanistan. It wasn't uncommon for soldiers to have difficulties upon their return home. After reading *American Sniper*, she felt she had some insight into Easton's psyche. And living in a shack because his medical expenses weren't covered? As an American citizen who enjoyed her freedom because of the sacrifices made by Easton and others like him, Chloe was outraged at his shabby treatment and planned to write a letter to the Department of Veteran Affairs. She'd do that first thing...she sighed...right after she finished her chores.

Chloe pulled her purse across the battered floorboards and retrieved her compact. She had to look at least somewhat presentable before seeing Easton. She opened the pink case, looked in the mirror, and released a horrified shriek.

The curtain slid across the rod. Easton looked down at her with an eyebrow raised. "I take it the mouse had friends. Where are they?"

His mouth moved, but whatever he said was drowned out by the theme song from the *Princess Bride*. His wet hair was slicked back from his beard-stubbled face, a white towel slung around his powerful neck while a droplet of water traveled down his sigh-inducing pecs and over the glorious slabs of his muscled abdomen to a thin line of dark hair. As that lucky little drop of water disappeared beneath unbuttoned jeans riding low on his hips, she bit the inside of her cheek to contain a moan.

She'd thought he was beautiful in high school. But even the gorgeous boy he'd once been couldn't compare to the stunning perfection of the man he'd become. Chloe pushed away the memory of the one glorious night she'd laid naked in his arms with the reminder that he was Cat's.

"Chloe, where's the mice?"

She blinked and jolted upright at his question. "There's another mouse?"

He sighed. "You screamed. I thought that's why."

"No, it's my hair." She scowled at him because that was better than fantasizing about him. "I told you my hair wasn't completely dry last night, and you made me go to bed anyway." She held up a hunk of her frizzed-out mane. "Are you happy now? It'll take me at least three hours to untangle the knots." A smug smile touched her lips. "Looks like I won't be able to help with your chores after all. That'll teach you not to listen to me, won't it?"

She'd been surprised when he'd ordered her to bed after they'd finished off the can of tomato soup she'd heated. When he'd set her on the counter, he seemed… different. His eyes were warm, his expression soft instead of hard and irritated. It reminded her of how he'd looked at her before everything changed. But then he'd gone back to responding to her attempts at conversation with those annoying grunts. He'd refused to let her massage his leg, too, which, she had to admit, she was secretly glad about.

"I bet I can get your tangles out in under ten minutes. Give me your brush." He wiggled his fingers at her.

She raised a protective hand to her head. "Thank you, but no."

His lips twitched, then he walked to the closet. He tossed her a ball cap.

"What do you want me to do with this?"

"Wear it. You won't get through your list of chores if you waste three hours fixing your hair." He pulled out a red plaid shirt and black sweatpants and tossed them onto the bed, then he went to the dresser, adding a pair of work socks to the pile. "I've got rubber boots you can wear."

"You expect me to wear these?" She pointed an offended finger at the clothes, ignoring the nervous flutter in her stomach at his mention of a list and rubber boots.

"Unless you've got a pair of jeans, a T-shirt, and a pair of sneakers in your bags, I do."

"Of course I don't."

"Didn't think so. Come on, Scarlett." He leaned over and pulled off her covers. "Time's a wasting. I want breakfast before I head out."

"I'm not stopping you. Go and eat."

"Can't eat until you make it." He winked and headed for the main room.

At the sight of his sculpted back, her ticked-off response sputtered in her throat. The wide expanse of golden skin and muscle were a work of art. She'd barely recovered from the sight when he returned with a bucket of steaming water. "Thought you'd prefer to wash up in here instead of the outdoor shower."

And poof, just like that, her anger totally disappeared. She smiled. "That was very thoughtful. Thank you."

A flicker of what looked to be surprise crossed his face, then he made a noncommittal sound in his throat and walked away.

Chloe didn't let his annoying grunt take away from his thoughtfulness. To her, his considerate act was a sign they were on the right track. But some of her pleasure dissipated once she'd washed and gotten dressed. It left her completely when she walked through the curtains and Easton looked up from his laptop and laughed.

She scowled at him. "I need something to hold up the pants." She let them go to make her point. They puddled at her feet.

He blinked and stopped laughing.

She stepped out of the legs and bent over to pick them up. She tossed him the sweatpants. His red plaid shirt fell to her knees; she didn't need to wear them. He tossed the pants back. "Put them on. You'll be feeding the animals."

"You can feed them." She draped the sweat pants over a chair.

"'Fraid not." He closed his computer, then stood up and walked to the refrigerator. Pulling a piece of paper off the door, he handed it to her. "I have to head into town for a job." He returned to the table and shoved his computer in a leather messenger bag, then hefted the strap over his shoulder. On his way to the door, he flicked the brim of her ball cap. "I'll get breakfast at the diner. I'll see you around five. I took out a roast for dinner. There should be some potatoes in the bottom cupboard."

She'd stopped listening to him at *see you around five*. She'd made the mistake of looking at the list. "Is this a joke? It better be because I can't do all this. I'm not a man, you know. I'm a woman with a heart condition in case you've forgotten."

He snorted. "You've just set the women's movement back a decade, Scarlett." He opened the door. "Don't forget to put the roast in the oven at three. I'll be hungry when I get home."

"And you think *I'm* setting the women's movement back?"

"It's called a partnership. I thought that's what you wanted."

"Well, yes...Oh"—she brightened—"you'll be with Cat. We need to talk about this before you leave. Come up with something really romantic to sweep her—"

"Your sister isn't exactly a hearts-and-flowers kind of girl. Trust me, I know better than you do how to win her over. I've done it before."

Chloe rubbed her chest. The sudden ache that blossomed under her ribcage was somewhat worrisome. No, she reassured herself, the hurtful twinge had nothing to do with Easton romancing her sister. Chloe was just concerned that he'd mess it up. "You were sixteen," she reminded him a little testily.

"Fifteen. And now I have seventeen years' worth of experience to draw from. She won't be able to resist me."

A pang of concern stabbed her in the heart. She hadn't given any thought to Easton's experience with other women. A miscalculation on her part. All you had do was look at the man and know he had tons. Women probably dropped their panties at one quirk of his dark, arrogant eyebrow or one sexy, come-hither smile. They wouldn't care if he was broke and lived in a shack and had a damaged leg. She cleared her throat. "You're not dating someone now, are you?"

"Not that it's any of your business, but no, I'm not."

She gaped at him. "Of course it's my business! We're talking about you marrying my sister!"

He rubbed a finger along his chin. "All right, relax. I haven't dated anyone in"—he cocked his head—"five months."

"Five months? Who were you dating five months ago? Does she live in Christmas?"

"Jesus, Chloe, what are you, a cop? She's a surgeon I met in Virginia. Long-distance thing wasn't working out. Satisfied? Can I go now?"

She nodded, absorbing what he'd just told her. There'd been a part of her that thought he'd never gotten over Cat. She supposed it was silly to think he'd been pining after her sister all these years. Maybe she was projecting. It had taken her a long time to get over Easton.

"Here's the boots. I stuffed the toes for you so they should fit. Be careful around Bessie. She's—"

"You stuffed the toes for me?"

"Yeah, stay with me here. Don't turn your back on Bessie. She'll—"

She frowned. "Who's Bessie?"

His broad shoulders raised on an irritated sigh. "The cow. Bessie's the cow."

* * *

Bessie was not a cow. She was the devil in disguise. Only moments ago, she'd head-butted Chloe into a steaming pile of manure. She was lucky she managed to stay upright. Chloe clung to the rail, sticking her foot out of the pen to wipe the cow poop off her boot. A wet snorting sound drew her attention. She glanced to her left. Bessie pawed the ground. Chloe shrieked, threw the bucket in the cow's direction, and ran. She'd buy Easton a lifetime supply of milk. Same went for eggs, she thought, inspecting the red peck marks on her hand as she slammed the gate shut. Easton should have told her to wear gloves.

Bessie charged the gate. Chloe held her breath as the wood creaked and shuddered. Thank goodness it held. She looked around for something to wedge across the latch. The last thing she needed was for Bessie to escape. Easton had been gone less than an hour, and Chloe was already exhausted. She'd never be able to catch the animal. It was obvious last night that he loved Bessie and his chickens. He'd never forgive her if she lost his precious cow. Though in her opinion, he could have provided them with a better home. The pens were haphazardly built. They were as run-down as the shack.

She felt bad comparing Easton's home to a shack, but it was true. He deserved better. He'd served his country with valor and had been grievously injured. It wasn't right. His country had failed him. Chloe's shoulders slumped, and so had she. She hadn't accomplished anything on her list. And even if she did manage to clean the house as he directed—she thought it was a little much that he wanted her to do the windows—it wouldn't matter. It was a disaster.

Scanning the list once more, she looked for at least one thing she could accomplish before five. Clean the outhouse? Was he insane? She'd be lucky if she crossed off three chores on his twenty-item list by the end of the day.

She imagined Easton's disappointment when he came home. She seemed to be good at disappointing people these days. She crumpled the list and walked dejectedly to the front of the shack...cabin.

The least she could do was write a letter to the VA on Easton's behalf. Thinking of how long it would take to wade through the red tape, she sighed. By the time Easton got the money to repair his home...Chloe stopped walking; she had money. She could fix the cabin for him. She could hire people, lots of people, and get every single item on his list accomplished and then some. But there was one problem with the plan; he had his pride.

As she thought of a way around that sticky little point, she came up with the perfect solution. She was living with him and, spoiled diva that she was, her accommodations needed to meet her demanding expectations. Easton would totally buy it. Which was kind of depressing, but she wouldn't think about that now. She had no time to lose.

She ran into what would soon be his fab new space and grabbed a pen, smoothing out the old list on the counter to start a new one. Ten minutes later, she was ready to make her calls. Not only was she going to help Easton, she'd hire as many veterans as she could find. She could barely contain her excitement. It would be just like an episode from *Extreme Makeover: Home Edition*. She looked down at herself. She couldn't let anyone see her looking like this. She had an image to uphold after all.

An hour later, the calls were made. Her twenty-man crew were on their way. New furniture and appliances would arrive at two. Food at three. Her hair was fab.

Makeup perfect. But as she waited on the gravel road for the trucks to arrive, Chloe realized she'd forgotten one thing.

She texted Easton: *What's your favorite color?*

Two minutes later, he responded: *This is Easton, not Esther.*

Her: *Ha-ha! Just answer the question.*

Him: *Black.*

Her: *Are u depressed?*

Him: *Pink.*

Her: *Yay!! Bye. Oh, are u making progress with Cat???*

Five minutes later: *Easton?*

Him: *Have u cleaned the outhouse yet?*

She didn't bother replying. And since he obviously wasn't making any headway with her sister, Chloe decided to give him some help and called Mr. Hardy at the Mountain Co-op. Disconnecting after ordering a gift guaranteed to win Easton some brownie points with Cat, Chloe smiled.

It was good to be rich.

* * *

Easton sprawled in a chair at the *Chronicle*. His sister-in-law Vivi Westfield, owner and publisher of the paper, looked at him over her computer monitor. "Not that I mind, but do you plan on hiding out here every day until Chloe heads back to LA?"

"I'm not hiding out. Just thought it would be more convenient working from here since it's my brother's favorite hangout." These days, Chance was reluctant to let Vivi out of his sight. She was almost eight months pregnant. His brother had lost his first wife and their baby girl in a car accident six years ago and was understandably overprotective of Vivi.

"Umhm," she said, glancing at her husband, who leaned back in his chair, resting his scuffed brown cowboy boots on the edge of Vivi's desk with a grin on his face.

Through the window behind his brother, Easton caught a glimpse of a familiar black SUV pulling in. "Ah, Chance, here comes Cat."

Chance dropped his booted feet on the floor and twisted in the chair. "She doesn't look pissed. Maybe she doesn't know."

"What did you do now?" Vivi asked her husband.

"It wasn't my idea. It was E's."

"Nice. Good to know you have my back, big brother." When Vivi arched a dark eyebrow at Easton, he sighed. "We didn't tell her we were doing the walk-through of the Martinez place today. Not that... Hey, Cat," he greeted her when she opened the door.

"Hey, yourself," she said with a grin. "Vivi, Chance."

Okay, that was good. She didn't seem upset. She walked over and gave him a kiss on the cheek. "Happy to see you, too," he said, a little surprised at her greeting.

"Don't play coy." She swatted his shoulder. "I know what you did."

"And you're not mad?"

"Mad? I can't wait to get to the practice range. But honestly, it's way too generous. The problems Grayson and I are having aren't your fault, Easton."

"Ah, Cat, I'm not sure I know what you're talking about."

"The Sig Sauer P320 you ordered for me. Mr. Hardy from the Mountain Co-op called to tell me that it'll be delivered in a couple of days." She cast a self-conscious glance at Chance and Vivi, and cleared her throat. "Your note was very, um, sweet."

His confusion over the gun was cleared up by the mention of a note. "Chloe," he muttered.

"What..." Her eyes narrowed. "You didn't buy me the gun or send me the note, did you?"

"No, your sister did."

Chance snorted. "Looks like you should have made a longer list, E."

"What list?" Cat asked.

"My little brother here thought leaving Chloe with a list of chores to do would keep her out of trouble."

Cat laughed. "You should know my sister isn't exactly a domestic goddess. She doesn't do chores."

"She made me soup last night," Easton said, feeling a bit defensive on Chloe's behalf.

His brother, Vivi, and Cat shared a look. One that made him uncomfortable, but he didn't have a chance to call them on it because Hailey from the Rocky Mountain Diner walked in.

"Hey, guys. Sorry I'm late with the copy for our column, Vivi. Computer issues, and we were swamped today." She handed Vivi a piece of paper and pointed a finger at Easton. "You owe me, buddy."

"For what?" And why did he have the uneasy feeling he wasn't going to like her answer?

"You'll be eating real well for the next month or two."

"How's that?"

"Chloe. She had me make up a freezer order of your

favorite dishes. We were all hopping today, including Grace. She sent something like ten dozen cupcakes out to your place earlier this afternoon. We sent the same amount of sandwiches. I've never been Chloe's biggest fan, but it's great the way she's supporting local businesses."

Easton shot out of his chair and headed for the door.

"I'll go with him, Cat. Do me a favor and take Vivi...Slick, what's wrong?"

At the panic in his brother's voice, Easton turned.

Vivi shook her head. "It's not me. It's Chloe."

Easton raked his hand through his hair. "What now?"

"I got a late start this morning, and didn't get a chance to look at the online edition of the paper until it was too late. Nell had uploaded the photo from Cat's engagement party. The one of Chloe in the pool. I thought I took it down in time, but it looks like the photo got picked up on the wire."

Cat pinched the bridge of her nose. "What does that mean?"

Vivi made a face. "It'll be everywhere. And the headline is even worse than the photo, which was pretty bad."

Lowering herself in a chair, Cat said, "Tell us,"

Vivi read off the screen, "Distraught after being fired from *As the Sun Sets*, America's Sweetheart, Chloe O'Connor, tries to drown herself."

* * *

Chance disconnected from Cat. "Ethan's on it now. He's trying to get the photo pulled from all media outlets. Estelle's putting out a press release saying Chloe's been in London auditioning for a part in a movie. So all you have to do is confiscate her cell phone and keep her away from TV and computers until we get a handle on it."

"Yeah, like that won't be difficult at all. Has anyone told Dad and Liz?"

His brother nodded. "They're over at Aunt Nell's right now. They're counting on you to take care of Chloe."

"No pressure there. I don't know how one woman can..." He trailed off at the line of cars and trucks extending from the main road all the way to his...No, it couldn't be. He rubbed his eyes. "She painted my goddamn cabin pink!"

Chance was practically rolling in the passenger seat with laughter. When he finally he got himself under control, he said, "And those pink and white flowers look real nice in your new window boxes. White shutters are awful pretty, too."

"Would you shut up? It's not funny. It looks like a freaking dollhouse." Easton pulled up behind a flatbed. "What the hell? That's my couch." He turned and saw his stove and refrigerator on the side of the road.

Easton slammed out of his truck. His brother met him around the front of the pickup and grabbed his arm. "Okay, calm down. Your furniture was crap anyway. And aside from the color, you have to admit the place looks a million times better than it did. She just should have talked to you before she went ahead and did the renovations, maybe consulted you on her color choice."

Easton scrubbed his hand over his face. "She texted me earlier and asked my favorite color. I told her pink, but I was joking. Do I look like a guy who likes pink?"

Chance started to laugh again, lifting his chin to the

left of the house. "Somebody does. She matches your house."

He followed his brother's gaze. Chloe sat in a white Adirondack chair under a pink, frilly umbrella. She had on sparkly shoes and a pink dress. Sipping on what looked like a cocktail, she called out orders to the army of men swarming his house and yard...in a Southern accent.

Chapter Seven

Y'all are doing such a wonderful job. Easton will be beside himself when he sees what y'all have done for him."

"He'll be beside himself all right," Easton muttered as he cut across the main road to the gravel drive.

"Yoo-hoo," she called out. An older man on the front porch turned. "Yes, you, sir. Would you do me a favor and adjust the shutter on the right? It's a teensy bit crooked. A little higher. Yes, that's perfect. Thank you so much."

How the hell did she notice that from where she was sitting? Jesus, the woman was a perfectionist. She must have driven the guys nuts. They probably wanted to toss Her Royal Bossiness off her throne.

"No problem, sweetheart. You see anything else you want fixed, just give me a holler."

"Forget old Ben, doll. You call me if you need anything, and I mean anything," a muscle-bound guy called out.

When several more men yelled the same offer, looking

at her like they wanted to eat her up, an overwhelming urge to punch someone came over Easton.

"Y'all are just the sweetest," she said with a tinkling laugh, then took a sip of her drink.

"So you going to play Rhett to Chloe's Scarlett?" his brother asked in an amused tone of voice.

"Why the hell would I do that? You can't think I'm jealous of those guys. I just…" He trailed off at the stunned expression on his brother's face.

"Whoa, little brother." Chance stopped him with a hand on his arm. "Where did that come from? I thought Chloe was staying with you so you could keep her out of trouble."

"A lot of good that did," he said, trying to think of a way to distract his brother. Easton didn't want to talk about his reaction because that would mean he'd have to think about it.

"It's none of my business—you're old enough to know what you want—but you and Chloe? I don't know, E, she's a little high maintenance for you."

"'Ya think? Look at her."

"I am, and I get why you're attracted to her. She's gorgeous and—"

"A pain in the ass."

"You know what they say, there's a fine line between love and hate. Just think long and hard before you get involved with her. A relationship between you two could cause big problems for Liz and Dad if it doesn't work out."

"I don't know where the hell this is coming from, but you can stop talking now. You're pissing me off. And I'm already mad enough."

"Yeah, I can see that. Just wondering if it's the guys

buzzing around your girl like she's a honey pot or your pink house setting you off."

"She's not my...What do they think they're doing? Do you see that? They stole those flowers they're giving her from my window boxes."

He didn't wait for his brother's response. Though he doubted Chance could make one since he was laughing again. Easton strode in Chloe's direction, the gravel kicking up dust under his boots.

One of the four men hanging around her chair looked up and said something to her. She leaned forward with a wide, welcoming smile. "Surprise!"

Now how was he supposed to stay mad at her when she was looking at him with excited anticipation on her gorgeous face? Easy, he told himself, she'd painted his house pink and threw out his furniture and appliances without consulting him. And she'd spent what must have been a crapload of money remodeling a place he planned to tear down. All because he'd lied to her. And if he told her the truth now, she'd be humiliated and hurt.

She looked away and said something to the men. They nodded and walked off, but not before a couple of them shot him warning glances. Chloe unhooked her umbrella from the back of the chair and stood up, smoothing a hand down her body-hugging dress. As she walked toward him, she searched his face with a nervous look on hers. "You're mad at me. You hate it, don't you?"

He shoved his hands in the front pockets of his jeans. "No, just a little surprised." He glanced at the cabin. "It's kind of...girly."

"But you said you liked pink." She looked up at him through her long lashes, and her shoulders sagged. "You were being sarcastic. Cat says I'm not very good at picking up on sarcasm." She caught her bottom lip between her teeth and glanced over her shoulder. Then she turned back to him and said, "I guess I could ask them to repaint the exterior."

"Jesus, no, don't do that. I'll get used to it." He only had to live with it for another couple of months.

A look of relief spread across her face. "They've all worked so hard today, I'd hate to ask them to stay longer."

"You wanna tell me why you're talking with a Southern accent?"

Her cheeks pinked. "I pick up accents easily. The foreman's originally from Savannah."

So that explained the British accent. She spent too much time with Estelle.

"Chloe, honey," his brother said, coming up beside him. "You completely transformed the place."

"You like it?" she asked with a hopeful smile.

"Are you kidding me? It's amazing. Suits my brother to a tee. He secretly loves pink, you know."

Easton shot his brother a look. There seemed to be a double entendre there. If Chloe was a color, she'd be pink.

She lit up. "Would you like me to show you around? You'll love the new pens they built for Bessie and the chickens, Easton."

"They're not pink, are they?"

"No, of course they're not."

She really didn't get sarcasm. He'd have to remember that. "Lead the way."

As she set off ahead of them, twirling her fancy umbrella, Chance lowered his voice. "Who's Bessie? And since when do you have chickens?"

"Since this morning. Bessie's a cow."

"Going for a little payback, were you? Making the princess slog it out on the farm. You should have remembered Chloe's not only beautiful, she's smart, and she always figures out a way to turn a situation to her advantage."

Chance was right. Easton used to play chess with her during lunch hour in high school. "Feel free to leave anytime," he said to his brother.

"No way, I want to see what she's done. I'm kind of in awe she managed to pull this off in what...eight hours?"

"She had her minions to do her bidding."

"Still, you have to admit it's pretty damn impressive."

It was. "Easy for you to say; she didn't turn your place into a dollhouse and your life upside down."

Chloe had stopped to speak with a good-looking blond guy. Easton and Chance were close enough to overhear their conversation. "No, *thank you*, Miss Chloe. A lot of these men haven't worked in months. You gave them hope, a sense of accomplishment. And you were more than generous. They appreciate the food you gave them, too," the man said with a Southern drawl.

"Well, I'll be," Chance said under his breath. "Ashley Wilkes in the flesh. You have competition, Rhett."

"You know him?"

Chance rolled his eyes. "He's the guy Scarlett was in love with. Mom wore out that book, and she made us watch the movie like twenty times. Don't you remember?"

"No. Hey, how's it going?" he said to Ashley, nudging Chloe out of the way to extend his hand. "Thanks for all the work you did here today. It's impressive."

"You're welcome. Always happy to help out a fellow vet. But it's the little lady here who deserves all the credit. She's a very special gal." He smiled at Chloe.

Easton slid his arm around her shoulders, angling his head so she didn't poke him in the eye with her umbrella. "She sure is. So all of you served?"

"Yes, sir. Miss Chloe wouldn't have it any other way. She got in touch with The Home Front Cares. They provide support for military families in Colorado, and Ruth put out the call. And don't you worry, they'll be looking into your medical claims, too."

Oh, Jesus. His brother shot him a wide-eyed look. "Ah, well, as much as I appreciate the offer, that won't be necessary." Sweat broke out on Easton's forehead as he searched his brain for a plausible excuse. "Chloe's brother Ethan is helping me out with the paperwork."

She tipped her umbrella back to look up at him. "That's wonderful. If anyone can help you, Ethan can. He's the district attorney," she told the other man. "I should have thought of that myself. I'll give you his contact information, Beau. You can pass it on to anyone else encountering the same problems."

Easton had some explaining to do. He'd think twice before he lied again. The rest of the men started walking over—and within minutes—they were surrounded. Beau introduced Easton around, and he thanked the crew. But they were more interested in hugging Chloe. It didn't seem to bother her that they were covered in dirt and sweat or that several of them looked like they crushed her ribs when they lifted her off her feet. She was polite and sweet and thanked them for whatever job they had performed. Oddly enough, she knew exactly what each one of them had done on the cabin and property. All twenty of them.

Chance and Easton watched as she accompanied the men to their vehicles to wave them off. "Okay, what happened to the Chloe O'Connor I remember? Did you see her with those guys? She was warm and sweet . . . and generous. One of the men told me she paid them each a grand and gave them a week's worth of food."

"She put out twenty grand today for labor alone?" Easton's voice went up an octave.

"Yeah, and do you want to tell me what was with the medical expenses thing? You better talk to Ethan before he starts getting calls."

"I'll let Gage tell him." His brother Gage, Christmas's sheriff, had been Ethan's best friend since grade school. "It was just shit I said to keep Chloe here and out of trouble. Now I'm in it so deep, I don't know how I'm going to dig myself out."

"Tell her the truth," his brother suggested.

Easton shoved his fingers through his hair. "Before today that wouldn't have been a problem. But now . . ."

"Yeah, I see your point." Chance looked beyond him. "Here she comes."

She gave them a wide smile. "Now for the grand . . . Oh." She went over on her ankle.

Easton took her by the arm. "You're going to kill yourself walking around in those things. You must own something without a four-inch heel."

"Slippers," she said.

"You mean to tell me you never wear anything without heels . . . ever?"

"No, and don't look at me like that. You don't have the

paparazzi constantly stalking you trying to get a picture of you looking less than your best."

He glanced at his brother who he imagined was thinking the same thing. Given Chloe's obvious concern at being caught looking less than perfect, Ethan better get that photo pulled. "So if you weren't in the public eye, you'd wear flats?"

She gave him a cute smile. "No. Now come on, I want to show you around."

Easton couldn't believe what Chloe and her crew had accomplished, and they hadn't even made it inside the cabin yet. She'd had the pens moved fifty yards from the house, the outhouse had been replaced with a state-of-the-art Porta-Potty, which now sat against the side of the cabin with a lit stone path leading up to it.

"Beau's applied for a permit to add an addition onto the back, so it'll take a couple weeks before you have your new bathroom. I wanted a custom-built hot tub, but it would have taken too long to install and the electrical is complicated. I settled on a portable one instead." She gestured to the beige acrylic six-seat tub sitting on patio slabs. "I read that hydrotherapy is good for pain management, so I thought..." She looked down and nudged a paver with the toe of her sparkly shoe.

"I love it, Chloe. It's perfect," he said, touched by her thoughtfulness. And a little irritated by it too, because she was getting to him. Big time.

"Really? I was worried..." She lifted her shoulder, then smiled. "I'm glad you like it. Now for the best part. Come on." She hurried ahead of them as if she couldn't contain her excitement.

"Jesus, I'm getting a little emotional here," Chance said, his voice gruff.

Join the club. "I think your balls shriveled up when you married Vivi. Either that or pregnancy hormones are contagious."

"Shut...Holy hell," Chance said as they walked into the cabin.

Easton opened his mouth, then closed it. The walls were painted a soft white, the windows had been replaced, the stove and refrigerator were top of the line, the cabinetry and sink were white, the countertop new and blue. The kitchen table and chairs he'd picked up at Goodwill had been upgraded to a glass table on a white stone base with high-back chairs covered in blue-and-white-striped fabric.

"It's a pullout," she said, drawing his attention to the blue sectional. The crates he'd used for a coffee table had been replaced by a white wooden one that sat on a blue shag area rug. "You used to like to read, so I had bookshelves installed." She gestured to the shelves on either side of the fireplace whose brick had been refaced and whitewashed.

He cleared his throat. "They're in storage." Until he moved them into his new home.

His brother held his gaze and lifted his chin at Chloe.

He nodded. Yeah, he was going to tell her.

"The bedroom was redone, too. There's a new bed and a door and—"

"I'd better take off," Chance said, interrupting her. He walked over and kissed her cheek. "This is amazing, Chloe. It really is. Thanks for everything you did for my brother. I hope he makes it up to you. If you're ever looking for a second career, you should go into home renovation."

Not exactly something you say to a woman who lost her job a couple of days ago. Especially a woman like Chloe. But since his brother was on a roll, he didn't seem able to help himself. "By the way, Cat loved Easton's present. He got a kiss out of it."

"She kissed you?" Chloe asked, looking less happy about the development than he expected. "I mean, that's perfect." She frowned at Chance. "You know about the plan?"

"Oh, yeah, I know all about the plan."

Easton didn't like the look in his brother's eyes. If he told Chloe what was really going on, he'd make everything worse. He tossed Chance his keys. "I'll bike into town in the morning and meet you at the *Chronicle*."

Chloe chewed on her thumbnail. "Did she like the poem?"

"You sent her a *poem*...from me?" He remembered Cat's reaction to the note. Now that he thought about it, she'd acted kind of weird.

"Yes. 'How Do I Love Thee' by Elizabeth Barrett Browning. Actually, I sent the poem to Mr. Hardy, and he was forwarding it along with the e-mail about the gun you bought her."

Chance smothered a laugh with a cough.

Easton scowled at him, then said, "*I* didn't buy her a gun, you did."

"I know, but...Excuse me, I better get that," she said when her cell phone rang.

His brother widened his eyes, nudging his head at Chloe a couple of times.

Right. He was supposed to keep her away from her phone. "Chloe, there's something I need—"

She raised a finger as she rushed to the kitchen table. "This won't take long," she said and picked up her phone. "Hello, Linda. I was going to touch base with you about the launch tomorrow. Can you believe it's only a month away? I'm so excited. Do you have a line-up of my inter...Pardon me? No, I'm fine. Why do you ask? I-I don't understand what you're talking about." She took the phone from her ear and looked at the screen. Her eyes rolled back in her head.

Chapter Eight

Easton didn't react fast enough. Typically, when Chloe fake-fainted, she crumpled to the floor in slow motion. The woman had the graceful swoon down to a science. Anytime something didn't go Chloe's way or she'd done something she shouldn't have, down she'd go. His bad knee hit the floor as he dove for her, reaching her in time to save her from cracking the back of her head on the coffee table, but he wasn't fast enough to save her ass from meeting the floor with a resounding thud. His bent leg at her back, he cradled her against his chest. "Chloe." He gently patted her cheek.

His brother held up her phone. "It's the photo Nell took. Whoever was on the line disconnected. She all right?"

Chloe's eyelids fluttered, a soft moan escaping her parted lips.

He nodded at his brother while keeping his focus on Chloe. "You're okay. You just fainted."

Her eyes blinked open, and she stared up at him for a couple beats, then blinked again. "What do you mean *just* fainted? No one *just* faints," she asked in a breathy but slightly ticked-off whisper.

He preferred ticked-off to the emotion now darkening her green eyes.

She rubbed her chest, a terrified expression coming over her pale face. "No. Heart. Must. Have. Stopped." She gasped between each word as she struggled to breathe.

"E, maybe we should call Dad."

"I'm dying, aren't I?"

Easton swore under his breath, then cupped her chin in his hand. "Look at me, Chloe. You're not dying. You're fine."

"I-I lost consciousness, and my heart is racing." She removed his hand from her chin and pressed his palm to her chest.

Her skin was soft and warm beneath his fingers and reminded him of the last time he'd touched her there. Only then his hand had dipped below her dress to...

"See?"

He cast her a sharp glance, worried she'd sensed the direction of his thoughts. But all he saw in those long-lashed eyes was fear. And while the emotion may have been unwarranted, he knew it was real. There was no way she could fake the tremors causing her delicate frame to shake in his arms or the faint sheen of perspiration on her pale face. So all this time they'd thought she was just an overemotional drama queen, her Scarlett O'Hara act as her sister called it, hadn't been an act at all. She truly believed she was having a heart attack.

He slid his hand out from under hers and reached up

to stroke her face. "I know you're scared, but it'll be over soon. I won't let anything happen to you. You're going to be okay. Just try and relax and take deep breaths."

"No, you don't understand. I can't breathe, and I have no"—she gasped for air—"feeling in my hands."

That's the thing—he did understand. The first few weeks after returning from Afghanistan, he'd suffered from panic attacks, too. Chance had witnessed one and had talked to him about it. But obviously, because Chloe was admittedly high-strung, no one recognized her symptoms for what they were. It made him angry to think she'd been dealing with this for years on her own. Angry at himself for not recognizing the signs. And worse, making fun of her along with everyone else.

"E, your leg," his brother said, crouching to take Chloe from him.

Easton didn't want to let her go, but the searing pain in his calf was getting harder to ignore. He grabbed the edge of the coffee table, unable to hold back a groan of pain as he pulled himself up.

Chloe drew away from his brother, twisting to face him. "I'm sorry. I didn't mean to hurt you."

He was about to tell her he was fine, but realized the best thing for her was to do something. She needed to get out of her head. He rubbed his leg. "Would you mind getting me an ice pack?"

"Me?" she asked, glancing from Chance back to him.

Easton groaned again and rubbed his leg. "Yeah, if it's not too much trouble."

His brother looked at him like he was being an ass, then seemed to understand what he was trying to do and helped Chloe to her feet. She took a moment to steady herself, then walked to the refrigerator with Chance following close behind.

"Well, little brother, it doesn't look like you'll have to buy food for the next six months. What all do you have in here, Chloe?" His brother began pulling containers out of the freezer and putting them on the table.

Chloe frowned. "What are you doing?"

"Thought I'd bring a couple home. Vivi loves Hailey's lasagna." He leaned around her and opened the fridge. "Hey, nice-looking roast."

"You can have it." She took out the roast and pushed the slab of beef into his brother's hands, then retrieved a container from the table. "But I'm keeping one of the lasagnas for us."

"What are you doing, giving away my dinner?" Easton teased, relieved to see her looking and acting more like herself.

She sighed. "Easton, I was too busy transforming your home to think about cooking a roast."

His mouth twitched, and over her head, his brother grinned. "You're right," Easton said. "After all the work you did today, I don't expect you to cook for me. Did I tell you how much I love what you did to the place? Because I—"

Her eyes widened, and she dropped the container on the floor, letting loose a high-pitched shriek. "My phone! Easton, where's my phone?" She put her hands on her head, tugging at her hair as her panicked gaze darted around the room. "I have to call Linda back. Call...I need to do something!"

He'd wondered how long it would take for her to remember the reason she fainted. Easton pushed himself off the coffee table and limped toward her. "What you have to do is settle down. Sit." He pointed to a chair.

"No, I can't sit." She gave her head a frantic shake. "You don't understand. There's a picture of me. Oh, my goodness, I have never looked so hideous. Why would anyone do that to me? I'm ruined." She sank onto the chair he held out for her. "They won't release my perfume now. I've spent over a year on the campaign. I worked with the best nose in the United States to get the perfect scent and…" She buried her face in her hands and started to cry.

Chance gave his head a slight bewildered shake as he went to clean up the mess on the newly laid laminate floor.

"Come on, you're overreacting. The picture isn't that bad," Easton said.

She lifted her head, swiping at her eyes. "You saw it?"

He pulled out a chair and sat down. "Yeah, I did. And your brother's already on it and so is Estelle."

"I don't understand. When did this happen and why didn't someone tell me?"

"A couple of hours ago. And we didn't tell you because we knew how you'd react," he said with a pointed look.

She blinked back fresh tears. "Oh, yes, because heaven forbid Chloe might get a little upset that someone decided to take a photo of her looking like a drowned…" Her eyes widened, and she slapped the table. "Nell. Nell took that photo of me, didn't she? That vindictive old woman has always blamed me for breaking up you and Cat. She would do anything to destroy me." She gave a bitter laugh. "Well, bravo, Nell. You succeeded."

"Are you done now?" Easton asked through clenched teeth, his earlier sympathy evaporating.

"My career or me, Easton? I'm hardly done, but my career and life are over. Over!" She threw out her arms dramatically.

"It's one picture, Chloe. No one is going to believe you were trying to drown yourself."

Her gaze shot to him. "Drown myself? I don't understand—"

"Forget about it." He scrubbed his hand over his face.

"No, I want to know what you meant about me drowning myself."

She'd find out anyway. Might as well get it over with. "The headline read 'Distraught over being fired from *As the Sun Sets*, America's Sweetheart tries to drown herself.'"

She flapped her hands in front of her face. "Oh, no. Oh, no."

His brother sat back on his heels. "Look, Chloe, Nell got carried away, but she had no idea the photo was going to get picked up on the wire. Vivi took it down as soon as she realized it was online."

"I'm suing! I'm calling my lawyer and suing."

Chance came to his feet with a look on his face that Easton imagined had scared guys a lot bigger and badder than Chloe. She lifted her chin. "Don't try and intimidate me, Chance McBride. I have no choice in the matter. If I don't sue, people will believe that it's true."

His brother looked like he wanted to strangle her, and Easton wasn't far behind. "Chance, go home. Don't worry about it. I'll handle this."

"You better," he growled and stomped out the door

with the roast and two containers of lasagna under his arm.

Chloe crossed her arms. "Where's my phone?"

"I'm not giving it to you until we've settled this." He raked his hand through his hair. "Chloe, a few days from now, no one is going to remember that photo. But here, in town, and in this family, if you sue Vivi and Nell, no one will forgive you or forget."

Her chin quivered. "It's not fair. How come I end up being the bad guy when I'm the victim?"

"'Cause, Scarlett, if you sue a seventy-something woman and your stepbrother's pregnant wife, you kinda are the bad guy." He leaned forward and took her hand. "I get it, okay. Nell shouldn't have put the picture online, and I'm going to talk to her about it. Dad and Liz already went to speak to her. But Vivi doesn't deserve to be hurt because of this. She took the photo down right away, and believe me, she'll be kicking Nell's ass, too."

"But if I don't do something... You don't understand what this will do to my career. The woman I was on the phone with said they no longer feel I'm a suitable representative for my perfume. It's *my* perfume, Easton."

"Seems to me, if you're going to sue anyone, it should be them. They shouldn't be able to fire you over this."

"I've worked so hard, and in less than a week I've lost everything. No one wants to hire me. And now with that photo and headline out there..."

He gently tugged on her hand to get her to look at him. This wasn't exactly the best time to come clean, but he didn't want to put it off any longer. Especially if she was worried about money. "You shouldn't have spent what you did on this place, Chloe. I'll—"

"Money's not an issue for me. I don't have to work. But I love what I do, and it's all I have. It really is my life." She looked away.

"I didn't realize soap stars made that much."

She shrugged. "We're well paid, or at least I was. And I've done several commercials that were lucrative. But the bulk of my fortune comes from the investments I made with the inheritance Daddy left me."

"Guess I shouldn't be surprised. You always were smart."

"Yes, I am. And that's why I have to initiate a lawsuit against the *Chronicle* and Nell. I'll tell my lawyer to—"

He stared at her, shocked and disappointed she still planned on going ahead with the lawsuit. Dropping her hand, he pushed off the chair. "There's a reason why all you have is your money, Chloe."

* * *

Chloe flinched as much from the slamming of the door as Easton's parting shot. He was being unfair. He had no idea what it was like to live in the entertainment industry's fishbowl. Sometimes she wished she didn't. It was soul-sucking and exhausting. But if he just would have let her finish instead of storming off, he'd realize the lawsuit was a public relations ploy. She had no intention of taking Vivi and Nell to court, although Nell totally deserved it if she did. In the end, Chloe would accept an apology, but she had to go through the motions.

She got up from the chair, about to search for her cell phone, when she heard Estelle's ringtone. Following the sound, she found her phone tucked between the pillows on the couch. She sank down on the blue sectional, taking a moment to prepare herself before picking up. If she didn't want a repeat of earlier, she had to remain calm.

She'd barely gotten out *hello* when Estelle started ranting about Nell. Although her manager undoubtedly had Chloe's best interests at heart, she couldn't help but think Estelle's adversarial relationship with Nell was behind the older woman's suggestion that they take Easton's great-aunt down. And as Estelle plotted their legal revenge, a sinking feeling came over Chloe. Easton was right. If she went through with it, everyone would hate her. But she couldn't allow her reputation to suffer. She had to think of a way...

"Estelle...Estelle"—she raised her voice to cut off her manager—"we're not going to sue. No, I haven't been drinking." Although that wasn't a bad idea. As she explained to Estelle why she couldn't go through with the lawsuit, Chloe got up from the couch and walked to the refrigerator. She took out a lovely bottle of Sauvignon Blanc that she'd ordered for her and Easton's celebratory toast this evening. Obviously, that wasn't going to happen now. Despite everything she'd done for him, they were back to being frenemies.

With the phone tucked between her shoulder and ear, Chloe unscrewed the cap and filled the wine goblet to the brim. "I know it isn't fair, Estelle, but that's the way it's always been. No one in this town has ever taken my side. You're right, I probably shouldn't care what they think of me. I really wish I didn't, but I do. So here's how we're going to deal with this: we'll say it was Cat in the pool, not me. Well, if she won't make a statement...No. What am I saying? Of course she will." Chloe sipped on her wine as she walked into the bedroom. She was about to stretch out on the bed when she happened to glance out the window. Easton was in the hot tub. His head was tipped back, his muscular arms stretched out and resting on the ledge, his naked, tanned chest on mouth-watering display.

"Yes, I'm still here." She dragged her gaze from the tempting view. She couldn't afford to be distracted right now, and Easton was very distracting.

As the conversation turned to how they'd deal with Linda and the launch of her perfume, Chloe's pulse kicked up. Estelle thought they'd been looking for an out since Chloe had been killed off *As the Sun Sets*. An extra-large gulp of wine did nothing to calm her now-racing heart. She found herself craving the feel of Easton's powerful arms around her, his strong fingers gently caressing her face. He hadn't told her the attack was all in her head or that she was being dramatic. He'd said exactly what she needed to hear—he wouldn't let anything happen to her. And she believed him.

"No, don't bother getting in touch with Linda, Estelle. I think it's best if we let the lawyers handle this from here on in. The plan? Oh, right, sorry, I don't know where my head is at." Only she did, and drained the glass of wine. "Yes, I thought the poem and gun were an inspired idea, too."

Until she'd heard that Cat had kissed Easton and an anxious knot had formed in the pit of her stomach. If she wasn't such a good actress, she probably would have given herself away. She didn't know what was behind her mixed emotions. Maybe spending more time with Easton had reminded her why *she'd* fallen in love with him all those years ago. Just like he'd proven earlier, he was her white knight. Easton was that guy, the one who rode to the rescue of a damsel in distress.

But Cat…she'd never be a damsel in distress. Preoccupied with the thought, Chloe missed what Estelle had just said. When she tuned back into the conversation, her head jerked up. "No! Sorry, I didn't mean to shout, Estelle. I just don't think giving Cat's phone to Grayson to show him the poem is a good idea right now." Because Chloe was second-guessing her win-Cat-back plan. Which wasn't something she could tell Estelle. Chloe racked her wine-soaked brain for a plausible excuse. "It's too soon to show our hand. We have to be patient. If Grayson and Cat guess what you're up to now, they'll kick you out of the house. Yes, of course I meant what *we're* up to. I've had a stressful day, Estelle. So if you don't mind, I'll talk to you in the morning."

Chloe disconnected and chewed on her thumbnail. She was so confused. Maybe if she talked to Easton… Yes, that's exactly what she'd do. Before she lost her nerve, she stripped down to her pink lace bra and panties. She pulled one of Easton's white T-shirts from the drawer and put it on. Once she'd piled her hair on top of her head, fastening it in place with a clip, she headed for the hot tub.

The warm night air carried the familiar smells of spring. The sweet aroma of cut grass, newly budded leaves, and the earthy scent of the ground heated by the sun, reminded her of her years growing up in Christmas before the magic was stolen. Overhead, it looked like a magician had waved his wand and sprinkled the night sky with fairy dust as the moon smiled down over the mountains. Her view from her beach house was spectacular, too, but there was something about the Rockies that spoke to her soul. Something she'd forgotten until now.

As she reached the hot tub, she slipped off her heels. Easton slowly turned his head and opened one eye. Watching as she awkwardly attempted to climb in, he didn't make a move to help. So much for her white knight theory.

Balancing on the ledge, she cautiously dipped her toe in the bubbling water and quickly pulled it out. "Oh. I didn't expect the water to be so hot."

"It's why they call it a *hot* tub, Chloe."

"Well, I know that. I'm just not sure the heat is good for my heart."

He sighed and reached over, fitting his big hands under her arms to haul her into the tub. "Your heart will be fine." He plunked her down beside him. "Okay?"

She nodded, biting on her bottom lip as she glanced up at him through her lashes. "I've decided not to sue Vivi and Nell."

"Glad to hear it. I don't have time to play your personal bodyguard for the next few days."

Her heart did a little flip, and she wasn't sure if the water's heat or his words caused the reaction. She rubbed her chest. "You would have protected me?"

"Umhm," he murmured, his eyes on her hand. He covered it with his. "Relax, you're fine."

"Are you fine? I mean, is it helping your leg?"

Water glistened on his broad chest as it expanded on an irritated sigh. "So that's why you did all this?" He gestured to the cabin and grounds. "You felt sorry for me?"

"No...Well, yes, I did it for you, but not out of pity.

You were injured serving our country, keeping people like me safe, and it wasn't right that you were treated so badly. I was going to write to the VA on your behalf, but thought, why wait when I could do it for you myself." A muscle in his jaw pulsed. She knew his pride would be a sticking point. Good thing she'd prepared for it. "Fine, I'll come clean. I'm used to a certain standard of living, and the cabin didn't cut it. I like my creature comforts, and since I was going to be living with you—for a few days, I mean—I decided to kill two birds with one stone. I took care of my share of the chores for like the entire time I'm here, and I got a nice place to stay."

A slow smile curved his lips, and he slid an arm around her shoulders. "You're full of it, Scarlett."

She frowned and tipped her head back to look up at him. "Why do you think I did it then?"

"Because despite what everyone thinks, you're not the spoiled drama queen you pretend to be. You're still the sweet, thoughtful, generous girl you were growing up." He shifted and faced her. "Is that why you did it, Chloe? To make up for what you did to me and Cat?"

She lifted his arm from her shoulders and moved away from his warmth. "It's funny how that's all everyone remembers. No one cares that Cat stole you from me first." Afraid she was about to get teary-eyed, she looked up at the stars and blinked.

"What are you talking about?"

A sad, brittle laugh escaped before she could stop it. "Even you didn't know. How pathetic is that?" She looked at him. "We were fifteen. We spent nearly every lunch hour together for four months."

"I know, we played chess in the library." He angled his

head as though thinking back to their high-school days, then he scrubbed his hand over his face. "Mom had just been diagnosed with cancer, and I didn't feel like being around anyone. You were the only one I could talk to. I forgot about that. It was a tough time; I guess I didn't want to remember."

"Sometimes I wish I could forget, too," she murmured. From the moment she fell in love with Easton, her life changed. For the better, and then for the worse. "Looking back, I realize it was silly to think the popular star quarterback could fall in love with me. But you made me feel special, as if you saw past the headgear and glasses and chubby face."

"You were special, Chloe."

"Not special enough. Only I didn't know that then. I mistook your pity and kindness for love. I thought about you all the time, talked about you to Cat. She knew I was in love with you, but she didn't care. She went after you anyway. I remember the day I saw the two of you together on the football field after practice. Cat was in her cheerleader uniform, and you said something to make her laugh. Next thing I knew, she was telling me you had a date, and you stopped coming to the library to play chess."

He grimaced. "I stopped coming because I had football practice. But I'm sure I told you that."

"No, you didn't. I would have remembered."

"Are you sure you told Cat you had a crush on me? Because that doesn't sound like something she'd do."

"I didn't tell her *who* I had a crush on. Maybe I was afraid she'd laugh at me. But she had to know. You were the only boy I hung out with."

He took her hand and tugged her back to his side, then pressed his mouth to her temple. "I'm sorry I hurt your feelings. I honestly didn't know."

"It doesn't matter. It was a silly schoolgirl crush." But the way he looked at her now and the tender touch of his lips to her temple didn't feel silly or foolish, and she was more confused than ever. She gave herself a mental slap. She was doing the same thing she did in high school. "What you and Cat had was real, and I messed that up for both of you. Now I have a chance to fix it."

"What if I told you I don't want you to?"

"Why not? Two days ago you were all for the plan."

"I wouldn't go that far." He looked down at her and lifted her chin. "But it's not Cat I want to kiss right now, it's you."

"You want to kiss me?"

Instead of answering her whispered question with words, he lowered his head and slanted his mouth over hers, silencing her surprised gasp with his warm lips. And for the first time, he was actually kissing her, not her pretending to be Cat. But this was not the kiss of the boy she remembered. This was the kiss of an experienced and confident man. Slow and languid, their hands and bodies moving in sync, they explored each other tentatively. Her fingers tracing the line of his jaw, down his neck to his hard pecs. She opened her eyes to find him watching her as he gently drew her bottom lip into his mouth. She whimpered at the erotic feel, at the desire turning his blue eyes black. He pulled her onto his lap, the moments of slow seduction over as he pressed a hot and possessive kiss to her mouth. There was no more gentleness now. Only heat and passion and hunger. This night wouldn't end with just a kiss. This was already more than a kiss. It was...

There was a distant pounding on a door, and someone called out, "Chloe, Easton, where are you?" And then another voice called to them. Chloe was still somewhere between heaven and earth; too far gone to make out who their visitors were. She just knew Easton had frozen with his mouth on hers. Until it wasn't and she found herself practically airborne when he launched her onto the seat across from him.

He stared at her, then he gave his head a slight shake and dragged his hand down his face. "Liz, Dad, back here."

Chloe groaned and briefly closed her eyes, opening them in time to see a white light streak across the night sky. It was a shooting star. A sense of wonder filled her at the sight. Had her father and Easton's mother sent her a sign from up above?

Chapter Nine

Chloe looked at him with a stunned expression on her beautiful, flushed face. He understood the feeling. Every memory he had of his relationship with the O'Connor sisters had been turned on its head by a simple kiss. Simple kiss? If only that was all it had been. He wished he could put his reaction down to experience, hers and his, but it was more than that. He'd kissed her when they were seventeen and had a similar reaction. But back then he'd put his feelings down to being a horny, inexperienced kid who wanted to get laid, and he'd mistaken her for her sister. Only the kisses he'd shared with Cat couldn't compare to what he'd experienced with Chloe. It's too bad he hadn't clued in to the difference all those years ago. They might have avoided the heartache that followed.

Caught up in his thoughts, he didn't notice Paul and Liz staring at them until his father cleared his throat. Their respective parents were looking at them like they were seventeen again, and they'd caught them making out naked in the hot tub.

Good thing they hadn't arrived a few minutes later or they might have been naked. His brother's earlier warning echoed in Easton's head.

"Chloe, honey, are you all right? Chance told—" his father began, only to be cut off by a furious Liz.

"Chloe O'Connor, I have never been so ashamed of your behavior as I am now. You have gone too far this time! Now get out of that hot tub and get on the phone to your lawyer." It was obvious where Chloe got her dramatic tendencies.

Only right then his little drama queen looked more hurt than anything else, and that pissed him off. "Town's rumor mill must be slow today, Liz. Chloe isn't suing Nell and Vivi, despite the fact she has every right to. Hope you let loose some of your temper on my great-aunt and didn't save it all up for Chloe." He swung his legs over the side, making sure to hide a wince of pain from his father when his feet hit the concrete.

Liz lifted her chin. "I didn't know."

"Now you do. So might be a good time to apologize to your daughter," Easton said as he helped Chloe out of the hot tub.

She gave him a sweet smile and whispered, "Thank you."

If he wasn't transfixed by the curves his transparent T-shirt revealed, the worshipful look in those leaf-green eyes might have made him nervous. "No problem."

"Son, there's no reason to get testy with Liz. It was an honest mistake."

"No, he's right, Paul. I should have given Chloe a chance to explain. I'm sorry, darling."

"It's okay, Mommsy. I'm used to everyone thinking the worst of me. But I'm a little surprised you believed I'd sue Nell and Vivi. They're family, after all."

Easton looked down at her and raised an eyebrow.

She shrugged, her kiss-swollen lips tipping up at the corner.

"You're taking it much better than I thought you would, darling. That photo Nell put up of you was horrible, not to mention—"

He felt Chloe stiffen beside him and quickly intervened. "So what do you guys think of the changes Chloe made to my place? Pretty amazing, eh?"

His father frowned. "Well, yes, but I thought—"

He widened his eyes, sending his father a silent message to keep quiet. Easton planned on coming clean with Chloe tonight. Preferably after she had several more glasses of the wine he'd tasted on her lips. She took his hand and beamed up at him. Okay, so maybe he'd wait until they'd made love. Because after that kiss, he had no intention of sleeping on the pull-out couch tonight.

Liz and his dad followed them to the front of the cabin. Easton held open the door. "Wait until you see what she's done inside."

From there, Chloe took over. She led Paul and Liz around the small space, pointing out each and every change. With every word of praise their respective parents showered on her, Chloe surprised him by redirecting credit to the crew. As she led her mother into the bedroom, his father walked over to where Easton stood at the sink, filling the coffeepot with water.

"You wanna tell me what's going on here, son?"

"A little miscommunication, but I'll handle it, Dad."

"See that you do. Your breakup with Cat put enough strain on our families. I'd prefer not to have a repeat now that I'm married to Liz."

A couple of days earlier, he would have laughed at his father's warning. The thought of him and Chloe ever dating was the furthest thing from his mind. But now… "We're not kids anymore. What happens between us has nothing to do with you and Liz."

"Oh my goodness, Chloe, you have a bruise on your bottom." Liz's voice came from behind the bedroom door.

His father's gaze jerked to his.

"Come on, you can't seriously believe I had anything to do with that?"

"How am I supposed to know? These days all you hear about is kinky sex."

"We're not having kinky sex." Although, if Chloe wanted to, he was totally down with that. But it's not a discussion he wanted to have with his father. Ever. "She fainted, and her ass hit the floor before I caught her."

A concerned frown creased his father's brow. "Your brother mentioned—"

The door to the bedroom swung open. "Paul, Chloe fainted today. And she wasn't faking like she usually does."

"Mommsy, how can you say that? I have never fake-fainted! Any other time I've had a weak spell, I've had my pills and…" She wrinkled her small, upturned nose when she realized what she said. If she weren't standing behind her mother wearing only a pink bra and panties that left little to the imagination—and Easton's was working over-time—he would have thought it was cute. She didn't look cute; she looked centerfold hot.

"Don't get upset, darling. Paul will check you over." Her brow pleated with worry, Liz motioned for his father.

In response to her mother's concern, a look of fear came over Chloe's face. Easton had planned to talk to her about her panic attacks and figured now was as good a time as any. "Chloe, get some clothes on and come join us at the table. Liz, Dad, sit down, and I'll get us all a cup of coffee."

"Son, what's going on?" his father asked, holding out a chair for Liz.

"I'll tell you in a minute," he said, looking over at the clicking sound. Chloe walked to the table wearing her fancy slippers. She'd changed into a short, cream satin robe that wasn't much better for his focus than her panties and bra.

The three of them looked at him expectantly as he placed the pot of coffee on the table along with sugar and cream. He handed them each a cup, then straddled a chair beside Chloe. "Liz, Chloe doesn't fake-faint. She has a panic disorder."

Chloe released an outraged gasp. "I do not have a panic disorder, Easton McBride. I have a heart condition."

"You *had* a heart condition. You don't anymore."

"That's not true! I'm not emotionally unstable or...or overdramatic. My symptoms are real. You don't know how it feels. My heart races, and I get dizzy and weak. I can't breathe, and I have tingling in my arms and fingers and get all sweaty. Those are symptoms of a heart attack, aren't they, Paul?" She cast a pleading look at his father.

Paul got up from his chair and patted Easton's shoulder as he went to crouch by Chloe's side. Liz sent Easton a helpless, stricken look. He reached over and put his hand over hers, giving it a reassuring squeeze.

"Chloe, honey, Easton's right. You don't have a heart condition anymore. A panic attack can mimic the symptoms of a heart attack. But it doesn't make what you're feeling any less real or frightening."

Her chin quivered, and she wrapped her arms around her waist. "I'm not crazy. I'm not making this up."

"Of course you're not. And I'm sorry I didn't pick up on this earlier. What you went through as a little girl was traumatic. You spent four years in and out of the hospital. That's tough on anyone, but especially for someone as young as you were."

She bowed her head. Long tendrils of her hair escaped from her clip to fall across her pink cheek as she murmured, "They said I wouldn't live to my fifth birthday."

Liz gasped. "Oh darling, I didn't know you heard that. Why didn't you tell us? You were always such a little trouper. You never complained, never once told us you were scared. All this time..." Her mother started to cry.

Chloe glared at Easton. "Now look what you've done."

* * *

"I know you're awake, sleeping beauty, so you might as well open your eyes and talk to me. I'm not leaving until you do." She felt the gentle brush of Easton's lips over hers and smelled the cool, minty freshness of his breath.

She kept her eyes closed and forced herself to remain stiff and unresponsive. She'd felt like an idiot last night, and it was Easton's fault. He'd ambushed her in front of her mother and Paul. Now everyone would know. At least if he'd told her his suspicions when they were alone, she could have handled the attacks on her own. "Go away, I'm not talking to you."

"Chloe, I get that you're mad, but you needed to know that it's panic attacks causing your symptoms, not your heart. And so did your mother." The bed creaked as he stretched his big, hard body out beside her. He nuzzled her shoulder.

She wriggled away. "Your hair's wet."

"I had a shower." He tugged her back against him. "You need to have one, too."

Offended, her eyes shot open. "I do not smell."

His mouth quirked. "Never said you did. But there are chemicals in the hot tub. Wouldn't want you to damage your silky skin." He drew a finger down her bare arm.

"Oh." She shivered in response to his touch, then took in the matching black stretch top and shorts that hugged his masculine frame and frowned. "Why are you dressed like that?"

"What are you, the fashion police?"

"Ha-ha. I, at least, have a sense of style."

"I'm biking into town. Comfort is my concern, not looking good."

"It doesn't matter what you wear, Easton, you always look good." She ignored his self-satisfied smile; of course he knew he did. How could he not? "But that outfit doesn't... What do you mean you're biking into town? What about your leg?"

"I bike every day. The exercise is good for my leg."

"If it was, you wouldn't be in so much pain. I don't think you should ride today. Call Chance and—"

"I don't want to talk about me. I want to talk about

you." He twisted a piece of her hair around his finger, then gave the strand a gentle tug. "I thought maybe we'd set up an appointment for you to talk to the doctor my dad suggested."

She crossed her arms and stared up at the ceiling. "You mean the psychiatrist."

He cupped her cheek and forced her to look at him. "Yeah. Dad says she has a lot of experience with PTSD. She does a rotation at Christmas General on…"

Her heart started to race, and her palms got sweaty. She had the same reaction whenever she went to the hospital, but she'd hidden it from her parents. She'd avoided hospitals for the last ten years. "I. Can't. Go." She forced the words past the lump in her throat, hoping he didn't notice she was breathless and…panicked.

"Okay, take it easy. You don't have to go to the hospital. She has an office in Denver." He drew her into his arms and rubbed soothing circles on her back.

She felt so stupid. The symptoms were all in her head. She wasn't weak. She should be able to control this. Taking comfort in the feel of his strong arms around her while breathing in his clean, spicy scent, Chloe felt her heart rate slow.

Easton leaned back to look down at her. "Better?"

Embarrassed, she nodded and pulled away from him.

"Hey, no beating yourself up over this. Now that you know what you're dealing with, it'll get easier. Look how fast you got it under control this time."

"It's because of you. I feel safe with you." She self-consciously lifted a shoulder. She hadn't meant to tell him that. And from the small pleating between his dark eyebrows, she shouldn't have.

"I'm glad that you do, Chloe. But I won't always be here. That's why you have to see someone."

"Did you see someone?"

"For what?"

"Your panic attacks. Don't try and deny it, Easton. That's why you were able to recognize mine when no one else did."

"Times like this, I wish you were the airhead you pretend to be."

"I do not pretend to be an airhead." Okay, so maybe she did. Sometimes it was fun to pretend to be a ditz; it lowered people's expectations. But she didn't like that Easton saw through her act.

"Umhm," he said with a knowing smile, then surprisingly answered her question. "No, I didn't. I knew what I was dealing with, and in a couple of weeks, they were gone. But I would have gotten help, Chloe. There's no shame in it."

"Really? So if there's no shame in accepting help, why don't you see someone for your pain?"

"Because they'd tell me to kick you out of my house, and I kind of like having you around."

"You do?" Her heart pitter-pattered in her chest, and she knew it wasn't the onset of a panic attack. No, this was real and much more dangerous. Her old feelings for Easton were back, and she wasn't sure how to deal with them or him. She lightly swatted his chest. "You can't distract me that easily. Answer my question."

"I have pills for the pain. It's my choice not to take them. I'll work through it without them."

"The doctor wouldn't prescribe painkillers if you didn't need them. You're just being stubborn and macho."

A muscle pulsed in his jaw as he got up off the bed. "Appreciate the concern, Scarlett, but I'm fine. I have to get into town. I should be back around...What's wrong with you now?"

Her mouth hanging open, she waved her hand at him. "You can't wear those. They...they show *everything*." She wasn't exaggerating. The stretchy black fabric clung to every dip and curve, every muscle and bulge.

He grinned and flipped back the covers, pulling her out of bed to draw her flush against all those hard muscles and bulges. "Tonight, you and I are going to talk, and then I'll give you a good, long look at *everything* you seem so interested in."

She was very interested. She cleared her throat. "Everything?"

"Oh, yeah, everything. Now come on, I'll show you how the shower works before I go."

"It's okay. I'm having lunch with my mother today, remember? I'll have her come early, and I'll stop by their place for a shower first."

"All right, suit yourself. But you don't know what you're missing." He leaned in and brushed his lips over hers, then headed for the door. "If your lunch runs late, text me, and I'll pick you up. Save Liz a trip." He glanced over his shoulder and started to laugh.

She touched the side of her lips to check for drool. The view of Easton's backside was as mouth-watering as the front. "I hope you have a change of clothes," she said, following him to the door.

He bent down and picked up a black knapsack off the floor. She sank her teeth into her bottom lip to hold back a moan. He winked and slung the bag over his shoulder.

"Yeah, and I have a helmet, too, so don't worry about me. See you tonight."

She swallowed and nodded, thinking of his earlier promise. Closing the door behind him, she looked up at the ceiling and said to Easton's mother, "Anna, I need your help. If I'm the one meant to be with Easton, you need to give me a sign." She waited, glancing around the sunlit room. "Please, just a little one will do."

And then, as though in response to her request, a memory of her ghostly visitors last Christmas flashed in her mind. Their midnight visit that snowy night in December had been a terrifying experience. One that made Chloe vow to change her ways.

Easton's mother had been the ghost of Chloe's past, taking her on an embarrassing trip down memory lane. She could almost hear Anna now, telling her once again that Chloe could make everything right. In a voice as soft and kind as it had always been.

Chloe's mother and Easton's had been best friends growing up. Chloe didn't have friends of her own, other than her sister, and enjoyed hanging out with the two women. Admittedly, the possibility of an Easton sighting had been a draw, too.

Anna used to brush Chloe's hair and tell her one day she'd be as beautiful as Scarlett O'Hara. She wondered if Easton knew his nickname for her was the same as his mother's. At the thought, Chloe smiled. She had her answer. Cat and Easton weren't a match made in heaven. Chloe and Easton were.

Chapter Ten

Everywhere she looked, Chloe was reminded of Easton. Even now, as she stood at the kitchen sink arranging the wildflowers she'd picked in the field behind the cabin, she noticed the flax petals were the same blue as his eyes. A pine-scented breeze drifted through the open kitchen window, ruffling her hair still damp from the outdoor shower she'd taken. Despite Easton's enthusiastic recommendation, she'd been hesitant at first, but at the thought of chemicals damaging her skin, she'd given in.

Once she was out there, standing naked under the soft, warm water with only the majestic mountains and their snow-covered peaks as her witness, she understood what Easton meant. She felt free. No paparazzi to worry about or judgmental neighbors, just her and nature. She snorted a laugh at the thought. She must have spring fever, there was no other explanation. Well, there was, but she thought it was a little early to be thinking about the L word.

Chloe hadn't felt this peaceful in...Gosh, she couldn't remember how long it had been. Every minute of every day for the last five years had been consumed by her career, wanting to get ahead, wanting to impress, wanting to be the best. The pressure of staying relevant in Hollywood was exhausting, and she hadn't realized how exhausted she was until today. And she had no doubt, as difficult as it had been to hear, that learning her heart wasn't to blame for her attacks contributed to her more tranquil state of mind, too.

If it wasn't for Easton pushing the issue, she'd still be walking around thinking she had a time-bomb in her chest. She froze mid-step, wondering if that was just one more sign that he might be *her* one. Unlike that long-ago spring when he'd been her sister's.

Chloe buried her face in the wildflowers as she carried the vase to the kitchen table, inhaling their sweet scent in an effort to avoid thinking of Cat. But her brain wouldn't cooperate, and neither would her stomach. Ever since Easton left, she'd had an uneasy feeling something wasn't right with her sister. A feeling Chloe had spent the morning ignoring.

Because the stories about the psychic connection between identical twins were true. At least they were for Cat and Chloe. She'd experienced her sister's heartache over Michael as if it were her own. And while Cat never came out and admitted it, Chloe was positive her sister had felt her pain over the years, too.

Then again, the heavy weight taking up residence in Chloe's stomach might be nothing more than guilt. After all, even if it was with the best intentions, she'd planned to break up Cat and Grayson. At the thought, a sense of panic shattered her earlier contentment. She should have come straight out and told Easton the win-Cat-back plan was off before he left for work. No, she was being silly, she reassured herself. She had nothing to worry about. Not after the kiss they shared and Easton's promise for this evening.

And that's what she wanted to focus on, a wonderful night of delicious food, a walk under the stars while they talked about their day. And then they'd end the night in bed. She glanced at her watch. It was almost noon, and she was past ready for her lunch date with her mother. At least as far as her face and outfit were concerned, she was ready. The yellow racer-back sundress with the zip front she had on was sexy, her red shoes totes fab. Sadly, she couldn't say the same for her hair. She'd blown a fuse with her professional blow-dryer and had to settle for pulling back her unruly mane in a ponytail.

Checking out her chipped red-polished fingernails as she reached for her cell phone, she wondered if she could convince her mother to stop at Ty's salon before lunch. The household chores were playing havoc on her manicure. She picked up her ringing cell. "I was just going to call you. Are you on your way?" she asked, when her mother's voice came over the line.

"Darling, I'm afraid I have to cancel."

"Oh, no, Mommsy, I'm so disappointed." She wasn't. She'd been afraid their entire lunch-date conversation would revolve around her "attacks," but she made sure to sound like she was. "Are you all right?"

"No. I mean, yes, I am. But I have devastating news. The worst news ever. Prepare yourself, darling. Are you sitting?"

Out of habit, Chloe's hand went to her chest, and she sank down on the couch. "Yes, tell me."

"It's... There's no easy way to say this. Grayson left Cat."

"What!" Chloe's heart started to beat triple time against her ribs, and she fell limply against the back of the couch, weakly flapping her hand in front of her face.

"Just breathe, darling. I knew I shouldn't have told you."

"I'm... I'm okay. Is Kit Kat all right?"

"I have no idea. She won't answer her phone. You know what she's like when she's upset. She shuts down. But I spoke to Chance, and he says Easton's with her."

Chloe jerked upright. "Easton's with Kit Kat?"

"Yes, he's such a good boy. I feel better knowing she has him to lean on. But I'm heading to the ranch right now and getting to the bottom of this. I guarantee Estelle has something to do with Grayson leaving. She's never approved of his relationship with..." For several beats, all she heard was the sound of Liz breathing. Chloe chewed anxiously on her bottom lip. Her mother knew her a little too well. "Chloe, you wouldn't happen to know anything about this, would you?"

"Of course I don't. I've been here the entire time. Stuck out in the middle of nowhere minding my own business."

"Umhm, you have. And that's something else I want to talk to you about. But I don't have time right now." Chloe collapsed against the back of the couch, sending up a silent prayer of thanks as her mother continued. "I'll call you once I've spoken to Cat. You should call your sister, darling. She needs your support now more than ever. She's always been there for you, you know."

A twinge of guilt pinched Chloe's heart at the reminder. It was true. Cat had always been there for her. And as soon as Chloe disconnected from her mother, she punched in Estelle's number.

Her manager picked up on the first ring. "We did it, my dear. Grayson packed his bags twenty minutes ago and left the ranch."

Afraid she was about to hyperventilate, Chloe stretched out on the couch. "What did you do?" she whispered.

"Are you all right, my dear? You sound—"

"Estelle, what did you do?" Chloe shrieked into the phone. At her manager's affronted harrumph, Chloe winced and, with some effort, calmed herself. "I'm sorry. It's just...Can you please tell me what happened?"

"No apologies necessary, my dear. I'm sure the excitement got the better of you. And really, I can't take all the credit. The poem you sent your sister from the McBride boy did the trick. All I had to do was casually bring it to Grayson's attention."

Chloe whimpered, biting down on her knuckle to keep from yelling as Estelle continued. "You would have been quite proud of me. Your sister left her phone in the kitchen, and I pretended that I thought it was mine. When I found the poem, I went on about it as if Fred sent it to me. Then I made a horrified face, it was quite brilliant. Anyway, at that point, your sister realized the jig was up. I must say, though, I felt terribly bad for my grandson. He didn't deserve to be treated—"

"Estelle, my sister didn't do anything wrong. It was us!"

"Really, my dear, you sound quite overwrought."

"Where are you?" *Please don't be at the ...*

"I'm at the ranch. Grayson was so upset, he forgot me. And he's not taking my calls. Perhaps I should have curbed my enthusiasm, but—"

"Estelle, my mother's on her way to the ranch. You have to leave before she gets there." Her manager didn't stand a chance against Liz. "Get one of the ranch hands to bring you into town. Tell them it's an emergency." It wasn't far enough away. Liz would track her down. "You know, Estelle, it's probably best if you head back to LA. Between the problems with the perfume and all the bad publicity, I really need you there taking care of my interests. I'll book a flight for you now. Take a taxi from town to the airport." Chloe was talking so fast that she could barely catch her breath.

"No, that won't do. Not at all. I can't leave my grandson in his hour of need."

"I'll…I'll take care of Grayson."

"Ah, I see where you're headed with this. You're right, it's the perfect way for you to get closer to him. Brilliant, my dear."

"Yes, yes it is. Now get Fluffy and run to the barn. Don't waste time packing, I'll send you your things." When the older woman started to waffle, Chloe said, "Estelle, trust me, you do not want to be there when my mother arrives."

While Chloe was booking Estelle's flight, she heard a vehicle coming down the gravel road. Thinking it might be her mother, she rushed to the kitchen window. It was Easton's red truck, followed by Cat's black SUV. Chloe ducked down.

Easton knew she'd sent the poem, but surely, since he was in on the plan from the beginning, he wouldn't tell her sister. And while Chloe worried about her family's re-action to what she had done, a bigger concern reared its ugly head. What if she'd misread the signs, the meaning behind Easton's kiss, his promise of this morning? She'd done so in the past, and if she'd done it again, Easton now had the perfect opportunity to make a move on her sister. And it was Chloe's fault. Everything was falling apart. What had possessed her to come up with the idea in the first place? While protecting Cat may have played a part in it, Chloe had to be honest with herself. She'd been jealous of what Cat had and wanted it for herself. And now that she'd possibly found it…

Chloe inched up, hiding behind the upper cabinet to stay out of sight. Easton thought she was at lunch with her mother and wouldn't be expecting to see her. Until she had a better handle on the situation, Chloe planned to keep it that way. They got out of their vehicles, and Easton joined her sister on the gravel drive. The first thing Chloe noticed was that her sister didn't appear to be too broken up. Which on one hand relieved Chloe, while on the other, it made her nervous.

"You sure you don't mind helping me out?" Easton asked her sister. Chloe was happy to see he'd changed from his riding gear into a navy T-shirt and jeans.

But really, what on earth was her sister wearing? She had on faded jeans with a pastel plaid shirt Chloe was sure she'd worn in the nineties. A sisters' shopping trip was in order. If Cat wanted to win back her fiancé, she had to start putting some effort into her appearance. Unless she had her sights set on Easton, who'd probably approve of her laid-back look. Chloe's chest tightened at the depressing thought.

"No, I'm glad of the distraction." Cat held up a hand when Easton went to speak. "I don't want to talk about it, okay?"

Easton shrugged. "Works for me."

Well, it didn't work for Chloe. She wanted to know what was going on in her sister's head.

Cat crossed her arms and looked around. "My sister doesn't do small, does she?"

Was that sarcasm she heard in Cat's voice? Chloe leaned closer to the screen and squinted, trying to get a better look at her sister's face.

"Nope, she went all out. And if you think this is something, you should see what she did inside."

A smug smile tugged on Chloe's lips. At least Easton appreciated her efforts. Then at the thought of them coming inside, she turned from the window, looking for a place to hide.

"Aside from the unfortunate color choice, it's kind of a shame you're tearing it down."

He's what? Chloe whipped her head around. She couldn't have heard that right.

But Easton grimaced as he and Cat began walking toward the cabin. "The new place won't be ready for a couple months. I'll decide what to do then."

"Paul showed me the architect's drawings. The house looks amazing. You must be getting excited."

"It'll be nice to have the extra space…and indoor plumbing." He laughed.

Chloe gaped at him through the window. How could he lie to her like that? Lie to all the men who'd come to help a fellow vet in financial trouble?

"I wish you would have gotten a picture of Chloe's

face when you told her she'd have to use an outhouse. I didn't think she'd last a day." Cat shook her head with a laugh. "So where's the cow and chickens we're supposed to be moving?"

Easton lifted his chin. "Out back."

The rest of their conversation was nothing but a low murmur as they walked around the side of the house. Chloe ran to the bedroom and opened the window, standing to the side to stay out of sight. She heard Cat laugh. "And she really believed you lived off the land and were raising a cow and chickens?" Again with a disbelieving head shake. "Too bad she'll be leaving now that she got what she wanted and Grayson and I are split up. You could have done a reality show."

How rude…and mean! But hearing the pain in her sister's voice, a thread of guilt wound its way through Chloe's anger. Not only had Easton played her, he'd told Cat what Chloe had done. Though she wasn't exactly thrilled with her sister's mean-spirited remarks, she supposed she couldn't blame her.

As they walked past the hot tub, Easton put a hand on Cat's shoulder. "I'm sorry about you and Grayson. If I had known Chloe was going to send you that poem and buy you the Sig, I would have stopped her."

"It's not your fault. I practically had to twist your arm to get you to go along with her plan and have her stay with you. I should have listened to you and told Ty to dis-invite her from the grand opening and put her on the first plane back to LA."

Chloe covered her mouth; reaching with her other hand for the edge of the mattress she slowly lowered herself onto the bed.

Easton put both hands on Cat's shoulders. "Let me call Grayson; I'll explain everything to him."

"I told him there was nothing going on between us, Easton. If he can't trust me enough to believe me, then we shouldn't be together. I don't know why I'm surprised. Look at how he's reacted to me working on the Martinez security detail. He doesn't even trust me to do my job."

"Come on, you know he loves you. He's just trying to protect you."

Cat rested her forehead against Easton's chest and shook her head. He put his arms around her. Her sister looked up at him, her gaze roaming his face. Then she lifted up on her toes and put her arms around Easton's neck and...Chloe rubbed her eyes. She couldn't believe what she was seeing. Easton was kissing her sister. It was like she'd been hurled seventeen years into the past and was watching her dreams shatter all over again. Her throat aching and her eyes burning, she raised her cell phone. If she was ever stupid enough to believe in signs and Easton McBride again, all she had to do was look at the picture she'd just taken.

She turned away from the window and packed her bags. Wiping furiously at her eyes, she grabbed the handles of her suitcases. As she walked toward the front door, she took one last look around the small space. In a matter of months, Easton would level it. Somehow it seemed fitting. At least she wouldn't be here to see the destruction he left behind.

Fighting the temptation to slam the door, she quietly closed it. She wouldn't give her sister or Easton the satisfaction of seeing the devastation their betrayal had wrought. The bags thumped on each step as she dragged them behind her and headed down the road. Dust kicked up from the gravel, covering her luggage in a thin layer of grime. Halfway down the gravel drive, she was out of breath. She didn't dare stop. Even as sweat trickled down her face, stinging her eyes, she trudged onward toward the shimmering blacktop in the distance. She told herself the erratic beat of her pulse had nothing to do with her heart. It was a result of her humiliation and anger at the thought of Easton and Cat cooking up their scheme and laughing at her.

In the distance, she heard Bessie moo, and Easton and Cat laugh. Chloe quickened her pace and hit a rut. She turned her ankle and winced in pain. Looking down, she released a small cry of frustration. She'd broken her heel! She lifted her foot and reached back to snap it off, then threw it in a ditch and hobbled on. And with every uneven step she took, she got angrier.

Once she reached the main road, her blood was practically boiling, and she dug her phone from her purse. She glanced back at the gravel drive, limping a few yards to a weeping willow that would hide her from view. She texted Grayson, attaching the photo. *I'm sorry, but you deserve to know*. She typed, then shoved her phone back in her purse and stuck out her thumb.

Chapter Eleven

Around this time last year, if someone had told him he'd be kissing Cat O'Connor in his backyard today, Easton would have given a resounding "Hell, yeah." And it wasn't because he'd been pining after her all these years. It was just that as he stood on the sidelines watching his brothers find their *one*, he'd wondered if his had gotten away. He inwardly rolled his eyes at the thought. He was becoming as sappy as his older brothers. But that was the thing: he wasn't getting any younger, and he wanted a family.

He wanted what his brothers had, what his father had had with their mother, what he now had with Liz. But Easton hadn't found a woman he wanted to share forever with. Forever? The longest he managed to stay in a relationship before the attraction fizzled was a couple of months.

Yet here he was kissing the woman he'd almost proposed to, and instead of being overcome with lust and thoughts of forever, he was wondering how he could extricate himself without hurting her feelings. He couldn't help but compare the explosive desire he'd felt while kissing Chloe to the...Okay, this was just getting weird. He felt like he was kissing his sister. Easton eased back, reaching up to gently remove Cat's arms from his neck.

She jerked away from him, dropping her hands to her sides. Her cheeks flushed. "I'm so sorry. I can't believe I kissed you." She did a faceplant into his chest and groaned.

"Hey, don't apologize. We're friends, Cat. You've had a crappy day, that's all." He hoped that's all it was.

She looked up at him through her long, wispy bangs. "Friends don't jump friends. Well, unless they're, you know..."

"Yeah, and we're not that kind of friends, right?"

"No, not at all." She pulled back. "Now I've made you uncomfortable. Don't try and deny it, I can see the panic on your face."

"It's just..." He scratched his chin. "Didn't it feel weird to you, too?"

She grimaced. "Yeah. It was really bad."

For a guy who considered himself a talented kisser, he was a little offended. "It wasn't bad, just...more friendly than hot. Kind of like making out with your sister. I don't mean Chloe..." Well, hell. He cleared his throat. "You know what I mean."

She stepped away and scrubbed her hands over her face. "I do, and this is all Chloe's fault. She's the reason I kissed you."

He stiffened. They hadn't talked about it, but he'd been

pretty sure Chloe was on the same page as him and her win-back-Cat plan was off. "You've lost me. How does Chloe factor into it?"

"Last Christmas, she had a dream, kind of like Scrooge in *A Christmas Carol*...Yeah, yeah, I know, but this is Chloe we're talking about," she said in response to his low laugh. "Anyway, she said your mom visited her and took her on a trip down memory lane. Back to high school, where, as you know, the memories weren't so happy. But your mom told Chloe she could make things right between us."

"Not exactly following you, Cat."

She looked away, then shrugged. "I guess with the problems Grayson and I are having, I wondered... Dammit, I wondered if maybe I was supposed to be with you and not him." She threw up her arms. "I know, it's crazy. But between Chloe and her plan, and Estelle and Grayson's dad, I started to think Grayson and I weren't meant to be together."

"Okay, I get it now. But the kiss pretty much cleared that up, didn't it?" For both of them.

"Yeah, it did."

He put his hands on her shoulders. "You need to call Grayson and talk this through. And you need to send Estelle back to LA. She's as big a shit disturber as Aunt Nell."

"I know she is. If she hadn't shown Grayson that poem...It doesn't matter. He obviously has trust issues, and I'm not sure we can get past them."

"It's not like you to give up this easily. You love him, don't you?"

She nodded and said quietly, "Yeah, I do. After

Michael, I never thought I'd feel this way about someone else."

"You had your own trust issues to get over. Maybe you should cut him some slack."

"You're right, I did. And I can understand why he overreacted to the poem. He caught his first wife in bed with another man."

"That's rough," Easton said with a grimace. He slung his arm around Cat's shoulders. "Let's load up Bessie and the chickens, and we'll figure it out. All it would take is one call from Chloe, you know. She can tell Grayson what she did and—"

"You're talking about my sister Chloe, right? You more than anyone know what she's like. She won't accept responsibility for this, she never does. She'll just pull a scene, then she'll fake-faint."

"I think you're wrong. And Cat, she doesn't fake-faint. She has a panic disorder," he said, then filled her in.

"Wow, do I feel like an idiot now. How did I miss the signs? I should have picked up on that." As soon as the words were out of her mouth, she sighed. "She sucks me in every time. She's screwed up my life, and I'm the one who feels guilty. How messed up is that?"

"Honestly, I don't think she means to, Cat. She's—"

"Whoa, *you're* defending my sister?"

He rubbed his chin. "Yeah, I know. But the past couple of days with her have been...enlightening. It's an act, Cat. She's not a spoiled drama queen...all right, so she's a bit of a drama queen," he amended at Cat's arched eyebrow, "but underneath it all, she's still the sweet, generous—"

"Oh. My. God. She's sucked you in, too."

"No, she hasn't."

"Yes, she has. You're falling for her."

Shoving his hands in the front pockets of his jeans, he looked out over the field. "Maybe. I don't know, but there's something there. She's changed, and if you'd just give her a chance to explain everything to Grayson, I'm sure she'd make it right."

Cat was staring at him when her cell phone pinged. She pulled it from her back pocket and looked at the screen. She briefly closed her eyes, then handed him the phone. "You were saying…"

* * *

The late-model orange pickup jerked to a jarring stop on Main Street. Chloe, sitting in the open bed, stopped chanting, "It's not my heart," and grabbed the wood side panels to avoid being hurled backward. Although the weight of the hound dog lying halfway across her lap probably would have held her in place.

Easton's neighbor, Mr. Hanson, shuffled around to open the gate. His weathered face broke into a wide smile. "Old Blue doesn't take to everyone, you know. Sure seems to like you, though."

"Yes, he's very, ah, friendly." And smelly. She gingerly patted the dog's mangy coat. "I have to go now, Blue. Up you go."

"Just give him a good push," Mr. Hanson said as he dragged her suitcases across the rusty floorboards.

She cringed at the sound of fabric tearing; her bags would never be the same. With a resigned sigh, she gave Blue a push. He snuffled deeper into her lap. Mr. Hanson chuckled as he set the luggage on the sidewalk, then returned to grab the dog by the collar, hauling the animal off her.

The older man closed one eye and scrunched up his face. "He made a right mess of your dress. You should have taken Gertrude up on her offer and sat in the cab. She wouldn't have minded sitting in the back, you know," he said, referring to his wife.

Chloe drew her horrified gaze from the blobs of doggy drool that stained her dress and forced a smile. "Don't worry about this old rag." It was an eight-hundred-dollar original Shelby Rae. If Mrs. Hanson wasn't on oxygen, Chloe might have considered the older woman's offer. "I appreciated the ride. It brought back fond memories of when I was a little girl." It wasn't true. She was only ever allowed to ride in the cab.

"It was our pleasure, Chloe. And I hate to ask, but would you mind taking a picture with Gertrude?" He held up his cell phone. "She'd be tickled pink. She never misses an episode of *As the Sun Sets*."

Instinctively, Chloe's hand went to her wind-blown hair. "Now?"

"Well that's wonderful, just wonderful."

He must not have heard the question in her voice.

Mr. Hanson took her by the arm and led her to the passenger-side. Opening the door, he smiled at the frail, white-haired woman in the front seat. "I have a surprise for you, Gertrude. Chloe's agreed to have her picture taken with you."

"Oh, I don't want to be a nuisance," the older woman said in a reed-thin voice. But Chloe didn't miss the hopeful light in Gertrude's eyes.

"It's no trouble at all," she said, moving beside the older woman. They put their heads together and smiled as Mr. Hanson directed. He turned the screen to show them the picture. Chloe swallowed a traumatized whimper. Her face was wind burned, there were dark smudges under her eyes from her mascara, and all she could think when she looked at herself was *fright night*.

"I'll have the picture blown up for you, Gertrude. We'll put it up in a place of honor in the TV room," he told his wife.

"What a wonderful idea." Gertrude beamed at her husband, then smiled at Chloe, who was doing her best to hide her horror at the thought of anyone other than the sweet elderly couple seeing that picture. "Did Harold tell you Mr. McBride responded to his text? He didn't want to keep the animals, but Harold did as you suggested and insisted he keep the cow and chickens," Mrs. Hanson said.

That piece of news just made the ride from Hades worthwhile. By the time the Hansons picked her up, Chloe had been half a mile from Easton's. She'd told them her car had broken down, and the tow truck didn't have room for her. While Mr. Hanson loaded her into the back of the pickup, the chatty couple filled her in on the goings-on in the area. They were charmed by their handsome neighbor who wanted to try his hand at farming. "You didn't tell him it was my suggestion, did you?" Chloe asked Mr. Hanson.

"No, but if you ask me, when you give someone a gift like that, you should get the credit. And I feel bad accepting your money. Like I told you, we're getting too old to take care of the animals anyway."

"I like to give back to my community when I can, Mr.

Hanson. It was lovely to meet you both, and thanks again for the ride." She gave them each a kiss on the cheek, then turned to walk away.

"Oh, boy, looks like you got some rust spots on your pretty dress," Mr. Hanson said and began brushing at Chloe's behind. "Whad'ya know, must have been chicken poop."

Chloe covered her mouth to contain the mewling sound before it escaped.

"You have a safe trip back to Hollywood, you hear. You can bet I'll be watching you on the boob tube from now on."

Chloe didn't have the heart to tell them Tessa was dead. She waved good-bye, then rubbed her chest, reassuring herself that the feeling she was minutes away from ending up like Tessa was all in her head. She had to stop thinking about Cat and Easton's betrayal. It was making her symptoms worse. And the best way to do that was to leave Christmas.

After everyone discovered what she'd done, they wouldn't want her here anyway. It wouldn't matter that Cat and Easton were in the wrong. Chloe's family would put the blame squarely on her. Although, maybe, if she hadn't sent the photo to Grayson...She couldn't think about that now. What's done was done. She'd acted without thinking. No, that wasn't quite true: she had thought about it, only her hurt and humiliation had overrode any worry about the consequences. Her broken heel and her walk of shame down the gravel road hadn't helped either.

And neither was reliving it all over again. She hobbled toward the sidewalk to retrieve her bags. If not for Ty, she'd be on her way to the airport by now. But she owed him an explanation as to why she couldn't attend his grand opening. She glanced at the pastel-painted buildings along Main Street and spotted his salon. He'd opted for sophisticated instead of charming. His shop was painted a creamy white with a large window overlooking Main Street, the black-lacquered door framed by black iron pots filled with lavender flowers. As her gaze lifted to the sign above the black awning, her chin began to tremble. On the ride into town, she'd vowed not to let her emotions get the best of her anymore, but her eyes filled when she read the curvy, lavender lettering—Diva. Ty had named his salon after her.

Sniffing back tears, Chloe pulled up the handles of her luggage and limped toward his shop. Through the window, she saw Ty laughing with the older woman sitting in one of the stylist chairs. Chloe recognized the red hair, and her panicked gaze darted down the street. She couldn't let Nell and Ty see her. But just as she was about to make a run for the bakery three shops down, they turned to look out the window. Ty slapped his hand to his mouth, then rushed to open the door.

Wearing a black silk shirt and impeccably pressed black pants, he stared at her in horror. "Diva, what happened to you? You look…"

"I know. I've had a terrible, awful day. And I don't have time to talk." She wanted to fall into his arms and tell him everything, but she couldn't. Not with Nell there. "I have to get back to LA. But I didn't want to leave without saying good-bye."

He blinked. "You can't leave. I've told everyone you'll be here for the grand opening."

"Trust me, Ty. They'll be happy I'm not." Because of

her, they'd probably boycott his grand opening, which made it a little easier to disappoint him now.

"Well, I'm not happy. And it's not just the people in town. I've spent a fortune advertising in four counties. Denver, too. We're having a fashion show in the park, and you're the main attraction."

"I wish I could stay, Ty. I truly do." Chloe had to come up with an excuse important enough that Ty would forgive her. And she had no doubt Nell was hanging on her every word. "Steven Spielberg has offered me a part in his next movie, and I have to—"

Ty gave a dismissive wave of the comb he held in his hand, then grabbed her bags and dragged her into the shop. "You're not leaving. I forbid it."

"But Steven..."

Ty gave her a you're-not-fooling-me look and parked her luggage behind a potted plant. Taking her by the hand, he scanned the space. It was as high-end as any salon in Hollywood, with modern lighting, four black stylist chairs lining one side with comfortable-looking lavender chairs under the space-age dryers against the opposite wall. And it was just as terrifyingly full.

"Honey, you look like you've been rode hard and put up wet," Betty Jean said in a thick Texan drawl. The older woman was Skye's stepmother, and she was currently sitting in the stylist chair beside Nell, wearing a lavender cape. Chloe preferred Betty Jean's comment to Nell's assessing silence. From under one of the dryers came a snort of laughter. Chloe cringed when she realized who was behind the contemptuous sound. The voluptuous bottle-blonde was none other than Brandi, a woman who'd made Chloe's high-school years miserable.

Ty tightened his grip on Chloe's hand, pulling her toward the two shiny black sinks at the back of the salon. There was no way Chloe was going to get through this with her pride intact unless she faked it. Thank goodness she was a pro at faking.

She pulled her shoulders back, mentally imagining herself looking fabulous, and smiled at Brandi, adding a friendly wave. Then she turned to Easton's great-aunt. "Nell, that color really is divine on you." Patting Betty Jean's shoulder as she walked by, Chloe said, "You have the most adorable sayings. And let me tell you, I could have used a man today. I blew two tires on my car and had to change them myself. Talk about a stressful day. Look at my manicure." She wiggled her fingers, then caught the squinty-eyed stares of the older women in the mirrors across from the last two stylist chairs. "Oh, hello, Ellen and Ella, don't you look marvelous." They were the biggest gossips in town, and Nell McBride's best friends.

Ella, the one with the white streak in the front of her long, dark hair, pursed her lips. "It's Stella and Evelyn."

"Of course it is." Chloe smiled while inwardly sighing. She passed a woman with her dark hair in a beehive and recognized another mean girl from high school. "Hello, Holly. You're doing a lovely job on that pedicure. Keep up the good work."

Ty took her by the shoulders and pressed her into the chair in front of the sink as his concerned gaze roamed her face. "It's bad, isn't it?"

"Really bad," she whispered back.

"Once I finish up with everyone, you can tell Uncle Ty all about it. But right now, I think you need a little pampering. Lie back," he said, then gently untangled her hair from the ponytail holder. Ty responded to Nell's grumbling with, "Cool your jets, Nellie. I'll be with you in five. Holly, blow-dry Evelyn for me, please."

Twenty minutes later, Ty had made good on his promise. He'd given Chloe's scalp a relaxing massage while he washed her hair. And then he'd applied a soothing treatment to her skin, draping a cool, moist towel over her face. One of his assistants was currently giving her a manicure, while Holly gave her a pedicure.

Chloe relaxed in the chair, feeling more like herself. Until she heard a deep, familiar ticked-off voice say, "Where is she?"

Chapter Twelve

"Where's Chloe, Ty?" Easton repeated his question when the stylist didn't respond the first time. Easton had met the Hansons on his way into town. They'd told him they'd dropped Chloe off on Main Street, so he figured it was a safe bet that she was here. And he wouldn't be surprised if she was the reason he'd seemingly inherited Bessie and the chickens.

Ty continued to ignore him, turning the blow-dryer to high as he rolled Betty Jean's blond hair around a brush. Easton supposed he shouldn't be surprised the other man was protecting Chloe; they were friends. But since the stylist had been friends with Cat first, Easton had to wonder if Chloe had confessed what she'd done. The other women in the shop had no compunction about giving her up. His aunt and her best friends, Evelyn and Stella, pointed to the back of the shop.

"What's going on, Easton? You look upset," Nell said with a tinge of excited curiosity in her voice.

When Cat first showed him the picture Chloe had sent Grayson, Easton had been both shocked and furious. But then he realized the only way she could have taken it is if she'd been there, and not out for lunch with her mother. Which meant she'd also heard his conversation with Cat. So his anger had subsided…a bit. He imagined she'd felt hurt and betrayed. In her shoes, he would have felt the same.

But right now, seeing her sitting without a care in the world, being pampered after she'd basically destroyed her sister, his anger was back in full force. And he wasn't only furious with her, he was disappointed. Cat was right. Chloe hadn't changed. She was a spoiled princess who didn't care who she hurt. Not that he planned on sharing that with his aunt.

"Nothing's going on, Aunt Nell. I just need to talk to Chloe," he said, keeping his voice even.

As he headed for the back of the salon, he heard the older women whispering. Obviously they'd figured out something was going on, and they wouldn't be leaving anytime soon.

Ty snagged Easton by the arm as he went to walk by. Shooting a nervous glance in Chloe's direction, then back to the older women settling into the purple chairs, Ty whispered, "If you want to talk to her, you can use my office. But don't upset her. She's had a difficult day."

Easton made an unsympathetic sound in his throat. "You might want to ask your friend Cat how her day is going, thanks to Chloe."

Ty grimaced. "What did she do?"

"I'll let her tell you," Easton said and continued walking toward the sinks. "Hey, Holly, do you and your friend mind giving me a minute with Chloe?"

"No problem, Easton," Holly said, getting up from her stool. "Lottie." She angled her chin at the other woman, who glanced at him then nodded, releasing Chloe's hand.

"Holly, Lottie, if you don't mind, I'd rather you finish now. I can talk to Easton later," Chloe said, her voice muffled under the towel.

The two women glanced from Chloe to him and skedaddled. Easton lifted the towel from her face, tossing it into the sink. "You'll talk to me now."

She blinked up at him, then crossed her arms over the purple cape. "I have nothing to say to you."

"Too bad, I have something to say to you. And if you don't want our conversation broadcast all over Christmas within the next ten minutes, you'll come with me now."

Her lips pressed into a thin line, she gracefully got up from the chair and walked on the heels of her bare feet to the closed door beside the sinks. He followed her, blowing out an exasperated breath when she glanced back at him with an arched eyebrow. As he reached past her to hold the door open, she lifted her nose in the air, tossed her long, damp hair over her shoulder, and hobbled inside the small office.

Shutting the door, Easton leaned against it and waited for her to get settled in the chair. She shifted and wiggled, rested her hands on the armrest and admired her red-painted nails, then bent to adjust the pink spongy thing between her toes. "Chloe," he snapped.

Her head jerked up, and she settled back in the chair with a snotty look on her face. "What is it, Easton?"

"You know damn well what I want to talk to you about, and don't pretend that you don't."

She blew on her nails, glancing at him through her lashes. "Actually, I don't."

He gritted his teeth. "Yes, you do. You were at the cabin when Cat and I were there."

"Would that be the cabin you plan to tear down? The one I spent thousands of dollars renovating for you?"

"Look, Chloe, I didn't mean for you to find out that way. I'm sorry. And I plan to pay you back."

"That's right, you're not broke, are you? Your medical expenses didn't tap you out. I guess it's a good thing I didn't write to the VA after all. Too bad you didn't lie only to me, you lied to your fellow vets as well."

Easton was tired of being put on the defensive. None of this was his fault. "I wouldn't have had to if you hadn't hired them to avoid doing a couple of chores."

"How dare you! That's not the only reason I did it. You were living in a shack, and ... and I wanted to make it nice for you." She rubbed her chest. "All along it was just a game to you. You and my sister must have had a good laugh at my expense."

He searched her face, looking for signs of a panic attack. Rubbing her chest indicated she might be having one, but other than that he couldn't tell. There was part of him that felt guilty for upsetting her, playing her, but then the memory of what she'd done alleviated some of his guilt. It was her plan to break up Grayson and Cat that had set everything in motion. "Is that why you sent the picture to Grayson, Chloe? To get back at me and Cat?"

"No. Grayson had a right to know what was going on between you and my sister. Or are you going to deny that, too?"

"Because of the poem you sent, Grayson packed up

and left the ranch this morning. Your sister was understandably upset."

"Is that what you plan to tell Grayson? That you were making out with his fiancée because she was…upset?" She laughed, and not in amusement. "Please, the man is smarter than that. You better come up with something else."

He weighed the consequences of telling her the truth. For Cat's sake, it was best if he took the blame for the kiss. "It wasn't what it looked like. I'm not in love with Cat, and she's not in love with me." He pushed off the door and closed the short distance between them, wrapping his hands around the armrests of the chair. "Do you actually think after that kiss we shared, after making plans to spend the night in your bed, I'd be making out with your sister a few hours later?"

"I heard everything. Kissing me, and…it was all part of the plan. The only reason I was with you was because of my sister. It was always Cat for you, Easton. I don't know why I thought it would be different now."

"You're wrong. What your sister and I had was a long time ago. We were just kids. But you and I…We could have had something, Chloe. I thought you'd changed, but you haven't." He straightened, angry at himself for getting sucked into her act. "Do yourself a favor, do everyone a favor, and go back to LA."

* * *

Chloe stared after Easton, repeating his words in her head. He'd thought *they* had something—not him and her sister. So what was she doing sitting here with her mouth hanging open? She lurched from the chair, grabbing the slowly closing door. She flung it open. "Easton, wait!" she called out.

He turned, and as she took in the hard line of his beard-shadowed jaw, and the anger in his piercing blue eyes, she remembered what he'd said next. It seemed she'd been waiting her whole life for Easton to see her as someone he could love. And her snap decision, made in the heat of anger and hurt, had ruined any chance she might have had with him.

Behind him, Brandi, Holly, Nell, and the other women were watching their exchange with bated breath. Chloe willed him not to say anything. She may not escape with her heart intact, but at least she'd have her dignity. She was almost certain Grayson wouldn't say anything and neither would her sister. And with Estelle on her way to LA…

When the door to the salon opened, Chloe's hope of escaping with her dignity intact faded. Her manager and mother pushed their way inside. "Where is she?" Liz demanded.

Ty's clients gave Chloe up in two seconds flat, pointing to where she stood at the back of the salon. There was only one way Chloe knew to save herself. Pressing the back of her hand to her forehead, her gaze darting left and right to ensure she wouldn't hurt herself, she let her body go limp and slowly crumpled to the floor.

Her mother, Estelle, and Ty cried out in alarm, and Chloe heard the sounds of running feet. She hoped Easton reached her first. It would give her the opportunity to apologize, to make things right. She released a quiet moan, then silently counted to ten before fluttering her fake lashes. As she slowly opened her eyes, she was disappointed to find Easton wasn't crouched at her side.

Ty, Estelle, and her mother hovered over her while the other women looked on. "Chloe, darling, are you all right?"

Chloe raised her head to search the salon and saw Easton walk past the front window. "No, Mommsy, I think it's my heart."

* * *

Chloe sat in the stylist chair, avoiding Ty's eyes in the mirror. Within ten minutes of her fake-faint, he'd cleared and closed the salon. Her mother, of course, was the last to leave. If Cat hadn't finally responded to Liz's texts, she'd probably still be here lecturing Chloe. Her mother's sympathy didn't last as long as Chloe had hoped. Ty was as unhappy with her as her mother was.

"Really, my boy. I don't understand why you're upset with Chloe," Estelle said from the stylist chair beside hers. "Someone had to warn my grandson that his fiancée was no better than Cora in *The Postman Always Rings Twice*."

Her manager was being overly dramatic. "Easton isn't a drifter, Estelle. And they're not trying to murder Grayson." She studied her nails. "I wish I'd never taken the picture."

"Why ever not? The whole point of your plan was to save them from making a mistake. You've done that in spades, my dear." Estelle reached over and patted her hand.

Yes, she had, and ruined her love life as well as her sister's. Chloe was done with plotting and scheming. She glanced at Ty in the mirror. He was being uncharacteristically quiet.

Holding her gaze, he tapped the end of his black comb to his lips, then said, "Estelle, it's been an emotional day for you." He dug keys from his pocket and handed them to the older woman. "Why don't you take Fluffy and have a nap at my apartment? It's three doors down above the Sugar Plum Bakery. The purple door."

Anxious to leave town, Chloe quickly interjected, "It's probably best if we head for the airport after you blow-dry my hair, Ty."

"No, you're not leaving until you make things right with your sister. And…" He reached around her to pluck a paper off the vanity. "…You have to attend the fashion show for my grand opening. Your fans will be disappointed if you don't."

She glanced at the glossy flyer with her picture front and center and thought of Mrs. Hanson. Her family might not want her here, but Ty was right, she did have fans in the area. And more importantly, Ty would suffer the consequences if she canceled. "All right, I'll stay."

"Excellent, so will I. I didn't want to leave without seeing Grayson." Estelle smoothed her elegant chignon from her face. "Fluffy and I are more than happy to be in the fashion show if you think it would boost attendance, my boy."

"Thanks for the offer, Estelle, but…" Chloe swiveled slightly in the chair, reaching back to lightly kick his shin. She didn't want him to hurt Estelle's feelings. Ty pursed his lips at Chloe then said, "That would be marvelous. I have another ad going in the *Chronicle*; I'm sure there's time to have you included."

Estelle beamed. "I'll have to let Fred and Ted know."

Maybe Chloe should have kept her mouth closed. From Nell's death-stare as she left the salon, she was already on the older woman's hit list. No doubt she'd blame Chloe for Estelle staying in town. Chloe dug in her purse for her cell phone. "I'll call the lodge and rebook our rooms."

Ty confiscated her phone. "No, you're both staying with me. That way I can keep an eye on you two." He helped Estelle out of the chair and walked her to the door. Once he'd sent the older woman and Fluffy on their way, hanging out the door to make sure they got there okay, Ty locked it and lowered the blinds. "All right, now you're going to tell me everything from the very beginning. And when I say beginning, I mean back to high school when the rivalry for Easton's affections began." He sat in the chair, swiveling to face her.

"There was no rivalry for his…I guess there was, but it was only in my head. I never stood a chance against Cat."

"Maybe back in the day, but not anymore."

She frowned. "How can you say that?"

He shrugged. "I may have been listening at the door. But only because I was worried about you." He got up and patted her head. "I'll grab us a bottle of wine." He jogged to his office, calling over his shoulder, "Do you want some cheese and crackers?"

She didn't think she could eat, but Ty obviously wanted to make it a thing, so she said, "Yes, please."

He returned and handed her a mug. "I only have those little plastic wineglasses." Placing a paper plate loaded down with cheese and crackers on the workstation, he unscrewed the cap and filled her mug to the brim. Once he poured himself a cup, he settled into the chair. "All right, out with it, and no holding back."

Ty punctuated her retelling of her high-school years with *You what? You didn't! OMG, he was your first! OMG, you must have died when he said that!* When she reached graduation day, she held out her mug. Ty refilled both his and hers.

"Okay, now tell me what's happened since you arrived in Christmas for the engagement party. And don't leave out a single thing."

Chloe nibbled on a piece of cheese, wishing she could skip over the plan to break up Cat and Grayson. But Ty already knew about it. So after she swallowed a mouthful of wine, a very large mouthful, she launched into the second half of her story.

This time, Ty's interruptions consisted of *Diva, you are just the sweetest! I think I might cry!* When she told him about the kiss she shared with Easton, some dramatic fanning ensued, followed by pleading for more explicit details. Once he calmed down, she told him about Easton diagnosing her panic disorder. *Aw, you poor thing, and all along we thought you were just a drama queen.* As she went on to relay today's events, she reached for the bottle of wine. They polished it off, and Chloe told Ty about the conversation she'd overheard between Cat and Easton. She showed him the picture on her phone. And then Ty made Chloe repeat her conversation with Easton in his office in case he'd missed something.

"That settles it. You're not leaving until you've made up with your sister . . . and Easton." He pointed the empty wine bottle at her. "He's your one, Diva."

"I thought he was my one in high school, Ty. And look how that turned out. And then I thought Lord Darby was, and after him, Grayson, so I don't really trust my one radar."

"The only reason you thought Grayson and Lord Darby were it for you is because they were British and had titles and money. At least we thought Grayson did. No, don't argue with Uncle Ty." He waved the wine bottle between them. "Remember, I stayed in your room last December. I saw the vision board you made when you were twelve. You wanted to be a queen. But you're all grown up now. You're an accomplished, wealthy actress."

"Without a job," she hiccuped. "I think I prefer my fairytale world."

"Forget your professional life for now. It's more important that you get your personal life straightened out. And that means making it up to your sister and coming up with a plan to win back Easton."

She shuddered at the word. She'd sworn off plans for good. "My track record with plans is as bad as it is with men." She traced the rim of the mug. "Why are you so sure Easton's my one?"

"Because you didn't care that he was broke, injured, and living in a shack. And for you, that's huge. Trust me, Diva, you're in love with the man. It's the real deal."

The more she thought about what Ty said, the more she realized he was right. Her feelings for Easton were real. He'd been her first love, and she wanted him to be her last. But she was afraid to admit that to Ty. It was hard enough to admit it to herself. "Maybe. But you heard him, Ty. He doesn't want me. He told me to go back to LA."

Ty set the bottle on the workstation and stood up. He

came around her chair. "Put yourself in my hands and I'll take care of everything. Consider me your fairy godfather, Diva." He lifted her hair with one hand, reaching around her for his scissors. "Now, I think we need to do something dramatic. Since Easton likes your sister's natural look, we'll just…" He snipped.

"No," Chloe shrieked, leaning forward with her hands over her head. "You are not cutting my hair."

He held up a hunk. "I think I just did."

She grabbed it from him. "You're fired!"

Chapter Thirteen

The next morning, Chloe and Ty snuck out of the apartment above the Sugar Plum Bakery. "We have two hours to put our win-over-Easton plan into action," Ty said, holding open the apartment's outer door for Chloe. "I have a blow-dry scheduled at noon, and we have to be at Naughty and Nice at two for the fittings for the fashion show."

Chloe touched her head. After Ty had nearly chopped off her hair, she was worried what he had planned for an encore. And he had one. He just didn't want to share it around Estelle. Since Chloe didn't know how to tell her manager the new plan included getting Cat and Grayson back together, it was probably for the best. So far, neither of them had responded to Chloe's voice mails. Which is what she should be concentrating on instead of participating in a Ty plan. "What about walk-ins? I don't want you to lose business because of me."

They stepped into the bright morning sunshine. "I'm not taking walk-ins until after the official opening. I've only been accepting appointments from people I know. Well, people your family knows. I wanted to work out the bugs and train the staff before I open to the public." He took her hand and smiled. "What do you think of your new look?"

"I feel naked."

He rolled his eyes. "All I did was tone down your makeup and dress you in more casual attire. You still have on your hooker heels." He gave her an up-and-down look. "You need to buy a pair of jeans."

"They're not hooker heels," she protested, lifting the hem of her wide-legged cream pants. She had on a gorgeous pair of petal-pink Michael Kors sling-backs that matched the camisole she wore beneath her cream blazer. "I'm not buying jeans. They're uncomfortable and ugly. I don't do ugly, Ty. And I want my false eyelashes back."

"You're not getting them back. You're not in Hollywood. Besides, they weigh down your upper eyelids and make you look older. And Easton likes a more casual look."

"Really? No wonder my driver called me ma'am. You could have told me, you know."

"I just did. And speaking of a more casual look"—he lifted her hair—"I need to fix this. Maybe take off a couple inches?"

Luckily, he'd chopped off a hunk from underneath where no one would notice. "No, I don't mind toning down my makeup and wearing pants occasionally, but I'm not cutting my hair. If Easton doesn't want me for me...then I don't want him either."

"Yes, you do. And he wants you, too. We just have to show him you're his perfect match."

"How are we going to do that?" she asked nervously,

when she realized they were headed in the direction of the Mountain Co-Op. "I'm not learning to shoot a gun. They scare me."

He shuddered. "Me too. But that wasn't what I had in mind. Easton's physically fit, so we'll show him that you are, too."

As Chloe had seen with her own eyes, Easton was in incredible shape. And while she was careful what she ate… "But I'm not. I have a heart condition, and I can't do strenuous…" He glanced at her, and she sighed. "All right, so I thought I had a heart condition. Why don't we just go for a walk along the boardwalk?"

"That's for old ladies. We'll go for a jog." He held open the door to the co-op. "I'm sure Mr. Hardy can suit us up," he said, referring to the owner.

She made a face. "We'll get all sweaty."

"I didn't think of that. Okay, jogging is out. Morning, Mr. Hardy." Ty waved to the gray-haired man behind the counter, then looked around the warehouse. Every type of sporting equipment imaginable was laid out on the concrete floor. Brightly colored activewear hung on the walls, and footwear for the corresponding activity lined the shelves beneath them. Ty pointed to an orange kayak. "How about…" He trailed off when she arched an eyebrow. "…Right, you can't swim."

Mr. Hardy sauntered over. "Can I help you two?"

Ty gave him an idea of what they were looking for.

"I see, so you want to appear to be active, but neither of you are. Nothing too strenuous or that will ruin your hair or make you sweat. Does that about cover it?"

"Yes, you're very good at this," Ty complimented the older man.

"You could go for a walk along the boardwalk. I have some tennis shoes over here."

Chloe crossed her arms and gave Ty an I-told-you-so look. He ignored her, and said, "No, that won't work." His brow furrowed as he glanced around, then he pointed to a row of shiny new bikes. "Why didn't I think of that? We'll go bike riding."

Seeing as how Easton was an avid cyclist, it was an inspired idea. There was only one problem. "I don't know how to ride a bike." Her parents had been so overprotective she'd never been allowed to learn.

Ty and Mr. Hardy shared a look, then the older man said, "It's probably for the best. You'd have to wear a helmet."

Thirty minutes later, Mr. Hardy helped them maneuver the bicycle-built-for-two out the doors. They'd settled on a pretty pink-and-white bike. It matched their new cycling outfits perfectly, and Chloe's sling-backs.

Mr. Hardy cast them a worried look. "I really think you should reconsider buying the helmets."

Chloe and Ty shuddered at almost the same time. They'd tried the helmets on. They looked hideous, not to mention what they'd do to their hair. "We'll be fine, Mr. Hardy. We're just riding up and down the boardwalk. Chloe, you get on the back."

Mr. Hardy rubbed the side of his nose. "The rear rider has to be clipped in, and unless Chloe will agree to exchange her high heels for a pair—"

"Oh my goodness, no. Did you see my legs in these stretchy shorts? They'll look like stumps if I wear tennies. You take the back, Ty."

It took another fifteen minutes for Mr. Hardy to get

them organized on the tandem bike. Once they were set, they turned to wave at him before heading off on the sidewalk. "Thanks for all your help, Mr. Hardy!"

The older man's eyes went wide, and he yelled, "Mrs. Tate, move out of the way!"

Chloe whipped her head around, accidently jerking the handlebars to the right. Ty overcorrected by jerking to the left, and they hit a parked car. Evelyn Tate backed against a store window, clutching her shopping bag to her chest. "Sorry, for the fright, Evelyn. Your next blow-dry is on the house," Ty yelled. "Pedal, Diva, pedal. I think that big guy owns the car we just hit."

Ten stores down, they both let out relieved breaths. "Okay, we'll just take a short cruise down Main Street. Make sure you wave and say hello to everyone by name. Easton will expect his girlfriend to be friendly."

This was true. "But I don't know everyone's names."

Ty sighed. "Just follow my lead."

Easy enough, Chloe thought. Only riding the bike while waving hello didn't go according to plan. "Stop yelling at me, Ty! I've never ridden a bike before."

"Oh, there's Vivi and Chance going into the *Chronicle*." Ty poked her in the back. "Work it, and look good doing it. Stop pedaling so we just kind of glide by. I'll peek in the window to see if Easton is...Diva!"

* . *

Easton walked into the *Chronicle*. Vivi was sitting at her desk with tears streaming down her face. "Oh my God, I've never seen anything so hilarious in my life," she was saying to his chuckling brother.

Well, that was a relief. At first glance, Easton thought she was crying. "You guys going to let me in on the joke?"

"You might want to take a walk on the boardwalk and check it out for yourself, little brother. Chloe and Ty were headed that way." Chance grinned at Vivi, who started laughing again.

The smile fell from Easton's face. He was still angry about yesterday. He couldn't believe Chloe had pulled a fake-faint. One more sign that she was a spoiled drama queen, and he'd fallen hook, line, and sinker for her act. "What did she do now?"

"Other than taking out half the shoppers and cars along Main Street, nothing much."

"But...but"—Vivi gasped for breath—"you have to admit they looked stylish doing it. Their outfits..." She was laughing too hard to finish.

His brother must have picked up on Easton's growing frustration and explained. "They're riding a pink-and-white tandem bike. And from what I could tell, neither of them knows what they're doing." Chance started laughing. "They were yelling at each other between waving hello to everyone." His brother got himself under control and wiped his eyes. "And you know how Chloe said she only ever wears high heels? It's true."

"Jesus. Tell me she at least had a helmet on."

"Well, we suggested that, didn't we, honey?"

"We sure did," Vivi said. "Once we got Ty back on the bike after they'd crashed into the building, we recommended they both should have on helmets."

"And?"

Chance's shoulders shook. "They didn't want to mess up their hair."

Easton clenched his jaw and dropped his messenger bag on the chair in front of Vivi's desk. "I'll be back."

He couldn't help but think Chloe riding a bike had something to do with him. He might be angry at her, but that didn't mean he wanted her hurt. And Chloe on a tandem bike with Ty had the makings of a disaster. As he headed down the path into the park, he searched for some sign of them on the boardwalk. It was a warm spring day with not a cloud in the sky, drawing more people than usual for a weekday morning stroll. At least, from what he could tell, they hadn't run anyone over. Yet.

That's when he saw them. He scrubbed his hand over his face, fighting back a smile. They looked like they were having fun. The two of them were laughing as they pedaled along the water's edge. At the pace they were going, he was surprised they remained upright.

Ty spotted him and poked Chloe. She turned her head and gave him a movie-star smile. The light breeze blew her hair back from her face, and she lifted her hand to wave. She looked beautiful and...Oh, shit. "Chloe, watch out!"

He didn't make it in time to save them from toppling over. At least the railing along the boardwalk saved them from a tumble into the fast-moving creek. And the mother pushing her baby in the carriage had quick reflexes. Easton made sure she was okay before moving to Chloe's side.

He righted the bike and helped her to her feet. "Did you hurt yourself?" he asked, as he did a brief head-to-toe scan. And he had to make it brief, otherwise he wouldn't be able to stop staring. Her pink cycling outfit hugged every curve of her petite body, and where her pink high heels should have looked ridiculous, they made her legs look incredible in the form-fitting shorts.

"Just my..." Her cheeks flushed, and she rubbed her chest.

Okay...so not much he could say to that. "Ty, how about you?"

From where he sat on the ground, Ty rubbed his ass and scowled at Chloe. "This is the second time she crashed into something and sent me flying."

"I didn't mean to. This was all your idea. I told you I've never ridden a bike before."

Ty threw up his arms. "I suggested jogging in the park, but you didn't want to get sweaty!"

"You didn't want to get sweaty either!"

Easton fought back a laugh. "Okay, you two. I don't know what's brought on the sudden urge to get fit, but maybe you should start off slow. Like walking."

Chloe put her hands on her hips and glared at Ty. "That's what I said."

Easton's lips twitched. She might be a total drama queen, but she was pretty damn cute. He looked over the bike. "Doesn't appear to be any damage. Why don't you take it back to Mr. Hardy and see if he'll give you a refund?"

Ty and Chloe stared at him. "We can't do that," they said at almost the same time.

"Why not? Was it on sale?"

"Well, no, but we bought matching outfits, and when we weren't crashing into things, it was fun," she said.

"Chloe's right. We just need some practice. Maybe you could work with us?" Ty said to Easton.

He looked down at Chloe. "Have you fixed things between your sister and Grayson yet?"

She wrinkled her nose. "I've tried, but they won't return my calls."

"Let me know once you have, and I'll think about teaching you both to ride." As the words came out of his mouth, Easton assured himself it had nothing to do with how smoking hot she looked. His father was married to her mother, which made her family. He was obligated to keep her safe. "And just so you both know, no helmets, no lessons."

* * *

"Say it again…Ty, you were right. It was a brilliant plan."

After they'd picked up their clothes at the Mountain Co-op, as well as two helmets, Ty went to work and Chloe went back to the apartment to shower. They were now on their way to Naughty and Nice for their fittings.

"Shush," Chloe said under her breath. His plan had worked brilliantly, which she'd already told him. And she wasn't about to repeat her praise now. Estelle was with them. Chloe still hadn't figured out a way to break the news to her manager, and walking across Main Street wasn't where she wanted to do it. But as she recognized several of the women entering the high-end ladies clothing store, that became the least of her worries.

She stopped in her tracks. "Ty, I thought it was just Estelle and me having our fittings today."

He looked at her and frowned. "No, everyone is."

"W-who's everyone?" she asked, rubbing her chest.

Taking both her and Estelle by the arm, he led them across the road while rhyming off the women involved in the fashion show. The long list included her mother, sister, Nell McBride and her friends, and the mean girls from high school. Basically, every single person in Christmas who had an ax to grind against Chloe.

She pulled her arm from Ty's hold. "I feel a headache coming on. I think I'll go—"

Ty leaned in to whisper in her ear. "Your sister won't take your calls. This is the perfect opportunity to talk to her. Remember what Easton said."

"Don't you worry, my dear. I won't allow anyone to say a single word against you. We're in this together."

Chloe gave Estelle a weak smile. She didn't agree with Ty. Apologizing to her sister within earshot of the women from town was far from perfect. He had no idea how catty and cruel some of them could be. But Estelle obviously had her heart set on going, and Chloe couldn't leave her to deal with Nell and Liz on her own. Drawing on her inner diva, Chloe lifted her chin and walked to the shop's door with her patented elegant grace.

Fifteen minutes later, her inner diva had curled into a protective ball.

From where Ty stood outside the fitting rooms, he cast her a concerned glance. The women had congregated in small groups, completely ignoring Estelle and Chloe. Every time Chloe made an attempt to speak to one of them, they'd pretend they didn't hear her or walk away. Her mother and sister hadn't arrived yet.

Brandi said something to her friends. They looked at Chloe and laughed before turning back to their conversation.

Chloe's stomach cramped. She didn't know how much more she could take. They were making her feel as awkward as they had in high school. Stealing the confidence she'd taken years to develop. It was always that way when she came home.

"Don't let them upset you, my dear. They're just jealous," Estelle said, staring down the women.

Chloe patted Estelle's hand. "They're not—" She broke off at the sound of the door chime and inwardly groaned when her mother, sister, and Nell entered the shop.

"Hey, Cat," several women called out, waving her sister over.

Tongue-tied with nerves, Chloe blurted the first thing that popped into her head when her sister approached. "Don't you look lovely, Kit Kat. Are those jeans new?"

Her sister stopped in front of her. "Really? That's all you have to say after what you did?"

Around them, conversation stopped. "I tried to call you..." She twisted her sweaty hands. "You're right. I'm sorry. I shouldn't have sent the picture to Grayson. I wasn't thinking—"

"What are you apologizing for? My grandson deserved to know his supposed fiancée was kissing another man."

"It wasn't my sister's fault, Estelle. Easton kissed her, not the other way around. And I'm the one who encouraged him." She had, and he did. And once again, she felt the sting of betrayal. She could only imagine how Grayson felt.

Cat frowned. "That's not—"

"Girls, this isn't the time or the place." Her mother forced a smile for their attentive audience. "Chloe, it would be best if you come for your fitting at another time."

"But Ty…" she trailed off. Her mother wore the same expression she had last December. Chloe clenched her teeth to stop her chin from quivering and glanced at her watch. "Oh my, I didn't realize how late it is. Estelle, we better leave. We're expecting a call from Steven, remember?" She raised her hand. "Ty, darling, I'm sorry I have to go. Pick out whatever you want me to wear. I'm sure you'll find something for me in this cute little shop. Size two, remember." She was a size eight, but Ty knew that.

"With that ass, more like a size twelve," someone said with a snort.

Heat rushed to Chloe's cheeks, and she grabbed Estelle by the hand. "Kit Kat, Mommsy," she murmured and dragged her manager to the front of the shop.

Nell held the door open with a smug smile. "Don't worry, we'll make sure you ladies get the perfect outfits to wear."

Estelle opened her mouth. Chloe hustled her out the door before she made matters worse.

"Your mother certainly makes no effort to hide that your sister's her favorite," Estelle said as they stepped onto the sidewalk.

"She blames me for the situation with…" Out of the corner of her eye, Chloe spotted Grayson getting out of a black Yukon in front of the sheriff's station. "Estelle, there's Grayson. Come on." This was her chance to make things right.

"Grayson! Yoo-hoo, Grayson," Chloe called out and waved. He glanced their way. Since he had on dark sunglasses, it was hard to gauge his reaction. But if she wasn't mistaken, his shoulders rose on an unhappy sigh. After her reception at Naughty and Nice, she wasn't sure she was up to another confrontation or rejection. But she had to do something. She couldn't stand to see that look of disgust in her mother's or sister's eyes...or Easton's.

"Go ahead, my dear. Don't waste your opportunity. I'll catch up with you."

Intent on her quarry, Chloe nodded and ran down the sidewalk. Since the outcome would hardly be what Estelle hoped for, it was probably best that Chloe speak to Grayson on her own.

He leaned against the hood of his SUV wearing an expensive black suit. And he wore it very well. Chloe had always been attracted to a man with a sense of style, and Grayson had been no exception. But now it seemed her tastes had changed. She found Easton's casually rugged look more appealing. When she reached Grayson, it took a moment for her to catch her breath. "Hi," she finally managed to say with a tentative smile.

"Hello, Chloe. What can I do for you?" His voice was tight. Obviously he was as angry at her as everyone else.

"It was my fault, Grayson. I set everything up." His expression didn't change, and she swallowed hard. She had to be completely honest with him to make him understand. "I heard about the problems you were having with my sister, and I thought maybe you weren't her one after all. I didn't mean to hurt either of you. I truly didn't." She looked at the parked cars along Main Street, then drew her gaze back to his. "It was me who bought the gun and sent the poem, not Easton. And that picture, I never should have sent it to you. She was upset when you moved out. Easton was just trying to comfort her. I'm truly sorry, Grayson. I'll do whatever you need me to do to make this right."

He sighed and took his cell phone out of his pocket. "Chloe, I appreciate what you're trying to do. But Cat kissed Easton, not the other way around."

"No, that's not true. Easton told me..."

"If that's what he said, he was trying to protect Cat." He handed her his phone. "Look at his face, Chloe. You'll see what I mean."

She took in Easton's expression. He looked...stunned. Oh, my goodness, Grayson was right! Why hadn't she noticed that when she took the picture? It must have been the shock of it all. But she didn't understand how her sister could kiss another man when she loved Grayson. Or why Easton lied. He had to know how Chloe felt after seeing that kiss. Had to know how much it hurt. Then again, she shouldn't be surprised. The only person's feelings Easton had ever cared about were her sister's. But given what he'd said to Chloe in Ty's office, maybe that had changed. And the thought that her sister had initiated the kiss and not Easton gave her hope. If Chloe wanted a relationship with him, she had to ensure her sister was happily married to Grayson. Now she just had to convince the handsome man standing before her that he still wanted the same.

As she studied her sister's body language, she knew how. "You're right. Cat kissed Easton. But it's not what you think, and I can prove it to you." She pointed out how Cat's arms and hands were positioned. She looked stiff, her feet turned as though ready to bolt. She didn't lean into Easton. Instead she held herself away from him.

Grayson shook his head. "Sorry, I'm not seeing what you do. It's obvious to me your sister's made her choice. And it's not me."

Chloe sucked in a panicked gasp. This was not going the way she had hoped. She looked from the photo to Grayson. There was only one way to convince him. She glanced around; there were too many people on the street. She took him by the hand. "Give me one more chance to show you what I mean. Please," she pleaded when he hesitated.

His broad shoulders rose and fell on a deep inward breath. "All right, Chloe."

She pulled him into the alley at the same time his grandmother appeared. That wasn't good. She had to get rid of her. "Estelle, would you mind giving us a little privacy? Grayson's upset. Maybe get him a coffee at the bakery? A . . . dozen cupcakes, too."

"I don't want—" he broke off when Chloe gently elbowed him in the stomach.

Estelle frowned, looking from Grayson to Chloe, who gave her manager an exaggerated wink, pretending some alone time with her grandson was part of their original plan.

"Cupcakes are just the thing to mend a broken heart. I'll get right on it." Estelle beamed, returned Chloe's wink, then headed down the street.

Grayson groaned. "You know what she thinks, don't you?"

"Yes, but don't worry. I'll fix everything with Estelle. She thinks I'm in love with you, but I'm not."

He angled his head, his eyebrows rising above the frame of his dark shades.

His reaction didn't surprise her. Several months earlier, she'd been vocal about her feelings for him. To everyone, including Grayson . . . and Easton. "I thought I was, but I was jealous of my sister. I think Easton might be my . . .

Never mind. Okay, so first, I'm going to kiss you like I would if I was in love with you."

"Ah, Chloe, I'm not sure this is a good idea." He curved his hands around her biceps, setting her away from him.

"Trust me. You need to see what I'm talking about to understand that the kiss Cat gave Easton meant nothing to her." At his skeptical look, she added, "You'll understand what I'm getting at, I promise. I'm an actress, Grayson. It's not real. We'll just pretend we're Rand and Tessa," she said with a cajoling smile.

Last year, Grayson had been undercover on *As the Sun Sets*. He'd played Rand Livingstone, Tessa's ex-lover. "Now give me your cell phone and put your arms around me." When he reluctantly did as she asked, Chloe wound hers around his neck, holding up his phone to get the best angle.

Then she kissed him. Passionately, like a woman in love. Kind of like she'd kissed him during the last scene in Christmas at the lodge. Embarrassment heated her face at the memory of that day. She'd made a fool of herself in front of Easton, her sister, and the cast and crew. And afterward, devastated by Grayson's rejection, she'd made one of the biggest mistakes of her life. She'd accused her sister of trying to kill her. No wonder everyone hated her. She really did have a lot to make up for, and this was one step toward doing just that.

She took the picture, then stepped back and showed him the screen, comparing the photo of Cat and Easton's kiss to theirs. "Do you see the difference now?"

"Maybe." She didn't miss the unconvinced look in his eyes.

Chloe sighed. "All right. If that didn't convince you, this will." She lifted up onto her toes. "Now this is how I believe my sister was actually kissing Easton." Holding up the phone, she pressed a soft kiss to Grayson's firm lips. No heat, no passion, just a woman searching for answers...and comfort. She heard the click of a camera and frowned. She hadn't snapped the picture yet. An anxious knot formed in her chest, and she slowly broke the kiss, turning her head. Estelle stood in the alley with a coffee cup at her feet, focusing on the cell phone in her hand. At the zip of a message being sent, Chloe's eyes widened. "Oh, no, you didn't!" she cried, seeing the self-satisfied smile spread across the older woman's face.

Chapter Fourteen

Easton flung open the glass door and stalked into the station. "Where's Alexander?" he asked Suze, the dispatcher at the front desk. Her eyebrows rose, and she glanced past him.

"Right here, McBride."

Easton turned. Grayson stood with his arms crossed over his GQ suit and a superior look on his face.

Easton strode toward him with his cell phone raised. "What the hell is wrong with you, Alexander? I apologized for kissing Cat. Explained that while it looked bad, it wasn't what you thought. We're just friends." He had, despite Cat telling him not to. Grayson hadn't responded to Easton's texted apology. "But that wasn't enough for you, was it? You had to turn the screws"—he shoved the cell phone in the other man's face, making sure he got a good look at the photo Cat had sent Easton five minutes ago—"and kiss her sister."

Last December, he'd witnessed a passionate kiss be-

tween Chloe and Grayson when they were filming a scene
for *As the Sun Sets* at the lodge. It had bothered him. A
reaction that had surprised him at the time because he
wasn't exactly Chloe's biggest fan back then.

But today's kiss had more than bothered him. And he
wanted an explanation, a reason why he shouldn't punch
Alexander in his sanctimonious mouth. A mouth that had
been on Chloe's.

Grayson briefly scanned the damning evidence. "You
might want to take a closer look, McBride. It looks bad,
but it's not what you think."

"Really, that's all you've got to say for yourself?"

"Like I said, take a closer look. Chloe was kissing me,
not the other way around."

Easton jerked back and turned the screen. He'd convinced himself that Grayson had kissed Chloe as a form
of payback. Yes, it took some convincing. The guy wasn't
the type to play games. Now Easton's chest tightened at
the knowledge that Chloe was the one who'd initiated the
kiss. Someone who had playing games down to an art
form. And while that grated on one level, proving once
again that she hadn't changed, he was almost relieved. A
few months back, Chloe made no secret that she was in
love with Grayson. So Easton would rather put her kissing the other man down to payback than an attempt at
following through with her original plan. Jesus, he hoped
he hadn't misread her. After this morning at the boardwalk, he didn't think he had, but…

"I, ah, didn't mean to eavesdrop…" Jill Flaherty, wearing a tan deputy's uniform, nodded at the desk behind
her. "…But I was sitting right there and couldn't help but
overhear. I'm not exactly Chloe O'Connor's biggest fan,

but I thought you should know the girls were pretty rough on her today. So were Cat and Liz. They basically booted her out of Sophia's place. She seemed upset. Might have had something to do with her...um, well, making out with you, Grayson."

Easton rubbed his hand over his jaw. He'd been so intent on laying into Grayson that he hadn't bothered to keep his voice down. But that was the least of his worries. No doubt the latest Chloe drama was burning up the telephone lines in Christmas. Right now, he was more concerned about what exactly had taken place at Naughty and Nice.

Before he had a chance to ask, Grayson said, "She wasn't making out with—"

Shuffling her booted feet, Jill interrupted him. "Just sayin', but I saw the picture. So did pretty much everyone at Sophia's. And if you two weren't making out—"

"We weren't," Grayson said from between clenched teeth. "Chloe was attempting to prove to me that I'd misinterpreted the photo of *my fiancée* making out with McBride here."

Jill's gaze shot to Easton. "You were making out with Cat? How come I didn't hear about it?" She didn't give Easton a chance to respond. "Wow, who needs to watch *As the Sun Sets*. We have our own soap opera playing out in town."

His brother stepped from his office in time to hear her last remark. He scowled at Grayson and Easton before saying to Jill, "Don't you have some work to do?"

"Sheesh, I was just trying to help," she said and stomped to her desk.

Gage ignored her. "You two, in my office now."

"I don't have time for this. I have to get back—" Grayson began, only to be cut off by Gage, who pointed at his office.

Grayson sighed and walked inside the wood-paneled room.

Easton followed him, then turned at the doorway. "Jill, how bad was it at Naughty and Nice?"

She grimaced. "Felt like we were back in high school."

"How did Chloe handle it?"

"Same as she did then. It was kind of surprising, you know, with her being a celebrity and all. You'd think she'd give them attitude, but she didn't." She organized the papers on her desk, then lifted a shoulder. "I felt sorry for her. She left looking like a kicked puppy."

Easton's chest tightened. He didn't like the visual. He could picture it all too clearly. Even though they were obviously protecting Cat—a woman who sure as hell didn't need protection—it made him angry that women old enough to know better were acting like catty bitches. And like Jill, he didn't understand why Chloe didn't stand up for herself. "Thanks for the heads-up, Jill. Appreciate it."

"Anytime, Easton." She eyed him speculatively. "So you and Chloe..."

"Don't you have work to do?" he asked, catching her eye roll as he closed the office door.

"Easton, sit down." His brother gestured to the chair beside the one Grayson occupied. While he did as his brother asked, Gage said, "Jill's right. Thanks to you two, we've got more drama going on than a soap opera. And I want it to stop before it gets out of hand."

"Why are you looking at me?" Grayson said. "I'm the injured party here."

"I thought you were, too, but I just got off the phone with my wife. She mentioned a photo of you kissing Chloe in the alley. And from what I hear, she wasn't pretending to be your fiancée at the time."

"Would that be my fiancée who was kissing your brother?" Grayson asked.

"I kissed Cat. She didn't kiss me. And I would have explained everything if you—"

"Don't try to protect her, Easton. I know what I saw." Grayson leaned forward in the chair and passed his cell phone to Gage. "Tell me, who's kissing whom?"

Gage thumbed through a couple of pictures, and his left eyebrow went up. "Okay, so I was wrong. The problem isn't you two, it's Chloe and Cat."

"Chloe may have been the instigator, but she came clean and apologized." Grayson went on to tell them what Chloe had been attempting to prove when she'd kissed him.

Easton relaxed in the chair. He wasn't exactly thrilled to hear Chloe had kissed Grayson more than once, but he had to admit to feeling a sense of relief upon learning why she did. Although now he was busted. Or more to the point, Cat was.

He didn't get the opportunity to defend her to Grayson because the other man continued. "And just so we're clear, Chloe also told me she's no longer in love with me. I guess I was a passing phase." His lips twitched as he turned to Easton. "But, if I'm not mistaken, she now has her sights set on you."

Easton felt a smile beginning to form at the news, then caught his brother's wide-eyed stare. And if he wasn't sure what that look meant, Gage enlightened him with a

groan and the next words out of his mouth. "Please tell
me you're not in love with her."

Easton didn't have to lie. He may be in lust with her,
but he wasn't in love with her. Although if his brother
questioned him further, he was afraid he'd shoot holes in
that theory. He had to divert Gage's attention. Besides,
Easton's relationship with Chloe wasn't the problem.
"I'm not in love with anyone." He jerked his thumb at
Grayson. "But if he doesn't get his head out of his ass,
he'll be alone, too." Did that sound as pathetic as he
thought it did?

Since his brother was frowning at him, it must have.
But thankfully Gage turned his attention to the other idiot
in the room. "We were talking about the case earlier, and
I didn't get a chance to mention the situation between you
and Cat, but Easton's right, Grayson. What's going on
with you two? Family's pretty worked up about you moving out, especially Liz."

"I know your family's big on sharing, but I'm not. This
is between Cat and me, and I'd like to keep it that way."

"Good luck with that," Easton muttered.

His brother shot him a look before he said, "If there's
anything we can do to help, let us know."

Grayson stood up. "I appreciate the offer. But until this
thing with Martinez is wrapped up, it's probably best that
Cat and I take a break."

Easton swiveled to look at the agent. "So what you're
saying is that the only reason you two are having problems
is because Cat's working security on the Martinez job?"

"Not entirely, no. It's become apparent that we have
things to work out. But because of the case, I can't do that
right now."

"Why not?" Both he and Gage asked at almost the same time.

"It's a conflict of interest. When we arrest Martinez, I can't afford to have even a hint of impropriety come out at the trial."

"That's the reason you want Cat off the case?" Easton asked.

"Honestly, no. But it is the reason I moved out of the ranch. I was going to talk to her about it that morning, then I saw the poem. I didn't handle it well and left. It didn't help that my grandmother was there at the time and Cat got defensive."

"So what's the real reason you want her off the case?" Easton asked.

The agent glanced at Gage before answering Easton. "Given the circumstances, all I can tell you is that I don't want Cat anywhere near Martinez when this goes down. And, Easton, it's going to go down. You're protecting a man who is about to piss off...Look, I can't tell you what we've got on Martinez because we're on opposite sides right now. But believe me, he's not who you think he is."

"I ran him, Grayson. Nothing popped. He inherited a pile from his old man, who was squeaky clean, by the way, and now Martinez uses his millions to collect art. We're advising him on security and updating his system."

Grayson shoved his hands in his pants pockets and rocked on his heels. "So you're not providing physical security?"

"Only for a couple of weeks when the pieces for the exhibit arrive. And during the exhibit itself." As the event had been well-publicized, Easton wasn't telling the agent anything he didn't already know. "If—and I highly doubt it will—but if anything went down, you have to know Cat can handle herself. And you out of anyone understands the hell the FBI and Denver PD put her through over Upton. She needs to know you trust her. That you have complete faith she can handle herself and the job. She's good at what she does, Grayson. One of the best."

"I know she is. And if I wasn't in love with her… Okay, tell me this: what if it was Chloe?"

Easton laughed. "Be serious…Chloe? The woman doesn't know how to shoot a gun, and at the first sign of trouble, she'd either be screaming at the top of her lungs or hiding under a bed."

Grayson sighed. "Don't be obtuse. You know what I'm getting at. If Chloe had Cat's training and was protecting a man you knew was about to make a move on the territory of one of the biggest drug car…" The agent swore and shoved his fingers through his hair. "This is what I'm talking about. I've already said too much."

Easton was glad he had for two reasons. For ten seconds, he'd walked in Grayson's shoes and understood why he didn't want Cat involved. If it was Chloe, Easton would react the same way. Which meant, no matter how much he denied his feelings for her, he was probably falling in love with the damn woman. And now that Easton had an idea what the FBI were looking at Martinez for, he had to figure out what they should do about it. He needed to have a conversation with his brother.

"Don't worry about it, Grayson. Nothing you've said will leave this room, right, E?" Gage said.

"Since McBride Security involves not only me, but my brother and Cat as well, no, I can't guarantee that." He held up his hand when both men began to protest. "Hear me out. Now that I have a lead, I'll dig deeper, widen my search. If there's anything to find, I'll find it. So the information will come from me, not from you, Grayson. Once we know what you know, we'll decide as a team how to move forward. But we don't provide security for drug dealers, so if my intel matches yours, you might want to start thinking how you can use that to your advantage. We're already on the inside, and Martinez trusts us."

"You'll take Cat off the case?"

"Don't put me in the middle. Like you said, this is between you and Cat. Have you talked to her?"

"After I reamed out my grandmother, I tried to call. She wouldn't pick up."

"You hurt her when you left the ranch, Grayson. And I'm sure the picture of you and Chloe only made matters worse. She's off today. Why don't you go to the—" Easton began.

"I have to head back to work. I'll try and stop by the ranch tonight."

"She won't be there," Gage said. "They're meeting at my place to plan Vivi's baby shower. Why don't you join Easton, Chance, and me at the Penalty Box tonight? Kick back and have a couple of beers."

"I might just do that. Thanks," Grayson said and headed for the door. He turned before opening it. "I've heard Martinez has a very interesting collection of sculptures with more on the way. I bet they'll be real popular at the art exhibit."

"I'll be sure to take a closer look at them." And at the Colombian artist for whom Martinez was holding the exhibition. Easton glanced at his watch. "Should have what we need to make a decision by the time we meet up at the Penalty Box."

"Look forward to hearing what you find out."

As soon as the door closed behind Grayson, Gage said, "This is out of my jurisdiction, so I'm not involved with the operation, but, E, Grayson's not bullshitting you just to get Cat off the case."

"I didn't think he was. Don't worry, Gage. I'll handle it."

His brother nodded and said, "See that you do." Then he rested his chin on his steepled fingers, his eyes narrowed. "All right, now that we've got that out of the way, it's time to come clean. What's going on between you and Chloe? And don't say nothing because I was watching you when—"

Easton got up from the chair and headed for the door. "Wish I could stay and chat, but I have work to do."

"Don't think you're off the hook," Gage called out as Easton closed the door. "Tonight we're getting to the bottom of the deal between you and Chloe."

"Big mouth," Easton said under his breath when he caught Jill's triumphant smile. And he didn't miss her reaching for the phone either.

* * *

Chloe stood beside Ty in front of the bathroom mirror. He spritzed her with a sample of her new perfume, then spritzed himself. "Um, that smells so delish, I wanna eat it. Are the lawyers making any progress with Linda?"

"No, and obviously I can't say it was my sister in the pool. After today, she's not going to cover for me. And because I listened to Easton, releasing a statement now that I intend to sue won't have any effect. I should have gone ahead and done it when I wanted to. Everyone despises me anyway."

"I understand what you were trying to do, Diva," Ty said as he picked up a can of hair spray. He lifted a piece of her hair and sprayed the roots. "And while well-intentioned, you really didn't think it through.'"

He was right. She'd been so intent on proving to Grayson that the kiss her sister shared with Easton hadn't been a passionate one that she hadn't noticed Estelle sneaking back into the alley. "I know. And now Estelle's mad at me, too. I should go back to LA, Ty. I know you want me here for your grand opening, but no one else does. I'll end up ruining your special day if I stay."

He set the can of hair spray on the sink. "You'll ruin my day if you leave." He moved behind her and put his arms around her, meeting her gaze in the mirror. "The Chloe I know and love doesn't give up. And she certainly wasn't the woman I saw cowering in the corner at Naughty and Nice today."

"You love me?" Emotion tightened her throat, and the words came out on a whisper.

He rocked her back and forth. "Of course I do, you silly goose. Now no more of this nonsense about leaving. Let's go have some fun at the Penalty Box." He smiled and fluffed her hair.

"What about Estelle?" Instead of breaking the news gently like she'd planned to, the older woman had found out Chloe had been attempting to reunite her sister and Grayson during a heated exchange. Realizing what Estelle had done and what that meant for Chloe's already strained relationship with her mother and sister, she'd kind of lost it on her manager. So did Grayson.

When they returned to Ty's apartment, Estelle had retreated to the bedroom with Fluffy and refused to come out. Once Chloe had calmed down, she'd tried to make it up to her manager through the locked door. It wasn't Estelle's fault, and Chloe was worried about her.

Ty steered Chloe from the bathroom. "She'll be fine, Diva. If she loves Grayson, and I know that she does, she needs to start focusing on his happiness and not her own."

On one hand, Ty was right. But Chloe thought it might be better if Estelle stopped living through Grayson, and in some ways Chloe. Maybe it was time for her manager to focus on her own career and love life. Just because she was seventy-seven didn't mean her career was over. As for her love life, Chloe already knew two men who were interested in Estelle. And they were just the ticket to cheer her up.

So when Ty stopped in front of the closed bedroom door and knocked, Chloe pulled her phone from her purse and sent a text to the cavalry.

Ty called through the locked door, "Duchess, Chloe and I are going out for a couple of hours. Call if you need us. And when we get home, if you don't come out of your room, we're breaking down the door."

Chloe smiled when she received an immediate response to her text. "Estelle, Fred and Ted are on their way over. You have less than ten minutes to make yourself..." She trailed off when the door flew open to reveal a disheveled Estelle.

Ty and Chloe exchanged a look, then they each took an arm and led Estelle to the bathroom. By the time Ted and

Fred arrived, the older woman had forgiven Chloe and was ready to receive her suitors in style.

Ty grinned and high-fived Chloe as he closed the apartment door. "Well done, Diva." But on the way down the stairs, his grin turned into a grimace. "Let's hope Nell doesn't find out you've been matchmaking. After today's escapade with Grayson, you're on the top of her shit list. And the top of Nell's shit list isn't a place anybody wants to be."

Chapter Fifteen

As Chloe soon discovered, she wasn't only on Nell's shit-list. Up the street, she spotted Easton with his brothers and Grayson. While the McBrides were dressed in worn jeans and T-shirts that showed off their broad shoulders and well-developed muscles, Grayson had on his black suit from earlier in the day. And the sigh-inducing foursome were headed for the Penalty Box, too.

Well, Ty was sighing. Chloe was inwardly dying. She hadn't spoken to Easton since the kissing photo went viral. Hers and Grayson's.

She drew back, tugging on Ty's hand. "I don't know if this is a good idea."

Ty frowned. "Why not?" He followed her nervous glance. "Right, you haven't explained what you were up to with James Bond to the White Knight. Seems like they're getting along okay. But don't worry, the way you look tonight, the White Knight will forgive you anything. You're totally rocking that black dress, Diva."

Her bandage dress was pretty fab, and her Prada sandals with the jeweled straps were totes awesome. She just wished Ty hadn't thrown away *all* of her false eyelashes. She still felt naked without them. But he'd made up for the loss by giving her smoky eyes and rock-star hair. Now if only her inner diva hadn't decided to take a hiatus.

Ty tugged on her hand. "Work it. Chin up, boobs out."

Maybe she didn't need her inner diva after all. She had Ty.

"Hello, boys. You're looking as studly as ever," he said when they were a couple of yards from the men.

The four of them stopped in front of the Penalty Box and, almost as one, crossed their arms. "Chloe, you are not going into the bar dressed like that," Gage said.

Chance and Grayson murmured their agreement while Easton's gaze moved intently, and slowly, from her shoes to her hair before he met her eyes. There was no denying he was as ticked as the other men, but there was also a gratifying glint of heat in his eyes. And the evidence of his desire was enough to give her confidence a boost. She added an extra sway to her hips and tossed her hair, about to say something along the lines of "you're not the boss of me" only better, when the next words out of Gage's mouth stopped her cold. "Ty, I thought you were supposed to be at my place helping the girls plan Vivi's shower."

Chloe's attitude shriveled up and died. She looked down at the sidewalk, hoping no one noticed the heat rising to her cheeks. Earlier, she'd called her mother to ask if she could come over and explain what happened with Grayson. But Liz told her she didn't have time to talk. Now Chloe knew why. Ty squeezed her hand.

Then she heard Gage say, "Why are you all...Oh, I wasn't thinking."

"Obviously," Ty snapped, pulling Chloe past the men. He held open the door to the Penalty Box.

She hung back. "I don't want to keep you from your plans, Ty. You should probably go—"

He gave her a gentle shove. "Please, why would I want to plan a baby shower when I can be hanging out at the bar with you?"

If Ty wasn't a hairstylist-slash-makeup artist, he would have been a party planner. She didn't want him to feel obligated to spend the night with her. "No, I'm serious."

"So am I." He pulled her the rest of the way into the rustic-looking sports bar with its exposed log walls covered in hockey memorabilia. The jerseys and hockey sticks belonged to the Penalty Box's owner, Sawyer Anderson, a former captain of the Colorado Flurries. Tall with a lean, muscular build, his dark blond hair half-hidden beneath a baseball cap, Sawyer manned the bar.

He lifted his chin when Ty and Chloe took their seats on the high-backed black leather barstools. "What can I get you two?"

Before she could respond, her barstool spun around, putting her eyes level with a wide white-T-shirt-covered chest. She looked up and met Easton's frowning gaze. "I know you're upset they didn't invite you to the planning thing, Chloe, but don't do anything stupid. Okay?"

She crossed her arms and looked away. "I'm not upset."

He cupped her chin, drawing her gaze back to his. "Yeah, you are. And I don't blame you. But you gotta know that little lip action you pulled with Grayson didn't win you any friends."

Now it may have been perverse, and perhaps not the smartest thing she'd ever done, but it kind of ticked her off that Easton didn't show any signs of being jealous of said *lip action*, so she decided to poke the bear. "It wasn't a *little* lip action, it was a lot."

He brought his face closer to hers. Close enough that his warm, minty breath fanned her cheek. "Are you trying to piss me off, Scarlett?"

"Yes, is it working?"

His eyes on her mouth, he nodded. "It is, but I wouldn't recommend you take it any further. I want to forget about that picture with you and Grayson. Just like I'm sure you want to forget about the one of me and Cat. Am I right?"

"Yes," she said, with a pout in her voice. She was having fun until then. She didn't appreciate the reminder. It didn't seem fair that everyone was mad at Chloe when what Cat had done was far worse. She was engaged and had thrown herself at Easton. Yet no one held Cat accountable for her actions. No doubt she was at that very moment planning Vivi's baby shower with the extended members of their family.

"Good, then we're on the same page."

She chewed on her thumbnail. "Are we?"

"I think so, but we can talk about it later." He pulled her thumb from her mouth. "Right now, I have a few things I need to discuss with Grayson and my brothers. Okay?"

"All right." She nodded. He swiveled her stool to face the bar. Ty, holding a pink frothy drink, grinned around the straw and waggled his eyebrows at them.

A group of men sauntered by, giving the three of them a once-over. They sat down at the end of the bar. Easton's eyes narrowed, then he shared a silent exchange with Sawyer, and the bar owner nodded.

"Stay out of trouble. I'll be keeping an eye on you," Easton warned, giving Chloe's shoulders a light squeeze before heading across the planked floor to where his brothers and Grayson sat. Both Ty and Chloe watched him walk away.

Ty grinned at her when Easton took a seat at the table. "Aren't you glad you listened to Uncle Ty? That man is totally into you." He nudged a pink frothy cocktail toward her. "Things are looking up. Sawyer even named a drink after us. He called it the Diva."

Three Divas later, Chloe and Ty were drawing attention with their laughter. They were having a great time reliving memories from their *As the Sun Sets* days. But while Chloe welcomed the attention from a certain hot man sitting with his brothers and Grayson, she didn't like the leering glances the five disreputable-looking men at the end of the bar were shooting their way. And a moment ago, she'd caught an off-color remark about Ty. The bar had steadily filled up as the night wore on and Sawyer was busy. Too busy to keep an eye on them as Chloe imagined had been the meaning behind Easton's earlier silent exchange with the owner.

She set her empty glass on the bar and took Ty by the hand before he could order another. "Let's dance."

"I'm so down with that. I thought you'd never ask." He jumped off the stool. As they wound their way through the tables to the dance floor, Sawyer called, "You two behave out there or I'll throw you in the box."

The penalty box, for which the bar was named, sat to the left of the dance floor. A white bench enclosed by white-and-black-painted boards, it had an electronic clock affixed above. "Oh, that sounds like fun. Does Sawyer get in the box with us? Because if he does, we are totally getting thrown in."

"He doesn't, "Chloe said, dragging Ty after her. They didn't need to draw any more attention to themselves. At the thought, Chloe wondered if maybe this wasn't such a good idea after all. But she forgot all about her misgivings when their jukebox choice blasted from the speakers, and she and Ty started to dance to "Heroes" by Alesso.

They each turned to face in the opposite direction and did some slow, perfectly timed body rolls. Out of the corner of her eye, Chloe caught a glimpse of Easton. His legs were stretched out, and he was watching her with an amused look on his face. Just for him, she added a couple of booty pops. His beer froze halfway to his mouth, and he slowly straightened in his chair.

"You're a tease, Diva." Ty laughed, and added a couple of booty pops of his own.

She didn't entirely forget about Easton's eyes upon her, but she let the music take over and began dancing for herself and not for him.

Pointing at each other, Chloe and Ty sang the lyrics while bouncing to the techno beat. She was so caught up in the song that it took a moment for her to sense the approach of the men from the bar.

Two of them crowded Ty from behind, pushing at him with their plaid-covered chests. "Your kind's not welcome here, faggot. Get lost."

Horrified, Chloe gasped. Ty staggered into her with

a humiliated look on his handsome face. Seeing his expression, Chloe acted without thinking and moved protectively in front of him. She pressed a palm on each of the men's chests and shoved back. "You're wrong, you no-neck Neanderthals. It's you who's not welcome here."

The taller of the two men leaned in and grabbed her arm. "Why don't you let a real man show you—"

Chloe put her hands on his shoulders and raised her knee.

"Diva, don't!" Ty cried from behind her.

She ignored him. There was no way she was letting them get away with hurting Ty. But just as her knee was about to connect with his manhood, Ty's attacker stumbled backward. Easton had him by the back of the collar. Spinning him around, he punched the man in the face while yelling, "Chance, get Chloe and Ty out of—" The man's friends jumped Easton before he got out the rest of his command.

Chloe launched herself onto the back of the man about to take a swing at Easton, and covered his eyes with her hands. "You leave him—"

Chance grabbed Chloe around the waist and dragged her off the man, then threw her over his shoulder. She lifted her head to see Gage and Grayson trying to reach Easton, but they were waylaid by several other men getting in on the action. "Put me down! Your brother needs you."

"After the little stunt you just pulled, I don't trust you not to take swing at someone else," Chance muttered as he reached for Ty.

"Are you crazy? I'm not going to swing at anyone. I already broke two nails!"

Chance snorted and plowed through the people converging on the dance floor. Once he lifted Chloe onto the bar, he put Ty up there, too. "Don't move," he ordered, then waded back through the crowd. Half the bar had joined in the fight, including Sawyer.

Chloe turned to Ty, searching his face. She took his hand. "You know they're just idiots, right?"

He nodded, then bumped her shoulder with his. "I've never had anyone stand up for me like you did, Diva. That was pretty awesome, you know. And speaking of awesome," Ty said, turning his attention to the McBrides and Grayson slugging it out on the dance floor. A moment later, he said to Chloe with a grin, "Now that's what I call heroes."

Watching Easton battle it out on the dance floor, she released a heartfelt sigh. "He always was."

Ty laughed. "I meant all of them."

She grinned. "Me too." Then let out a small shriek when a man lurched toward Ty and tried to drag him off the bar. Chloe grabbed a bottle off the bar and broke it over the man's bald head.

Ty stared at his assailant lying on the floor at his feet, then lifted his wide eyes to Chloe. He hugged her. "You're my hero."

* * *

As the deputies led the last of the men away, Grayson and Easton righted the overturned tables and chairs. "So what was it you said about Chloe this afternoon? At the first sign of trouble she'd be screaming her head off or hiding under a bed? Called that one wrong, didn't you, mate?"

The agent's memory could be annoying at times. But

he was right, Chloe had shocked the hell out of Easton by standing up to the men on Ty's behalf.

He glanced to where she sat on the bar, her body-hugging black dress riding up on her thighs as she crossed her long, shapely legs, dangling her right shoe from her toes. She and Ty had their arms around each other's shoulders, singing "Heroes" into a wine bottle. Grayson followed his gaze and laughed, then winced and touched his fat lip.

Gage walked up to them and glanced over his shoulder. He grimaced and brought the tips of his fingers to the edge of his black eye. "In less than a week, she's caused more trouble than my wife ever did. Saturday can't come soon enough."

At the reminder she'd be leaving town, Easton made a noncommittal sound in his throat. He'd spent half the night watching Chloe, and the other half listening to his brothers warn him against dating her. Other than Grayson, Easton was the only one who seemed to think it was a good idea. But now, at the reminder she'd be heading back to LA in a few days, even he wondered what he'd been thinking. That wasn't true—he knew exactly what he'd been thinking watching her gorgeous face light up with laughter and her sexy moves on the dance floor. But now that his brain wasn't totally fogged by lust, he had to think realistically.

The long-distance thing hadn't worked for him and Kelly, the orthopedic surgeon in Virginia, so no doubt it wouldn't work for him and Chloe. And his family hadn't had a vested interest in his previous relationships, but they would in this one. The last thing he wanted was to cause problems between his dad and Liz.

"If you don't need me, I'll be heading out. Thanks for the entertaining night, boys." Grayson lifted his chin at Gage, who'd answered his cell. "I'll touch base with you in the morning, Easton."

For all his talk that he'd come up with a lead on his own, Easton was no further ahead on the Martinez case. Maybe because he'd gone by the book. He didn't think Grayson would appreciate, or condone, him hacking into the Bureau's computers. "We should know how we're moving forward by ten tomorrow." Even if he had to work all night to catch the break he needed. "Are you headed to the ranch to see Cat?"

Grayson raised an eyebrow. "Your interest in my love life is bordering on obsessive."

Possibly, but only because he wanted the heat off Chloe. And if he was honest, he felt guilty for his role in their breakup, too. But that wasn't something he planned on sharing. Grayson had already figured out it was Cat who'd initiated the kiss. Something Easton would rather not get into now. So far tonight he'd done a good job not talking about it. "What can I say? I inherited my great-aunt's genes."

"Guess we all did," Gage said as he shoved his cell in his back pocket. "That was Madison. She thought you'd like to know Cat is on her way home."

"Okay, you win. I'll head to the ranch. Happy now?"

"Over the moon." Easton grinned as the three of them walked toward the bar. Chance, who was helping Sawyer sweep up the broken bottles, leaned on his broom to look them over. "How is it that you're the only one of us not bruised and battered?" he asked Easton.

"What can I say? I'm just that good." He turned to

Chloe and went to help her off the bar. "Okay, Scarlett, time to get you home." She gave him a sweet smile that hit him almost as hard as she did when she launched herself into his arms.

She wrapped her legs around his waist and looped her hands around his neck. "You were amazing," she said with a look in her beautiful green eyes that he was oh-so-familiar with. And knowing what he had to tell her, one that punched him in the gut.

"Geezus, Chloe, what are you thinking? Get off him before you hurt his leg." Gage reached for her.

His brother's attitude toward Chloe was starting to piss him off. He got that she reminded Gage of his first wife, Sheena. She'd left her family for fame and fortune, but Chloe was nothing like her.

She slid off him, her cheeks flushed with embarrassment. "I'm sorry. That was stupid of me. Did I hurt you?"

He shot Gage a back-the-hell-off look before responding. "No, you didn't. I'm good." And he was, he just wished he could pound that into his overprotective brothers' thick skulls. "Ty, you need a hand down?"

"Maybe two?" He gave them a loopy smile. "And I should warn you, I'm going to hug you all. So be prepared."

Grayson and Chance helped him down, and Ty made good on his promise. "You all get free haircuts for life."

"Ty, you don't owe us anything. We were happy to clean up the floor with those clowns. You're one of us now. We look after our own," Gage said.

Easton was glad his brother tried to make Ty feel better, and he knew all of them felt the same. Intolerant bullshit wasn't tolerated in town. He just wished Gage was as quick to defend Chloe. "But I'm not sure you really needed us, Ty. You had Chloe looking out for you."

"I don't know about that." Chance laughed, and told them what she said about her nails.

Easton couldn't help it; he laughed along with everyone else. Everyone except Chloe, who scowled at his brother.

Ty put his arms around her, rocking her back and forth. "I don't care what you say, she's the best friend I've ever had."

"Well your best friend owes me for a two-hundred-dollar bottle of Scotch. If you had to hit the guy over the head, why didn't you grab the twenty-dollar bottle of wine?" Sawyer asked Chloe.

"We don't like Scotch," Ty informed him with a straight face.

Sawyer sighed. "Yeah, and that makes perfect sense."

"I'll take care of any damages, Sawyer." Chloe glanced around the bar. "You know, if you're looking for bouncers, I have a couple of friends who could use a job."

"I'll give it some thought," Sawyer said.

Chance looked at Easton, and he knew his brother was thinking the same thing. That was sweet...and thoughtful. The girl he remembered. Only lately, more often than not, that's the girl he saw all the time. And right now, he kind of wished he didn't. It made it more difficult to do what he had to do.

"We better clear out and let Sawyer lock up," Gage said, ushering them toward the door.

"I'll walk you two home," Easton said, following Ty and Chloe onto the sidewalk. It was a nice night. The air was warm and sweet with the smell of spring, or maybe that was Chloe's perfume. She was walking by his side, glancing up at him every so often as though trying to get a read on him. Ty kept up a running commentary of the night. It made it easier for Easton not to talk, but that was about to end as they reached the bakery.

Ty, as though sensing the tension, looked from Chloe to Easton. "I'll go up now. Thanks again, Easton."

He shoved his hands in the front pockets of his jeans. "Don't mention it, Ty."

As the door closed, Chloe looked up at him. "Do you want to come in? You could put your leg up, and we can talk…"

He'd been hoping she'd forgotten what he'd said earlier. "Chloe, I don't…" He couldn't do it. She'd had a rough few days, and he didn't want to hurt her. "I can't come up. I have a crapload of work to do on a case, and I have to get it done before the morning." He didn't know why he kept talking—maybe it was the disbelieving look in her eyes—but he told her why the case was so important that he had to pull an all-nighter and filled her in on what he had so far.

"Well that's easy. It's the wife."

"What do you mean it's the…Jesus, you might be right." He lifted her off her feet and kissed her. And as soon as his lips touched her soft, pliant mouth, he knew he'd made a mistake. Letting Chloe O'Connor go would be one of the hardest things he'd ever done. But for everyone's sake, he had to. He slowly lowered her to the sidewalk and stepped away, forcing a smile. "If you ever want to give up acting, you could get a job as a PI."

Chapter Sixteen

Chloe checked her messages for the tenth time in less than so many minutes. She was becoming obsessive. She hadn't heard from Easton since the night of the barroom brawl. That was two days ago.

"Still no word from the White Knight?" Ty asked from where he sat in the stylist chair beside her.

She held out her wineglass for a refill. "No. If we were dating, I'm pretty sure that kiss was the breakup kind."

Ty filled her glass, then his own. "Show me how he kissed you again."

She lifted her palm to her lips and demonstrated the brief, unsatisfying kiss they'd shared. Actually, it had been a very nice kiss. But with Easton, she'd never be satisfied with a quick lip-lock. And then there'd been that look in his eyes. The one that said he was thinking of an excuse to take off. Work had always been hers. It seemed they had something else in common. Within minutes, he was headed for his pickup. Though he did turn to tell her to get inside before he reached his truck. The man was nothing if not protective...

She blinked. "Ty, I think I know what the problem is."

He nodded sagely. "Me too. His brothers don't like you."

Even though that hurt to hear, she made sure the emotion didn't show on her face. "You're right, but that wasn't the problem I was referring to. I guess I didn't think this through. Easton and I never had a chance. It's probably for the best that we didn't take our relationship any further. I'll be going home after the fashion show anyway."

"You're not giving up on Easton. He's your one. His brothers are just being overprotective. All we have to do is prove to them that you've changed. And the only way you can do that is to stay in town. There's nothing for you in LA. You got an audition for Estelle in London next week, and we both know she's a shoo-in for the part."

In her bid to keep Estelle from interfering in Cat and Grayson's life, Chloe had called her former agent yesterday morning. By nine that night, Estelle had an audition for a docudrama about the queen of England. Ty was right, Estelle was perfect for the role. It was kind of depressing that the older actress had received an offer for an audition in less than twenty-four hours while...

Ty cut her off mid-thought as he continued. "I don't like to think of you by yourself in LA, Diva. You don't need to be in Hollywood to get work, you know."

Given her recent experience with Estelle, obviously that was true. And if Chloe was honest, she didn't like the thought of being alone in LA either. At least here she had

Ty and her family. Cat had texted her yesterday and extended an olive branch—more like a twig, but whatever. At least her sister no longer hated her. Grayson had explained their kiss, and he'd also told Cat about Chloe's heroic defense of Ty at the Penalty Box. All right, so Cat hadn't exactly said heroic. She was just glad Chloe had been there to defend Ty. As to her sister's engagement, from what Cat said, they still had issues to work out.

At the ping of an incoming message, both Ty's and Chloe's eyes jerked to her phone. They reached for it at the same time. "Ty, it's my phone," she groused when he grabbed her cell.

He reluctantly handed it over. She opened the message and couldn't help releasing a disappointed sigh. The text wasn't from Easton. "It's from Kit Kat," she told Ty. "Grayson just told her about Estelle's audition. She thanked me for arranging it."

"Okay, so say something like 'I've got your back, sista.'"

Chloe pursed her lips and arched an eyebrow at him. When Cat texted her yesterday, Ty had insisted she let him help with her responses. He didn't want her to blow her chance at a reconciliation. "I think I can take it from here, Ty," she said and typed. *I've got your back, sista!*

"Oh, shoot," she said when she realized what she'd done.

Ty leaned over and angled the screen. He smirked.

At the sound of another incoming message, they both leaned in to read the text. *Tell Ty to quit hijacking your phone.*

He laughed. "She knows me so well."

For several minutes, Ty and Cat texted back and forth

while Chloe sipped her wine, contemplating her disappointment that it wasn't Easton texting her. Obviously she wasn't ready to give up on him just yet. If he really was her one, they deserved a chance. Which she told Ty as soon as he put her phone down.

He clinked her wineglass with his. "Your fairy godfather is back on the job. Now here's what I think you should do. Are you ready for it?" When she nodded, he said, "Convince the citizens of Christmas you've changed. Win them over. What do you think?"

"That your plan is doomed to fail. It's a small town, Ty. Everyone knows everyone's business, and they don't forget a single thing. They don't let you live down your past mistakes or let you change."

"Okay, so you do something for the town. You're rich, buy them, I don't know, a new...Oh, wait, I do know. They're up in arms because the school board plans to close Christmas High. Maddie's been working day and night trying to save the school."

"I'm not helping save Christmas High. Some of my worst memories are from my years attending that school."

He nodded and topped up her wineglass. "I forgot. Don't worry about it, we'll think of something else. But the most important thing we need to do is come up with a plan to get Easton to call. Now don't argue with Uncle Ty, he's your one. He just needs to spend more time with you."

"I think I know why Easton isn't interested in me anymore."

"Oh, please, that man is so hot for you he nearly—"

"Let me finish. You didn't see him the other night, Ty. I did. We both agree that Easton's a protector, right?"

"I didn't name him the White Knight for no reason, Diva."

"That's what I mean. Everyone knows I needed protecting or at least I acted like I did. But that night at the bar, I didn't. And now that I know my panic attacks don't have anything to do with my heart, I'm not as, well, emotional or high-strung." She caught Ty's smirk and sighed. "Okay, so I'm a little emotional. But do you see what I'm getting at?"

"Umhm, and I need to ponder this a moment." He tipped his head back and closed his eyes. After a couple of minutes of humming to himself—it sounded suspiciously like the theme song from the *Princess Bride*—he turned his head and smiled. "I've got it. The White Knight to the rescue."

When he explained the plan, she said with a nervous hitch in her voice, "Ty, I don't know about this. If Easton finds out—"

He waved her off. "You're a brilliant actress. You'll pull it off. And I'm going to help get you into the role." He walked to the back of the salon and disappeared into his office. "Cross your fingers I don't blow..." There was a pop and what looked like blue sparks shooting from behind the door, then the lights went out.

"Ty, are you all right?" she called out at the same time her cell phone rang. Searching the workstation, she found her phone and picked it up. "Hello." There was nothing but heavy breathing coming over the line. Her pulse kicked up. "Who is this?"

"I'm watching you. I'm coming to get you," someone said in a creepy falsetto. The line went dead. There was a loud crash to her right, followed by an eerie moan. "Ty!"

she shrieked, jumping from the chair. Her heart pounding, she raced to the back of the salon and slammed into someone. She ran on the spot, screaming. Ty screamed, too.

She stopped screaming and running and swatted him. "That's not funny! You scared me half to death."

"I scared myself," he panted. "Just let me sit for a minute." He put out his hands and felt for a chair. She heard him taking long, steadying breaths, then he got up and moved away from her. "Okay, call Easton now."

"I don't think this is a good idea, Ty."

"Do you want to see Easton and talk this over with him?"

"Well, yes, but can't I just call him?"

"Diva, you're the one who said he's lost interest because he no longer has to protect—"

"All right, I'll do it." She quickly punched in his number before she changed her mind.

He answered on the second ring. "Chloe?"

"Hello, ah, East—" Something grabbed her leg, and she screamed. Ty looked up from where he lay on the floor with a ghoulish smile on his face. She screamed again.

"Chloe, what's going on?" Easton shouted over the line.

"Stalker, deep breathing on the phone, and a really creepy voice saying he's watching me…" The front door rattled. She looked down. Ty wasn't there anymore. "I think he's trying to break into the salon." Even though she knew it was Ty, she was freaked out, her heart thumping against her ribs.

"Calm down. Where's Ty?"

"I don't know where—" The receptionist chair rolled

across the floor with Ty in it. He looked like he was...
"Dead!"

"I'm on my way. It'll take me about fifteen minutes to get to you, but I'm calling Gage as soon as I get off—"

"No. No Gage. That's not a good—"

He talked right over her. "Stay away from the windows and lock yourself in Ty's office. Gage'll call you on your cell to let you know when he gets there."

He disconnected. Chloe stared at the phone. Ty rolled the chair to her feet. "He's sending Gage, isn't he?" She nodded. "We're so screwed," he said and fell back in the chair.

"I told you this was a bad idea!"

He threw up his arms. "It would have been fine if you hadn't told him I was *dead*!

"I know. I know. Now we have to figure a way to get ourselves out of this." She paced in front of him, chewing on her thumbnail. "All right, I have an idea." She ran to the front of the salon and peeked out the closed blinds. She saw movement outside the police station and turned. "Do you have a back door or window?"

"Both. Good idea, I'll hide in the alley until I see Easton arrive. Then I'll—"

Chloe's cell phone rang. "Go, go," she whispered. Ty ran to the back of the salon. She took a second to get into character, then answered in a tremulous voice, "H-hello."

"Hang tight, Chloe. I'll be there in a minute. Have you had another call?" Gage asked.

"No, no—"

"Diva, the painters sealed the door shut," Ty called out in a panicked whisper.

Chloe threw her arms up to silently say *what am I sup-*

posed to do about it? then responded to Gage, "No, no calls."

"Okay, just calm down. I'm here now; you can let me in." The front door rattled.

As Ty stood there staring at her, Chloe disconnected from Gage. "Go out the window."

* * *

Easton's tires squealed as he turned onto Main Street. He'd broken every posted speed limit to get there. When he pulled in front of Ty's salon, the lights of his truck shone on Gage's pissed-off face. The tension in Easton's shoulders eased slightly. At least it wasn't panic. His brother in his sheriff's uniform stood outside Diva yelling into his phone.

Easton jumped from his truck. "Where's Chloe?"

Gage disconnected. "Inside. She won't open the door because she says I could be the stalker impersonating a sheriff. Do I look like a stalker?" his brother gritted out from between clenched teeth.

No, but he did look kind of scary. "I'll call her. Any sign of Ty?" he asked as he pulled out his cell phone.

"Cat said she was texting with them about an hour ago, and everything seemed fine. Although she thought they might have been drinking. She's on her way. And Estelle hasn't seen them for a few hours. They were here setting up for tomorrow's grand opening."

Chloe's cell rang five times before going to voice mail. He pounded on the door. "Chloe, it's Easton. Open up."

His brother's eyes narrowed. "Where were you?"

"Out for a drink with a...friend. Why?"

"Did Chloe happen to know you had a date tonight?"

"No, and it wasn't a date." At least he hadn't thought it was. Nell had asked him to do her a favor and meet with a friend who needed computer advice. Easton hadn't realized he'd been set up until he arrived at the restaurant. But there's no way Chloe could have known about it.

"Good jeans, button-down shirt, and a jacket...It was a date. Keep trying to get Chloe to open the door while I check around back."

He tried Chloe once more. Disconnecting when her cell went to voice mail again, he fought back a wave of panic. If he hadn't known how much he cared about her before, he did now. The last twenty minutes had been hell.

Easton once again pounded on the door. It swung open to reveal his brother, who had one hand wrapped around the back of Chloe's neck, the other wrapped around Ty's. Gage was furious.

Easton frowned. "What's going on?"

"That's what we're going to find out. I caught them trying to sneak out the window." Gage steered them into the dark shop. His brother switched on a flashlight and aimed it at the stylist chairs. "Sit," he snapped. "Easton, open up the blinds."

He did a quick scan of Chloe before he did as his brother directed. She looked cover-model perfect in a peach wrap dress and matching heels. More importantly, she didn't look like she'd been hurt. Though she did look nervous. But just as he registered the hint of nerves, her expression smoothed over.

She lifted her chin. "The only reason we were sneaking out the window was because we thought you were the stalker, and you were trying to break down the front door. Right, Ty?"

Ty nodded. "Right."

Gage crossed his arms over his chest. "I thought Ty wasn't with you. You told Easton—"

"Well, that's the funny part of the story. I mean, it wasn't funny at the time. But I was in the loo, and Ty told me he was going to grab us a bite to eat. And then the lights went out, and I couldn't see a thing. Not even the hand in front of my face." She gave them a quick demonstration before continuing. "Then I heard a crash, and someone moaning. I didn't realize it at the time, but Ty had fallen over…the chair. And then when I walked by, he grabbed me by the leg. That's when I called Easton."

"Really, so did he also tell you he was watching you?" Gage said in an exasperated voice.

Easton raised an eyebrow at her, wondering how she was going to get around that one. He probably should be pissed at her, but oddly enough, he wasn't. Indirectly this was his fault. He'd been avoiding her, and he imagined this was her way of getting his attention. Most people would just pick up the phone, but not Chloe. He supposed that was one of the reasons he was attracted to her. Life with Chloe would never be boring. And, he was beginning to think, worth the effort he'd have to put into a long-distance relationship.

"Well, as you know, I have a vivid imagination. And Ty and I had been talking about our favorite stalker movies. Mine was *Wait Until Dark*. You may not have heard of it—the movie came out in the sixties—but Audrey Hepburn's performance was brilliant." She turned to Ty. "What was your favorite again?"

"Okay, I've heard enough. I don't believe any of your story. And if your mother wasn't married to my father, I'd throw you in jail right now for public mischief. This is serious, Chloe. While you were wasting my time playing games, someone could have—" He broke off when Chloe raised her finger.

"I don't mean to interrupt you, Gage, or would you prefer Sherriff McBride? Anyhow, just so we're clear on this, you have no grounds to arrest me." His brother looked like he wanted to strangle her. "Easton called you, not me."

"Consider this your last warning, Chloe. Next time you pull a stunt, any stunt at all, I'm throwing you in jail." As Gage pivoted and strode for the door, his cell rang. "Hey, Liz, no, she's fine. It was just Chloe being Chloe. She probably found out about Easton's date tonight."

Chloe stared up at him. "You had a date tonight?"

Chapter Seventeen

Chloe adjusted her sunglasses as she and Estelle stepped into the early morning sunshine. At the sound of yelling and hammering, she glanced to her left. The park was a hub of activity. Men and women were busy setting up chairs and the stage for this afternoon's fashion show. She couldn't see it from where she stood outside the bakery, but she knew a tent was being erected behind the stage. They were getting their hair and makeup done at the salon, but they'd be changing in the tent.

"Thank goodness the press hasn't arrived. The last thing either of us needs is a photo without our makeup on appearing in the tabloids." Estelle said, and looped her arm through Chloe's.

Chloe shuddered at the thought. With her recent spate of bad publicity, that was the last thing she needed. "It's a little early for them to arrive, but to be on the safe side, maybe we should forgo picking up a coffee. I'm sure Ty will have a pot on."

"Good idea, my dear," Estelle said as they headed to the salon. She patted Chloe's hand. "I'm going to miss you, you know. If I get the part, I probably won't be back in the States for some time."

"I'll miss you, too. But this is a fabulous opportunity for you, Estelle, and I have no doubt it's the first of many. Just look at Betty White. Besides, I'm already making plans to visit you in London. And we can Skype every day."

The older woman sniffed and nodded, then stopped walking to remove a handkerchief from her purse.

"Oh, Estelle, I'm sorry. I didn't mean to make you cry," she said, rubbing the older woman's arm. "Do you not want to go?"

"No, I'm excited about the thought of being in front of the camera again. But..." She offered Chloe a small smile. "You've become very dear to me. I'm closer to you than my own grandchildren. And I'd hoped one day, in the not-too-distant future, you would be family."

"You're going to make me cry." Chloe sniffed, then gave Estelle a heartfelt hug before saying, "We don't need to be related by blood or to have a piece of paper to make it so. You're the grandmother of my heart, Estelle. And if you give Cat a chance, you can have two granddaughters."

"I don't know, my dear. I think I may have ruined any chance of that happening. My grandson is barely speaking to me."

"That's as much my fault as it is yours. And I plan to repair your relationship with Grayson, and my sister, before you leave for London. You just leave everything to me." She took the handkerchief from Estelle's hand

and gently dabbed at the older woman's damp cheeks. "We'll start with Cat first. She's in the fashion show, so we'll…Oh my, goodness, this is too perfect. While you distract my sister, I'll get hold of her phone and invite Grayson. Knowing Cat, she hasn't told him she'll be making an appearance. We'll kill two birds with one stone. You'll have an opportunity to talk to your grandson face-to-face, and Cat will look so fabulous that Grayson will forget about their problems."

Chloe chewed on her bottom lip. There was one problem with her plan. "We'll have to sneak out to the tent to see what she's wearing. If the outfit's casual or tailored, we'll switch it up with something sexy. Actually, I have the perfect dress in mind. No one will know it wasn't from Naughty and Nice."

"You're a wonder, my dear."

Chloe smiled absently as she went over the plan in her head. She had to talk to Ty about Cat's hair and makeup. Maybe Chloe would do it herself. The time had come for her to take her sister's beauty regimen in hand. And her love life. She winced at the thought, reminding herself that's what had gotten her into trouble in the first place. But now that she was honestly acting in Cat's best interest, everything would—well, should—turn out just fine.

Her excitement faded a little as they reached Diva. The salon was packed. Through the front window, she saw that Nell and her friends were already in the stylist chairs. As she went to open the door, Chloe squared her shoulders and lifted her chin. Without her makeup on and hair styled, it wasn't easy swanning into the salon like she owned the place, but she did. Ty had warned her that he'd kick her behind if she played the shrinking violet as she had at Naughty and Nice.

She pasted a confident smile on her face. "Good morning, ladies. Is everyone excited for the big show today?"

Nell, with red dye in her hair, swiveled in the stylist chair and gave Chloe an up-and-down look. "I see you've recovered after your close encounter with your fake stalker. Though you are looking a little the worse for wear."

Before Chloe had a chance to respond, Ty, standing behind Mrs. Tate's chair, pointed his scissors at Nell. "Another word out of you, and you'll have pink hair. I'll wash out your color before it's set."

Estelle tittered.

Nell's eyes narrowed. "I thought you were heading to London. Hope you didn't stick around for this. We already have—"

Estelle interrupted her. "I was supposed to leave today, but Ty begged me to stay. He needs at least one mature woman who knows what she's doing on stage. And I didn't have the heart to disappoint Fred and Ted."

Ty's eyes went wide. He looked at Chloe and lifted his chin to the back of the salon. He didn't have to tell her twice. Chloe was already on Nell's hit list, and if Estelle shared . . .

"By the by, Nell, did Fred tell you he planned to join me in London? Oh, my, I can tell by your expression that he didn't. I never was very good at keeping—"

Chloe tugged on Estelle's arm. "You can chat later. We have to get started on our treatments."

The door opened, and her mother and sister, along with Brandi, entered the salon. Cat had already had words with

Chloe about her and Ty's stalkercapade. Last night, her sister had arrived seconds after Chloe had learned that Easton had been on a date. Two days after he'd sort of kind of broken up with her, he'd been out with someone else. So of course she hadn't been in the mood to be lectured by her sister, who had kissed Easton. And Chloe left the salon without speaking to either one of them. She also hadn't spoken to her mother since Gage had ratted her out.

But she didn't have much choice now. She gave her mother and sister a wide, welcoming smile. "Good morning, Mommsy and Kit Kat. We're all going to have so much fun today, aren't we?" She could hope, couldn't she? But she was already feeling overwrought, and that feeling only intensified when she caught the gleam in Nell's eyes.

"Brandi, you're looking beautiful, girlie. Ty won't have to do a thing with you. Probably just as well since some of these ladies need a whole lot of help." She cast Chloe and Estelle a pointed look before continuing, leaving no doubt who she was referring to. "Nothing like love to put a twinkle in your eye and a flush in your cheeks. How was your date with Easton, by the way?"

Chloe's jaw dropped. Then, despite the knife-like pain in her chest, she pasted a smile on her face. But when Brandi, looking as beautiful as Nell said she did, opened her mouth, Chloe knew she couldn't stand there listening to a blow-by-blow of their night together without her reaction showing on her face. Even she wasn't that good of an actress.

"Pardon me, nature calls," she said, and speed-walked to the bathroom. She shut the door, leaning against it for support. Her legs were shaky, and she felt sick to her stomach. She was about to lock the door when Ty pushed his way inside.

He took one look at her, lowered the toilet's lid, and sat her down. "Don't let Nell get to you, Diva. She pulled a fast one on Easton. He didn't know it was a date until he got to the restaurant. And if you would have stuck around last night, instead of flouncing off in a huff, he would have told you himself."

"But you don't understand, Ty. Brandi is exactly what Easton's looking for. She's beautiful, and she needs his protection. Truly needs it. Her ex-husband's an abusive alcoholic, and she's raising her son on her own."

"Oh, I thought you were upset because she was one of the mean girls who bullied you in high school."

"She was." Chloe glanced at the door. "I don't think I can go out there. They all know how I feel about Easton. How I've always felt about him. And now—" She broke off when the door opened.

"You okay?" her sister asked.

"I can't face them," Chloe said, repeating her fears to Cat. Her sister turned to Ty. "Can you give us a minute?"

"Sure thing, Pus..." He looked at Chloe and sighed. "Kit Kat."

When Ty shut the door behind him, her sister crouched in front of her. "You can't let them get to you. You did the same thing back in high school, Chloe. You're the perfect target. You don't stand up for yourself and fight back. You even did it again at Naughty and Nice the other day." She angled her head, her gaze roaming Chloe's face. "I don't get it. You weren't like this in LA."

"I know, I was a bully."

"No, you weren't a bully. You were aggressive and ambitious. You went after what you wanted, and you weren't afraid to stick up for yourself."

She gently pushed her sister's wispy bangs from her eyes, and smiled. "Thank you for saying that, Kit Kat. And thank you for being here for me now. I don't like when we fight. I've missed you."

"I've missed you, too. And I'm sorry about what you saw and overheard at the ranch the other day. I didn't know there was anything between you and Easton." Her shoulders went up around her ears when she drew in a heavy breath. "Not that I should have been kissing him. I still can't believe that I did."

"Why did you?"

"I'm not blaming you, Chloe, but all that talk about him being my one...I guess I was scared I was making another mistake. Grayson and I were having problems, and then I invited his dad here, and that made everything worse. I think the man hates me more than Estelle does."

"Estelle doesn't hate you. She was just afraid of losing Grayson. He's the only one who's ever shown her any affection. They're kind of a dysfunctional family. I'm sure that's why you and Grayson are having problems. He has trust issues, and after Michael, so do you. And don't get mad at me, but when you're upset, you shut yourself off. You need to be honest with Grayson and let him in."

"When did you get so smart?"

"I always was, only no one ever took me seriously."

"Does Easton?"

"I think so." She wrinkled her nose and looked down at her hands. "Well, he did. I'm not sure how he feels after last night." She lifted her gaze to meet her sister's. "I'm falling in love with him, Kit Kat."

"Yeah, that's pretty obvious."

She frowned. "How come you're not rolling your eyes like you usually do when I tell you I'm in love with someone?"

"Chloe, you told me you were in love with Grayson an hour after you met him on the set."

"Oh, right," she said, her cheeks heating at the reminder.

"Besides, Easton was always the one for you. And it must be true love because he's not perfect. He has a damaged leg. And there's nothing you hate more than imperfection."

"How can you say that? He's perfect in every way. He has a little scarring, sure, but the strength in his leg will eventually improve." She crossed her arms. "I'm very disappointed in you, Kit Kat. You never used to be this shallow."

Her sister laughed and pulled Chloe to her feet. "Oh yeah, definitely true love. And just so you know, Easton isn't interested in Brandi. He's interested in you."

"Were you not listening to me earlier? Easton is a protector, and Brandi needs protection. I don't."

Cat pressed her lips together as though trying not to laugh, then said, "Ah, Chloe, I don't know how to break it to you. But you're the type of woman a man will always feel the need to protect. You're a girly girl."

"Are you being sarcastic?"

"No, just telling it like it is."

"Well, don't be offended, Kit Kat, but I think you should be more like me. Did you ever think that your macho fiancé might like to feel you need him to protect you every now and again?"

Cat scoffed. "I don't need anyone to protect me."

"You will this afternoon when you're walking down the stage in four-inch heels." She followed Cat out of the bathroom. "Is Grayson coming to the fashion show?"

"Are you kidding me? I don't want him to see me looking like an idiot. The only reason I agreed to do this is for Ty."

Chloe made a show of looking around the salon. "You know, Ty's really busy. So why don't I do your hair and makeup for you? "Without giving her sister a chance to respond, Chloe called Estelle over on the pretense of helping with the makeover. It was time to mend some fences. "Now, you just sit down and relax, Kit Kat. Oh, do you happen to know what you're wearing in the fashion show? That way we can coordinate your makeup to your outfit."

Cat sighed. "A pair of jeans and a frou-frou top."

Honestly, her sister had no idea how much she needed her help. "All right. Give me your phone: I want to take before-and-after pics."

* * *

Chloe sat beside Estelle in the chairs at the sinks with warm towels draped over their faces and wrapped around their heads. Ty was saving them for last. He'd ordered hair and facial treatments for them while they waited. Though the treatments actually felt more invigorating than calming. Her skin and scalp were tingling. But other than that, and despite the incident with Nell and Brandi,

Chloe was happy and relaxed. Her sister's makeover had gone brilliantly. She looked stunning. And best of all, Cat and Estelle had made significant headway in improving their relationship. Chloe was excited to see Grayson's reaction to both. And there was no doubt he'd be in the park this afternoon after the text Chloe had sent him. Thinking of what she'd promised her sister's fiancé, she grinned, then grimaced at the twinge the movement caused.

Pushing herself upright, she removed the towel from her face and called out to Ty, who was at the workstation to Chloe's right, blow-drying her mother's hair. "I think I'm done, Ty."

He glanced her way, then did a double-take and dropped the brush. Her hands went to her face. "What's wrong?"

Estelle sat up and removed her towel. Chloe took one look at the older woman's beet-red face and screamed. Estelle looked at Chloe and did the same. "Mirror, I need a mirror," Chloe said, flapping her hands in front of her face. She felt faint.

"No, no mirror," Ty said as he hurried to her side. He reached for a container on the shelf behind the sink. He unscrewed the cap and sniffed. "Holly, which treatment did you use on Chloe and Estelle?"

Chloe's nemesis from high school twisted her hands. "I-I thought you wanted me to use the red one."

"No, I told you to use the gold jar. The red jar is an intensive peel that—"

"Burns the skin!" Chloe shrieked.

Her mother and sister rushed to her side. Instead of telling Chloe to calm down like she expected them to, they stared down Holly. Estelle turned to add her glare to theirs, and her towel slipped off her head. Chloe gasped. "Y-your hair is…red!"

Estelle collapsed in the chair. "Water, get her some water," Chloe cried, and then brought a trembling hand to her own head. She pointed to the towel and whimpered. "Kit Kat, take it off."

Her sister did as she asked and grimaced. "Is it red?" Chloe whispered.

"No." Relieved, Chloe sagged in the chair. "It's purple."

Ty buried his face in Cat's shoulder while her mother stormed to the front of the salon, shutting off the hair-dryer Nell sat beneath. "You have gone too far this time! Look what you've done to my daughter. You've ruined her face and her hair. Oh no, don't you try and deny it," her mother said when Nell opened her mouth. "I know your handiwork when I see it. I'm calling Paul right now."

"Mommsy's right. I can't go out there like this. I'll be ruined. She blinked back tears as the expression on Ty's face registered. He was devastated. "This isn't your fault, Ty. I'm…We're not blaming you, are we, Estelle?"

"No, it's that old battle-ax's fault."

Ty removed his glasses and swiped at his eyes. "It doesn't matter. I might as well cancel. They're here to see you, Chloe. The press has come from all over. Even *Access Hollywood* sent a correspondent."

She took in Ty's crushed expression and, despite her heart pounding an erratic beat, rose weakly to her feet. "I guess we better get this show on the road then."

Chapter Eighteen

Easton searched the rows of chairs in front of the runway for Chance. Movement in an oak tree to the left of the stage drew his attention. A man straddled a branch, aiming a long-lens camera at the white tent set up several yards behind the runway. Another scan of the park revealed several more professional photographers. Easton gave his head an irritated shake at the sight of the paparazzi. The negative attention Chloe had received in the tabloids had begun to die down. If Easton had his way, he would have banned the press from the fashion show. No doubt he would have been overruled.

"Easton." His brother waved him over.

He weaved his way through the crowd to where Chance and Vivi stood to the right of the runway in front of an ice cream truck.

"How did it go? You get the tracking device on the wife's phone?" Chance asked when Easton reached them.

He nodded. "Yeah, and I added another camera feed

from the room where they're housing the private collection of sculptures." Getting the device on Tara Martinez's phone was easy; escaping the woman's attention, not so much. She was friendly, overly so. Something her husband didn't fail to notice, and hadn't been pleased about. If she didn't stop with the flirting, Easton wouldn't be surprised if Martinez booted him off the security detail. Which wasn't something he planned on sharing with his brother right now. The last thing Easton wanted was to be taken off the case. Because Grayson was right; something was going down. And Easton wasn't about to let Chance and Cat go in blind.

"Good job. You've got the estate covered from all angles now," his brother said, then glanced at the entrance to the park and chuckled. "Looks like Ashley plans to give you some competition."

"What are you talking about?" he asked, then spotted Beau and the rest of the crew who'd worked on his house near the back. It was standing room only now. The Southerner nodded. Easton gave him a chin lift, wondering if Chance knew something he didn't. But if he asked, his brother would put two and two together and ride him for the rest of the afternoon, so he changed the subject. "Thought the fashion show was supposed to start at two; it's twenty after."

He'd busted his hump to get here on time. Along with protecting Chloe from the press, he was worried the guys from the Penalty Box might show up to cause trouble. So far, he hadn't spotted them in the crowd.

"You didn't hear?" Chance asked.

His brother's question made him nervous. He had an uneasy feeling the reason for the delay had to do with Chloe. The woman had an unerring ability to both cause and attract trouble. And after her reaction to his being on a *date* last night, the last thing he wanted her to discover was that he'd been out with Brandi. "Hear what?"

"Aunt Nell was up to her tricks again." Chance looked down at his wife. "What was that stuff she put on their faces?"

As soon as Vivi finished filling Easton in on what happened at the salon, he turned to walk away. He planned to tear a strip off his great-aunt, but first he wanted to check on Chloe.

His brother grabbed him by the arm. "Where do you think you're going?"

"To the apartment to see Chloe."

"She's not there."

"She left town?" After the last few days, he supposed he shouldn't be surprised. But he didn't think it was too much to expect a good-bye call. Though she obviously felt he didn't deserve one since he'd been out with another woman. She hadn't given him a chance to explain last night. He'd planned to make her listen to him today. From the expressions on his sister-in-law's and brother's faces, if they didn't know how Easton felt about Chloe before, they did now.

"Nope, she'll be hitting the runway in about fifteen minutes," his brother said.

"There's no way she'll take part in the fashion show. Not with all the press...Wait, did Ty manage to fix her face and hair?"

His brother's cell rang, and Vivi answered Easton's question. "No, and you guys are a little too quick to judge

Chloe if you ask me. She's loyal to Ty. She wouldn't let him down."

His brother took his phone from his ear and scanned the screen. He grimaced, then said to whoever he was on with, "Thanks for the heads-up. Yeah, I'll tell her. Hopefully she isn't pulled over before she gets…That fast?" His brother let out a low whistle. "Okay. Thanks again, Jake."

"What's going on?" Easton and Vivi asked at almost the same time.

"Found out the reason for the delay. Chloe and Estelle hit the tanning salon."

"Chloe wouldn't go to a tanning salon," Easton said. The way the woman hid from the sun, it was like she was a vampire.

"There's a salon in the same strip mall as Jake's automotive shop that does spray tans. They're probably trying to match the color of their faces to their arms and legs so it's less noticeable. Not a bad idea actually," Vivi said.

"Wouldn't have been if she stopped at that, but she didn't. Cab didn't show up, and Chloe was in a panic that she'd be late for the fashion show. But unlike most normal people, she doesn't just ask for a ride, she buys a Mustang. And from what Jake said, she was driving hell for leather out of the lot. He didn't get a chance to give her the paperwork."

"Jesus, where's Gage?" Easton had to make sure his brother didn't find out or he'd arrest her on the spot.

"At home. Maddie's…under the weather," Vivi said.

His brother grinned. "Is that what they're calling it now?"

Vivi nudged her husband with her elbow, and Easton

had a feeling he was out of the loop. As long as Gage wasn't around, he was fine with that.

Grayson strode toward them. "Where is she?" he asked.

"Cat?" Easton said, hoping to hell that's who the man was looking for and not...

"No, Chloe." He leaned to his left, looking in the direction of the tent. At that exact moment, two women crept out of a back alley and fast-walked across the grass to the tent's entrance. Oversize rainbow-colored golf umbrellas hid them from view so it was hard to tell who they were.

Grayson straightened and turned to Easton. "That woman is a menace on the road. What were you thinking letting her drive a souped-up Mustang? I clocked her doing eighty miles per hour around a hairpin curve. She drove me off the road."

Easton rubbed his jaw. "Didn't happen to be any law enforcement on the road at the time, did there? Other than you, I mean." At the sound of sirens in the distance, Grayson cocked his head and raised his eyebrows. As Easton was trying to figure out how to cover for Chloe, Ty and Sophia, the owner of Naughty and Nice, took their places behind the podium and welcomed everyone to the show.

"Is that why you're here or did it have something to do with the Martinez case?" Chance asked Grayson. The audience was clapping so he didn't have to lower his voice.

"Cat asked me to come." He shrugged at Easton's disbelieving glance. "I know, I was surprised, too. But she texted me this morning, and no way was I missing this."

There was something about the man's grin that made Easton study him closer. "What exactly did she say in her text?"

Grayson laughed. "No way I'm sharing that with you, mate. But I will say our relationship appears to have taken a turn for the better."

"Seriously, Cat O'Connor was sexting you?" Chance laughed. "Doesn't sound like the woman we know and love."

"No, it sounds like Chloe," Easton muttered.

Grayson's jaw dropped, and he reached in the pocket of his black suit for his phone. He thumbed through his messages and stared at the screen.

"Check for winky faces and exclamation marks. You find them, you've been had," Easton said.

"Bloody hell," Grayson clipped out. "I'm going to strangle the woman."

"I don't know, buddy. I think Chloe did you a favor. You might want to look at the stage," Chance said.

Easton looked up at the same time as Grayson. Cat stood by the podium wearing thigh-high black leather boots and a short black leather skirt and matching bustier. Grayson stared at her and swallowed hard. Cat looked smoking hot, but it was the woman in a white robe with a hood hiding her face who held Easton's attention. She crept alongside the stage. Cat looked down at her. The woman, who Easton was pretty sure was Chloe, made a walking sign with two fingers. Cat's lips flattened, and she started to walk—clomp might have been a better word for it—when Ty introduced her, talking about her hair and makeup.

"You're not John Wayne," Easton heard the woman

stage-whisper and recognized her voice. He was right; it was Chloe. "Pretend you're me."

Chloe's instruction seemed to do the trick, and while Sophia described the outfit, Cat walked the stage like a pro. When she turned at the end of the red-carpeted runway, Cat caught sight of Grayson. The agent smiled at his fiancée, then put his fingers to his lips and whistled.

Cat blushed, but she smiled, too. If Chloe's plan had been to heat up the action between the couple, it looked like it may have worked. Distracted by Cat and Grayson's interaction, Chloe had disappeared before Easton could warn her she had a few things to answer for. And so did the older woman now taking her turn on the runway in a bright blue dress. When Ty started his spiel, Nell fluffed her hair and batted her eyes to the amusement of the audience.

Easton didn't realize his father had joined them until he saw his great-aunt look their way. She quickly turned her head and made a show of waving to the crowd. Ted and Fred encouraged her when she swiveled her hips in what Easton imagined was her version of twerking.

"Good Lord," his father said, "I didn't need to see that." But when Liz took to the stage wearing a tight red dress and high heels, a lovesick smile replaced his dad's previous look of horror.

Chance looked at Easton and rolled his eyes. Easton grinned.

A few minutes after the last woman left the stage, the crowd got antsy. People started whispering Chloe's name, and Ty cast a nervous glance at the tent. The stylist visibly relaxed when the flap opened to reveal Chloe. Even with her long, lush mane a dark shade of purple and her overly tanned face, there was no denying she was the star of the show. But as she walked toward the stage, Easton sensed there was something wrong. Instead of her usual graceful stride, she was…shuffling. The hot pink dress she wore appeared to be several sizes too small.

Her mouth formed a startled "oh," and she looked down. She walked another couple of feet to the sound of fabric ripping. The tearing sound continued as she took to the stage. From where he stood, Easton could see the edge of her pink lace panties. He expected her to turn tail and run, but she didn't. She said something to Ty that made his eyes go wide, then angled her body to him. Beau and his crew called out her name and others joined in. She glanced over her shoulder and waved with a movie-star smile on her face.

"I hate to tell you this, E. But I think Ty just cut…" Chance didn't get to finish because as Chloe stepped out onto the runway, she whipped off the dress like a seasoned stripper. Tossing it over her shoulder, she strutted her stuff. And her stuff consisted of a golden tanned body wearing only a pink lace push-up bra and panties. She played to the crowd, and the men hooted and hollered. As she turned at the end of the runway, she looked straight at Easton, blew him a kiss, and tossed her dress onto his head.

He pulled it off, expecting to see his father, brother, and Grayson watching him for a reaction. But no, they were watching Chloe sashay her way back up the runway while cameras furiously clicked. Including Vivi's. "You are not putting that picture in the *Chronicle*," Easton growled at his sister-in-law.

"Hate to tell you, mate, but in the next fifteen minutes,

that photo will be on every social media site," Grayson said.

"Chloe, Chloe, Chloe," the chant grew louder, and she turned. When she looked like she was about to take another stroll down the runway, Easton jumped onto the stage and strode toward her. He heard whistling, and thought it was Chance and Grayson, maybe even his dad, but ignored them. His sole focus was the half-naked woman staring at him open-mouthed and taking a startled step back. He grabbed her before she fell off the stage and lifted her into his arms. "Scarlett, you have some explaining to do," he said as he headed for the tent.

But she didn't get a chance. A deputy blocked their way. "Chloe O'Connor, you're under arrest."

*   *   *

Chloe sat in the passenger seat of Easton's truck wearing a tan deputy's uniform, a champagne-colored cowboy hat, and dark shades. The disguise was the only way they could get her past the press staked out on the sidewalk outside the station.

She sat huddled next to the door. "It's not fair. Gage had no business having me arrested."

"His deputy clocked you doing forty miles per hour over the speed limit," Easton informed her as he backed out of the parking space. "And you ran Grayson off the road, so quit complaining. You're lucky all you're getting is community service and not jail time."

But if Gage assigned her to the project Easton thought he had in mind, Chloe would probably prefer jail time. And while assigning her to community service might be overstepping the bounds of his brother's authority, Easton wouldn't be the one complaining. It worked in his favor. At least she'd be in town long enough to figure out if their relationship would stand the test of time and distance.

"It was an emergency. Ty was depending on me."

"You wouldn't have been much good to him lying in a hospital bed, now would you? Tomorrow you're returning the Mustang. If you need a vehicle, we'll get you something sensible to drive." Like a tank. "And if you weren't arrested for dangerous driving, you just as easily could have been arrested for indecent exposure. What were you thinking pulling a stunt like that? You could have caused a riot."

"I don't understand why you're all making such a big fuss about it. My bra and panties were no more revealing than a bikini. Besides, it wasn't my fault. It was your aunt's. The dress was a size two!"

"Nell admitted she bribed Holly to change the treatments for your hair and face, and she apologized. But you're the one who said you were a size two."

"Do I look like I'm a size two to you?" She chewed on her thumbnail. "And for your information, the last thing I wanted to do was stand half naked on a stage with hundreds of cameras and cell phones pointed at me. I've been so stressed these past few months, I've gained weight. I'm probably a size ten now."

Out there on the stage, no one would have guessed how she felt. But he could tell something more was bothering her, and he took his hand off the wheel to stroke her face. "You're beautiful whatever size you are."

"So is Brandi. She looked lovely, don't you think?"

"Didn't notice." At her raised eyebrow, he said, "I was

too busy reading the text you sent Grayson. And just so you know, the only one you'll be sexting in the future is me."

She gave him a cute grin. "I think it takes two to sext."

"I can handle that." He cast her a sidelong glance when she went quiet, her smile replaced with a preoccupied look on her face. "Chloe, I'm not interested in Brandi. The only woman I'm interested in is you."

"Are you sure? Because Brandi needs a man to look out for her, and she's popular. Everyone likes her. No one likes me, Easton. Even your family—well, other than your dad. I'm not like Cat. Remember when she was arrested? Everyone came to the station and demanded her release. No one did that for me." She glanced out the window.

So that's what was bothering her. Instead of heading to the ranch for the barbeque Liz and Cat had organized to celebrate Ty's grand opening, Easton took the next turn. He drove down a deserted road toward Lookout Point—a popular make-out destination back in the day. For Chloe's sake, he figured they could be a little late.

Easton pulled up to the guardrail and shut off the engine. He leaned over and unsnapped her seat belt, then undid his. "Come on. Let's go for a walk." A few yards down the path there was a bench with a great view of town.

She glanced out the back window. "What about the press?"

"It'll take a couple of hours for them to realize you're not at the station. We'll be at the ranch long before they clue in that you're gone. Besides, they'll never find us here." He got out of the truck and walked around to her side, opening the door.

She peered out the windshield. "Where are we?"

"You mean to tell me no one ever took you to Lookout Point?"

"I wasn't that girl, Easton. No one asked me out."

"Because you were hiding in the library. But I can't believe no one asked you out our senior year." The summer before twelfth grade, Chloe disappeared off the radar. Easton later found out she'd been reinventing herself. She'd gone from the cute, awkward girl he knew and liked, to a knockout. Her transformation had been all anyone could talk about the first day back at school.

At his comment, she looked at him and raised her eyebrows. Right, there'd been only one guy she'd been interested in. Him. "Their loss," he said, and helped her out of the truck.

She tossed the cowboy hat onto the seat, making a face when her hair tumbled over her shoulder. "I have purple hair."

"Ty told you it would wash out in a few days," he said and tugged her into his arms, kissing the pout from her face. He pulled back and looked down at her. "Chloe O'Connor, I don't care what size you are, if your hair is pink, purple, or green; you'll always be the most beautiful woman in the world to me."

She gave him a sweet smile, then touched the corner of her mouth. "My face is on fire."

Well, there went his plans for their alone time. It looked like they'd have to wait for another day. But right now, he was more worried about her. "Should you be wearing makeup?"

"No, but I couldn't go on stage without it."

"I'll never understand women." He leaned past her and

picked up her hat. "You better keep this on." He put the hat on her head. "You sure you're up for a walk?"

She nodded and glanced at his leg. "As long as you are."

He took her by the hand and drew her away from the truck to shut the door. "Stop wasting time. I'll be lucky to have you to myself for another twenty minutes before they send out the cavalry."

"We probably have less than that. Your brothers won't want to leave you in my clutches for long. I wouldn't be surprised if Nell has a voodoo doll that looks like me and she's sticking pins into it right now."

"The doll didn't look exactly like you, but I took it from her anyway," he teased, then tugged on her hand and started across the blacktop to the path through the woods. She held back, and he turned.

Standing there in the too-large uniform shirt and pants with an earnest expression on her face, she looked small and vulnerable. "I know you think I'm joking, but I'm not really. You're close to your family, as close as I am to mine. I don't want to cause trouble between you and your brothers. Between my mom and your dad. "

He stayed quiet. There was some truth to what she said. If they crashed and burned, it wouldn't only be the two of them who got hurt. But when he looked down at her upturned face, there was only one answer he could give.

"Scarlett, I don't give a damn."

Chapter Nineteen

Chloe sat in the back of Grayson's black Yukon with Ty. They'd just come from dropping off Estelle at the Denver airport. Chloe couldn't have asked for a better send-off for her friend and manager. Although Estelle did the whole stiff-upper-lip thing, Chloe could tell that having Cat and Grayson there meant the world to her. Her plan to bring Estelle and Cat closer, and remind her sister and Grayson how much they loved each other, had worked brilliantly. At least their improved relationships made everything Chloe had gone through at the fashion show worthwhile.

Ty bumped her shoulder with his. "I'm going to miss the old girl. It's just you and me now, Diva. Unless you're moving in with Easton. You're not, are you?"

She caught Grayson's eyes in the rearview mirror and her sister's glance from the passenger seat. It was as bad as the barbeque at the ranch on Saturday night. Chloe had felt like she and Easton were under a microscope with everyone watching their every move. Within five minutes, she'd wanted to go back to Lookout Point or to his cabin. But Easton hadn't asked, and if she was honest, she'd been a bit disappointed. Not that she let him know.

But maybe it was better if they take things slow. If she wanted proof that it was, all she had to do was look at her track record with men. She'd rushed headlong into her relationships. And, invariably, a few weeks later, they'd fizzled out and died. Leaving her beating herself up for making another mistake.

"No, we're dating. It's not like we're engaged or anything." Chloe O'Connor and Easton McBride. How many times had she scribbled that in her binders, making a heart around their names? Too many times to count. You'd think now that her long-ago dream had come true, she'd be over the moon. But all she seemed to do was worry, waiting for the other shoe to drop. He'd always been the unattainable guy. He'd been the prince, and she'd been the frog.

"Dating here, right? You're not going back to LA."

After spending the past three days hiding out from the press, the last thing she wanted to do was go back to LA. If she'd thought the picture from the engagement party was bad, it had nothing on the ones of her getting arrested. The gossip rags were running the photos side by side. And wasn't that a ringing endorsement? Like any director would hire her now. And the thought of roaming around the beach house by herself, with nothing to occupy her time, wasn't all that appealing. Of course Easton wouldn't be there either. At least here she had a personal life, one that was looking up if she dealt with her insecu-

rities. "No, I think I'll stay in town for a while longer,"
she told Ty. "I'm sure, a month from now, someone will
bump me out of the actor-behaving-badly tabloid wars."
It was then that she realized even if she wanted to go back
to LA, she couldn't. The sheriff was issuing her community service assignment today. If she weren't dating his
brother, she'd be tempted to file an abuse of power against
Gage. And wouldn't that further endear her to the citizens
of Christmas?

Her cell phone rang. "Speak of the devil," she murmured, then took a deep breath and put a smile in her
voice. "Good morning, Gage. How are you? How's the
family?"

Her sister looked back and grimaced, then picked up
her phone. Cat's reaction made Chloe wonder if she
should be worried, but Gage was being pleasant enough.
"Yes, thank you. Estelle got off okay. We're on our way
back now. Four o'clock at...Pardon me, could you repeat
that? I think we have a bad connection." Chloe prayed
she misunderstood him because her pulse had already begun to flutter in her throat, her body becoming warm and
clammy beneath her buttercup-yellow halter dress.

He repeated the assignment. She'd been right the first
time. "No, you can't force me to do this. I refuse, I absolutely refuse to chair the committee to save Christmas
High. I'll run a drama program or a literacy program. I'll
do anything but this, and if you try and force me to, I'll
sue—"

Cat leaned over the seat and grabbed the phone from
Chloe and handed her hers. "Talk to him. It's Easton."

Of course Cat called her partner. They all thought he was
Chloe's sugar pill. The one person who could keep the dra-

matic diva calm and make her see reason. Maybe they were right, but this time it was different. It was his brother who was bullying her and sending her into a panic attack. And she wasn't exactly happy with Easton at the moment. He was in Aspen on a job. He'd left town the morning after the fashion show and had been gone three days. The man was not big on conversation and phone calls. She'd spoken to him briefly yesterday morning. No wonder she was feeling insecure.

Ty gave her hand a commiserating pat. He, out of anyone, would understand why she couldn't go back to that school. Easton should, too. She lifted the phone to her ear. "Do you know what your brother just asked me to do? No, correction, told me I have to do."

"I can guess. He wants you to work on the committee to save Christmas High, doesn't he?"

"No, he wants me to head up the committee. I'm not doing it, Easton, and he can't make me. I'll call my lawyer."

"Seriously, you're going there again? First you were going to sue Nell and Vivi, and now you're going to sue *my brother*. Didn't we have a conversation about this on Saturday?" His tone was clipped. "I don't understand why you're making a big deal out of this. Yes, I get that you were bullied in high school, but, Chloe, that was years ago. You have to grow up and move past this once and for all. It's a couple weeks out of your life. It's not like you have anything going on right now."

She rubbed her chest and fought back angry tears. "Did you just tell me to grow up and get over the bullying I withstood for four years? Is that what you're telling me, Easton?"

She heard him blow out a breath over the line. "Look, Chloe, I know—"

"No, Easton, you don't know. Out of anyone, I expected you to support me. Maybe stand up for me to your brother." Her fingers tightened around the phone. "But you're right, this is exactly what we talked about Saturday, so let's end this now before someone gets hurt. Good-bye, Easton."

"Chloe, you're overreacting. Let's—"

Ty gaped at her when she disconnected. "Did you just break up with the White Knight? The only boy you've ever loved."

"I never would have given you the phone if I thought that's how your conversation was going to go," Cat grumbled. "Just once I wish you'd think before you speak, Chloe. Maybe try and be a little more like me."

"Oh, yes, because it's so much better to keep your feelings locked up inside. So no one knows they've hurt you or said something that makes you mad or—"

"I agree with Chloe," Grayson interjected. "At least you know where you stand with her. Whereas you—"

"Really, Grayson, we're going to go there now?"

Chloe widened her eyes at Ty, who mouthed, "uh-oh." They both sank down in their seats as the couple finally opened up about what was really bothering them. On the one hand, Chloe was glad that they did, while on the other, it would have been less uncomfortable if they'd done so in private. Something she'd have to remember.

Ty handed her an earbud and stuck the other one in his ear. He held up his iPhone. "I'm listening to the audio version of the first book in Nell's series, *The Trouble with Christmas*. Gage and Maddie's story."

Chloe supposed it was better than listening to her sister and Grayson squabble for the next three hours. Thanks to Maddie's antics, the long drive back to Christmas passed quickly. And by the time Grayson pulled in front of the Sugar Plum Bakery, Chloe felt she had learned some valuable insights into her hometown…and Gage McBride. Obviously, she reminded Gage of his first wife. And oddly enough, that made Chloe feel better.

"We'll listen to the end tonight," Ty said, unbuckling his seat belt. "I have back-to-back appointments for the rest of the day. Thanks for the ride, you two." He leaned forward and patted Cat's head, then opened the door to the SUV, helping Chloe onto the sidewalk. "Stop by later and we'll talk."

As Cat got out of the truck, Ty jogged down the street with a wave. When her sister handed Chloe her phone, she had a hard time holding back a smug smile. During the last twenty minutes of the drive, the couple had shared soft, loving looks. She'd even caught her sister tenderly stroking Grayson's stubbled jaw. And Cat was far from a touchy-feely kind of girl.

"Don't look so pleased with yourself," her sister said. "Your big mouth might have gone a ways in improving my love life, but it didn't help yours."

Chloe had been doing her best to forget what she'd said to Easton. In under ten words, she'd ended their relationship before it really got started. Maybe Chloe had to learn to strike a balance between how her sister dealt with her anger and hurt and how she did.

"Thank you for reminding me because I'd totally forgotten that."

Cat smirked, then handed Chloe her phone. "He knows you're upset. All you have to do is call and apologize."

Now that was a problem. "I went too far. I shouldn't have broken up with him when I was angry and on the phone. But I don't owe him an apology, Kit Kat. He owes me one."

Cat held up her hands. "Okay, I didn't hear the entire conversation, so you and Easton will have to figure that out on your own. But Chloe, for everyone's sake, can you please just do as Gage asked? Maddie was heading up the committee, but she hasn't been feeling well, and Gage is worried about her."

After listening to their story, Chloe had become somewhat invested in the couple's happiness. "Is it serious?"

"She's pregnant."

"How nice. Connor, Lily, and Annie must be excited."

Cat stared at her. "You remembered their names."

"Of course I know their names, Kit Kat. They're our step-nieces and -nephew now." Until she'd listened to the book, she'd never remembered their names before. She supposed it had been her way of leaving Christmas and her bad memories in her rearview mirror. She never let herself get sucked into the town's drama. She stayed above the fray and far away. And here she was stuck right in the middle of it.

"Speaking of nieces, Skye and Ethan aren't happy you haven't dropped by to see them and Evie."

"I thought I was supposed to see them at the barbeque on Saturday night."

Her sister grinned. "They couldn't make it. Skye's sick, too. And they have some news they want to share."

"They're pregnant, too?"

Cat raised her hands. "You didn't hear it from me."

Chloe was happy for the parents-to-be, but she couldn't help feeling a little jealous. As the years flew by, she was beginning to think she'd never have a baby of her own. She wondered if Cat felt the same. Probably not, since she already had a ring on her finger.

Chloe hugged her sister and waited until Grayson disconnected from his call, then bent down and blew him a kiss. "Bye, my favorite brother-in-law-to-be."

He winked at her. "If you need backup at the meeting, give me a shout. You've got my number."

"Thank you," she said.

"You're going to the meeting then?" her sister asked.

"Yes, I am. And I'm going to sit there and not say a single word."

"Chloe!"

* * *

Chloe slunk down in the driver's seat of her Mustang in the parking lot of Christmas High. She watched the women walk beneath the caramel-colored brick arch to enter the double doors of the school. Suddenly overcome with a feeling of impending doom, her heart beat triple time against her ribs. Lightheaded and disoriented, it took a moment for her to realize she was having a panic attack. Once she did, she tried one of the strategies she'd found online, distracting herself by counting backward from a hundred by threes. It wasn't working, and it became more difficult to breathe. In an effort to calm herself, she put her hands over her mouth. That didn't work either. Now her ears were ringing. Then she realized it was her phone. She fumbled for it in her purse. She needed help.

"Hello," she said, her voice a strangled rasp.

"Chloe, where are you?" Easton asked. He sounded angry, but it didn't matter. She pressed the phone tight to her ear as though she could absorb his strength.

"In my car. Parking lot at the high school. Can't breathe."

"Okay, just sit back and relax. You're going to be fine. You know it's a panic attack. You talked yourself out of one before, you can do it again."

"It's worse. Feel sick."

"Pretend I'm there with you, that I'm holding you in my arms. I wish I was, you know."

"I wish…you…were, too," she whispered, still having a hard time catching her breath.

"We're not over, Chloe. Not by a long shot. I'll be home tomorrow, and we'll talk."

"That's what you said…last time, and then you went out…with Brandi. She's here, you know. I saw her walk in the school…with her posse. I can't do it, Easton. I know you want me to, but I can't. I'm having a panic attack, and I haven't even gone in the school yet."

"Good girl. You did it."

"What are you talking about? I just told you I haven't been inside the school. I'm going to embarrass myself. I'll start sweating and—"

"I am listening. Your breathing's evened out. Your panic attack is over."

"Oh, I-I didn't notice." She hated the attacks. They embarrassed her and made her feel weak. How could Easton want to be with her?

"Hang on a sec." There was a long pause before he came back on the line. "Listen, I was calling to say I'm sorry. When you started talking about suing Gage, I got mad. But it—"

"I understand. He's your brother, and I shouldn't—"

"Chloe, would you mind letting me finish?"

"No, but I just wanted you to know I'm not suing. And even though it's unfair, I was going to chair the committee. But now, after this—"

Easton cut her off with a sigh. "Can you give me a minute here? What I'm trying to tell you is that I wasn't thrilled you threatened to sue Gage, but it's not why I was mad. I was mad that you keep sabotaging yourself. You get your feelings hurt because you think everyone in town hates you, and then you pull crap that makes them hate you. Maybe *hate*'s too strong a word."

"I prefer *despise*. It doesn't sound as harsh."

Easton laughed at the same time someone knocked on Chloe's fogged-up window. "Just a minute," she said to Easton, then rolled it down. It was Gage and Madison's oldest daughter. "Hello, Annie."

"Hey. Uncle E told me to come and get you and show you where the meeting is. He figured you haven't been here for a long time and wouldn't remember where to go."

"Thank you. That's very nice of you. I'll just be a minute, all right?"

Annie shrugged. "Sure."

Chloe smiled and rolled up the window, swallowing past the wedge of fear in her throat. She put the phone to her ear. "Annie's here."

"I heard. She's one of the student reps. She'll be attending the meeting, too. If you don't want to go, I'll call Gage. Get him to assign you to something else. But Chloe, I think you should."

"Of course you do. Conquer your fears and all that, I get it. I just don't know if I can, Easton. I'm sure this will sound stupid and immature to you, but I don't want to save Christmas High."

"The girls bullied you, Chloe, not the school. They're women now, and life's knocked a few of them around. Hopefully that's knocked some sense in them. If it hasn't, that's their problem, not yours. Don't let them get to you. Call me after your meeting."

"All right. Thank you for calling and sending Annie."

"Wouldn't be much of a white knight if I didn't look after my girl, would I?"

"You know Ty's nickname for you?"

"Small town, remember?"

They said good-bye, and she reluctantly disconnected. She didn't want to get out of the car, but she'd already kept Annie waiting long enough. "Sorry, I didn't mean to keep you." She apologized to the teenager, then shut the door and beeped the lock button on her key fob.

"It's okay. I know you don't want to be here. I overheard my mom and dad talking. They didn't know I was listening."

"I'm sorry you had to hear that, Annie." She didn't know what else to say. She wasn't going to pretend it wasn't true. If Annie was in the meeting, she'd find out soon enough.

The young girl shrugged. "I'd probably feel the same if I were you. I was bullied in eighth grade, and I didn't want to come to school either."

She stopped Annie with a hand on her arm. "You're not still bullied, are you?"

"No, Mom told me I had to stand up for myself, and it worked. You should, you know, stand up for yourself. I heard what Aunt Nell did. She pulled stuff like that on my mom until she stood up for herself."

"I know, I read about it in *The Trouble with Christmas*." Something else that made Chloe feel better. After listening to the book, she no longer took Nell's attacks personally. Well, mostly she didn't.

Annie held open the door, and Chloe forced herself to walk inside. The common area's beige tiles were polished to a high sheen. Sunlight streamed through the domed ceiling while potted plants and comfortable-looking brown cushioned chairs decorated the space. To the right was the secretary's office. There'd been two when Chloe attended Christmas High. Behind that the principal's. She'd spent more time in the nurse's office than Mr. Lowry's.

Classes were dismissed at three, but there were still students hanging around. A couple of them waved at Annie and said hi, looking at Chloe with interest. One of the girls appeared to recognize her and shyly approached. "Can I have your autograph?"

Chloe smiled. "Of course," she said, taking the proffered glitter pen and signing the girl's notebook.

Before long, a crowd gathered around them, and Annie, looking at her with a mischievous gleam in her eyes, said, "Chloe's taking my mom's place. She's the new chair of the Save Christmas High committee. Isn't that great?"

Chloe narrowed her eyes at the teenager who she was beginning to think had inherited a manipulative gene from her great-aunt Nell. But she didn't get a chance to refute Annie's statement because the students began talking at once. They relayed their thoughts about their school and why it should be saved. While they did, Annie stood off to the side texting and occasionally taking pictures of Chloe.

She heard from them all: members of the football team, debate team, drama club, and band. They were wonderful kids who obviously loved their school and their friends. Friends that would be, Chloe learned, separated, in some instances, by the new boundary lines being drawn up so as not to cause overcrowding at the other schools.

She happened to glance at the clock on the wall and realized they'd been talking for more than thirty minutes. "It's been lovely meeting you all, but I don't want to be late for the meeting."

As she started to walk away, the boys and girls invited her to come and watch their respective teams. "I'll try and—" Chloe began before Annie interrupted her.

"Text me the times and dates, and I'll make sure Chloe is there," her self-appointed social secretary said.

Chloe crossed her arms and tilted her head. Annie grinned, then shrugged. "Christmas High isn't how you remember it. If you get to know everyone, you'll want to help save the school."

"You're pretty smart, aren't you?"

"Yeah, Dad says I take after my uncle E. He helps out at the football practices when he can, so you'll want to go to those," Annie informed her as they walked down the hall. "Computer club, too. And you should definitely try to make a rehearsal for the drama club. They're really good."

Chloe heard a whooshing noise. It was the sound of her getting sucked into Christmas. "Send me the details, and I'll try to make it," she said, stopping in front of the glass cases that held the athletic trophies. The McBride boys had their names on more than their fair share. Her brother and sister did, too. Chloe pressed her nose to the glass to get a better look at the football trophy from their final year of high school. Easton had been captain and star quarterback of the team. Cat had been head cheerleader. They were voted prom king and queen, too, but after what Chloe did, they were no longer talking at that point. Chloe didn't go to the prom. She couldn't face Easton. Her sister did though.

Chloe turned at the camera's flash. Annie shrugged. "Uncle E wanted another picture of you."

"Have you been texting and sending pictures to him the entire time?"

"Yeah." Annie read the incoming text and rolled her eyes. "He said to tell you he likes your jeans."

Chloe smoothed her hand down the dark denim. When Ty found out she was attending the meeting, he insisted she attempt to fit in by dressing down. He'd badgered her for two hours. She'd finally given in and picked up a pair of skinny jeans from Naughty and Nice and a long-sleeved black T-shirt with pink sparkles. She'd completed the outfit with a pair of her favorite black-and-pink peep toes.

"Do I look okay?" Chloe asked self-consciously.

Annie nodded. "Better than the dresses you always wear. You look younger."

"Really?" Chloe said, not quite believing her. But if it was true, she might have to revisit her opinion of jeans.

Annie angled her head, then nodded again. "Doc Martens might look better than your high heels though."

Chloe no longer trusted Annie's fashion sense. "You sound like my sister." She looked down the hall. "Do we have time to stop at the library?"

Annie's eyes dropped to her cell phone. "Sure," she said, then led the way. And as Chloe stepped into the room, it was like walking back into her past. This was the one place she'd felt safe at school.

"Chloe O'Connor, is that you, dear?" She turned to see the librarian, Mrs. Woods, behind the desk. Chloe ran over and hugged her. "It's so good to see you," she said and meant it. Mrs. Woods had been the one person other than Easton who she'd opened up to at school. It had been the librarian who'd encouraged Chloe to follow her dreams.

Mrs. Woods hugged her back. She smelled like books and lavender powder. "It's good to see you, too. Your mother always lets me know what you're up to. And I never miss an episode of *As the Sun Sets*."

A pang of guilt twisted in Chloe's chest. "I'm sorry, Mrs. Woods. I should have dropped by when I was in town. I will from now on."

"You're old enough to call me Vera, dear. And I'd love to see you more often, but you know the board is talking about closing the school." The older woman looked around the room with its brick walls lined with bookshelves. "I'll probably retire. It wouldn't be the same working anywhere else. But you can drop by my house anytime."

"Chloe's not going to let them close the school, Mrs. Woods. She's the new head of the Save Christmas High campaign."

Chloe arched an eyebrow at Annie. The teenager gave her a smirk that was scarily similar to Nell's.

Vera pressed her hands to her chest. "Chloe, that's the best news I've had in ages. If anyone can change the board's mind, it's you. Your celebrity alone will have them sitting up to listen. I hated the thought of retiring, and now, because of you, maybe I won't have to."

Chloe glanced around the library, her eyes lighting on the table in the far corner of the room. It was where she and Easton had played chess. The place where she'd fallen in love with a teenage boy who'd been dealing with his mother's cancer diagnosis. Chloe had been there for Easton, but the woman standing behind the desk, at risk of losing a job that she loved, had always been there for Chloe. "I'll do my best, Vera."

Chapter Twenty

Easton pulled up beside Chance's log home on the lake. As soon as he got out of his truck, he heard his brother's dog Princess barking her head off. "We're up front, E," Chance called out.

His brother had texted him to stop by on his way home. He planned to make the visit a brief one. Chloe was holding a committee meeting tonight, and he wanted to be there. He'd driven straight to his brother's place from Aspen. He'd ended up having to add another two nights to his stay. Something that a few months ago wouldn't have bothered him. Now, with Chloe in his life, it did. Easton planned to keep that piece of intel to himself. His brothers would razz him if they found out he was as whipped as they were.

Stepping back to shut the door of his truck, a searing pain shot from his knee to his foot. One more thing he had to hide: his leg was killing him after the drive. *To hell with it*, he thought and leaned across the driver's seat to retrieve the unopened prescription bottle from the glove box. Chloe was right: there was no shame in taking the pills for his pain. He unscrewed the lid. Since he was driving, he popped only one in his mouth instead of the prescribed two. Grabbing the cold cup of coffee from the holder, he took a mouthful.

Of course his brother chose that exact moment to come around the side of the log house. "What's keeping..." Chance's gaze dropped to the prescription bottle in Easton's hand, and he grinned. "About time. Guess we have Chloe to thank for you finally getting your head out of your ass."

Great. No doubt Chance would be sharing the news with the rest of the family. "Off your game if you think Chloe has anything to do with me—" Easton began, as he tossed the plastic bottle onto the front seat.

Chance cut him off with a snort. "Right. You've been away for almost a week, and you're telling me you won't be making up for lost time with your girl tonight? If you're not, then it's you who's off your game, bro."

Since that was the plan, he could see his brother's point. A little hard to make up for lost time when you can't think straight with the pain. He probably should have thought about that and taken the pill sooner. Easton shut the driver's-side door. "You wanna tell me what's so important we had to have a meeting now instead of in the morning?"

"I wanted your thoughts on the feed that came in from the Martinezes about an hour ago. We have a problem," Chance said, as they walked through the grass to the side of the cabin.

Easton groaned inwardly as his hope of a quick escape

faded fast. He followed his brother down the stone steps
and onto the patio. Vivi sat wrapped in a striped throw
with her feet up on a chair, eating a...

He stopped and stared at her. "In case you didn't notice, you have a dill pickle on your s'more."

She grinned and wiped marshmallow from her upper
lip. "I know. Chance will make you one if you want."

"I think I'll pass." He nodded at her baby bump.
"How's Chance Junior?"

She opened her mouth, then narrowed her pretty violet
eyes at him. "You almost got me that time. We're not
telling you if it's a boy or a girl, so quit fishing."

Chance smiled at his wife and gave her baby bump a
tender pat. "Easton and I have a couple of things to discuss. You need another s'more before I go inside?"

"No, thanks. I think I'll go in, too. I'm a little tired."
She fake yawned and stretched.

"Yeah, you look real tired, honey. You go on in and lie
down; I won't be long."

"But I thought... You're annoying, McBride. I don't
know what the big deal is."

"The big deal is that you're my very pregnant wife
who likes to stick her nose where it doesn't belong, and
inevitably that means trouble comes a-knocking."

"I haven't..." Chance crossed his arms over his black
T-shirt. "Fine," she said, pushing herself up and off the
chair. "Since your brother won't let me hang out with
you, I'll see you later, Easton. Are you going to the meeting?"

"I was thinking about it," he said, careful not to give
himself away.

"You might want to get there early then. After Chloe's

op-ed, they're expecting a packed house." She pressed her lips together, shooting a glance at Chance. "I should be there, but your brother's being an overprotective pain in the butt."

"Can't fault a guy for looking out for his wife and baby girl, honey."

Easton laughed at the oh-shit look that came over his brother's face when he realized what he'd just revealed, then said, "Well, hell, I just lost fifty bucks."

"You share the news, and you'll lose more than fifty bucks," Vivi warned Easton as she opened the patio door. She scooped up the Yorkie dancing at her feet, glaring at his brother through the glass door as she slammed it shut.

"Looks like you're in trouble, big brother. And your wife's kind of scary." Easton grinned, then recalled what Vivi had said before the big reveal. "What was that about Chloe writing an op-ed?"

Chance drew his gaze from the patio doors. "Yeah, no doubt I'll be paying for that. And if you think Vivi's scary, you should read Chloe's op-ed piece. Pretty sure it will be standing-room only at the meeting."

He'd talked to Chloe yesterday, and she hadn't mentioned anything about her op-ed piece to him. And there was only one reason she'd hold back, because the woman certainly didn't hold back anything else. "How bad was it?"

Chance took a seat and put his feet up on the ledge of the fire pit. From his brother's shit-eating grin, Easton figured he'd better sit, too, and took the chair beside him.

"I can get you a copy if you'd rather read it yourself. Vivi has a couple lying around the house," his brother offered.

"No, just give me the condensed version."

"You know that her first meeting didn't go so well, right?"

He nodded. That he'd heard about. Brandi and her friends had given Chloe a hard time. They thought one of them should have been made chair of the committee instead of her. Knowing how difficult it had been for Chloe to attend the meeting, Easton had been tempted to hop in his truck and head back to town. But there'd been a spate of home invasions in Aspen, and every celebrity within a thirty-mile radius had wanted him to advise them on their security systems.

It'd been great for the company's balance sheet, not so great for taking any personal time. At least Cat, Ty, and Liz had been there for Chloe after the meeting. Annie and the other student reps, along with deputy Jill Flaherty, who'd been assigned to keep the peace, had stood up for her during the two-hour-long session.

"I guess Chloe decided she'd had enough. She basically said how she was the least likely person to champion the school after her experience at Christmas High and in town. But that Annie and her friends and Mrs. Woods had changed her mind."

Easton relaxed. "So what was with the shit-eating grin? That doesn't sound—"

"I didn't get to that part yet. She also listed everyone who'd bullied her past and present, including the little incident at Diva. Aunt Nell got a mention and so did our brother. But you wanted a condensed version, so I skipped over it."

"So that was the reason for your grin?" he asked hopefully.

"Nope, saved the best part for last. Turnout was low at the last meeting, and she called out the parents for their lack of support. Told them if they weren't invested enough to fight for the school, why should she."

Easton didn't understand what the big deal was. He was proud of Chloe. "Seriously, you're a little touchy if you think that's a problem."

"Really? I thought you'd be pissed she was making waves."

"Nope. Happy that she finally stuck up for herself." And he wanted to tell her that himself. Easton stood up. "I'm going to head out. Whatever you saw on the feed can wait until tomorrow. Or I can check it out after the meeting and call you."

"No, we need to deal with this now." He stood and nodded at the computers set up on the glass table under the trellis. When Easton joined him, Chance said, "Five-thirty-two in the kitchen. You're better at this than me. See if you can zoom in on the screen." It took Easton a couple of minutes to find what Chance wanted. Tara Martinez was on a laptop.

He looked at his brother. "She's watching the fashion show in the park, and she's stopped it twice. First time when Cat's on the stage and Grayson's in the picture whistling. You and Vivi show up, too. Second time when I jump on the stage." Easton played with the feed, getting an angle from the camera across from Tara. "She's nervous, and the only reason for her to be nervous would be that she knows Grayson is FBI, and they have them under surveillance, and it's obvious he's connected to us."

"Got that. She knows we're on to them. But here's the bigger problem." He nodded at the screen.

"She's smart. She's removed the tracking device from her cell phone." Easton watched as she dug around in her purse and pulled out another phone. "It's a burner."

"So we can't trace who she called. But five minutes later, she's in Martinez's office demanding he dismiss us."

Easton brought up the feed from five-forty in the office and picked up the conversation. "Shit. He's buying that I made a move on her."

"Did you?"

He shot his brother an are-you-kidding-me look. "No. She made one on me, and he walked in. I should have told you. Didn't realize it would come back to bite us. You hear from Martinez yet?"

Chance shook his head. "Last shipment for the exhibit is set to arrive tomorrow at ten. I figure he'll tell me then. He's probably trying to line up another security team as we speak."

"Wanna bet that Tara has one already lined up?"

"Never thought of that, but makes sense."

"We need to let Martinez know what's happening. He's been had. His wife and the artist are having an affair. Once they get the big payout, they're on the wind. And he's left holding the bag if things go south. Or worse, she makes sure things go south and gets it all, including the insurance money when he gets popped."

"Can you prove it?"

"Need a day or two to connect the dots, but I have enough on her to give him something to think about. Arrange a meet with him away from the estate and bring in Grayson. Put the fear of God into Martinez, tell him he's going down for this, too. Then bring him on board."

"Sounds good. Show me what you have on her first."

Once Easton had laid everything out for his brother, he glanced at the time on the screen. He scowled at Chance. "Thanks a lot, there's no way I'll make it in time for the meeting now."

His brother frowned. "You didn't sound as though you cared if you went or not." A slow smile creased his tanned face. "Baby bro's got it bad. Looks good on you, E," he said and pulled out his phone. "I'll text Gage, see if it's worth you making the drive."

So much for playing it cool. Easton pulled his laptop from his messenger bag and e-mailed Chance a copy of his file on Tara Martinez and cc'd Grayson.

Chance laughed to himself as he typed on his phone. "Chloe just gave Gage hell for texting in the meeting. He figures they'll be wrapping up in ten minutes, and it's standing room only. Gage says you shouldn't bother making the drive." Chance looked up with a grin. "But I think you should go, baby bro. Ashley Wilkes is there. Saw him hanging out with Chloe a couple times this week. Wouldn't want him to get a leg up on you."

That was news to Easton, and not particularly good news. Chloe would already be disappointed that he hadn't made it to the meeting like he'd promised. He had to think of a way to make it up to her. Something romantic. Her sister might not be a hearts-and-flowers kind of girl, but Chloe was. And what was more romantic than a picnic under the stars at the place they'd first made love? He glanced at his brother, not exactly thrilled he'd give himself away, but there wasn't much he could do about it." You mind if I borrow a blanket, a bottle of wine, and some...I don't know, cheese and grapes or something?"

Chance blew on his knuckles, then rubbed them on his chest. "Good to know you were paying attention to your big brother. But you forgot a couple of things. You gonna do this right, you need chocolate and flowers. While you're getting the stuff from inside the house, I'll make you up a couple of s'mores to go. You can pick some tulips from the flower bed at the side of the house." He grinned when Easton raised his eyebrows. "What can I say, I'm good at the romance shit."

By the time Easton collected what he needed from inside the cabin, with some romantic advice from Vivi as well, Chance was wrapping four s'mores in tinfoil. "You didn't put any pickles on them, did you?"

"Please, I told you I'm a pro at…Wait a minute, there's no reason Chloe would be craving pickles, is there?"

"No, of course not. We haven't…" he began without thinking, then shut his mouth and took the s'mores from his brother.

"Whoa, really? Guess you don't take after me. Maybe you're more like Dad. Ah, hi, honey," he said sheepishly to Vivi, who stood behind the screen door with her arms crossed.

Just as he opened his mouth to give Chance a much-deserved shot, Easton's cell rang. He checked caller ID. "Hey, Dallas. Yeah? That's great. I'll tell her. I'm sure she'll be in touch. Thanks."

Easton no longer had to worry that his plan to romance Chloe wouldn't be enough to sweep her off her feet. He'd gotten her a job.

* * *

Chloe got up from the black fold-up chair behind the table and searched the auditorium for Easton. With the parents and students beginning to file out the doors, she was hoping to catch a glimpse of him. But there was no sign him of sitting in the emptying bleachers or standing against the wall. As several parents approached, along with Vera Woods and the principal, Chloe covered her disappointment, accepting their thanks with a smile. "You're welcome. Yes, I think the meeting went really well," she said, then continued chatting with them for a few minutes. Mr. Lowry, the principal, shook her hand, and Vera gave her a warm hug before making way for a petite brunette and her daughter.

The woman offered Chloe a tentative smile. "I'm not sure if you remember me, Chloe. I'm Jenny Ryan, and this is my daughter Lindsey."

"Of course I do." She didn't have a clue who the woman was. "It's lovely to see you again. I met Lindsey the other day. You have a talented daughter, Jenny." Chloe smiled at the young girl, who blushed.

Jenny smiled at her daughter, too, then returned her attention to Chloe. "You're all she's talked about for the past few days. We appreciate what you're doing. If they close the school, I don't know how I'll manage to get Lindsey to drama club. I'm a single parent now. Dave passed away three years ago."

"I'm so sorry to hear that," Chloe said. At the mention of Dave, she remembered Jenny. She'd been a member of Brandi's posse. But Easton was right, life hadn't been easy for some of the women who'd tortured Chloe in high school, and it was time for her to move on. And while she wasn't entirely confident their case was strong enough to sway the board, at least not yet, Jenny didn't need the added stress of hearing that. "We have a strong case to bring before the board. I'm hopeful for a positive outcome."

Chloe sensed someone watching her and, thinking it was Easton, turned. It wasn't. Gage stood a couple feet away, looking like he was fighting back a smile, which was an improvement over how he'd looked at her lately. "Hi Jenny, Lindsey," he said as he closed the distance between them. "Great meeting, Chloe. Seems like you have everything well in hand."

"Yes, although *some* people chose to ignore my no-cell-phone rule."

"We better be going. Thanks again, Chloe. Sheriff." Jenny smiled and moved away. Lindsey hung back. "Chloe, are you coming to help out the prom committee with the decorations tomorrow?"

"Yes, absolutely. I wouldn't miss it." Since she hadn't attended her own prom, she'd enjoyed helping out the last couple of days. For the juniors' sake, she hoped this wouldn't be the last one held at the school.

"Great." Lindsey smiled and ran off to join her mother.

"Prom, too? When you do something you go all in, don't you?" Gage said.

She shrugged. "I have the time. And they're nice kids."

"So maybe I'm not the big, bad bullying sheriff after all? Come on, admit it. I won't tell anyone."

"Fine. I admit it ended up being a good idea. But you were a bit of a bully. All you had to do was ask nicely, Gage, and I would have agreed to chair the committee."

He snorted. "Yeah, right." When she opened her mouth to object, he said. "Did you forget who your shadow was the first day? Annie told me everything. And my brother called to give me hell." He shoved his hands in the front pockets of his tan uniform pants. "I'm sorry, Chloe. I should have realized this would be difficult for you. I was around enough to know you didn't have an easy time of it here. But I figured..." He gave an apologetic shrug. "I didn't know about the panic attacks."

And she wished he still didn't. Embarrassed, she waved her hand. "That was in the past, Gage. So let's leave it there, shall we? And next meeting, do me a favor and turn off your cell phone."

He gave her a smile that indicated he knew she was trying to change the subject. "I'm the sheriff; I can't turn my phone off. But you can blame Easton for me breaking your rule."

"He's not back from Aspen?" she asked, unable to keep the disappointment from her voice. She understood Easton was busy with his job, but this was the second promise he'd broken to her. And she was beginning to wonder if he was using work as an excuse not to see her.

"He's back, but he got tied up with my brother on a case. Chance texted to see if it was worth Easton heading over for the meeting. I told him it wasn't."

"Why did you do that?" Chloe asked with a touch of censure in her voice. At Gage's grin, she realized she should have been more careful. She'd just given away how much she wanted to see his brother. Something she didn't want everyone in their respective families to know. She wasn't even secure enough in her relationship with Easton to want him to know.

"Don't worry, I'm expecting him to show up any minute now."

"But you just said—"

"I told Chance to let Easton know Ashley Wilkes was here." He nodded at Beau, who sat at a table signing up volunteers. She noticed Nell in the long line. As a former electrical engineer, the older woman would provide valuable help, even if she was a pain in the behind. Beau and the volunteers were the most important piece of Chloe's plan. The board's argument for closure of Christmas High was not based on low enrollment, but the expense of expanding the school.

As though he sensed their attention, Beau looked over and smiled, then gave Chloe a thumbs-up. She returned the gesture and looked at Gage. "His name isn't Ashley Wilkes, it's Beau…" She trailed off as she recalled the character from *Gone With the Wind*. So they thought Easton was her Rhett, did they? Well that had to be a good…No, she was done with signs. "Development" was a much better word.

"I know." Gage waggled his eyebrows, then said, "Looks like Beau is going to be at it awhile. I'll stick around until he's done, and you can head out. Jill will walk you to your car."

Chloe looked to where Jill leaned against the far wall and followed the direction of the deputy's narrowed gaze. She was watching Sawyer and Brandi, who were chatting on the upper row of the blue bleachers.

"You're not concerned that Brandi will pull something, are you?"

"No. Why would you think that?" Gage said.

Chloe gathered her files and notes from the table, then shoved them in her black hobo bag. "So why's Jill following me to my car then?"

Gage helped her into her leather jacket. "We've heard that students and parents from the other two schools on the chopping block were coming tonight. They have a lot to gain if you can't make a good case for keeping Christmas High open. If you do, one of their schools will close."

"I wish you would have told me, Gage. I wouldn't have revealed our four-prong strategy."

"I didn't know until I arrived for the meeting. Annie saw it on Facebook. Don't worry, I'm not overly concerned. But I can't take chances with my brother's girl."

She glanced at him. He'd called her Easton's girl, and hadn't said it like it was the biggest mistake his brother had ever made. And she couldn't deny that made her happy, and being thought of as Easton's girl made her happy, too. But she had to play it cool. If things didn't work out between them, she didn't want everyone feeling sorry for her. It would be hard enough seeing him at family gatherings without the added stress of pretending she was fine.

"I'm not really his girl, you know." Gage's eyes narrowed at her. "I mean, we're dating, but it isn't serious." He crossed his arms. "Well, it could be serious if we actually spent some time together...Never mind. It's none of your business anyway." She hooked the strap of her bag over her shoulder. "Thanks for coming...Oh, I nearly forgot to ask, can you investigate the board members for me?"

"No, *I* can't, but your *boyfriend* can." He waved Jill over.

Chloe rolled her eyes, said good-bye, then walked to where Jill stood waiting for her in the middle of the auditorium. "Why do you keep staring at Brandi? Do you think she's going to try something?" Chloe asked again, concerned Gage didn't want to worry her by telling the truth.

Jill drew her gaze from the couple. "I'm not staring at them."

She caught the *them* and murmured, "Oh, I see." And she did. Jill Flaherty had had a crush on her brother's best friend, Sawyer Anderson, since high school.

"What do you see? They're not dating, you know," Jill said, glancing back at the couple as she and Chloe walked toward the exit doors. "They're just...Do they look more than friendly to you?"

Chloe glanced over her shoulder. "Well, no, but—"

"Yeah, they're just friends. And Nell's setting up Brandi and Easton to be the couple in her..." She trailed off, her cheeks flushing a dull red.

Ten days ago, that might have bothered Chloe, but it didn't now. She trusted Easton. He'd explained his non-date with Brandi. "You know, Jill, if you're interested, you should just ask Sawyer out."

"Why would I do that? The guy's a total player. Besides, I'm not interested in him."

"Of course you're not." As someone who'd pretended not to be interested in Easton, Jill couldn't fool Chloe.

"It's not dark enough that I can't see your smirk, you know." They'd just walked outside. It was after eight, and the sun had set, leaving a nip in the air. Jill gave her head a slight, disgusted shake. "I don't know what's gotten into everyone. It's like they have spring fever."

"Well, if you change your mind, let me know. It'd be fun to make you over. Ty would help—"

Jill's hand went to her dark hair, an affronted look on her face. "You think I need a makeover?"

Of course she needed a makeover. Jill was as bad as Cat. She didn't put any effort into her appearance. And while Jill wasn't a typical beauty, she had the most fabulous skin Chloe had ever seen. She also had amazing blue eyes and bone structure. With a little effort, she'd turn heads. Possibly Sawyer's. "Of course you don't. I just thought it would be fun. But if you don't mind me saying, you should change hairdressers. Your cut is uneven."

"I don't have time to go to a hairdresser. I cut it myself."

Chloe stopped walking and stared at her. "Are you serious?" She didn't bother waiting for an answer because obviously she was. Chloe pulled out her phone. "When's your next day off?"

"Friday, but I'm not…" She sighed when Chloe pressed her lips together and arched an eyebrow.

Chloe texted Ty as they continued across the parking lot. They'd reached her Mustang when he responded. She glanced at Jill. "Ty scheduled you at two. If you're not there, I'm coming to get—" Chloe's gaze swung to the left as something hurtled through the air. She jumped back and a football landed at her feet.

Jill laughed. "I think someone wants to play."

Chloe picked up the football and turned. In the fading light, she made out Easton standing on the edge of the football field. He had on jeans and one of his old yellow-and-white Cougar football jerseys. "Come on, Scarlett. Show me what you got," he called to her.

"Have fun," Jill said.

Chloe was so happy to see Easton that she wasn't sure if she returned Jill's good-bye. Taking off across the parking lot, Chloe weaved to avoid the cars pulling out. For maybe two seconds, she wished she'd traded her four-inch wedge sandals for tennies. But she forgot her discomfort as she ran across the dew-dampened grass, tossed the football, and jumped into Easton's arms. And her thought about playing it cool—she didn't exactly forget that—but as his strong arms went around her, she no longer cared who knew he was her one.

Chapter Twenty-One

"Missed me?" Easton asked with an amused smile on his gorgeous face.

She didn't hesitate or hold back. She wrapped her arms around his neck, tightened her legs around his waist, and returned his smile. "Yes, it felt like you were gone forever."

"Guess we better start making up for lost time then," he said, and lowered his head.

At the touch of his warm mouth on hers, a small sigh of contentment escaped from her, and she closed her eyes. He smiled against her lips. She would have done the same, but at that moment, he deepened the kiss. And the slow dance of his mouth on hers transported her to another place. A place where hopes and dreams came true, and the man she'd been in love with since she was fifteen loved her, too.

Because if a kiss spoke, that's what his would say. And as he brought his hand up and under her hair, his fingers caressing the side of her neck, there was a promise, too. A promise that this night would not end with just a kiss. And no matter how perfect his kiss was—how he made her stomach clench and her toes curl with the teasing strokes of the tip of his tongue—she wanted more. She wanted him to keep that promise.

He gently pulled away and slid his lips across her cheek to her ear. "In case you can't tell, I missed you, too, Scarlett."

She opened her eyes and smiled. "I can't. I think you need to show me some more."

He laughed, then gave her one last deep, passion-filled kiss before lowering her to her feet. "Plan to," he said, and scooped the football off the grass. "But I thought we'd eat first and catch up."

"You want to go out for dinner?" She worked to keep the disappointment from her voice. She wanted to be alone with him.

"Not exactly," he said, taking her by the hand. Instead of walking toward the parking lot, he turned in the opposite direction.

"Where are we…" She trailed off at the sight of a glowing lantern under the goalposts. As they drew closer, she made out a yellow-and-white team blanket, a picnic hamper, and a bouquet of yellow tulips. "Is that for us?"

"For you mostly." He scratched his chin. "I grabbed a couple of burgers on the road. But if you'd rather go out for dinner—"

"No, this is perfect." It was better than perfect, if such a thing were possible. Easton had gone out of his way, and out of his comfort zone, to do something romantic for her. She wondered if he'd picked the location because of the meeting or if he remembered the night they'd made love. It had been the first time for both of them. And while, given the circumstances, it hadn't been perfect, she remembered every moment of that night. Sadly, she remembered the fallout afterward just as clearly.

"You wanna play catch first?" He tossed the ball above his head, catching it easily with one hand.

Obviously she'd misjudged his reason for choosing the location. He wanted to relive his youth. She arched an eyebrow at him, raising her foot to show him her shoe. "I'm not exactly dressed to play football."

"You sure about that?" he said with a wicked gleam in his eyes. And before she knew what he was up to, he tackled her to the ground. Breaking her fall with a hand at the back of her head and an arm around her waist, they tumbled onto the blanket.

He smiled down at her. "Bring back any memories?"

So maybe he hadn't forgotten. But she had. She hadn't remembered that their first time together had begun playfully. They'd met here on the pretext of studying for exams, then Easton had goaded her into playing catch with him. Afraid he'd figure out she wasn't Cat if she didn't agree, Chloe had gone along with him. Flirting to distract him. Even back then, she'd been a good actress. She traced the dent in his chin. "Yes, but I thought you'd forgotten or maybe you'd want to."

He searched her face, then rolled off her to sit up, helping her to do the same. She pulled her knees to her chest and glanced at him. "Sorry, I didn't mean to spoil the mood."

"You didn't. Okay, so you kinda did," he said when she raised her eyebrows. "I'm just surprised that after these last few weeks, you'd think I haven't forgiven you. We talked about this, Chloe. I wouldn't be with you if I hadn't. We were kids, and kids do stupid things."

"You think us making love was stupid?"

He looked out over the field, then turned his head to look at her. "I think we're real lucky you didn't get pregnant. And you were young, Chloe."

"So were you."

He shrugged. "Not that young for a guy. But for a girl... And your first time shouldn't have been on a football field with a guy who thought you were your sister. It should have been with someone who loved you."

It was her turn to look away. He was right, but it didn't take the sting from his words. She should have let it go. If she had, she wouldn't be remembering what he'd said the night he'd found out he'd made love to her instead of Cat. She'd never seen him so angry, or heard such spiteful words out of his mouth. "Not with someone who thought you were a slut."

He took her chin between his fingers and forced her to look at him. "I thought you'd played me, Chloe. I didn't know you had a crush on me. But even so, I never should have said that to you. I'm sorry." He dropped his hand from her face. "Maybe this wasn't such a good idea after all. Why don't we—"

He twisted to pick up the picnic basket, and she covered his hand with hers. "No, I want to stay." She gave him a tentative smile. "Please, can we start over?"

"You sure?"

"Yes, absolutely." She moved to kneel beside the picnic basket and picked up the bouquet of tulips. She buried her nose in the petals, lifting her gaze to his. "They're beautiful." She leaned over and kissed the cleft in his chin. "Thank you."

He smiled, and the hard angles of his face relaxed. "You're welcome. How did the meeting go?" he asked, as he pulled out a bottle of Chardonnay and uncorked it.

"It went really well, I think," she said, and told him about the meeting. He asked questions as she laid out how she planned to move forward, more interested, it seemed, in the part Beau would be playing to win over the board than anything else. When he asked his fifth question about the handsome Southerner, Chloe tilted her head and arched an eyebrow. "He's not my Ashley, you know."

His lips flattened, and he handed her a glass of wine. "My brother has a big mouth."

She took a sip. "A few days ago, I would have agreed with you. But Gage was very nice tonight. He apologized."

"That's something at least. You're doing a great job, Chloe. Bet your mom and Cat were proud of you, Ethan too."

She shrugged and carefully set down the glass of wine to pull out the food from the hamper. "They weren't there. Ethan had a meeting, and my mom and Cat went over to help Skye. Her dad and Betty Jean are in Texas. Evie's teething, and Skye has all-day sickness. She's pregnant."

Chloe kept her head down in case she didn't do a good job hiding her disappointment over her family's no-show. Easton seemed to have a talent for reading her when no one else could. She didn't begrudge Skye their help. But it would have been nice if they'd been at the meeting. Her family didn't think much of Chloe's chosen profession.

They were all about careers that made a difference in the world. Her dad had especially felt that way. So now that Chloe was actually doing something she thought they'd be proud of...

Easton tucked her hair behind her ear. "I should have been there. I'm sorry I wasn't."

"It's all right. Gage said you were at Chance's talking about the case," she said as she placed the crackers, cheese, and grapes on a paper plate. She set it between them on the blanket.

While they ate, Easton filled her in on the Martinez case. She liked that he was comfortable confiding in her, even when he wasn't supposed to. She laughed when he told her how Chance had unwittingly revealed their baby's sex and promised to keep the secret.

"Well, no one can say the McBrides and O'Connors aren't doing their part in contributing to the population of Christmas. You know, I should probably factor the baby boom into the forecast for the school board. Maybe I'll do a survey of the thirty-somethings in town and see how many are planning to have children and raise them here." She pulled out her iPhone and gave him a smile, feeling a little sneaky about how she was going to get the answer to a question she'd been thinking about. "You can be my first respondent. How many children are you hoping to have, and will you be raising them in town?"

He choked on a cracker. She offered him her wine, but he shook his head and pulled out a bottle of water from the hamper instead. "So I'm taking that to mean you don't want to have any children." She hoped he didn't pick up on the disappointment in her voice.

"No, I inhaled some crumbs when I went to give you

my answer." He looked up at the stars like he had to think about it for a minute, then said, "Five, maybe six."

She stared at him. "Five or six . . . children?" Her voice sounded like she'd been the one who'd choked.

He grinned. "Yep, and I'll be raising them in town."

"What if your wife doesn't want that many children or to live in Christmas?"

"Then I'll find one who does."

"Oh, I guess . . . That doesn't sound very romantic."

"Scarlett, I'm teasing you. I'd be happy with two or three kids. What about you? You're a thirty-something, too, you know."

"Thank you for pointing that out," she said a tad grumpily, then took a sip of wine before answering. "I'd like two or three babies, too, but I don't think I can use my response in the survey. I can't see myself raising a family here." But she couldn't see herself raising her children in LA either. And the thing was, the only person she wanted a family with was Easton. She glanced at him from under her lashes. "If your wife didn't want to live in Christmas, would you move?"

He lifted a shoulder. "Anything's possible, I guess. But I'd prefer to live in town. Family's here, and we'd have a good support system. Built-in babysitters. And I'm building my dream house, so that'd be kind of tough to leave behind."

"I can understand that. My beach house was my dream home, too." It was once, but not anymore. And Easton made a good point about a support system. What would Skye have done without Liz and Cat around? If Chloe ever had children, she'd want her family close by. Ty too. But living in Christmas? She didn't think she could handle that. But could she handle losing Easton because she didn't want to move home? She didn't bother answering the question; she was putting the cart before the horse.

"You said *was*; are you having second thoughts about living in LA?"

She nodded. "It's not the same without Ty, Cat, and Estelle around." And now that Estelle had the part in the docudrama, the older woman wouldn't be back anytime soon. She loved London, and surprisingly, she was enjoying spending time with her son. "And I don't have many friends, and no job..." She gave a disheartened shrug at the reminder there still were no offers. She'd been too busy the past few days to think about it.

"I might have a job for you. Have you heard of the director Dallas Howard?" Easton asked, then went on to tell her about meeting the man who'd been trying to convince one of Easton's big-name clients to come on board his new project. After overhearing the actress reject Dallas's offer, Easton had mentioned Chloe to the director. Obviously the adage "no press is bad press" held some merit, because Dallas had heard of her. She'd heard of him, too. There'd been some Oscar buzz about his low-budget film last year. And although he didn't receive a nomination, he was considered an up-and-coming filmmaker. Chloe would have been more excited if Easton didn't also share the premise of the movie.

"Sounds great, doesn't it? World's ending and only one woman can save the day. You'd be a hero." He grinned, and she had a feeling he was thinking of her and Ty singing "Heroes" by Alesso at the Penalty Box. "Nothing like a good action-drama to get the blood pumping."

Her blood was pumping all right. And that was the

problem. Chloe wasn't a hero, nor did she want to play one. Heroes had to do crazy action stuff. And since money would be tight on a low-budget film, they'd cut costs where they could. No doubt she'd have a stunt double, but they'd expect her to do a lot of the action sequences herself. And while everyone told her her heart was fine, deep down inside she didn't quite believe them. Even now her heart was thumping erratically in her chest.

But she couldn't disappoint Easton. "It's a fantastic opportunity. Thank you for putting a good word in for me. That was so thoughtful of you." It was, and she'd have to find a way to get out of it without him knowing how she really felt.

"Always looking out for your best interests, Scarlett," he said, digging his wallet from the back pocket of his jeans. He pulled out a card and handed it to her. "I told him you'd contact him."

"I'll get in touch with him first thing tomorrow," she said brightly and tucked the card in her bag. Then she deftly changed the subject by asking him how his jobs in Aspen went.

Twenty minutes later, Chloe suggested they pack up. Listening to him talk about his job had gotten her worked up. Not only did he look good doing it, she loved his confidence and admired how technically savvy he was. There was nothing more attractive than a smart man, at least to her. And his voice... Yes, she was more than ready for him to fulfil the promise in his kiss.

Once they'd packed everything away, Easton moved the picnic basket to the edge of the blanket, then he leaned over and blew out the candle in the lantern. Stretching out on the blanket, he said, "It's too nice a night to leave just yet." And tugged her down beside him. He slid his arm around her shoulders, and they lay on their backs looking up at the stars. For several long moments, there was only the sound of their breathing, crickets chirping in the field, and a horn honking in the distance.

Then Easton turned his head to look at her. "This is the last time we're going to talk about it, but you need to know Cat and I wouldn't have lasted."

She outlined the cougar on his football jersey with her fingertip. "Why not?"

"Because while there was a lot I liked about Cat when we were dating, there was more I liked about you. My relationship with Cat didn't go to the next level until you pretended to be her. I liked the changes. Really liked them. You were softer, sweeter. You didn't mind me holding your hand. I liked how you kissed me and touched me like you couldn't keep your hands off me. And I liked how you weren't afraid to talk about your feelings and made me talk about mine. Maybe, in some ways, Cat and I are too much alike. We make better friends than lovers."

Her gaze jerked to his. "I didn't know that you and Cat had been...intimate."

"We weren't."

"Oh, okay, that's good." She was happy to hear they hadn't been, and even happier to hear that he'd noticed the differences between her and her sister. Best of all that he appreciated them. There was just one problem. And while part of her didn't want to mess things up now that they seemed to be in a good place, there was something he needed to know. "I'm not that girl anymore, Easton.

I mean, for the most part, I guess am. But I'm much stronger now, and I don't need you to protect me. A lot of people don't know this about me, but I'm actually pretty tough."

His lips twitched, and his eyes danced with amusement. "Oh, I know you are, Scarlett."

She narrowed her eyes at him. "Are you being sarcastic?"

"Kind of." He grinned and turned onto his side, bringing her with him. "I think it's time for us to make a new memory here."

"Here...now?" She went up on her elbow to search the parking lot. It was empty.

"Oh, yeah, right here and right now," he said, and then his mouth was on hers, his hands moving between them. His fingers dipped beneath the waistband of her jeans and his kiss went from amazing to off-the-charts in twenty seconds flat. She closed her eyes on a low moan, the muscles in her stomach tightening in anticipation. At his frustrated groan, her eyes blinked open.

"Love the way you look in your jeans, Scarlett, but they're a pain in the ass to get off. Next time, wear a dress."

*   *   *

Easton sat beside Chloe on the rocking chairs. He'd picked them up in town the week before with this exact moment in mind. The two of them spending quiet time drinking coffee on the front porch before the day got underway. But the moment he hadn't envisioned had taken place fifteen minutes ago in the outdoor shower, and it was one he'd be thinking about for the rest of the day. And one he planned to repeat every morning. And night if he had his way.

"You haven't said anything about the chairs. What do you think?"

Chloe wore an old robe of his with her damp hair piled on her head and her feet tucked beneath her on the rocker. "They'll be lovely once you finish them."

"Scarlett, they're not a make-work project. I bought them from a local artisan. They're actually in pretty high demand." And cost a small fortune.

She wrinkled her nose. "Really? But they're made of sticks and need to be sanded and painted."

"If I come home and find you painted them pink, I won't be a happy man."

"I was thinking white." She gave him a cute grin. "Don't worry, I won't have time. I have too much to do today. Oh, and that reminds me, would you be able to investigate the board members for me? I think something hinky is going on."

"Hinky?"

"Yes, hinky, suspicious. It's almost as if Christmas High is being slated for closure to increase the enrollment of the two other schools, and I want to know why."

Jesus, she was cute. He hooked his arm around her neck and pulled her in to kiss the top of her head. "Nothing gets past my girl. I'll look into it for you, Scarlett."

She fluttered her eyelashes. "You're my hero."

"Remember that when you're meeting with Ashley today. Actually, what time are you supposed to meet him? I can probably move some stuff around and join you."

Her eyes narrowed at him, then she pursed her lips

as if thinking about something, and a self-satisfied smile spread across her gorgeous face. A smile that made him nervous.

"You know what, that's a good idea. You should meet with Beau. I'll text him and see when he's available."

"Okay, what are you up to now? No, don't try and deny it. You get a look in your pretty green eyes that gives you away every time."

"It's nothing nefarious. It's just that, well"—she chewed on her thumbnail—"I may have mentioned to Beau that you'd hire him and his crew to build your new house. So it's probably a good idea for you to talk to him."

He took her thumb from her mouth. "Stop chewing on your nail. I'm not mad, but I'd appreciate it if you talked about stuff like this with me first."

"So you'll hire them?"

"I'll think about it. And—" He broke off at the sound of an orange pickup turning off the main road. "Looks like the Hansons have come for a…Chloe, what are you doing?"

She was up and off the chair, duck-walking to the cabin door. "I can't let them see me."

"Do not tell me this has anything to do with you not being dressed to the nines and having no makeup on."

She touched her cheek and gave him a horrified look. "I didn't even think of that. But no, I don't want them to think I'm that kind of girl," she said as she opened the door and disappeared behind it.

"What kind of girl would that be exactly?" He had a feeling he wasn't going to like her answer.

"The kind that lives with a man before they're married."

"They'll figure out sooner or later that you're living here, Scarlett." He lifted his hand to wave at the Hansons as the truck trundled down the drive.

Chloe peeked out from behind the door and frowned at him. "Whatever gave you the idea I was moving in?"

"I thought after last night—"

"Unless you proposed to me and I missed it, you thought wrong."

Chapter Twenty-Two

Chloe sat in the stylist chair at Diva while Ty blew her hair dry. "Maybe a little less movie star and more… PTA," she suggested. Her presentation to the school board was at seven, and she wanted to look professional. She'd paired a conservative black-and-white-striped wrap dress with a fab pair of black heels with white leather piping. The shoes were more movie star than PTA, but she'd only go so far in her bid to win over the board.

"I don't tell you how to act, so no telling the Dallas Howard of hair how to do his job."

She never should have told Ty about the director's offer. He'd been stalking Dallas on social media for the past five days. The thirty-four-year-old director was gorgeous, unattached, and gay. "The analogy doesn't work. And you can quit bringing him up in every conversation. I'm not changing my mind."

He whimpered.

"Don't be so dramatic. It's not as…What's wrong with you?" she asked.

He was staring out the window, the blow dryer hanging limply in his hand. Ty turned her chair to face the door as it opened. Easton walked into the salon. Chloe had a feeling she might have whimpered, too, but she couldn't be sure because the soundtrack from the *Princess Bride* drowned out everything else. Easton had on an expensive black suit and white dress shirt with its top button undone.

Dark eyebrows raised, he cocked his head.

"If he asked me to move in with him, I wouldn't say no," Ty murmured.

Easton heard him, and his mouth lifted at the corner. She really had to stop sharing with Ty. "Hi," she said. It sounded more like a breathy sigh, and she cleared her throat. "You look incredibly handsome."

Easton smiled and rubbed his head. "Glad you think so. My brother says I need a haircut."

Like always, he had a sexy bedhead going on. Chloe loved it, but since he was attending the art exhibition to-day, she supposed she could see Chance's point. "Maybe just a…"

Before she got out *trim*, Ty had tossed his blow-dryer on his tray and reached for Easton.

"I have been wanting to get my hands on you—"

Chloe wanted to get her hands on him, too, and jumped off the chair. She took Easton by the arm. "You need to get your own boyfriend, Ty. I'll wash Easton's hair while you do Stella's. I think she's cooked," Chloe said, nodding at the older woman under the dryer with her nose buried in *People* magazine. Thankfully they were no longer publishing Chloe's pictures.

Ty pursed his lips as he released Easton's hand. "If you didn't reject Dallas's offer, I would have a boyfriend." Chloe stared at Ty. She couldn't believe he'd outed her that way. He knew she hadn't shared the news with Easton, and he knew why. But her livid stare didn't seem to bother Ty, and he kept talking. "That man is perfect for me. I would have come to the set and done your hair, his too. Aspen isn't that far from Christmas."

Easton looked down at her, his brow furrowed. "You didn't tell me you rejected Dallas's offer. Was he not offering you enough money?"

She took Easton's hand, leading him toward the sinks and, more importantly, away from Ty. "No, money wasn't the issue. After I read the script—"

"She was afraid her heart wasn't up to the action," Ty piped up from behind her.

Chloe whirled around. "Ty! How could you? I told you that in confidence."

Ty crossed his arms. "He needed to know. You're letting your fears rule your life, and it's not healthy. If anyone can get you to listen to reason, it's Easton."

"This has nothing to do with me. You're mad because you think I ruined your chance to meet Dallas."

Ty's face fell. "I care more about you than meeting Dallas Howard, Diva."

She would have felt worse about hurting Ty's feelings if Easton wasn't watching her with a concerned look in his eyes. She forced a smile. "We better get your hair washed. The exhibition starts at five, doesn't it?" Avoiding his gaze, she kept talking, "Let's take your jacket off. We wouldn't want it to get wrinkled or wet."

"Ty, I'm going to use your office for a minute," Easton said, then tugged Chloe after him.

"Easton, we don't have time for this." And she didn't want to talk about it to him or anyone else, other than Ty. And obviously that had been a mistake.

Ignoring her, Easton opened the office door and pulled her inside. Once he'd closed it, he lifted her onto Ty's clutter-free desk. Easton crossed his arms, the fabric of his jacket pulled tight across his broad shoulders and muscular arms.

When he opened his mouth, she reached up and gave a gentle tug on his sleeve. "It's a little tight. You should—"

"Chloe, we're not here to talk about my damn jacket. Do you remember what we talked about at dinner the other night?"

She drew her hand away. They'd had their first "real" date two days earlier. Other than that particular point in the conversation, she'd had a wonderful time. So wonderful that, when he'd made a case for her moving in with him, she'd almost said yes. But as difficult as it had been, she'd held firmly to her convictions. If she moved in with Easton, there would be no reason for him to put a ring on her finger. As old-fashioned as it might seem, she wanted to be at least engaged before she agreed to live with him.

Easton released an impatient sigh, bringing her back to the conversation at hand. She preferred the one she'd been having in her head. "Yes, I remember *everything* we talked about, Easton." As she made her point, his throat worked on a quick swallow. It didn't look like he'd be proposing to her anytime soon. She pushed her disappointment aside and continued. "And I told you the truth.

I haven't had a panic attack since the day in the school's parking lot, and that's weeks ago. I don't need to see anyone."

"So Ty's lying?"

When she began nibbling on her thumbnail, Easton removed it from her mouth. She gave him a grumpy look. "No, he's not lying. But that's not the only reason I didn't accept the role. There's problems with the script, and I don't think the producer is right for the project."

"I don't care if you take the part or not, Chloe. It's your career, and you know what's best. But if you're not accepting the role because you're worried about your heart, that I care about, and it's something we have to talk about."

"For twenty-eight years, I've believed my heart was damaged, Easton. And I've lived my life accordingly. It takes time to unlearn that behavior and change my belief system. I'll get there. You just have to be patient with me."

"You're right, it will take time. But you don't have to deal with this on your own. You shared with Ty, but you didn't tell me, and I guess that worries me a bit."

He was right. She should have talked to him about her fears. He'd opened up to her about his frustration with his injury and how much he disliked being pitied. He'd even started taking his pills. Not all the time, but he no longer let it get so bad that the pain showed on his face. It wasn't fair she hadn't been more open with him. "I'm sorry. I guess I don't care if Ty thinks that I'm being silly or weak, but I do care if you do. No, that came out wrong. I do care what Ty thinks, but it's…different."

He moved into her and framed her face with his hands.

"Looks like we've got a ways to go if you don't feel safe telling me stuff like this."

She winced. She was making a mess of this. Maybe it wasn't only her fear about her heart holding her back; maybe it was a fear of rejection. She'd loved Easton for so long that she was afraid to do anything that would put their relationship at risk. She'd told Cat she had to be more like her, to open up to Grayson or she'd risk losing him. And here Chloe was doing the same. She took a deep breath and covered Easton's hands with hers, about to confess her feelings. At the last minute, she chickened out and smiled. "Of course I feel safe with you. You're my white knight."

"I'm not kidding around, baby. We're not living in a fairy tale. You need to trust me with it all, good and bad." He turned his hands and held hers, then stepped back. "I haven't exactly been easy on you these past few years; maybe that's why you're afraid to trust—"

"No, you haven't. But let's face it, I had it coming." She looked at their joined hands, then raised her gaze to meet his. "Easton, I'm in love with you. No one's opinion matters more to me than yours. I want to be someone you can be proud of. You're strong and smart and good and kind, and everyone loves you." His eyes were intent on hers, a muscle pulsing in his tense jaw. Her cheeks warmed, and she once again dropped her eyes to their hands. "I guess I sometimes wonder if I'm good enough for you."

He let go of her hands and lifted her chin. "Chloe, look at me." A cold knot formed in her chest. His harsh tone worried her, and it took a moment before she did as he asked. "Don't put me on a pedestal. I'm just a guy. Sometimes I have my shit together, and sometimes I don't."

"I know you're not perfect."

"You sure about that? Because it sounded like you think I am, and that's a lot to live up to."

"I don't expect you to be anyone other than who you are, Easton. You may not be perfect, but you're perfect for me."

His expression softened, and he took her in his arms. "And you're perfect for me. So don't try and change. I love you just the way you are."

"You do?" she asked more out of habit than anything else. She saw the emotion in his eyes, felt it in the way he held her. Easton McBride loved her. He really, really loved her. And as that knowledge flowed through her, a sense of wonderment and peace settled over her. She could finally put the past behind her. Because if a man as amazing as Easton loved her, she must be pretty amazing herself. He wouldn't settle for anything less. It was time for her to say good-bye to that shy, awkward little girl she used to be.

"Yeah, and I mustn't be doing a very good job showing you if you have to ask."

Before she had a chance to disabuse him of the notion, there was a light knock on the door. "I don't want to interrupt you two, but Stella's gone, and I have twenty minutes before my next appointment."

"Be right there, Ty," Easton said, then smiled down at her and lowered his head, giving her a kiss that said, *Chloe O'Connor, you're my one*. While she responded with a kiss that said, *Easton McBride, you've always been mine*. And because she'd been waiting for what seemed like forever for the opportunity to let him know that he was, she put her heart and soul into the kiss.

"Ah, guys, what exactly are you doing in my office? My next client will be here in ten minutes," Ty said through the door.

Easton drew back, his eyes dazed, his breathing ragged. "I know how you feel about sleepovers, but you're staying with me tonight. So you better tell Ty you won't be coming home after the meeting. And, Scarlett, we've got more to talk about. But we'll save the conversation for the morning when we're watching the sun rise over the mountains."

* * *

Chloe sat in the front row with Ty on her left and Jill on her right. The board members had yet to take their places at the table across from her. The meeting was scheduled to start in fifteen minutes. She glanced over her shoulder, searching the audience for Easton, Cat, and Chance. They'd promised they'd be here. They expected the players in the Martinez drama to make their move within the first hour of the exhibition. At that point, the case was in the DEA's and FBI's hands. Which was a relief.

Chloe had assumed Easton wouldn't be in the thick of things. He was a computer expert after all. She supposed his suit would have been a giveaway if she hadn't been mesmerized by the way he looked in it. It wasn't until Cat had come to get him at Diva that Chloe realized he'd be in the middle of the action. She thought she'd done a good job covering her dismay, but Easton saw through her. And while she knew he was as well-trained as her sister and Chance, a few minutes ago an unsettling feeling had come over her, a heaviness in her stomach that she couldn't will away. She needed to see Easton. See all of them safe and out of harm's way. She had a better understanding of Grayson's concerns now.

Chloe's sister-in-law, Skye, looking pretty but wan, entered the room with her brother. The couple waved, and Ethan got his wife settled a few rows back before making his way to Chloe.

He greeted Ty and Jill, then leaned in to kiss Chloe's cheek. He pulled back with a frown. "You're not nervous, are you?"

Chloe was surprised he asked. She loved public speaking and had every angle of their defense covered and memorized. Beau had done an incredible job on the renovation end of things. With donations of materials and a mostly volunteer workforce, they could come in fifty percent below what the board had projected—with the added bonus of providing much-needed jobs for veterans. And Easton had come through, too. Three board members had a vested interest in the outcome; a definite and provable conflict of interest. They had grandchildren enrolled in the other schools, and two of their children taught there. Chloe planned to demand they recuse themselves from the vote. "No, not at all. Why?"

"You're pale."

"He's right, you are." Ty tutted.

While Ty pinched color into her cheeks, Chloe asked her brother, "Have you heard from Cat?"

"No, they're probably on their way. The Martinez estate is eighty miles west of here." He glanced around the crowded room and lifted his hand. "There's Gage, Madison, and Annie. Mom and Paul should be here any minute. They had to pick up Nell."

Chloe turned, and the McBrides smiled and gave her a thumbs-up before taking their seats beside Skye. She spotted Vera Woods and the principal, Mr. Lowry, a couple rows behind. The seats around them were filled with other members of the staff, as well as students and their parents. And as Chloe returned their waves and smiles, she realized the reason behind the unsettling weight.

Ethan crouched in front of her, a look of concern on his face. "Chloe, what's going on? You're rubbing your stomach."

She stilled her hand and glanced once more over her shoulder. "They're all depending on me to save Christmas High. I don't want to let them down."

"No matter the outcome, we're all proud of what you've done. Madison said you've accomplished more in a couple of weeks than she did in months. None of us believed the school could be saved, but you've made believers out of us, Chloe."

She sniffed, a little emotional at her brother's praise. She'd never doubted Ethan's love for her, but her older, conservative brother hadn't exactly been her biggest fan the past few years. She didn't blame him.

Ethan stood up and leaned over to give her a quick hug. "Love you, Chlo Chlo," he said, using his childhood name for her. "Give 'em hell."

Ty fanned his hand in front of his face. "He's so hot, and that was so sweet, I think I'm going to cry."

"Don't," Chloe said, feeling the same. "My mascara isn't waterproof."

Ty gave her a horrified look and took her purse from her. Digging through her makeup bag, he found her mascara and held it up. "Really, Diva, what were you thinking?"

"You threw out my false eyelashes, and I couldn't find the brand you use at the drugstore in town," she said a little defensively, though secretly relieved the conversation had distracted her, and she no longer felt the urge to cry.

"What's wrong with that mascara? I use it all the time," Jill said.

Chloe and Ty shared a look. "And why am I not surprised," Ty said to Jill, then wagged the mascara at her. "You're lucky I'm still speaking to you after you didn't show up for your appointment last Friday."

Jill grimaced. "Sorry about that. I meant to call, but I had to work overtime." Chloe arched an eyebrow. As promised, she'd gone looking for Jill. Caught in her lie, the other woman sighed. "Fine, I was at the shooting range, but it was work related. Besides, I don't want or need a makeover."

"If you want Sawyer Anderson to stop seeing you as his best friend's baby sister, you do, too." When Jill opened her mouth, no doubt to argue, Chloe added, "I saw you watching Brandi and Sawyer." The couple had been the first to arrive, and Jill had glanced at them so often that Chloe wouldn't be surprised if she had a crick in her neck.

Ty twisted in his seat. "Sawyer's dating Brandi? How come no one told me?"

"They're not dating. They're just friends," Jill gritted out.

Ty said something that had Jill whipping her head around, but Chloe was no longer engaged in the conversation. A sharp pain lanced through her back and upper abdomen, causing her to double over.

"Diva, what's wrong?"

"Chloe, are you okay? Do you want me to get Gage?" Jill asked. Gage had been a paramedic before going into law enforcement.

"No," she said, breathing through the pain. "I'll be okay." She carefully straightened, slowly turning to look over her shoulder. There was still no sign of Easton, Cat, and Chance. Or her mother, Paul, and Nell. She caught her brother's eye. He mouthed *What's wrong?* Afraid she was overreacting, and not wanting to worry him, she mouthed back *Nothing* and managed a smile.

The pain subsided a bit, but not her fear that something had happened to her sister. Chloe pulled her cell phone from her purse and checked for messages, then texted Cat. She had to know that she was all right.

But she didn't have time to wait for a response; members of the school board were taking their places at the table. The chairman, a white-haired man with bifocals, called the meeting to order and introduced the other board members. Her eyes drawn back to her phone, Chloe willed her sister to respond.

Ty gently nudged her. "Chloe, you're up."

She handed him her phone and whispered, "Keep trying to reach Cat. Let me know as soon as she responds."

As Chloe made her way to the podium, the people who'd come out to support both her and Christmas High cheered, reminding her that she had a job to do. They were depending on her, and she wouldn't let them down. She said a quick and silent prayer for her sister. Then pushing her worry aside, addressed the board members. She walked to the table and handed each of them a twenty-page copy of her proposal. Two-thirds of the way into her presentation, she asked Beau to join her to take questions from the board.

From the attentive expressions on their faces, they were obviously impressed with both Beau and his plan. At least the members who didn't have a vested interest in the closure of Christmas High. It was then that Chloe alerted the board to her findings. Outraged at the charges, the three members threatened to sue. Out of the corner of her eye, Chloe noted that both Jill and Gage were headed toward her. They walked to where she stood, taking up their positions on either side of her. Arms crossed, feet shoulder-width apart, Gage and Jill stared down the angry board members. The chairman covered the mic and addressed the three men. After a brief but heated exchange, he called the meeting to order.

"Ms. O'Connor, I assure you we will be looking into the charges you've made. Now, if you'd like to continue."

Just as she was wrapping up her presentation, thanking the committee members for their time, there was a chirp of a cell phone, and then another, and another. It sounded like half the cell phones in the room had gone off at the same time. On either side of her, Gage and Jill reached for theirs. Chloe glanced at Ty. With a worried look on his face, he shook his head.

As the chairman called for order, Chloe looked back at Ethan. He was heading for the door.

Chapter Twenty-Three

Easton paced in front of the entrance to the hospital. He wanted to be here for Chloe when she arrived. It would be hard enough on her knowing that Cat had been injured, doubly hard dealing with her own issues. A few weeks ago, she'd had a panic attack at the mere thought of meeting the psychiatrist at Christmas General. Given that, he should probably ask his dad to write her a script for anti-anxiety meds.

He looked up to see his brother coming through the doors. Chance shoved his cell phone in the inside pocket of his black jacket and stepped outside. "Gage says they should be here in fifteen minutes."

"How's Chloe?" Easton had been trying to reach her for the past ten minutes. He'd thought it best to wait until they knew the full extent of Cat's injuries before calling her.

"Don't know. Gage said it was like she already knew something had happened to Cat. He'd barely gotten two words out of his mouth, and she was gone. Jill mentioned Chloe had been acting strange before the meeting started. She kept rubbing her back and stomach like she was in pain. Weird thing is, timing coincides with when Cat got hit."

When the first hour of the exhibition passed without incident, Martinez got antsy. They should have realized the man wouldn't be able to hold it together for long. Cat got a read on him right away and took him to the room that contained the private collection of sculptures to calm him down. She didn't realize Tara Martinez had followed them until it was too late.

Neither did Easton and Chance. Easton was shadowing the artist while Chance kept an eye on two men he suspected were the buyers. From what they could piece together, Tara overheard her husband's and Cat's conversation. The room was dimly lit, and she hid behind a display pedestal, pushing it and the heavy, bronze sculpture onto Cat. Once Cat was down, Tara went after her husband.

Because of the lighting, it was difficult to pick up much movement in the private viewing room. But when Grayson, who'd been monitoring the situation from the surveillance truck, swore he saw a shadow moving behind the exhibits, he searched the other screens for Tara and noticed she was missing. He alerted Easton and Chance through their earpieces, and they headed for the private viewing room. Easton didn't know how the agent got there so fast, but Grayson was right behind them. Members of the DEA and FBI surrounded the place, rounding up the artist and the two buyers when they tried to leave the estate.

Cat had been conscious, which was a good sign, but she had excruciating pain in her side and upper abdomen. By the time the ambulance arrived, she was vomiting. The doctors were in with her now.

"E, did you hear me?"

"Yeah, sorry. I'm just worried about Chloe. And Cat obviously. Any word on her condition?"

"They're looking at traumatic kidney failure."

Easton swore low and viciously under his breath. "We should have brought in extra security."

"There was nothing to indicate Tara would react like she did, or for that matter, Martinez. Up until then, he hadn't given any indication he'd break under pressure. If he had, we wouldn't be here right now."

"Grayson will never speak to us again." Easton wouldn't, if he was in the other man's shoes.

"He's angry, and he's scared right now...What the hell?"

Easton turned at the sound of squealing tires. A black Mustang with red racing stripes roared into the hospital parking lot. "What kind of moron...Wait, that's Chloe's car, and she's driving. What was Gage thinking letting her get in her car in the state she's in?" Easton reined in his temper as he strode across the parking lot. She didn't need his anger right now. She needed his support. He'd save the lecture for when they knew Cat was okay. And she would be okay, dammit.

His brother followed after him. "Doubt he could have stopped her if he wanted to, but Ty and Jill are with her."

"Lotta good that did," Easton muttered.

The Mustang had barely jerked to a stop when the driver-side door flew open and Chloe jumped from the car. Her gaze shot to him. He took in the panic in her glassy green eyes and the black streaks tracking down her ghostly pale face, and opened his arms. She ran the few yards that separated them.

He closed his arms around her, holding her tight, murmuring words of comfort as she buried her face in his chest. Ty and Jill got out of the car. If possible, they were paler than Chloe. Ty leaned against the trunk with his palm pressed to his heart and said, "I thought we were going to die."

His voice was a hoarse whisper, and Easton laid odds he'd been screaming the entire ride there.

Jill pointed at Chloe and opened her mouth, then closed it.

Chloe stepped away from him. "How is she?" she asked, wiping her cheeks. He was a little surprised at the steadiness in her voice. He'd been preparing for the worst.

"Doctors are with her now. She's conscious, and she's not in pain," he said.

She nodded and rubbed her side, then searched his face. "Are you all right?"

"I'm good. What about you?"

"I just want to see my sister. I need to see her." Her chin trembled, but she held it together.

He took her hand. "Okay, come on." He glanced back at his brother and mouthed *Give us a minute*. Chance nodded. Easton knew how Chloe felt about people witnessing an attack and wanted to save her from embarrassment. He watched her closely as he held open the door, noting her momentary hesitation. But just as he was about to reassure her, she squared her shoulders and headed for the bank of elevators.

As they reached the elevators, he heard raised voices and glanced to his left. Ethan, Skye, and Gage were coming through the front doors followed by Ty, Chance, and Jill.

Ethan threw up his arms when he spotted his sister. "Chloe O'Connor, what the hell were you thinking?"

"Calm down, Ethan. She's fine," Easton said, drawing her closer.

"You weren't trying to follow her. She's lucky to be alive."

"So are we," Ty murmured from behind.

Chloe didn't say a word. She just stared at the elevator doors. Easton looked at Gage and lifted his chin. His brother leaned in to Ethan and said something only he could hear. Ethan pinched the bridge of his nose and nodded.

As the elevator doors slid open, they all crowded inside. Skye rubbed Chloe's shoulder. She gave her sister-in-law a weak smile. Gage asked Chance what happened, and his brother filled them in. Easton kept his eyes on Chloe, noting the instant she raised her hand to her chest. But just as he was about to take her into her arms, she let her hand drop to her side.

He drew her against him and whispered, "You're doing great, baby."

She reached back and touched his face.

He glanced over to see Ethan watching them and saw the moment Chloe's big brother clued in. Ethan briefly closed his eyes before he said to his sister. "Chlo, Chlo, Cat's going to be fine."

She nodded, rubbed her side again, and said, "I know."

Easton was beginning to think he'd prefer a panic attack to her eerie calm. From the looks of everyone in the elevator, they were as concerned as he was. When the doors slid open, he held her back. As the others headed for the fifth-floor waiting room, Easton pressed the hold button, then turned her to face him.

"Talk to me," he said, as he searched for signs she was in shock.

"Don't worry about me. I'm focusing on Cat. I'm trying to send her healing energy..." She lifted a shoulder, a hint of pink coloring her pale cheeks. "Does that sound weird?"

"No, baby, it doesn't sound weird." He brought his hand to her face, caressing her cheek with his thumb. "You keep rubbing your side. Are you in pain?"

"It's duller now." She touched her upper abdomen, bringing her hand around to her back. "Is that where your kidneys are?"

He nodded. "Yeah, they think they were damaged by the blow she took to her back."

"Did they arrest the woman?"

"Yeah, they did. Her husband feels real bad about it. He's offered to pay Cat's medical expenses. He blames himself for what happened." He rubbed his chin. "We all do."

"Don't do that. Don't feel guilty for something that was beyond your control. The only person responsible is Tara Martinez." She leaned over and released the hold button. "I need to talk to the doctors and see my mother."

There must have been a part of him that worried she'd hold him responsible for what happened to Cat, because something loosened inside him when she made it clear that she didn't. As they stepped out of the elevator, he tugged on her hand. She looked up at him. "You know you don't have to be strong for me, right?"

"I have to be strong for Cat."

"You don't have to do this alone. I'm here for you to lean on. Remember that."

"I won't pretend this is easy, but having you by my side makes it better. I love you, Easton McBride."

"I love you, too, baby. And I'm not going anywhere."

They walked toward the waiting room hand in hand. The room was packed. Two doctors stood talking to his dad, Liz, and Ethan, who sat in the waiting room chairs. They looked up when he and Chloe entered the room. Chloe let go of his hand and went to her mother. Liz started to cry. Several of the other women in the room did, too. So did Ty.

Ethan stood up, motioning for his sister to take the seat beside Liz. He looked at Easton as though asking if Chloe was okay. He nodded. She was better than okay, she was amazing. But the man standing alone by the window was not okay. Grayson was barely keeping it together.

Easton sensed his presence wouldn't be welcome and instead focused on the doctors.

"Urinalysis, blood tests, and scan indicate that her one kidney is barely functioning and the other one is at a limited capacity. It's possible we'll see some improvement over the next several days after the initial swelling goes down, but I'm afraid we're not hopeful."

"What does that mean?" Liz asked, sending a panicked look from the doctors to his dad.

Before Paul could reassure her, the older doctor said, "We recommend a transplant."

"What's my sister's prognosis without one?" Chloe asked, over her mother's quiet sobbing.

The two doctors shared a look. "If her kidney function doesn't improve, she would have to be on dialysis every day for the rest of her life."

Easton felt like he'd been gut punched at the thought of Cat on dialysis day in and day out. The woman couldn't sit still. She always had to be doing something. Face pale, his eyes haunted, Grayson strode from the room. Chance followed after him. His dad, with Liz in his arms, watched the two men leave.

"And with a transplant?" Ethan asked.

"She would lead a normal life. Although, unless we found a match her body wouldn't reject, she would have to take anti-rejection medication for the rest of her life. There can be side effects, but I think you would agree in comparison to—"

"I'll do it," Chloe said. "I'll donate my kidney."

"Oh, darling," her mother cried, clinging to Chloe's hand. "They're identical twins. She's the perfect match, isn't she?" Liz asked the doctors.

Easton didn't hear the doctor's response or Ethan's or his own father's or any of the other family or friends praising Chloe for her selfless act. He could barely breathe as he stared at her. She was ashen, her hand trembling as she brought it to her chest. No one noticed. Not one of them noticed.

"Damn it, would you look at her? She can't do this. You can't ask her to. She's scared shitless. She had a heart condition. She's terrified of hospitals. The only reason she volunteered is because she's desperate for all of your goddamn approval."

The room went silent as everyone turned to stare at him. He didn't care. There was only one person in this room he was worried about. "Chloe baby, you don't have to do this," he said as she stood up and walked toward him.

A tender smile on her face, she put her arms around him and held him tight for a couple beats of his racing heart, then she looked up at him. "Yes, I do. You know Cat as well as I do. It would kill her to live like that. And watching her slowly fade away a little bit every day, that would kill me."

He rested his forehead against hers. "And it would kill me if I lost you."

* * *

Chloe was scared spitless. But it wasn't something she could share with the man sitting beside the hospital bed holding her hand. She'd learned a few things about the man she loved this past week. One, he got grumpy when he was worried. Oh, who was she trying to kid? He wasn't worried, he was afraid for her. He had been from the moment she'd volunteered to give Cat her kidney. And that's why she had to put on a brave face. The other thing she'd discovered is that Easton dealt with his fear by looking at a problem from every angle. And she meant *every* angle. When he wasn't checking on her, pampering her, nagging her, loving her, he was on his computer. He'd spent countless hours researching the operation, possible complications, proper diet. It had gotten to the point he knew almost as much as the doctors. Though if you asked him, he'd probably tell you he knew more than they did. His brothers thought it was hilarious, and were now calling him Dr. McBride Junior. The nurses and doctors at Denver Memorial didn't find him quite as amusing. She was pretty sure they called him the pain-in-the-behind boyfriend.

His thumb slid to the inside of her wrist, and she slanted him a look. "Are you checking my pulse again?"

"No, but now that you mention it, it seems a little fast." He reached behind her for the call button. She tugged it out of his reach. "No, you're not ringing for the nurse again. They'll throw you out."

"I'd like to see them try," he muttered, looking up when Grayson walked in.

Her sister's fiancé was handling the upcoming surgery about as well as Easton. The two men had been friends before this, but now they were more like brothers.

Grayson lifted his chin at Easton and came to Chloe's side. He bent down and kissed her cheek. "How are you doing? Are you nervous?"

She waved her hand airily. "No, I'm an old pro at this stuff. Three hours and it will be over." Easton grunted. She ignored him and said, "You shouldn't have left Kit Kat alone to check on me, Grayson. I'm fine. Honestly."

"She's not on her own. My dad's with her, so is Ty and GG," he said, referring to his grandmother.

Estelle had taken the first flight out of London upon hearing the news. She'd told the director her granddaughters were having surgery, and if he didn't give her the time off, she'd quit. He gave her the time. She'd also convinced Lord Waverly that his son needed him. It had been a little tense the first couple of days, but Grayson and his father seemed on better terms now. Mostly due to her sister's intervention. And in thanks for giving him a second chance, Lord Waverly had been throwing his title around, making sure his daughter-in-law-to-be got the best care available. He was running a close second to Easton in driving the hospital staff crazy.

"How is Kit Kat?" Chloe had spent several hours every day with sister. At first Cat had tried to refuse Chloe's kidney. It had taken a few days to get her on board. She finally gave in when she realized Chloe wouldn't back down. And she wouldn't have. As the tests had revealed, Chloe's kidney was a perfect match.

Of course anything was possible, and Cat's white cells might still reject the kidney. But in her heart, Chloe knew that wouldn't happen. Just as she knew, no matter how scared she was, she had to do this for Cat. And it had nothing to do with guilt, or making up for past mistakes, or winning her family's approval—she didn't have a hero complex. She just loved her sister too much not to do everything possible to give her the life she deserved.

"Your sister is pretending everything's fine, just like you are. Only she's a little grumpier." Grayson took her hand. "And she's worried about you."

Chloe didn't get a chance to respond. Her mother and brother walked in the room. Liz gave them all a wobbly smile. She looked like she hadn't slept in a week. "Are you okay, darling?" she asked as she approached the bed. "No difficulty breathing or heart palpitations?"

She'd had a panic attack the first day of testing, but Easton had called Dr. Reinhart, the psychiatrist, and she'd given Chloe some techniques that had helped. She hadn't had an attack since. "Mommsy, I told you, I haven't—"

Easton cut her off. "Her pulse is racing, but she won't let me call the nurse."

She sighed. He'd done it now. Her mother, who apparently thought she was a doctor too, started firing questions at her as she checked her pulse and temperature. Chloe closed her eyes and fake-snored.

Her brother and Grayson laughed, and Easton said, "Are we boring you, Scarlett?"

She cracked one eye open, happy to see the tension lessen on his face. "No, you're annoying me. I..." She trailed off when Paul walked into the room dressed in scrubs. It was time to go.

Clasping her hands so no one would see them shake, she forced a lighthearted tone to her voice. "Party's over, guys. I have an appointment with a hot surgeon, and I don't want to be late." Her surgeon was seventy. Paul would only be there to observe.

Easton spoke to his father while Chloe's mother, brother, and Grayson kissed her before heading to her sister's room. Paul left with them, giving Chloe and Easton a moment alone.

He took both her hands in his and brought them to rest on her chest. "You know I've read everything there is to read on your surgery and on your recovery, right?" She gave a jerky nod, unable to smile. Her throat ached from fighting back tears. "And if I thought for one minute you wouldn't come out of this okay, that you wouldn't be able to lead a normal, healthy life afterward, I would do everything in my power to stop this."

"I know you would. You're my white knight."

"I am, and we'll get our happy-ever-after, Scarlett. We all will," he said, then gave her a tender kiss.

He lifted his head when a short nurse in scrubs, her powder blue mask covering the bottom half of her face,

entered the room. While they'd kissed, Chloe had curled
her fingers in Easton's white, button-down shirt. She
didn't want to let go. She finally managed to force her ice-
cold fingers to release him. He helped the nurse raise the
rails on the bed and wheel it out into the hall. The woman
responded to Easton's questions with a grunt, nod, or
head shake.

Paul joined them and kissed Chloe's forehead. "Everything's going to be fine, honey. I'll be with you and Cat
the entire time."

She nodded and tried to smile, but couldn't. Her body
trembled as her heart thumped an odd beat in her chest.
She didn't want to say good-bye to Easton. He raised
his hand as they started to wheel her down the hall. She
was about to call out to him when Ty and Estelle scooted
around him. They each gave her a quick kiss and hug,
moving away when Paul told them they had to go.

"Hair and makeup as soon as you're out of recovery,
Diva," Ty promised.

She laughed at Easton's exasperated expression, some
of the tension releasing in her chest. It made it easier to
say good-bye. To blow Easton a kiss. They were almost
at the doors to the operating room when another doctor
flagged down Paul. As soon as he walked away, the nurse
moved to her side. She lowered her mask. It was Nell
McBride.

"You can't fool me, girlie. I know you're scared. But
that's okay." She took Chloe's hand in hers. "You can
handle it. You're like me, we're tough broads. Nothing
keeps us down for long." She glanced over her shoulder at
the sound of Paul's returning footsteps, then whispered,
"Just remember, you're not alone."

"Aunt Nell," Paul gritted out.

Nell pulled up her mask, winked at Chloe, and patted her cheek, then turned and hurried off. Paul didn't get a chance to say anything. The doors to the operating room opened, and the other doctors and nurses took over. The room was bright, white, and cold—sterile. Chloe shut her eyes and focused on her breathing while they attached the tubes and monitors. Opening them when she heard the squeak of wheels rolling across the tiles as her sister was brought in. Cat turned her head and looked at Chloe. She was scared, too. And that worried Chloe more than anything else. Not only did her sister rarely show emotion, Chloe had never seen her scared. Beaten down, yes. But never, ever scared.

"Kit Kat, did I tell you about the tattoo I'm going to get?"

Cat gave a weak snort. "You want to talk about tattoos now?"

"Well, yes, I'm going to have a scar. So Ty and Estelle and I came up with a plan. The scar will be the butterfly's body. How fab is that?" she asked her sister.

Cat gave an annoying snort. But the nurses agreed it was a totally fab idea. "I know you're identical twins, but it's amazing how much you look alike. If you weren't wearing different-color hospital gowns, I wouldn't be able to tell you apart," one of the nurses said. "By the way, I've never seen a pink one before. Where did you get it?"

Cat tilted her head. "You do not have a pink hospital gown on."

"Of course I do. I tried to get a matching hat, but I couldn't find one online." When Cat released a dry laugh, Chloe smiled inwardly and gave herself a mental pat on the back. She was doing a brilliant job distracting her sister.

"All right, ladies. Time for your naps," one of the nurses said.

Chloe repeatedly swallowed, then stared up at the bright fluorescent lights. She couldn't look at her sister. "Night-night, Kit Kat. Have a good sleep."

"I love you, Chloe," her sister whispered.

She managed to get out "Love you too" just before they were told to start counting backward.

* * *

Chloe blinked her eyes open and looked around. She wasn't in the operating room. She was in a never-ending space illuminated by a white light that was beautiful and warm, joyful. It was a place she recognized. She'd been here before. When she was a little girl. But this time she wasn't afraid. She stood and listened as voices raised in song reached her. They were mesmerizing and tugged on her soul, pulling her in their direction. She moved to follow the sound, and that's when she saw them, her father and Easton's mother. People in long robes stood behind them, but she couldn't make out their faces. The brilliant white light caused them to shimmer in and out of focus. Anna and her father smiled, and Chloe started to run toward them. Her father raised his hand and gently shook his head. She heard his voice, but it wasn't the same; it was more like she heard him in her mind. "It's not your time or Cat's," he said. "You need to find her and bring her home."

"She's lost?"

"She's scared."

Chloe knew all about being scared. She'd lived her life that way for years. As if her father heard her thoughts, he smiled again. "Not anymore. You're free. I'm proud of you, sweet face," he said.

Anna smiled. "So am I, Chloe. Now hurry, I don't want my son to worry."

They faded, and Chloe felt bereft at the loss. She wanted to follow them, but then thought of Easton waiting for her, of her family, of Cat. A low mewling, like a kitten in pain, drew her attention. She turned. Cat was curled in a ball, whimpering. "It's okay, Kit Kat. You're not alone. I'm here."

Her sister lifted her head. "I don't know how to get home."

Chloe held out her hand. "I do. Come on."

Chapter Twenty-Four

Easton opened the door and entered the O'Connors' ranch house. He didn't bother knocking. It was his home away from home. He'd basically been living there since Cat and Chloe were released from the hospital three weeks earlier. He hadn't wanted to let Chloe out of his sight. They hadn't known until both of the women were in recovery that Cat's heart had stopped on the operating table. Less than two minutes later, so did Chloe's.

The surgeon felt the trauma Cat had suffered led to the episode, but they didn't have an explanation for Chloe. Up until that point, her vitals had been stable and strong. They ran tests on both sisters and monitored them closely for ten days before releasing them. According to the doctors at their last appointments, they were recovering remarkably well. Cat still had to check in at the hospital every couple of days, but knowing what the other option had been, she didn't complain. Much.

Chloe didn't complain at all. Which is why he'd felt reasonably comfortable taking on a job out of town four days ago. He hadn't wanted to take it, but with Cat off indefinitely and Vivi's due date fast approaching, Easton didn't have much choice.

Being away from Chloe had been tough. He was anxious to see her and more than anxious to take her home. Having family around was great, but the 24/7 thing was getting on his nerves. He wanted time alone with Chloe. He wanted her to move in with him. And he had the ring in his pocket to guarantee that she said yes. To seal the deal, he had Beau and his crew add a bathroom off the bedroom. Nothing fancy. The new place would be ready in early fall. Easton planned to keep the cabin and either rent it out or use it as an office.

Everything was set but the how and when of his proposal. His fiancée-to-be had an affinity for the dramatic. She'd expect it to be special. He patted the blue box in his messenger bag and smiled. He'd knocked it out of the park with the ring. As soon as he saw the pink, princess-cut diamond in the jeweler's case, he knew it was meant for Chloe.

Easton's gut tightened as he walked toward the kitchen, and it had nothing to do with being nervous about losing his bachelorhood. His dad, Liz, and Grayson looked exhausted. The three of them sat slumped on the stools around the island.

He dropped his duffel bag on the hardwood floor. "What's going on? Is Chloe all right?"

"Chloe? Chloe's wonderful. She's a perfect angel. She doesn't complain. She rests like she's supposed to..." Grayson lifted his coffee mug to his mouth, then slanted

Easton a look. "You wouldn't be up for trading sisters, would you?"

Easton laughed. "Cat giving you a hard time, is she?"

"Hard? Understatement, mate. The woman is a bloody tyrant. Not twenty minutes ago, she—"

The tyrant in question chose that moment to appear. And from the scowl on her face, she'd obviously overheard her fiancé's loving remarks.

Easton cleared his throat to save Grayson from digging a deeper hole, lifting his chin at the entrance to the kitchen. Grayson gave him a bloody-hell-why-didn't-you-warn-me-sooner look, then swiveled on the stool to face Cat. Arms crossed over her white hoodie, she pinned Grayson with a pointed stare from under a navy ball cap.

"There you are, love. I was just telling Easton what a perfect patient you are," he said with a British accent.

Paul and Liz smiled into their coffee mugs while Easton fought back a grin. The couple had met when Grayson had been undercover as a British lord. But from the look on Cat's face, the fake accent wasn't going to save him now.

"Oh, please, I heard you complaining about me. And you wouldn't think I was such a pain if you weren't comparing me to Miss Perfect Patient."

"I have to agree with Cat, Grayson. It's not really fair to compare her to her sister. Chloe's used to following doctor's orders. She never complained once when she was a little girl. She always did what she was told with a sweet smile on her face. Her father used to call her sweet face," Liz said with a nostalgic smile.

Cat angled her head and looked at her mother. "You're not being helpful, you know." Then she returned her attention to Grayson. "I'm not like Chloe. I can't lie around reading and gossiping with Ty all day. It makes me crazy. I need to stay busy, keep active."

"I know it's hard on you, Cat. But in another week, you'll be cleared for more activity," his father interjected in a soothing tone of voice.

"And you know, darling, your sister isn't lying around reading and gossiping. I mean, yes, she does that, too. But she's conducting her business from bed. I'm sure Easton could give you something to keep you busy, couldn't you, Easton?" Liz asked, the expression in her eyes saying *For the love of God give her something to do*.

"Yeah, I have a ton of paperwork I can pass on to you, Cat."

"Thanks a lot," she muttered.

Grayson got up from the stool and reached for her hand. "Come on, I'll take you for a drive. We'll stop at the bakery, and I'll buy you a cupcake."

"Okay. That'd be nice," Cat said, sounding slightly mollified.

"Uh, uh, low fat and low cholesterol, my cranky sister. You have to take care of my perfect kidney," Chloe said, coming up behind Cat. Looking gorgeous and glamorous in a robe trimmed with the same feathery stuff as her pink slippers.

Cat crossed her arms and scowled at her sister. "How long have you been listening in the hall?"

"Long enough to know I'm the perfect patient and you're not. And long enough to know that my boyfriend's been here like forever and hasn't come to see me yet." She gave him a playful pout, then ran and threw herself in his arms. "Close your eyes, family. PDA coming your way."

Easton laughed. "You're turning into a brat," he said, then kissed her. It felt good to have her back in his arms, so good that he almost dropped to his knee and proposed to her then and there.

"She is. And now that you're back, you can keep her in line," Cat said.

"Happy to," he said, looking into Chloe's sparkling green eyes.

"I missed you. Next time I'm going with you."

Ty and a tall, good-looking brunette joined them in the kitchen. There was something oddly familiar about the woman, but Easton couldn't place her. "You can't go with him, Diva. You'll be busy with your new movie," Ty said.

Easton frowned. "What movie?"

"She took the role—"

"Ty, do you mind?" Chloe said to the stylist. Sometimes they reminded Easton of an old married couple. She turned back to Easton. "I wanted to surprise you. I agreed to do the movie with Dallas."

"That's great. But I thought you weren't happy with the producer or the script."

"Oh, that's the best part. She's rewriting the script and taking on the role of producer, too," Ty said.

"Ty!" Chloe stamped her slipper. "That's not fair. I wanted to tell him."

"I saved the best part for you. I didn't tell him you bought the rights to your perfume..." He grimaced. "Sorry. Jill, we better go."

Easton stared at the woman. "That's not Jill."

"Yes, it is. Doesn't she look amazing?" Chloe said, her anger at Ty forgotten.

Now that he looked at the woman more closely, the

blue eyes were the same and so was the shape of her face. But it was the long hair that was throwing him off. And possibly the figure she'd been hiding under her uniform. She wasn't hiding much of it in the red dress she had on.

Jill, her lips pressed in a flat line, said, "Extensions."

"We've convinced her to grow her hair out. Her own is even more gorgeous than the extensions. Sawyer won't know what hit him when he sees her."

"Chloe!" Jill said, stamping her high-heeled boot. The woman had obviously been spending a lot of time with Ty and Chloe. But Sawyer? Guess Easton shouldn't be surprised; she'd been the guy's shadow growing up. Though he figured Sawyer might be surprised, and not in a good way.

"Don't worry, Jill. No one will say anything. We're good at keeping secrets." Chloe arched an eyebrow at Ty. "Well, most of us are. Jill's going to ask Sawyer to the prom."

When the seniors at Christmas High found out about Chloe's surgery, they'd voted to delay the prom until she could attend. It was being held Friday night. The same day they were to get word as to whether the school would remain open or close. Chloe was touched and excited—overly so, Easton had thought—until he remembered she hadn't attended their prom. He smiled to himself. He'd just figured out the when and how of his proposal.

"We just need to work on her walk. But we've got a few days, so we're good."

"And her." Ty moved his eyebrows up and down behind his glasses at Chloe. "You know…"

"You're right, I forgot," Chloe said.

"They're kind of scary," Jill said to the room at large.

"You're telling me," Cat said, tugging on Grayson's hand. "Let's get out of here before they set their makeover eyes on me."

"Too late," Chloe told her. "We're having an at-home spa day on Thursday. Mommsy, you're invited, too."

As Grayson, Cat, Jill, and Ty headed out, his father said, "Okay, Mommsy, why don't we go for a walk and leave these kids alone for a bit?"

"Come on," Chloe said, taking Easton by the hand. "I have a surprise for you." She opened the door to her bedroom and stood back. "What do you think?"

Before he'd left, her bedroom looked like it had been designed for a princess. With its canopied bed and lacy bedding and over-the-top femininity, it hadn't exactly been a place he'd wanted to spend time. But she'd redecorated in creams and blues and exchanged the canopied bed that had barely held the two of them with a king-size one. And while he was happy with the changes, he was a little worried they meant she wanted to live at the ranch with her sister and Grayson. Though it wasn't something he could bring up without spoiling his proposal.

"Looks amazing," he said, lifting her into his arms. He closed the door with his foot and carried her to the bed. Settling her carefully on the middle of the mattress, he took off his boots before stretching out beside her. At the sound of paper crinkling beneath him, he raised his hip. "Sorry," he said, holding up the paper. "I hope it wasn't important."

She turned on her side to face him. "No, it's the design for my butterfly tattoo, but I've decided not to get one."

"You were going to get a tattoo?"

"Yes, I planned to transform my scar into a beautiful

butterfly." Right, he shouldn't be surprised. She didn't like ugly. "But I've decided I want to leave my scar just the way it is."

Now that was a surprise. "Why the change of heart?"

"Because in a way it's beautiful, too. Just like your scars. They're proof that we're strong, we're survivors. We were hurt, but now we're healed." She lifted a shoulder and gave him a small smile as if embarrassed.

He stroked her cheek. "I love you, Chloe O'Connor." And if he hadn't already decided to ask her to marry him, that would have done it for him. "Now, if you don't mind, I think I should check out your beautiful scar."

She laughed. "As long as I get to check out yours."

* * *

Chloe sat in the backseat of the limo with Easton, Grayson, and Cat. She was both nervous and excited. She was going to the prom with Easton McBride. The thought made her practically giddy. At thirty-two, she knew that was a little silly. But she didn't care. From now on, she planned to enjoy each and every minute of her life. She wasn't going to let fear or worry stand in her way.

Though she was nervous about the outcome of the vote. In case it didn't go the way she hoped, she'd talked to Madison about setting up an after-hours bus service so the kids didn't have to miss out on school activities if single parents like Jenny couldn't afford the time and money to get them there.

"We're here," she said when they pulled into the parking lot. The trees had been decorated with white lights, a class banner draped above the front doors.

"Honestly, you'd think it was your prom," her sister said, then her eyes narrowed. "Wait a minute, isn't that the dress you were going to wear to prom?"

She had on a pale yellow, floor-length dress with a sweetheart neckline trimmed in crystals. "Yes," she admitted, and while it was, her shoes were new. She'd found them online. They were beaded with the same crystals as her dress. They were totes fab, and Chloe loved them.

"Really?" Easton said with a low whistle. "If you'd come to the prom wearing that dress, I would have forgiven you in a heartbeat."

"You would have?"

"Yeah, but it's probably better it worked out the way it did. I don't think my seventeen-year-old self could have handled you."

"And you would have had to follow me to Hollywood." She kissed the underside of his jaw just before the driver opened the door and helped her out.

"Did you decide what to do with the beach house?" Cat asked, when she joined her on the sidewalk.

"I thought I'd rent it out as a vacation home. That way, if family want to use it, I can block out their time. Why don't you and Grayson have your honeymoon there?" They were getting married this fall.

"So you've decided you're going to make Christmas your home base then?"

She nodded. She'd told Easton when he came back from his business trip. He hadn't said much, just smiled. She'd found his reaction odd and somewhat disconcerting. Then again, they'd been making up for lost time when she'd mentioned it.

"That's great. Now the whole family will be in town.

Grayson, what do you think?" she asked when he joined them. Chloe just offered us the beach house for our honeymoon."

Chloe stopped listening to the couple when Easton got out of the limo. He had on a black tux and white dress shirt. He'd refused to wear a tie. But with it or without, he was the most handsome man she'd ever seen. She looped her arm through his, and he smiled down at her. "Happy?"

"Very," she said as they walked toward the doors. There was a long line waiting to get into the auditorium. "It looks like everyone in town is here. I didn't know Ethan and Skye were coming. Oh look, there's Nell, Madison, and Gage."

Easton's lips twitched, and he shared a look with Cat and Grayson before saying, "Guess the whole family decided to show up."

"Do you know something I don't?"

"Nope, not a thing."

While they waited in line, they talked to pretty much everyone in town. And again, it felt like they all knew something Chloe didn't. There were sly glances exchanged, secret smiles, good-natured chuckles. But she forgot everything when she saw the auditorium. To get into the room, you had to walk on boards made to look like a castle drawbridge. Cardboard cutouts of castle exteriors were staggered throughout the room. And miniature pink, white, and blue lights were twined in tulle and draped from the ceiling to the walls, while artificial trees in containers were bunched in each corner of the room and wrapped in white lights. Round tables covered in white tablecloths ringed the dance floor. They'd transformed the auditorium into the fairy world Chloe had once envisioned as a child.

Within minutes of entering, Chloe was whisked away by the excited prom committee. She looked back at Easton and gave him an apologetic smile. He had his hands in his pockets watching her with an indulgent look on his face. By the time she found her way back to him half an hour later, he was surrounded by former members of the football team. She was beginning to think popularity was overrated.

"Chloe." She pivoted to see Vera Woods waving her over. Trumpets sounded, and the principal walked onto the stage. "It's time," Vera said in an excited whisper. "Get up there."

The older woman gently pushed Chloe toward the stairs.

Mr. Lowry tapped the microphone. "Ladies and gentleman, let's give a warm round of applause for Chloe O'Connor. She'll be reading the results of the vote to you." He waved a sealed envelope over his head.

Chloe walked across the stage to the cheers and whistles of the crowd gathering below her. It was as exciting as when she'd been awarded a Daytime Emmy. But more nerve-racking given that the results would impact so many people. She thanked everyone who helped with the proposal, then turned to the band behind her and asked for a drum roll. She picked out several members of her family in the audience, including the most important one, Easton. He smiled and winked as she opened the envelope.

She looked down, silently reading the results. The room went utterly quiet, then sounds of disappointment started to come from the audience. Chloe figured she'd left them in suspense long enough. She looked up and smiled. "Christmas High is saved!"

She waved the paper, laughing when the principal picked her up and spun her around. The band played the school song, and everyone sang along, including Chloe. She looked for Easton in the audience as she made her way off the stage, but she was immediately swept up in a crowd of people who wanted to thank her for saving the school. It felt as though an hour had passed before she made it to the refreshment station. The DJ was playing a mix of current songs and ones from the 90s, and the dance floor was packed. She spotted Jill wearing the ruffled red dress and matching heels Chloe and Ty had picked out for her, standing by the punch bowl.

"Congratulations. You did good," Jill said, filling a glass and handing it to her.

"Thanks. Where's Sawyer?" Chloe asked, accepting the punch.

Jill waved a hand to her left. "Over there somewhere with Brandi."

"You didn't ask him, did you?" They'd been afraid she'd chicken out at the last minute.

"No, I—"

Chloe put her drink on the table and took Jill's from her. "Go ask him to dance."

"He's with Brandi."

Chloe stretched up on her toes to see if she could find the couple. She spotted them leaning against the far wall talking. And she wasn't the only one looking at them— so was Nell McBride. The older woman, arms crossed, head cocked, studied the couple. As if Nell sensed her attention, she glanced back and caught Chloe's eye. Nell grinned, nudged her head in Sawyer and Brandi's direction, and held up seven fingers. Oh no, she'd picked them for the couple in her next book! Chloe frantically shook her head, pointing at Jill, then Sawyer.

Nell looked like she was mulling the idea over, then slowly nodded and gave Chloe a thumbs-up. Yes! This was perfect.

"All right, Jill, I'll go with you and distract Brandi." But just as Chloe was about to lead her away, the music stopped, and the principal once more took the stage.

"It's that time you've all been waiting for. We're going to announce this year's prom king and queen." The kids cheered.

Chloe smiled and turned away, saying to Jill, "Let's work our way toward them, and then it won't be so obvious what we're up to when the music starts."

Jill was looking at her, her blue eyes dancing with amusement.

"What? Do I have lipstick on my teeth?" She smiled and rubbed her finger across them.

Jill laughed. "No, you were just voted prom queen. Get up there."

"I was not." But when people started yelling at her to go get her crown, she realized it wasn't a joke. She was the queen. As Chloe walked across the dance floor, she searched for Easton. She heard whistling and turned. Cat, Easton, and Ty, who had on a powder-blue tux, were standing on chairs, yelling, "Hail, Queen Chloe!"

Laughing, she covered her face with her hand, then headed up the stairs to accept her crown. She waved to her loyal subjects as the principal read off the name of her king. "And this year's prom king is...Easton McBride!"

The crowd cheered, and Chloe looked up, surprised to see Easton already walking across the stage. He grinned at what must have been her stunned expression, bending down so the much-shorter principal could place the crown on his head. Then Mr. Lowry joined their hands together and presented them to audience.

"This is what all the secret smiles were about earlier. You set this up," she whispered out of the side of her mouth as they bowed to their subjects.

"I might have had a little something to do with it," he said and took her other hand in his, turning her to face him, and then he started to go down on one knee.

"Easton!" She reached for him. Afraid his leg had given out, she tried to hold him up.

He raised an eyebrow. "Scarlett, do you mind? I'm trying to propose to you here."

She dropped her hands from under his arms and took a startled step back. "You're what?"

He gave his head a slight shake and lowered himself on one knee, holding up an open ring box. "Chloe O'Connor, will you do me the honor of becoming my wife, and making me a very happy man for the rest of my life?"

"I...You're serious." And as it finally dawned on her that he was, she was overcome with happiness. There was only one other time she'd been filled with such a feeling of warmth and joy. She smiled, knowing in her heart it was a sign they truly were a match made in heaven. "Yes, Easton McBride, I'll marry you. And I'll do my very best to make you a happy man for the rest of your life."

"You already have," he said, rising to his feet. And as

he slid a pink, princess-cut diamond ring on her finger, the crowd whistled and clapped, their family and friends gathered at the front of the stage. "But I have to tell you, Scarlett, you had me a little worried there," he added.

She wrapped her arms around his neck. "I don't know why, you had me from the day your white knight captured my queen."

"You're telling me you fell in love with me the first day we played chess?" he said with a laugh.

"Yes, when did you fall in love with me?"

He put his arms around her, resting his forehead against hers. "The day you turned my cabin into a doll-house."

Behind them, the DJ played Ed Sheeran's "Thinking Out Loud." And as they swayed to the music on stage, Chloe said, "Did you pick the song?" She smiled knowingly when he nodded. "You've loved me since you were seventeen. You just didn't know it then."

Listening to the lyrics, he smiled. "You might be right, Scarlett." And then he kissed her, and it didn't matter how long he'd loved her. They had now and forever to make up for lost time.

Jill has had a crush on Sawyer for *forever*, but her chance to share her true feelings is right now . . .

Please see the next page for a preview of

Happy Ever After in Christmas.

Marry me?"

Jill Flaherty squinted behind her sunglasses at the elderly man hunched over his walker, smiling up at her. He'd forgotten his dentures again. But Mr. Gorski was determined, she'd give him that. This was her third marriage proposal in a week. If he was five decades younger, Jill might consider his offer. Her chances of striking a proposal off her life-goal list by the time she hit thirty were bleak. She'd be lucky if she was in a relationship by then. Heck, she'd settle for a date. The approach of the big 3-0 hung over her like an ominous black cloud. Her mother had died two days before her own thirtieth birthday. October was only five months away.

"No!" Jill ordered in her cop voice when Mr. Gorski bent his knee, his walker listing to the right on the concrete. She winced when several white heads turned her way. She was here, at her boss Sheriff Gage McBride's directive, to learn a kinder, gentler approach. Jill would have protested the assignment at Mountainview Retirement Home, but she wanted her boss's recommendation, and his job. Rumor had it Gage was joining his brothers at McBride Security and wouldn't be running for another term.

She gave Mr. Gorski a kindly smile and wrapped her hands around his thin arms to keep him upright. He grimaced. *Shit. Brittle bones.* She loosened her hold and said in a sweet voice, one she heard her sister-in-law Grace use, "We don't want to break anything, do we?"

Her smile faltered. Was that a shimmer of tears behind his dark glasses? Wonderful, just freaking wonderful. She didn't have to worry about his bones; she'd broken his heart. "I'm flattered, Mr. Gorski. I really am. You're a great catch. Really, really great."

The words had barely left her mouth when a determined glint replaced the tears. He leaned toward her. "You are bootiful. I make you happy."

Relax. You've got this. She'd distracted him easily enough the last two times. Once by pretending she didn't hear him and continuing her self-defense class. The second time she'd been saved by vision testing. It had been a slight blow to her ego to learn Mr. Gorski was legally blind.

She needed to put a stop to this before he hurt himself. Or scarred her for life, she thought, when he stuck out his tongue to wet his dry lips. Letting go of his arms, she stepped back and blurted, "I have a boyfriend."

One by one the residents of the retirement home stopped searching the manicured grounds for the weapon Jill had hidden for the murder mystery game. They turned their heads, craning their necks in her direction.

Mrs. Sharp looked up from digging in a bed of yellow tulips beneath the gurgling fountain. A naked cherub, or maybe it was supposed to be an elf, spurted water from his mouth. Whatever it was, the statue seemed a weird choice for a nursing home, but what did she know? And the elf had provided her with the perfect hiding spot for the knife. "Who is he, dear? Do we know him?"

Jill drew her gaze from the well-endowed statue. Mrs. Sharp was, well, sharp . . . and relentless. She had to give her something. The best way not to get caught in a lie was stick close to the truth. And while Jill might not have a boyfriend, she'd been fantasizing about the man she wanted for a long time. Too long, actually. He was the reason for her practically nonexistent love life. No one compared to Sawyer Anderson. "No, he, ah, lives in Denver."

He didn't now, but he had while he played for the Colorado Flurries, a professional hockey team. Sometimes she wished he would have stayed in Denver instead of moving home. It was hard to avoid him in their small hometown. Especially since he was her brother's best friend. And it wasn't like she could leave. She'd had her grandmother to take care of and, when she died, her sister-in-law and nephew.

Mrs. Lynn, of the tight salt-and-pepper curls and freakishly pale eyes, drove her motorized scooter closer. "What's he look like? Is he handsome?"

"Yes, tell us," several of the other women urged, awaiting her answer with breathless anticipation.

Anxious, Jill imagined, to relive their youth through her and her make-believe love affair with a man who didn't know she exists. No, that wasn't entirely true. He knew she existed. Sawyer had been a part of her life since the day Jill and her brother Jack moved to the small mountain town of Christmas, Colorado. The problem was he still saw her as Jack's kid sister, not as a woman.

It would be easier if she saw him as the tall, skinny boy he'd once been and not the man he'd become. "He's beautiful. But not pretty-boy beautiful, more like Viking warrior or Norse God beautiful. Rugged. He broke his nose, and it's a little crooked, but it suits him. Just like the dimple that shows up on his left cheek when he smiles. He has a great smile," she told her attentive audience. She didn't want to disappoint them. And sadly, for her and her heart, it was true.

"Dark hair or light? What about his eyes?" Mrs. Lynn and Mrs. Sharp uttered their questions in rapid-fire succession.

A smile playing on her lips, Jill stuffed her hands in the front pockets of her khaki shorts and rocked on the heels of her combat boots. This was kind of fun, talking about Sawyer as if he was hers. "Straight hair, dark blond. Always messy and it comes to about here." She pointed mid-neck. "It lightens to a caramel color in the summer. His eyes are dark, same as his eyebrows and scruff."

"I like scruff. Manly. He is manly, isn't he, not metrosexual?" Mrs. Lynn asked.

"Metrosexual is passé, Edith," Mrs. Sharp said to Mrs. Lynn. "It's lumbersexual. I read it in *Cosmo*."

Jill hoped she stopped there. She didn't want to hear what else she'd read in *Cosmo*. She'd interrupted a heated debate over vibrators the day before last.

"I'm manly, strong," Mr. Gorski said, glaring in the direction of the women while flexing his arms. And that started a who's-got-the-biggest-biceps competition between the men.

"Oh, stop it, you old coots. We want to hear more about Jill's boyfriend. Go on, dear," Mrs. Lynn said.

Mr. Gorski muttered something in Polish and headed for the glass doors.

"Be right back," Jill told the older woman, sprinting ahead of Mr. Gorski. She held the door open. She hoped she wasn't making a mistake, but she felt bad for the old guy and said, "You've got great muscles for a man your age, Mr. Gorski."

"Ninety-five is not old."

Not only determined, but a good attitude. She admired that. "Ouch." Dammit, he'd pinched her. Mr. Gorski gave her a toothless grin. She sighed and rubbed her butt cheek. He had strong fingers, too.

"How tall is he? I hope he's not short," Mrs. Sharp said when Jill returned to her place on the patio. "Short men have a chip on their shoulder." The older woman made a face. "My Barry was five four."

"He's tall. Six three," Jill said, warming to the subject. "In great shape. His arms..." She trailed off when Mrs. Lynn looked beyond her. The other women seemed to have lost interest too, fluffing their hair and fanning themselves. Must be the heat. It was warm today. She probably should have kept them indoors. All she needed was for one of them to drop dead...

Mrs. Lynn smiled and said, "Sawyer."

Jill's jaw dropped. Mrs. Lynn of the freakishly pale eyes told her she saw dead people. Jill hadn't believed the older woman. Now she wasn't so sure. Maybe Mrs. Lynn was psychic. It's fine, Jill reassured herself, totally fine. Sawyer wasn't an uncommon name. She'd just...

"How's it going, Mrs. Lynn? Shortstop?" said a deep voice from behind her.

Jill froze. Her heart stuttered to a stop in her chest. Slowly the muscle came back to life, flooding her face with heat. And other parts; parts that should not be heating. It was that whiskey-smooth voice of his. But this was not the time for lust; it was the time for panic. Panic that he'd overheard her and knew she was talking about him. She'd never live it down. She couldn't face him. Maybe if she ignored him he'd go away. He was used to her ignoring him, sniping at him. Her defense mechanism. The one that saved her from prostrating herself at his feet and declaring her undying love.

Thankfully, she didn't appear to be the only member of the Sawyer fan club. And while she surreptitiously fanned herself with her sweatshirt, he greeted the rest of the home's residents.

"Doing good, Mr. Applebee. You?" He laughed at something Mr. Applebee said. Jill's brain hadn't completely recovered so she didn't make out much of the conversation. Sawyer's close proximity wasn't helping. She could feel him behind her, smell his clean outdoor scent. And dammit, he had a sexy laugh. "You're on. Flurries'll take them four games straight."

Right. Playoff hockey. He'd come to watch the game with his old hockey coach. He visited him on a weekly basis. And that was the thing about Sawyer Anderson: not only was he beautiful on the outside, he was beautiful on the inside, too.

Jill had just about got it together enough to face him

when she noticed the speculative gleam in Mrs. Sharp's eyes. Her gaze moving from Sawyer to Jill, from Jill to Sawyer. Dammit. Old sharp-eyes had figured it out. Jill had to distract her. She clapped her hands. "Okay, people, what is the problem? You've had an hour to find the murder weapon. If you worked for me, I'd fire your ass...butts. Come on, get it together and find the knife."

She heard a choking sound behind her and turned. "What?"

Sawyer's eyes crinkled with amusement. "Looks like your sensitivity training's going real well, Shortstop."

"Bite me." She hated him calling her by her childhood nickname. The one Sawyer and her brother had christened her with. She wasn't short. She was five eight. Why couldn't he call her Legs? She had great legs. They were her favorite and best body part—long and lean with well-defined calf muscles. Or Hot Cop? Not that she was beautiful; she wasn't. The only way she stopped traffic was by turning on her siren. But since women pretty much thought all male cops were hot, men must think women cops were, too.

He smiled that slow, easy smile of his. The one that made her toes curl every single time. "So, how many more weeks do you have to put in before Gage lets you off for good behavior?"

"Four." Her assignment officially ended tomorrow. But something was going on in the retirement home, and she wasn't leaving until she knew the residents were safe. She'd noticed suspicious bruising on a couple of them. Cash and jewelry had gone missing, too.

Sawyer glanced at the older men and women as they wandered off to hunt for the knife. He rubbed his hand over his chiseled jaw and manly stubble. "Why exactly do you have them looking for a knife?"

She shrugged. "Murder mystery game. It keeps them active. Makes them use their brains." And like her self-defense classes, hopefully keeps them safe. "You're getting warmer, Mrs. Sharp. Real warm," Jill called out encouragement, relaxing a bit now that the older woman was focused on the hunt. Jill noticed Mr. Appleby looking up at the Aspen trees that bordered a steep hill on the edge of the property. "Mr. Appleby, buddy, you're not even close. Get back here."

"Maybe if you weren't talking about your boyfriend for the last ten minutes, we would have found the murder weapon by now," Mr. Appleby shouted at her.

Danger. Danger. Jill turned to Sawyer and faked a smile. "Better get going or you'll miss the National Anthem. I know how much you like to sing along."

He crossed his arms over his broad chest, the movement putting his biceps on sigh-inducing display. *Show-off.* He raised an eyebrow. "What boyfriend is he talking about?"

"Don't listen to him. He's losing it." She gave him a light shove. "Nice seeing you. Say hi to coach for me."

"Her lumbersexual. He sounds wonderful, doesn't he, Alice?" Mrs. Lynn looked to Mrs. Sharp for confirmation, then turned to Sawyer and said loud enough for the entire town of Christmas to hear, "We're so happy she has a beau. We thought she was a lesbian, you know."

Jill briefly closed her eyes. Now what was she supposed to do? Maybe she should put in for a transfer. She opened her eyes and stared straight ahead, refusing to look at Sawyer. No doubt the interrogation would begin once he stopped silently laughing his ass off.

Movement near the statue drew her attention to Mr. Appleby. The older man stuck his hand in the elf's mouth and triumphantly pulled out the plastic knife. *There is a God.* Jill pumped her fist. "Way to go, Mr. Appleby! Time to celebrate the man of the hour, folks."

Sawyer leaned into her, his warm, spearmint-scented breath caressing her cheek. "You're not getting off the hook that easily, Shortstop," he said, then gently tugged on her two-inch stub of a ponytail before walking away.

She glanced over her shoulder, following his loose-limbed stride. He pulled his cell phone from the back pocket of his jeans. "Hey, Jack, heard something interesting. Jill has a boyfriend. Yeah, I was thinking the same..." She didn't hear anything else as the doors closed behind him. But she didn't have to to know what the next few days would bring. Sawyer and her brother wouldn't let up until they knew every last detail. Every last detail about her fake boyfriend. She needed a real one. Fast.

She glanced at the tall, wiry man standing in the fountain with his black toupee sliding down over his eyes, the knife still raised over his head. He hadn't groped her or pinched her butt, and he was ambulatory. "Hey, Mr. Appleby, how old are you?"

KISS ME IN CHRISTMAS
by Debbie Mason

Back in little Christmas, Colorado, Hollywood star Chloe O'Connor is still remembered as a shy, awkward schoolgirl. And there's no one she dreads (and secretly wants) to see more than her high school crush. While Easton McBride enjoys the flirtation with this new bold and beautiful Chloe, he can't help but wonder whether a kiss could have the power to bring back the small-town girl he first fell in love with.

Fall in Love with Forever Romance

"No one writes a sexy love triangle better than Tiffany Snow."
—JILL SHALVIS, New York Times bestselling author

GREAT LOW PRICE!

PLAY TO WIN

TIFFANY SNOW

THE RISKY BUSINESS SERIES

PLAY TO WIN
by Tiffany Snow

In the third book of bestselling author Tiffany Snow's Risky Business series, it's finally time for Sage to decide between two brothers-in-arms: Parker, the clean-cut, filthy-rich business magnate...or Ryker, the tough-as-nails undercover detective.

Fall in Love with Forever Romance

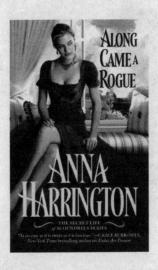

ALONG CAME A ROGUE
by Anna Harrington

Major Nathaniel Grey is free to bed any woman he wants...except his best friend's beautiful sister, Emily. But what if she's the only woman he wants? Fans of Elizabeth Hoyt, Grace Burrowes, and Madeline Hunter will love this Regency romance.

Fall in Love with Forever Romance

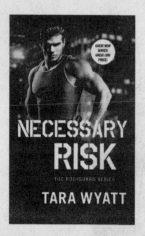

NECESSARY RISK
by Tara Wyatt

The first book in a hot new action-packed series from debut author Tara Wyatt, which will appeal to fans of Suzanne Brockmann, Pamela Clare, and Julie Ann Walker.

SEE YOU AT SUNSET
by V.K. Sykes

The newest novel from *USA Today* bestselling author V.K. Sykes! Deputy Sheriff Micah Lancaster has wanted Holly Tyler for as long as he can remember. Now she's back in Seashell Bay, and the attraction still flickers between them, a promise of something *more*. Their desire is stronger than any undertow...and once it pulls them under, it won't let go.

Find out more about Forever Romance!

Visit us at
www.hachettebookgroup.com/publishing_forever.aspx

Find us on Facebook
http://www.facebook.com/ForeverRomance

Follow us on Twitter
http://twitter.com/ForeverRomance

NEW AND UPCOMING TITLES

Each month we feature our new titles
and reader favorites.

CONTESTS AND GIVEAWAYS

We give away galleys, autographed copies,
and all kinds of exclusive items.

AUTHOR INFO

You'll find bios, articles, and links to personal websites
for all your favorite authors—and so much more.

GET SOCIAL

Connect with your favorite authors, editors, and
other Forever fans, and share what's important to you.

THE BUZZ

Sign up for our monthly romance newsletter,
and be the first to read all about it.

VISIT US ONLINE AT

WWW.HACHETTEBOOKGROUP.COM

FEATURES:

OPENBOOK BROWSE AND
SEARCH EXCERPTS
•
AUDIOBOOK EXCERPTS AND PODCASTS
•
AUTHOR ARTICLES AND INTERVIEWS
•
BESTSELLER AND PUBLISHING
GROUP NEWS
•
SIGN UP FOR E-NEWSLETTERS
•
AUTHOR APPEARANCES AND TOUR
INFORMATION
•
SOCIAL MEDIA FEEDS AND WIDGETS
•
DOWNLOAD FREE APPS

BOOKMARK HACHETTE BOOK GROUP
@ WWW.HACHETTEBOOKGROUP.COM